Reap
the
Whirlwind

Valerie M. Noon

by Valerie M Noon

First published in the UK in 2019 by
Tyne Bridge Publishing, City Library,
Newcastle-upon-Tyne, United Kingdom
www.tynebridgepublishing.org.uk

Design & Edit David Hepworth

This book is a work of fiction.

For
Linda

For
Dee and Michael

In memory of
my parents and grandparents
with their generations

'... they sow the wind,
and they shall reap the whirlwind'

Hosea 8:7

1

1909, The North East of England

It was pitch black apart from the glow of a safety lamp.

Two in the morning, with a tight feeling Ben Hawthorne stood alert an hour before the shift. He checked and rechecked the cage, the platform, the steel ropes that were greased and running smooth.

Opening up the lamp cabin for the lad with the smashed leg to serve the pitmen, he ran an eye over stacks of pouches, battery headlamps then rows of safety lamps and tapped his own 'Geordie' named affectionately for Stephenson. The flame was steady. A flicker or snuffing out meant killing gas wafting in the seams. Firedamp, their nightmare.

Holding a rattle-like hydrometer at arm's length, he spun it and checked the mercury level in dry and damp thermometers for humidity and heat, then clipped the rattle to his belt. Last he picked up a square cage, stroked a sleeping canary awake, closed the door and watched the bird flutter against wire staves. Gas in the air and it might perch or jump to the floor, wings spread, tiny lungs closing. Ben always revived them, he never let a bird die.

The morning was freezing but he hung his jacket on a peg as the seams would be hot before long. He touched a heavy tin bottle of water at his belt. Long pit stockings under trousers would keep him warm enough. Hewers could work naked at the coalface come summer, in boots, helmet and belt but not Ben. Safety officer must come to the surface and be respectable. His hobnailed boots rang with a sound of confidence. No one listening would tell how he felt.

Nearly an hour later the miners arrived, stabled pushbikes and took a last drag on tobacco smoke before stepping into the cradle. He made them crush out their tabs and grind them with their heels. His belly was queasy as he went down, checking and rechecking the

Geordie's flame as he walked the seams. It burned steady. He whirled the hydrometer creating a breeze. From time to time he stopped, reached up and ran a middle finger along the top of an unlit tunnel feeling for moisture, very slowly touching ceilings in the inbyes that forked off a main mothergate and narrowed to the coalface. The roof was damp but not dripping.

The layout of the pit in his head was like a wheel, the square shaft central, haulage roads running off like spokes to break away from the circle to narrow inbyes and taper to the T of the coalface. Tramping the warren of passageways, brushing through canvas fire doors that kept the airflow, he sometimes felt guilt that they stole the earth's black diamonds from her. He fussed, testing each route for gas and damp but paused smiling to watch a mouse or insect skitter across his path, creatures that shared the pitmen's darkness in the belly of the earth. All morning he spot-checked, getting in the way of fillers who strained to empty and refill heavy coal tubs for young lads, the putters, to haul out walking alongside pit ponies. Ben shrugged at their curses.

After the break when he'd eaten a bait of bread, jam and cheese he came to watch stonemen close off a dangerous old tunnel and blast a fresh one. A handkerchief over his nose and mouth he stood back as they fired a shot of high explosive. White cloud settled then they clawed at the rock and lifted down huge blocks of stone. Slowly the beginnings of a ceiling showed through the haze.

'Careful with those massive canches.'

'Handled bigger than these.'

'When you were pissin' in a pot as a bairn!'

Men at his back pressed to come through to clear a path, others waited with heavy timber props. 'Stand back, you lot. Let stonemen do their job!'

Ben wiped a hand across his eyes, cleaning a white fringe from his lashes, the pollen of the pit. The stonemen were men of dust as they shifted canches to uncover a floor. He watched them, like moving grey statues as they dug the tunnel. 'Get back! Give them space!' The team behind him poured in and he tested that thick props were steady and would not split. A thin young lad fetched and carried, ducking under them as they inched forward.

He turned his back on them, breathed easy and took a step before the crash flung him flailing onto his face.

The ground spun, ears pressed onto his brain, the world flickered, went black.

He thought he was dead but a noise knocked on his skull. Knock, knock to bore into his head and wake his senses. Something dug sharp into his brow. He told his body to turn, heaved swearing and found a body lying beside him. Moaning joined the knock, knock knocking.

'Hell!' He sat up slowly, clicked his headlamp and a faint beam slit through churning dark. He looked at the body. It was the young lad. 'Are you hurt, son?'

'Aye.' A groan. 'I am'

'Can you sit up? Quick, sit up! … Can you stand?' Ben painfully felt about for his safety lamp, talking the boy into movement. 'Is your battery working? That's better, a bit light. Stand up. You're all right. Take a step. Pull your strength together and find the overman. Do you know him?'

'Me uncle.'

'Find him, tell him to send men down here to the rescue - picks and shovels, at least four. Shout for the rest to get out from the coalface. This could just be the beginning.' The lad's mouth quivered. 'Do as I say then lean on somebody else to get you up on bank. Tell them at the top what's happened.'

The lad stumbled. 'What do I say?'

'Ben thinks the roof's come down after the blast. Stratas've collapsed. You say they're to send stretchers - get ropes, pullies, slings ready in case we need them at the other vent.' Find the St John's Ambulance man. Then stay out. Scoot! Quick as you like.'

His eyes focused. The Geordie was shattered under a rock. The little cage was battered and the canary lay still. Hell! There might be gas about. The knock, knock started up and he heard a faint voice.

'Knock back if you can hear me.'

His tongue was leather in a dry mouth but he rasped back. 'Aye, I can hear ye … team's on its way. Switch your headlamps off to one. Keep the batteries. If a lit candle's survived snuff it right out. I'm staying. Overman's coming with help. I can hear them now. Is the roof gone?' Two knocks. 'Thought so. Everyone alive?' Again two knocks … Thank God! Keep still. Don't talk.'

The overman was behind and hiked him out of the way. Ben pressed up from all fours, stood and leant weakly against the rock face. 'Has your laddie gone up to the surface?'

'Aye, he's all right, shocked that's all. Now get yourself back, will ye?'

Ben reeled against the wall. Beams cut the darkness. He flattened to let the hewers past. Picks and shovels attacked the sharp edged stack of rock and rubble, a prison for their marras. The overman had a Geordie but didn't dare light it. One flame would blast them to kingdom come.

Seconds, minutes, hours? Steel wrestling stone. A gap appeared and rock pelted in. He could hear men from the top trampling the tunnels. Dazed he watched them make a clearance big enough to haul a body through, the first man choking on dust. They formed a chain and dragged the miners out, passing them from hand to hand to the stretchers.

He could see no spark but Ben's horror was coal dust at the face or in tunnels inbye. Dust swirling in its black dance, fast and faster, whirling, colliding till specks created heat, set fire to each other and burned for an instant to flare drifting gas.

One man screamed as they moved him. 'Me leg's gone!' They passed a stretcher up and laid him down gently as a bairn.

'Air vent's a closer way out than the cage.'

'We're onto it, Ben. Get yourself out, man!'

4

'I'm here till the last man's up.'

Frantic heaving, sweat, curses, shouts.

Ben could feel it in his bones, a big one was coming.

Distant cheers echoed as the pitmen were yanked and hoisted up on bank, naked but for helmets, dust streaming on their skin. He followed last on a canvas sling and held his breath. Someone threw a blanket round him, he counted heads, no one missing, he thought. God, they'd been lucky! Broken bones but it was an ambulance needed, not a hearse.

Then it came, the angry roar, the earth's breath of fury that could have been their tomb. He wept.

For weeks he struggled in his sleep thrashing, panting to breathe, seeing lightning flare cut the black. Then the foretelling of his nerves came true again.

The West Stanley pit exploded. A hundred and sixty-eight lives lost, men and boys.

Ben drowned himself in the pub.

After a lively night he stumbled as he walked home from the local in darkness, reached for the wall, flailed and hit the pavement. He rose to his knees and found blood streaming over his eye, down his nose, and onto his shirt front.

'Mary'll kill me,' he muttered, 'Doesn't she realise ...' he licked the metallic tasting blood, 'doesn't she realise,' he said out loud talking to the wall, 'I can afford to buy NEW?' A pair of feet walked up, stopped in front of him and he watched in a trance as his blood dripped onto black boots.

'I'll help you up, lad.'

'Don't need it.' Ben snivelled onto the back of his hand.

You're in a state, man. That's a nasty cut.'

'Can handle meself. Used to it in the ring.'

'Better get you to the station. Just across the road.'

'Leave me, I said!'

As PC Martin put a hand on his shoulder Ben aimed a punch at his chest and hit an arm.

'No nonsense, now. Come on!' The constable reached under his armpits and heaved while Ben commanded his hands to land another one. They hung limp at his sides. 'That's it. One step over the kerb ... over we go,' the constable panted. 'One step up now. Another and we're in ... help me with this 'un. Fetch a chair!' His voice was cracking from the effort of holding a man. 'I'll need a damp cloth and a plaster.' He raised Ben's face talking. 'Now don't try any funny business. That's a deep cut but we'll clean you up.'

'It's been opened there before.' Ben's speech slurred. 'In a fight.'

'Aye, it's gushing, keep still, man. You should keep out of fights.'

'Champion bantam weight, I'm talking!' The constable lifted Ben's chin and pressed a cloth on the gash over the eye. Ben jerked his head. 'Trying the one/two, are ye?'

'Another time. We'll try that one in the ring if ye like. Not now. Hold him for me, will ye? That's better. If I can just get the sticking plaster on I can let his wife sort him. There!' He swiped the nose and chin with the cloth. 'Now we're gonna lift ye. One on each arm? Grand! ... Out the door, Ben, down the step. Keep yer feet goin'. Help us out. Up the kerbstone, over we go,' the constable panted. 'One step up now. Another now. Past your shop front and here's the door. At last!'

'Don't hammer on that door. You'll wake the bairn.'

PC Martin nodded to his friend as the door opened and a woman's face appeared. 'I'll manage him now. Don't be frightened, missus. I'm bringing him home.'

'Again!' The woman stood at the threshold in a long white night dress, a deep crocheted shawl over her shoulders.

'I'll get him up these stairs for you. Lift your feet, Ben. Just go ahead and open the door at the top and we'll get him into a chair. Up the dicky dancers now.' Ben moved automatically. 'Sit here. Just leave him, pet. Let him sleep it off.'

'Thank you for this.' Mary's hair fell over her shoulder in a plait that shone in soft silver gaslight. 'Send your wife in. I'll give her my special tatey pie next time she calls.'

PC Martin straightened up. 'Just in a night's work. If you're all right then, I'll bow out.' She nodded as the constable backed awkwardly to the door. 'I'll see myself out.'

Mary brought a bowl of water and began to dab at her husband's face with a clean rag. 'The shame of it,' she muttered.

'No sermons.'

'I can't see you properly and I'm not turning the gas up for you to waste.' She picked up a brass handled poker and stirred the embers of the fire.

'No sermons, I said. Get me a cup of tea.'

'It's too late for tea.'

'I'll decide that.'

'The fire's nearly out and I'm not wasting good coals to heat water at this time of night.'

'Just get me a cup of TEA!'

Mary stood over him, the poker still in her hand.

'My wife doesn't defy me. Now get moving,' He raised his fist.

'I'll move you out of that chair, Ben Hawthorn, if you dare touch me.' She raised the poker as his fist hit her belly. He lurched forward to try to catch her as her head glanced off the fender and he blacked.

Next morning he woke in the chair, cold with stiffened shoulders, a wrenched neck, tongue like drying leather and a head that felt it would fall off his body. There was no fire, no coals laid in the grate.

'What the...? Why aren't I in bed?' He slumped back and laced his fingers behind his neck. 'Mary?'

There was a whirl across the room and she bent her face in front of his. 'Mr Jekyll? ... Aye, wake up. Take this from Mrs Hyde!' A sharp burst of pain broke on his brow and across his cheek with hot needles, a second jab squeezed breath and brought a drowning feeling, pressing down from the bridge of his nose so he gaped, mouth open. 'Aye, you're like a fish on the hook now, Ben. Look up. This is what I think of your precious wedding gift!'

Blood forced from the trap of his eyelashes and one eye was closing. A final blow thudded on his scalp and he heard the shattering of glass on the hearth. She was gone and he heard the front door bang. He got up and reeled crunching over the slivers of glass in the shoes he'd slept in, the cut glass jug shattered, a rainbow of splinters as he caught the door to the bedroom, half leaning in. 'The bairn? Where's the bairn?' He caught himself on the bedstead and made out the cot was empty. 'Baby? Patricia?' His foot twisted, he sprawled onto the satin eiderdown and passed out.

A week passed with no sign of Mary. Ben knew where she was. Saturday he walked into town to take a bus to her parents' house. They'd shelter her in their colliery village straggled against fields near the pit. He hadn't visited with her for months, letting her struggle humping the baby back and forth to see her family. Ben got off the bus and strode in swift ringing steps, to the second row of houses, ready, mouth set.

Two raps at the door and a figure loomed dark behind the frosted glass over the letterbox. The door flew open like a wind and a fist bunched the collar tight on his Adam's apple. 'You! In the back yard!'

The hand released so he could speak. 'Steady, Peter, lad!'

'In the yard!'

The reddened hand almost lifted Ben from behind and flung him through a passage way, through the back door that half opened at the top, stable wise, and he landed on the stone beneath the threshold. Another brother stood square at the back door as he turned to face Peter and braced himself.

'You want to fight? You'll fight with a man! This is no Bantam weight ring.' Ben ducked but willed his hands by his side. 'No bloody Marquis of Queensbury's rules, yer little runt!' Ben side stepped and again commanded his clenched fists to stay down. His knuckles were white, the nails digging his palms. He could take a man twice his size if he wanted to. His feet were dancing, though, to their own tune.

'Want me to hold him, Pete?' A rough voice and beer breath came behind him.

'No! I'll knock the bugger's lights out meself.'

But there was less room for dancing. Peter closed in and Ben braced his stomach muscles. It took the second blow to wind him, a punch in the eye to have him on his knees. They would play dirty now. He covered his head shielding brain and eyes as fists peppered him before he sagged onto the rough paved ground and pretended to be out. He caught a whiff of Mary's sweet lavender but she couldn't get near him.

'Leave him, pet.' He heard Peter's gravel voice. 'Let'im come round where he's lying. I'll lay odds drunk or sober he'll not lay a finger on you again except in love. I'd kill him next time.' an all!' the beer breath grunted. 'Then stuff'im down the midden.'

2

1925

Late afternoon Ben cycled home from a back-shift at the pit, pedalling against a breeze, glad to get the evil stench of the ash-heap from his nostrils, wondering how many weeks or days the wrangling would last. Mary wanted an unopened pay packet but he'd already slipped a note away in his shirt pocket. They'd make do. He'd eat herring till he looked like one. Mine owners were taking the gloves off.

He smiled at a big woman walking easily up the rise of a street sloping towards the Tyne, skirts billowing behind her, a huge basket of clean linen was balancing on her majestic head, one hand steadying it, showing her bare arm pink as a ham.

'You can wash my overalls!' His teeth flashed white against the coal dust blackened face.

'They'd walk into the washhouse themselves today. You need chucking in a copper to get all that muck off you.'

'That's it, hinny. Hoy 'im in!'

He nodded back to them and glanced at the women coming to their front doors from houses with windows bricked up for the long past Government tax. They'd tax the sun if they could. Children pushed past their mothers clutching pieces of jam and bread, mouths smeared red, rushing to play before bedtime. A little knot of them made a swing from a long rope heaving and helping the smallest one to shin up a lamp-post and tie their borrowed treasure to the bars that jutted on either side. They whirled out, trying not to clatter knees against the hard iron. Ben ran an eye across the group to see if any of his bairns were out there. Six girls set up to play skippy rope with two lines lifting inward, one after the other. The girl who was 'on' hopped dancing into the loop while handlers started the swaying rhythm slowly then faster and faster till they caught her. Another set of lassies tied one end of their rope to a lamp-post further down. None of his girls was there. They had a back yard to play in.

Two women with identical headscarves over hairnets brushed their front pavement clean, one brushing down, the other brushing back. They tussled over muck passing up and down the path, glowering till the long brushes clashed against each other and showered dust upward that rained back onto flowered headscarves, forming a dirt river along the front door steps they'd chalked fresh yellow ochre. Ben snorted and got back on his bike as they screamed, shrieking abuse like mad seagulls tearing for food then smiled to himself at a little gang of lads playing knocky nine doors, rapping at front doors then running for their lives.

He pedalled home then caught sight of his eldest daughter pushing a pram up the street. He stabled the cycle inside the back yard and came out to rest his shoulders against the chipped brick by the window of Mary's bakery.

The women noticed Patricia and stopped their battle. 'There goes Miss High and Mighty.'

'Can't come over on our side of the street. We're not good enough!'

'How old's ya mam, pet, ter have had a baby?'

'Forty if she's a day.' They cackled.

'Passin' yor bairn off as her own, as the late one.'

'Ah will say ye've got ya figure back.'

'But the man that did it should be strung from that lamp post.'

'And we'll nor say by what!'

'I'm having none of that.' Ben stepped onto the street. 'My wife's bonny enough and strong enough to have given me a son - a little laddy. Keep your tittle tattle for yourselves and leave my lass alone. Leave us all alone.'

The headscarves laughed and shrilled, duel over. They made mock curtsies, sniggered and went in. He helped Patricia push the pram into the yard and lifted the baby up for her.

'I'll take him, dad. You're dirty.'

'Don't let those women get you down. Empty headed gossips.'

'I know. I don't answer.'

'That's best. Can you warn your mam Wilf's going to drop by and ask if she can fill another plate. I saw him on the way home.'

'I don't think I know him. She won't be pleased.'

'You can handle her. He's a best mate, my marra, though he hasn't been to the house much.'

'I'll pour water for your wash.'

'I'll see to myself in the bedroom, out of your way. Just check that the girls are all in while I scrape this muck off. They're forming a little gang these days. Our Louise should be out of that.'

'She's young for her age. She'll be all right.'

Carpet slippers stood ready in the scullery and he groaned as he shook pit boots off, relaxing to the sweet welcome of crust pies from the bakery. The baby in his cot, Patricia reached for the kettle spitting on the hob by the fire to pour a steam of water into the zinc tub the girls still used. Hair was sticking to her forehead.

'I'll take that, pet. Don't strain your back.' She smiled and handed him a towel warmed on the staved brass fireguard. Other brasses on the hearth glimmered from the flames. He felt a cord loosen in his head. As he put the tub in the bedroom a shiny blackened face edged slyly round the door. A girl four foot high jumped in, eyes looking twice their normal size in a circle of white. He slopped the water. 'It's you who've got my boot black, then?'

She started a tap dance, spread her arms to sing *I'm sitting on top of the world, just moving along, just singing a SOOoong.'*

He chuckled at the Al Jolson voice. 'Out! Your mother'll kill you. We've got company coming. Patricia'll clean you up.'

'She's changing the baby.'

'Then you'll have to take what's coming to you. Go on. Douse yourself from the tap in the yard. I have to get out of these pit clothes.' She disappeared laughing and he heard his wife's voice rise. The tune hummed in his head as he peeled sweat-caked, dust-coated clothes from his body and knelt on the lino to dip his head and lather the hair with a bar of green laundry soap then stepped lightly into the tub. When he was dried and dressed he heard a timid knock. 'Come in.'

A taller girl, so thin her clothes hung on her looked in. 'Mam says can you come to the table. And where's your friend?'

'If I'm not mistaken that's him rattling the knocker. Take these clothes to your mam, Louise. And help clean Katharine up.'

The girl lifted a bony shoulder and shrugged out.

'You've been at the coal face again,' Mary's voice accused. These'll mean a stint at the poss tub. I could do without this.'

'Pit props had weakened.'

'You shouldn't be down there.'

'It's my job. I'll not have blood on my hands.' He noticed his other daughter by herself in a corner, Diane, fair hair and pale rose complexion like a china doll.

'I'm not doing anything wrong.'

'You're the perfect one.' He clattered downstairs to open a creaking door.

Wilf Robson stooped awkwardly into the room and held his cap while Patricia brought in white china tea cups then ducked out to stop the girls in the scullery from quarrelling. Wilf smiled at the commotion.

'Four lasses?'

Ben nodded and sat back in his captain's chair, hands on the polished red wood of the arms. 'And we've a lad, not a year old. I couldn't quit before getting a little spout, a son and heir.' Patricia came in again with a teapot and poured.

'You're lucky. King of your castle. I've only got lads. Not waited on like this. How old's this one?'

'She'll answer for herself.'

'I'm seventeen, Mr. ...?'

'Robson.' Wilf looked straight at her but spoke to her father. 'She'll be getting married soon I expect, Ben.'

'I can keep my daughters yet a while. She doesn't have to take the first comer. And we need her at home for a bit to help look after the bairn.' Ben winked at his daughter as she went out. 'Fetch Christopher in when he's seen to, pet, when we've got a sup of soup.' He turned to his friend.

Patricia hurried out and came back with steaming bowls and freshly baked rolls.

'Reach up, Wilf. The vegetables here were all grown in the allotment.'

'Very good too.' They ate in silence for a minute and looked up gratefully when Patricia brought them a hot pie with a crusted potato top and chopped buttered cabbage.

'Thank you kindly. By, that feels better.'

'What I want to know is, would your lot be with us or not?'

Wilf shifted in his chair, his usually ruddy face a deepened red from the heat of fire and food. 'It's a hell of an undertaking, Ben, a strike.'

'So, the rail men are not with us. Same old story.' Ben knocked out his pipe over the live coals

'Divn't be like that, Ben. Ah didn't say we weren't with ye, just it's not to be entered into lightly. And are we sure there's no alternative? Strikes are hardly ever won and everybody loses.'

'But we're not as far as a strike.'

'Not what I heard.'

'Not by a long chalk. Not yet. I only want to see the lie of the land *if* we're pushed to it.' He offered Wilf a pouch of sweet Virginia tobacco. 'It's not us spoiling for a fight, it's the bosses. And they want to have it out. There's lively talk we could be locked out from the pits if we won't work longer hours for less pay. Would you do that?'

His friend waved a briarwood pipe. 'It's hard …'

'You wouldn't! And you don't have to haul your guts out in the bowels of the earth or sweat hours on end in a dark seam to wrestle coal with a pick head, sometimes on your belly.'

'We know, we know! The miner's life's a hard one … *but* you're not the only ones that know what work is.'

'*And* you don't go to work every day thinking it could be your last and that you could be blown to kingdom come by firedamp, the damned methane.

'No. But in the war years and till now, it has to be said, the miner's lived fairly well …*deserved* … before you get on your high horse again. But some of your gain's been at tax payer's expense though, first in the war and now to tide things over till both sides …'

'Are *we* not tax payers?' Ben thumped the table.

'Of course ye are. Divn't be so het up, man. I'm just trying to point out that a government subsidy can't go on forever in peace time.'

'Then pits should be taken over by government.'

'That's another issue. And somehow the war's got to be paid for. We're runnin' a debt'd frighten the devil `imself, payin' a fortune in interest every day!'

'And the miner has to pay for the damned war, soaking in sweat on his belly so the country can keep running?' He was on his feet swearing.

'Ben!' He saw his wife's frightened face at the scullery door.

'It's all right, Mary. I'm not going to throttle him.'

'Glad to hear it,' Wilf coughed as Mary ushered her daughter in with fresh tea. 'But where you're right is that Baldwin wants to take the subsidy off. Pit owners feel they can't make up the difference. Coal's losing money.'

'While their tables groan.' Ben felt a gentle hand on his shoulder and sat down to please his daughter. 'They want to up the shift by an hour to eight and pay us less for it. "Not a penny off the pay. Not an hour on the day." '

'I can just hear you lot chantin' it.'

'Be fair, Wilf. An' I'll tell you who else is payin' for the damned war. It's the German miner as well. France and Italy want free coals for reparation, bleeding poor German beggers white and starvin' their bits of bairns.'

'Now that's not patriotic talk!'

'Patriotism be damned! Keir Hardy said British and German people shouldn't have had to fight each other at all. There's a brotherhood of man and we violated it.'

'Stop bein' so high falutin!' Everybody bloody violated it!' And Keir Hardy, well we're not all soft pacifists. It's a wonder the white feather brigade wasn't after him.'

Ben laid a hand on his friend's arm. 'Worse than the white feathers.' He leant forward. 'Some people stoned the lad in the valley he represented.'

'Well, that's horrible to hear, Ben, but there's a time to keep your mouth shut.'

'And let wholesale slaughter go on? Working lads on the other side. There'll be more fight, what with the state Germany's in. That war to end war did no such thing.' Ben pulled out a drawer in the table and rummaged. 'I've got a cutting somewhere from the Journal from 1914.'

'Never mind your cuttings from the Journal.'

'It's a letter sent home from the trenches by a Gateshead lad.' Ben was in full flow.

'Here we go!' His friend sighed and stared at his cup pretending to read the tea leaves.

'Christmas Eve. Krauts started shouting "Merry Christmas" across the no man's land from one lot of trenches to the other and German and English troops ended up walking to meet each other in the middle'. Soldier that wrote the letter home said if it were left to the men on both sides there'd be no war at all.

'That's a touching story,' Wilf put his cup away, 'but it's not really the point, Ben.'

'The point is reparations hurt everybody and miners here'll be put out of work or have empty bellies while they bring up the coals. D'you know the cost of coal? It's bloody lives.'

'Nobody wants you working on an empty belly, man.'

'Right. But will you stand with us if the bosses lock us out and then there's a vote for a strike?'

'I can't speak for the whole of the rail industry but ...'

'Always the same!'

Patricia came in with the baby then little apple pies and smiled at Wilf. Ben bounced his son on his lap and watched his daughter break in with a tackle.

'Will you be going to St. James' Park this Saturday, Mr. Robson?'

The railman turned to her. 'I never miss, lass. Mind that referee last week needed his eyes seeing to. They must recruit them especially for defective sight.' Patricia began to eat with them as Wilf forgot who should own what and set off on his other passion. 'No, you don't see it all, Ben. Once a month on the terraces, and it's about your lot for the football. You don't see the half of it.' He turned and nodded to Patricia. 'It was a very nice meal, pet, tell your mam.' She got up and went to play a tune on the piano Ben had bought at auction. Wilf lit a pipe and their feet began to tap.

1926

Ben cycled home with a slim envelope in his pocket. It weighed a ton. He bolted the food ready for him on the table, scolded the younger girls, had indigestion and demanded bicarbonate of soda. Patricia took the girls by the hand to serve them at the scullery table

'You're going to wear a path on that good Wilton carpet.' Mary handed him the remedy in a glass of water.

'I bought it. I can tramp it.'

She took the kettle and went into the scullery to wash dishes talking over her shoulder. 'What's the matter? You're like a cat on hot coals.' Steam pearled on the green painted walls.

'It's not opening time yet. That's what's the matter. And don't shake your head at me! Where's my jacket?'

'Where you put it, I expect.'

He rattled the hangers in the wardrobe, found the missing item, brushed it to a beat in one direction, looked for a flower from the allotment for his buttonhole then went into the girls' bedroom to forage. 'Just because I work at the pit head doesn't mean I can't dress like a gentleman.' He found a flask of lavender on Patricia's chest of drawers and shook four spots onto his handkerchief.

She leaned in the doorway. 'I'll miss that, Dad. It's gone down by a quarter.'

'Evaporation,' he said.

'Aye, like a whisky bottle,' Mary said.

'I'll buy her fresh!' He glared at his wife then took the brown envelope from his working coat. 'You'd better read that.'

Mary took it but didn't open it. 'What is it?'

He turned, hunted beneath anger. 'Warning of the lockout. Let me dress like a gentleman while I can.' He slammed the door. 'Don't wait up!'

*

Saturday came, the fateful day. Ben reached over to switch the alarm clock off a few minutes before it was set, awake five minutes before he needed to be up. He never used a knocker up, hammering on the house to wake everybody.

He got out of bed quietly, later than on many a day for the early shift but still he tried not to waken Mary, picked up his work clothes from a chair and went downstairs to the range. The hot plate was warm from the ash-banked fire and the big black kettle on the hob to the side of the grate was simmering.

He took a blackened frying pan, placed it on the hot plate, melted lard for bacon and set it to fry while he made tea in the earthenware pot then swilled the rest of the hot water into a bowl and refilled the kettle to warm the water for Mary. His wash was thorough and swift, dousing his head, sweeping a sponge, waking body and mind as the bacon sizzled and the tea massed forming a brown moss under the lid. He added an egg to the pan and dressed in one minute.

Breakfast in the warm fug of the kitchen with the yeast sharp smell of proving bread was a pleasant solitary moment. He would have liked to linger with an early pipe but there was never time on workdays. Instead he slipped a twist of baccy to chew into his pocket. He reached down a warm plate from the range and served his bacon and eggs. A good breakfast to take him through the shift, a good hour spent seeing whether tunnels and whole pit lay out were safe before the miners arrived, only one break and then checking machinery when the hewers and putters and surface men were gone. He drank his tea hot, packed the bait tin in his haversack and was ready. The morning ritual took thirty-five minutes and he would cycle to the pithead in another twenty. The remains of a hangover cleared in the surge of cold air.

Men would turn up regardless of that letter. They were not on strike. Ben pushed his bicycle out into the blanket of lifting dark. He'd turn back if a whistling woman crossed his path but there was no bad omen.

Great wheels that meant work and energy showed stark and beautiful, carved against a gold-barred, lightening sky. In spite of the cold Ben felt warmth as he neared the pithead machinery. Working rhythmically, smoothly it was alive. Idle it stood against the sky sculpted in power, a statement of human mastery of the earth, ready to receive its tribute in lives. Gas. Collapsed seams. Rock fall. Fire. A fall down a shaft.

But a baton barred his path. There'd be no safety check this morning. Hadn't he heard? He stood back and waited in the cold, chewing a wadge of tobacco as a bitter solace, stained teeth or not.

Men cycled through the pit gates, bicycle lights on, protected with thick coats and flat cloth caps against morning keenness. He could see shock in their eyes at the sight they knew would meet them and thought they were ready for.

Broad ex-army types, imports from the South, from London, surplus muscle power from outside the region ranged in two ranks round the entrance. About fifty, human dross with long wooden truncheons. As the men approached their place of toil and comradeship, lamps on foreheads he knew they shared a sense of desecration with him, men who trusted each other with their lives hacking black gold.

The full number turned out for the Saturday morning shift in spite of warning of the lockout. No-one spoke as they dismounted and stacked bicycles one on another against the railings instead of the locked shed. They stood together facing an unfamiliar enemy moving together in silence to meet the invader. Five or six bobbies watched the scene to see Law and Order preserved.

The miners' hands were at their sides. The enemy lifted long weapons but held their charge. Miners advanced. The enemy strained to hold fire till the last moment as a spearhead of the brave made for the entrance. Truncheons lifted but held as a threat of worse to come. The men at the tip of the spear tried to pass but cudgels slammed to unbalance them, then iron shod toes kicked in hard. Another assault and the batons raised in unison like a military parade. A rush and they battered hands, arms, chests, legs when a man keeled over. The first line crawled and was dragged from the path of crippling boots by friends before staggering to their bicycles, determined to return. Others took their places. Ben joined them.

This was the start.

He cycled through the cold morning hardly feeling a blackening bruise that spread on his shin, sick at heart.

*

For days time hung at home. Wilf at work, no men to talk to, under everyone's feet. Mary was baking a wedding cake, an all-day affair, her table covered with sultanas, raisins, bits of peel on separate trays that had dried out over a couple of days from a fierce rinsing. He chewed his breakfast down. Better go into the town, a day in the library or the reading room at the Miners' Institute in refuge from his wife's creative madness. The calm of books and all the newspapers.

A thick atmosphere of quiet was broken by feet shuffling or clicking on hard floor, coughs, sighs, rustling of papers. But the stillness offered no comfort. Every movement echoed and he finally put down the *Manchester Guardian* after reading a paragraph three times. The covered market might be better.

He wandered under green light under glass panes in the roof, looking at stalls piled with vegetables and fruit stacked in bright colours. Produce from his allotment was less regular but he was sure it tasted better.

He turned coins in his pocket but left them and moved away from the earthy sharp smells to nose into the dust of old books at the other end of the market. Finally the clock showed four and he could go back.

A spice of dark treacle drifted from the range in the bakery oven door that was tight shut but he sniffed, separating aromas like a wine taster, drinking in nuts and cherries, cinnamon, nutmeg.

'There's long faces. Have you burnt that wedding cake? We can't afford for good ingredients to get burnt. I'm not made of money.'

Mary flounced her apron. 'Since when did you pay for my ingredients?'

'Well, there's something wrong. I can see crumbs on this floor.'

'There's nothing burnt, dad.' Patricia took his coat. 'You'd smell it right away. There's no fooling your nose.'

'So where are these crumbs from?' Irritation pressed against his throat and burst out. 'Have you lost your minds and eaten the whole thing? And what's that damn dog doing under the scotch chest? I can see its nose.'

Patricia settled him in his carver and gave him a cup of tea and a borrowed evening paper. He looked over his glasses, shook the thin leaves out and took a gulp of smoking liquid. He held his mouth and let the cup clatter onto the table, the newspaper slid onto the floor. 'Good God Almighty! Are you trying to kill me? You've scalded my mouth off!' His glasses had fallen to the tip of his nose and Louise began to giggle. 'Does no-one know how to serve me a cup of tea?' He stood up and trampled on the newspaper, trying to get the dog out from under the chest of drawers with his walking stick. The spaniel snapped at the rubber end. He pushed it further in.

'More crumbs under here! What's gone on?'

Mary's apron creased as she gripped its crisp white starch. 'If you must know, the dog got at the cake and ate a piece. Come and get your tea.'

'I knew it! A whole wedding cake ruined! What do you think this is? A home for criminal dogs? If I had a gun, I'd drag the thing out and shoot it.'

Patricia came in and picked up the crumpled paper. 'Dad, come to the table. 'You'll have a heart attack.'

'So, you're a doctor as well, are you, miss?' He sat down as she sat opposite trying to calm him.

'And the cake's all right. Mam always makes a little 'tryer' to see if the nuts are rancid. I've patched it with a wedge from the tryer, stuck it in with jam. I'll ice it and nobody'll know the difference.'

'The whole street'll know now,' Mary said.

'Living here's enough to give anybody a heart attack. I'll have an ulcer, never mind a heart attack.'

He stood up but fell back on his haunches, wiped his brow and felt Mary's hand touch his hair.

'It's not your fault, Ben.' She caressed the back of his head. 'It's not your fault.'

3

Ben breathed the comforting scent of baking as Mary beat up cake batter, vanilla reminding him of a warm meadow. Gashes appeared as she whisked the pale sugar and butter that folded over on itself like satin against the warmth of her hand.

So, what's this committee going to be about?' she asked.

A damp sour smell of coal from outside overcame the vanilla as he tipped a bucketful into an empty brass scuttle. Then he stirred the flames in the grate and watched greens and blues bounce back from the polished black lead of the range, putting off his reply.

'It's the Central Strike Committee.' He laid a weathered tweed jacket against the back of his chair to brush it. 'We've got to co-ordinate the Trades Unions.' He took long strokes down the heather blend.

'There's been a lot of agitation and talk.'

'Hot air,' Mary concentrated on her mixing bowl, comfortable on a three-legged stool, her cracket.

Ben looked up. 'By God, it's exciting, though. First time the Unions have actually stood together.' He stood up, shook the coat out and leant to kiss her neck as she whipped her blend. 'Almost as exciting as the first time you make love.' He ducked away. 'There'll be problems, though, when we really start the organising.'

She slopped the creamy mix. 'Think you can arrange anything, you men.'

'Not a bit of it. We've got a couple of capable women on the committee. I expect they'll keep us in order. We don't make distinctions. There's no need for you to wait on me hand and foot, you know, Mary.'

'You love it and you expect it, so don't give me that. Anyway, I don't interfere with your politics. I'll thank you not to interfere with the way I run my home. I won't have anybody talk about me round here.'

'I'd push Christopher's pram but you won't have it.'

'You'd better get to your meeting. Give Bessy Parker my regards. I expect she's one of them.'

'Aye, she's one of them.'

'It wouldn't be a show without Punch.'

Ben picked a bud from a vase for his buttonhole. 'I don't know what time I'll be back. It might go on a bit.'

'Don't worry. I've got plenty to do. People are going to have to eat through this lockout and strike. And no unemployment money.'

He paused at the door, 'We'll have to make sure you're stocked up for a month at least.' He came back, kissed her hair then clattered down the stairs shouting over his shoulder, 'I'll be back when I'm back,' and whistled as he snapped the latch on the front door.

Last to arrive, he took his place to sit round a table on the bare boards of the Co-op's upper floor. Fresh distemper from the walls and sawdust from knotty pine, smells of a meeting.

Bessy Parker sat opposite in a smart tailored coat of navy blue. Ben knew she'd picked out an old greatcoat, turned and re-cut the fabric, but this made her more handsome in his eyes. Strands of grey against black were curled smooth on her brow. She nodded to him.

'Now you're here, Ben, we can make a start.' Wilf was chairman. 'As I see it, the first problem here is transport.'

'And power, Wilf.' Bessy leant forward. 'Gas and electricity.'

A babble of voices broke out, echoing from the ceiling as Wilf held his pencil in the air like a baton.

'Right! We'll deal with that first. Show we're in charge if we shut the juice off.'

'Wait on, though, Wilf.' Ben took his jacket off. 'That's a thorny one. We can't blithely start shutting power off in hospitals or housing.'

'You have to make it bite, man, Ben! It's no good pussy footing around. This isn't make believe, not the bloody school yard – sorry, Bess – and everything put away after playtime.'

Ben put both elbows on the table and stared in his friend's eyes. 'Nobody said it was, but you'd be making ordinary people suffer.'

'That's right,' Bessy stopped writing. 'Punishing our own. What about sick children? What about a woman in labour?'

'She should have joined the Party,' Wilf said.

Bessy flushed and pushed her chair back and made towards the door. 'I haven't come here for a pantomime! There's enough work to do at home.' She turned round. 'These are serious matters. What about an accident down the pit? You could be responsible for deaths.' Her voice rose.

'She's right, Wilf. Please come back, Bessy.'

'You want to take over this meeting, Ben Hawthorne?'

'Not unless you give up on it. Bessy's right. In a hospital we'd make everybody suffer if we just pulled the plug on the juice.'

'Another opinion?'

'Yes, but we could shut down factories and stop blackleg labour.'

He nodded, 'Put the mockers on industry. So, we leave emergency services. And the women have to be able to cook a dinner. Hadn't thought of that.'

Bessy scraped her chair back to the table. 'Are we going to follow an agenda or not?' She smoothed her note pad. 'That's the principle then. We have to keep emergency services going, transport as well.' She made notes as she spoke.

'Not easy,' Wilf said. 'We're not going to run any trains. Any!' He stared at Ben. 'The railway men are out and that's that! We'll not be blamed by the miners this time round like the affair in `21. Men from buses and trams are out as well.' He banged the table and voices let loose again. 'Trams and buses are simply not going to run.'

'It'll be a hell of a job to control individual vans and lorries.'

'Can't control non-unionised labour.'

'We could barricade the streets!'

'So nobody can pass at all?' Bessy made herself heard. 'We're not here to cause unnecessary suffering.' She lobbied for essential foodstuffs and supplies to hospitals.

'Right! The colonel does without his whisky bur bread and butter get through,' Ben said. 'Luxury goods are another matter.'

'But how'll we know who's carrying what?' Bessy asked.

'A system of permits!' Wilf hit the table and glared round. 'Drivers'll have to come to us and declare what they're carrying. We'll issue permits to the right people for humanitarian supplies.' He grinned in triumph at the long word. 'But factories, public transport depots and the like'll be picketed. All in favour?' He checked for a show of hands. 'Take that down, please, Bess.'

'It's already down,' Bessy's neat handwriting slowly covered two sides. Argument after argument, resolution after resolution.

Ben took his pocket watch out. 'After ten, Wilf. Some of us have homes to go to.'

'Right, then. Any other business is for next time.'

Ben pulled his jacket on, clapped Wilf's shoulder and turned to Bessy. 'How are you getting home, lass?'

'I've my push bike, thanks, Ben.'

'I could cycle with you to make sure you get home all right.'

'I'll be O.K. thank you, Ben.' She looked up quickly. 'But there's no-one whose company I'd rather have.'

'No man to meet you, Bess. I'll cycle a little way at any rate. I wouldn't like Mary out on her own at night.'

'Just as you like,' Her voice was warm.

They rode in silence keeping their breath for the push up the hill, stopped at the end of her street and dismounted.

'Will you come in for a bite to eat Ben?'

'I'd better get back, I think. Mary sends her regards.'

'Thank her kindly. It would have been nice to have shared my supper. I'll not say it doesn't get lonely.'

Her eyes in the moonlight glimmered white round the edges. He smiled without thinking, feeling a tug of warmth at a woman's

27

invitation. 'You do very well, bonny lass, holding everything together, the bairns and all. Eight years, is it, since Charlie got killed?'

'Nearly nine. And I'll not say I'm not bitter.'

'It's got a lot to answer for, the Great War.'

'We're all called on to make sacrifices,' her voice hardened.

'Mass slaughter. Miners had to stay in the pits. But Churchill wants to make us pick up the tab now to put the country back on the Gold Standard, Longer hours, less money.' He checked himself. 'Sorry, I'm ranting and we've had enough of politics for one night. Is somebody with the bairns?'

'The eldest can look after them now.'

'You've brought them up right, Bessy, and given time to the Movement.'

'It's nice to be appreciated.'

Bessy's face was level with his. He was not a tall man 'Everybody appreciates you, lass,' he said putting a foot in the pedal and swinging over the saddle. 'I had to see you safe home. See you at the next meeting.'

'Night, Ben.'

The air was cool on his face as he rode back. He'd worked with Bessy before on Labour Party business and had looked after her as he hoped another man would look after his wife or daughters. She was a fine woman, Bessy. No mistake she'd held a door ajar for him. He rode against the breeze, pedalling weights of air and felt pleasure that she let him know there could be caring for him. If he were alone he'd make a beeline for her. He'd always been soft toward women. His mind wandered as he heaved up a hill. Twenty-four when he tied the knot with the woman he loved. Marriage was marriage. The warm pleasure of Bessy's glance stayed, though.

Dorothy Thompson had been his first. He remembered card games at his father's house at weekends. She came with the others, playing for coppers, the winner providing tea next time. Dorothy must have been all of twenty-three and he an apprentice of seventeen. Old gossips had a field day about Dorothy, watching who knocked, how late they stayed, callers after ten o'clock at night! - white hair straggling onto their cheeks, red in the face with indignation. Or was it regret? Young woman like that shouldn't be living on her own! But it wasn't her fault her parents were dead. Why shouldn't she stay if she could pay for the flat?

He slowed at a cross roads in the darkness then quickened his pace in the stirrups. Golden red hair, swept up on the top of her head, and a swan's neck. Lots of young men came courting Dorothy. He remembered the pouffe´ his mother had given her and that he'd had to lug up the stairs then had the offer of a cup of tea. He'd brought a bucket of coal in to show he was a man and banked the fire up.

'Do you have milk and sugar, Ben?'

'Please.'

'Or would you like something else in your tea? I think I have a drop of rum.'

'Er ... Yes, please, Dorothy. I'd like that.'

Spirits were new to him. The rum was warm, half sweet in tea, relaxing him. Dorothy's face glowed as the red light of the fire glanced off her face, making her blue eyes deep in a gaze that was for him. Heat from the fire, rum and Dorothy's stare made him flush.

'Take your jacket off if you're warm.' He slid it over the back of the chair. 'Don't you have a girlfriend yet, Ben?'

'I did have, but not for long.' He squirmed. 'Nothing came of it, nothing important. You're not settled yourself, then?'

'Haven't met the right man. If I'd gone through school with you now, I don't think you'd have escaped with that golden hair.' He blushed. 'Don't be so shy, Ben.' She'd been framed in a glow with her back to the fire. 'Come here.' She sat on the two-seater couch and he joined her, stiff as a board and took another shot of rum from her.

'Have you kissed a girl before?'

'Yes.'

'Would you like to again?'

He smiled through awkwardness then gave her a hard peck on the mouth before she slid her hand round his neck, nuzzled an ear and kissed him three times across his mouth. He copied her, not sure what to do next till she put a soft mouth against his and led his hand to her breast.

'You must go on kissing me, Ben, when you undo buttons. You need a lot of kisses. There are a lot of buttons.'

He was always grateful for Dorothy. He learned to kiss tenderly as she gradually showed him how to undress a woman, loving her gently all the while. Then what a fool! He almost skidded on a stone at the memory and swerved on the road that showed oily in the moonlight. Dorothy's voice, like the rest of her was soft. 'No-one does perfect first time.' She'd gazed at him as he looked at the floor in shame and patted his rosy rump. 'Come back to me, Ben. You're a man now.'

After that clumsiness she'd seen him off at the top of the stairs, wearing her nightgown with her hair unfastened on her shoulder. Third time had been better, in front of a roaring fire. He smiled in the darkness as he remembered the tash he grew to look older, how he slicked his hair with brilliantine. Dorothy knew how to obtain 'marital aids'. She was beautiful and he loved her fair smoothness, but his heart stayed aloof.

Bessy was another matter. Not a woman to play with. Perhaps Wilf should see her home next time. Twenty years and Mary was still his love. She'd kill him if he strayed! He was nearly home. Nice to know he could interest them, though. At forty-two if this lockout hadn't come and the big strike now planned with no money attached, his life would have been be damn near perfect.

Mary was sipping hot milk by the fire. 'The vicar called.' Her limbs showed through a cotton nightdress.

'John? What did he want?

'Wanted to talk to you about the strike, I think.'

'Give me a lecture, no doubt.'

'He wants to know the ins and outs of it - what you think. You know he likes to talk to you.'

The low gas lamp hissed behind an alabaster shade spilling splinters of light on Mary's dark head. He heard the spits and whisperings of the dying fire that licked shadows on the ceiling and stood slipping into the shape of this second, trying to hold it.

'He could want to help,' she said

'Maybe God isn't such a mean old bugger after all, then.' He broke the spell.

'Don't talk to the vicar like that.'

'He's got a sense of humour, old John. And God can take it! If he's as great as they say – if he's there.'

He sat opposite her. 'The trouble is nobody thinks things through till there's a crisis. Only concerned whether they've got money in their pocket and a nice woman in their arms to cuddle.'

'There has to be more to life than sex and money,' she said.

'A lot more.' He winked and knelt beside her. 'You're a fine figure of a woman, Mary.' He made a web of her fingers in his, tenderly kissed them and saw the young girl he'd married in this dream of silver light. A gossamer web of illusion wrapped them as they slipped into their bed, as he held her then fell into the void. Mary smelled of starch and lavender, spiked grass from a woman's own ointment ... too much to lose. But drowsing against her back consciousness spun back.

... She thinks I'm away too much on the politics. But for us our politics mean hope. John Hargraves gets it from religion. My father did that and look what happened to him. You just have to fight sometimes ...

A vision of the hard men guarding the entrance to the pit came back and a worm of doubt bored in his mind.

*

31

Committee after committee meeting in the next few days, mornings and evenings. Some afternoons he was free and looked after the bakery for an hour or two.

He was reading the strike paper and looked up as the door opened and the brass clappered bell fixed to the top rang. Two women stood meaningfully by the counter and Ben stood up. Mrs Snowball was brick faced and fishy eyed. He could tell from the set of her shoulders the bairns had been up to something.

Had he heard what those girls had done at the Salvation Army Citadel? He listened respectfully as Mrs. Snowball relayed it to him before he heard the girls' version. He could almost smell the soup kitchen and pictured the scene as she talked.

Before the nostril tickling broth was served they'd had to sing rousing hymns and settle down for a talk. The Major was used to speaking outdoors and could be heard in every corner. There was no escape. His idea of time was his own. Two minutes to Ben's children was eternity.

They spotted responsible people dotted about the Citadel to keep an eye on the unruly but couldn't sit still. A large man sat in front of them and craned round to give them a noisy "Shush!" The girls knew him. They knew the tribe and hated those who got up to do 'turns'. It wasn't called that. Here it was glorifying the Lord.

Mr. Snowball's back had become steadfast and immovable. He lost interest in them and was following proceedings from the platform. Gradually Diane's attention became riveted on this impressive back. It was not the back itself that was fascinating, but the attached large and ponderous bottom. The excesses of fat Mr. Snowball carried round seemed to have met and congealed at the base of his spine. It happened that a large and lethal safety pin for Christopher's nappies was in Diane's pocket. She fingered it, clasped and unclasped it till it was hot and sticky. The heat stiffened. The talk continued and the pin was in her hand. At last the Major drew to a close.

He coughed. 'And now to continue the word, Queenie will bring us a message in song.' Mr. Snowball shifted his weight as his daughter stepped up to the platform.

Queenie stood up, bashful but smart in her bonnet, tied in a large bow at one side and the dark uniform hugging a just-sprouting figure. Her father shuffled expectantly in his seat. The bottom shuffled with him. To a hush Queenie sweetly began her song. Diane's pin was poised. This was a particular 'thorn in their flesh' … everyone looking at the hated girl. The notes of the song rose higher as Queenie's voice dipped and swayed.

' … into His Kiiiiingdom!!.' Mr. Snowball listened in rapture. 'Come, come. COME!' rang out.

Diane took aim, Queenie's soprano climbed and was joined suddenly by a tenor top C. Diane put the pin back in her pocket. Mr. Snowball shot out of the bench dancing and clutching his rear. The hall was in uproar as the three girls raced for the exit waiting neither for soup nor the kind invitation to be saved.

Ben looked his visitors in the eye and kept a straight face as he heard scuffling up the stairs.

'That's them, Mr. Hawthorne. They think they'll get away with it by running round the back.'

'I'll send them straight to bed and every evening for the rest of the week. Can we help out at the soup kitchen? We sometimes have bread left over from the bakery. Yesterday's, you understand, but fresh enough to eat and I'll fetch you some vegetables from the allotment for the soup.'

The shoulders relaxed. 'We won't turn away help from any quarter, Mr. Hawthorne. But I want you to guarantee that not one of your daughters enters the Citadel again.'

'I'll guarantee that absolutely.'

'Our Queenie was most upset.'

'I'll investigate the whole thing. I'm really sorry you've had disruption at the meeting. They've no business to be cadging soup at the citadel.' He rummaged under the counter for a few loaves. 'I appreciate what you do for the very poor. It's not everyone who'll get their hands dirty. I know you've been helping families of the men on strike who've got nothing.' He meant it and came round to open the door for them. 'That's not forgotten. We'll send bread down on Tuesday. We don't bake on Sunday.'

'All right, then.'

... Banished from the halls of salvation ... what next?

Mary came in from the baby's afternoon walk, wondered why the girls had been put to bed and found him crying with laughter.

4

Ben grinned as the door opened for the Reverend Hargraves and he waved the clergyman to a seat.

'Not coming to try to convert me are you, your Parsnip?'

'I'll let the Almighty handle that himself, Ben.' The clergyman sat comfortably as Mary brought a cup of tea and a roll each from the bakery. They bit into the delicate crusts.

'Well, we can smoke a pipe together,' Ben said. Noisy chatter rose from the backyard where the youngest girl had her friends in. He looked out, saw Katharine had wrapped herself in the best chenille tablecloth for a concert and drew the sash down for quiet.. Hargraves politely drank his tea. 'What can I do for you then, John?'

'Wondered if you'd seen this latest copy of the British Gazette?'

'Government propaganda!' Ben almost spilt the tea. 'Lies printed to put the mockers on the strike effort, a lot of it from Churchill as well. Put it on the fire'

'Calm down, fill your pipe, Ben.' Hargraves offered his bag of Golden Virginia. The bitter smell of the leather pouch blended with a fragrant hay scent of tobacco, relaxed them before they lit up. 'You can be a bit hard on Winston, you know. He did decent things as Home Secretary. I know he went personally into prisons to forbid the caning of the men. Did you know that?'

'Probably sent by Lloyd George.' His friend shook his head. 'Anyway, if he did, then worms have got in his brain since.'

Hargraves sat back and crouched over the bowl of the pipe concentrating till the baccy glowed. 'One of the worst things about this strike is that good national papers aren't delivered to the shops. I miss my Manchester Guardian.'

'Half price to clergy!'

'The only perk, and it ends up round here.' He unfolded the latest copy of the Gazette from his outer coat. 'The Archbishop of Canterbury's quoted in this.'

'For or against us?'

'It reads as if he's against.' Hargraves jabbed a finger at a paragraph. 'His lordship's quoted saying the strike's so intolerable the government should make every effort to end it.' Ben snorted. 'Wait, they've reported only half of what he said. My 'phone line's still working – thank you - I rang a friend who works for the Archbishop. He wasn't attacking the miners. What he really **said** was ... and the government should explore **everything** to reach a settlement between all sides, miners, owners **and** government, all round the table. The paper's distorted it and this gets quoted on, of course.'

Ben looked up from his pipe. 'Where does the rest of your lot stand?'

'Bishop of Manchester's strongly for the miners, no surprise with William Temple.' Ben nodded and sucked on his pipe stem. 'There's a division of opinion among the others. The other point they left out in this Gazette is fear.'

'Oh aye?'

'Canterbury said it was desperate fear that's motivating this strike. Widespread fear that if miners take a cut everybody's wages will go down as well.'

'Well, he's not wrong there.'

'I thought I'd let you know about the misquote.'

'The damned rag's turned it on its head.' Ben relit his pipe, shook the match and puffed into the fireplace. Smoke circled on a draught into the chimney over unlit coals. He pointed the stem of his pipe at his friend. 'Churchill's also printed that the government'd back the actions of armed forces to the hilt if they came in to help the Civil Power. If that's not a threat! ... Send the troops in like he did at Tonypandy in 1910!'

'That whole incident of the Tonypandy riots was a tragedy.'

'It was a damned disgrace. He sent the troops and the Met into Wales against miners on strike.'

'But I think he tried to avoid the confrontation and I'm not sure the order to fire – **if** they did fire - came direct from Churchill. There's more than one story goes round.'

'You're not sure about nowt, John. And it was putting troops in to threaten civilians in time of peace - at the very least.'

'Anyway, did you know the king protested to the War Office about that? The next day!'

Ben's pipe went out again, he knocked it on the bricks above the coal dislodging soot that hung in a frail fringe of black lace and glared up. 'Surely that proves the troops were out of order.' He felt a wall building between them. 'So where do you stand in all this, John?'

'Honestly? I'm struggling with it. That's why I came round. But I'd like to ask you a personal thing first.'

'Ask away. I may not answer.'

Hargraves pulled at his dog collar. 'Set aside what other people say.' He leant forward. 'What drives **you** in all this? Your family could suffer from a strike. You know it always results in hardship.'

'I'm not offended, John.' Ben took down a sepia photo from the mantelpiece of Mary in a long tailored costume and wide brimmed picture hat. He passed it to the clergyman. 'I love my wife and you can see why. But the grit to strike goes back to my father. He had nine of us to bring up.' The photo clicked back into its place on the mantelpiece. 'He was clerk to an accountant and he worked very hard, my dad. He had a head on his shoulders for figures, could add a four figure column in his head quick as you like, more accurate than a ready reckoner. In the end he was almost doing the accountant's job but not getting paid for it.

'What went go wrong?'

Ben kicked at the fender. 'One of their clients, a big firm had a massive shortfall on the books and the taxman caught up with it. 'Huge amount of money'd gone missing. It looked like they'd been cheating colossally on taxes for years, the accountant and head of that firm, and they could both have gone to prison.'

'Did they?'

'What do you think? My dad carried the can and lost his job. He never had anything to do with that account but they dismissed him with one week's wage. Bosses found a scapegoat and the big firm got away with it.' Ben's mouth set in bitterness as he sat down.

'What happened to the family?'

'He had to take shop work and my mother had to go out cleaning. They were religious people and they put up with it. That's how I saw religion, as helping keep people down. My father's life was wasted. I don't hope for heaven. I want to right wrongs here on earth.'

'So do I, Ben. It was the prophet Isaiah who first coined the phrase "grinding the faces of the poor", not Karl Marx. The prophets fought for social justice, prophet against king.'

Ben lifted his pipe in salute. 'One to you. If my father'd had more formal education, he could have been an accountant himself. As for me, I want the working man and his family to have a decent life. Is that so much to ask?' Katharine burst in wrapped in her cloak, burnt cork marks on her face and scraped, eyes wide, to a halt on the polished lino. Ben caught her before she slipped. 'The vicar's not going to eat you, but you'd better get out of that tablecloth before your mam sees you.' Black eyes nodded but she went on staring at the man in grey with his collar the wrong way round. 'Here.' He untied and folded the soft bronze cloth.

'It's time for bed'.

'Can I wake up and listen to the wireless for the boxing?'

'No, you can't!'

'Louise told me it's from America and you listen to it in the middle of the night.'

'I haven't got to get up for a shift in the morning.' Her lower lip jutted. 'All right. If you're awake, you can listen to it.' She smiled and danced out. 'Let's take a turn outside, John. It's light, we'll be in the way here. My friend Wilf's on a bowling team up at the park, though I don't know how he finds time at the minute.' Ben lowered his voice. 'Little girls have big ears.'

'It's on my way home. Goodnight, Mary!'

They hurried downstairs and sauntered out hatless into the dying sun that had moved from the clock tower over the fire station casting a shadow over half the street. Women sat outside on three-legged stools or wicker chairs to gossip, younger ones holding babies against their shoulders or on their hips if they leaned against the doorframe. Men had no money for the pub, little girls chalked a hopscotch frame on the pavement.

'Be careful where you draw that line,' one squeaked.

'Why?'

'Don't want to land on a crack.'

'Why?'

'You'd have a black baby.'

They avoided two men illegally playing 'shove ha'penny' at the kerbside and Ben pointed out that the Almighty seemed to be with the slaves in the Old Testament. Not on the side of the big boss Pharaoh. John laughed and they walked up the street in good humour.

By the iron railings of the park they could hear the tock of balls. Ben sneezed when they went in to the freshly cut grass, dropped onto a faded wooden bench and watched the game intently. 'Old man's marbles. Anyway, can I do something for you, John?'

Hargraves watched a shot curl. 'I wondered if I could make a car journey or whether the pickets would stop me.'

'You'd need a permit. What's so important?'

Hargraves shifted on the bench. 'I'm afraid I have a murky past. My family has ties with the mines, on the owners' side. Money from seams of coal paid for my education. My father says it was money well spent and I'm giving something back now.''

'I suppose … I suppose, you didn't ask to be born into that family, choose any of it.'

'No.' He sat back. 'Most of my parishioners are suffering badly, though, and I feel it. We've got a welfare fund going to help. In fact, I've had to fill something in on the parish return for the diocese. I'm asked about whether there's serious poverty here.'

'Oh, aye. What did you say?'

'What could I say? Many of my parishioners are ill clad, malnourished and can't afford a doctor. I've given them the information. They want to know what we're doing about it – the welfare fund's not nearly enough, I know that.'

'It's a start. They should know, though, a lot of families can't afford shoes for all their bairns. And where there's a hard choice the little lads go bare foot. I've seen them hopping from one foot to another to try to get some warmth."

Hargraves sighed as they watched the game. 'I'd like to visit my family and hear what they have to say - to be fair to them. It might help clear my own mind. I feel like I'm in the middle of a tug of war. And my father's been a decent man according to his own lights, and he'll put his hand in his pocket for other people.'

'Can't argue against fairness. Do you have the juice?'

'A full tank, some jerry cans. I should be able to make it. I'll be careful with petrol after my trip - if I can go.'

'Do what your heart tells you, John. Wilf here'll sort you out some kind of permit if you think you need it, something to wave at them if you're stopped.'

They stood up to clap as a bowl nudged in by magic to touch the white jack.

*

Mary spat on the flat of her electric iron next night with a report like a gun. Ben started and almost dropped the cut throat razor he'd been smoothing across his cheek.

'I wish you wouldn't do that. And be careful, that's the only electric point we have.'

'How else am I to get your things ready?' She sprinkled water on a shirt. 'It heats up quickly, this. Better than that charcoal-packed thing on the hearth. Anyway, what's happening tonight?' She tested the beautiful electric iron on a shirt tail and raised a hiss of steam. The room filled with the smell of hot steel on scorching cloth.

Ben dipped his brush in water and worked a soap lather in his shaving bowl. Vapour from the ironing board made him catch his breath but the scent of fresh clothes airing was like his mother's kitchen. He looked carefully in his angled shaving mirror. 'Just speakers at the Bigg Market tonight.'

'Some people have been arrested for doing no more than opening their mouths, you know.'

'Nobody in this part of the world.' He lathered his cheeks. 'Police here have helped in organising concerts for the Miners' Welfare and played football matches with the pickets. There's been no bother here. You'd be surprised how many people are helping us with little bits and pieces. The bairns at any rate are getting fed, usually something hot, at least once a day.' The lethally sharp razor ploughed a smooth furrow through a froth of white soap.

'There's always a first time, and you've done your bit with all those committee meetings.'

'It's better to be busy, Mary. Believe it or not, I miss the pit. It pursues me in dreams. I often wake up feeling coal dust on the back of my throat.'

'Well, I don't miss the stale baccy on your breath.'

'I'll try and do something about that.' He took a hot towel from the fireguard and patted his face. 'It's men who're not doing much who're getting nervous. Anyway, you've got enough on your hands with the bakery without worrying about me.'

She stood the iron on its heel. 'I've got a problem with that, Ben.'

'Have you, lass?' He sat down to face her. 'You don't often admit to problems.'

'People are running out of money. There's some want to run up a tab.' Her shoulders hunched and deep lines creased on her forehead.

'Once you start that, Mary, there'll never be an end to it. Word'll fly round and you'll have everybody at your doorstep. There'll be those who're really hungry and those who're not.'

'But I know some of them, Ben. I know they're genuine. How can you be that callous when people have little bairns?'

Ben shook his head. 'You'll regret it,' his voice became hard. 'I saw a broken clock on a shop wall once with a message underneath. "This clock doesn't tick, and neither do we." Take that as your motto. If people are really hungry there are soup kitchens and they're doing a good job. A body can get by on soup for a while. No need for them to cadge off you. I want to see reform, you know that. That's why I'm involved in all this. But a business isn't a charity, Mary.'

'Yes, Ben.'

'You'll get hurt.' He shook her shoulders gently. 'You're not listening, are you?'

'I'm listening.'

He kissed her cheek. 'I'll be off then. Don't worry about us.' He reached a clothes brush from the mantelpiece for his ritual and stroked the pile up on his jacket. 'Last week we had up to five thousand men on a mass picket at the Central Station.'

'I didn't know that.'

'The police super just asked the Union secretary to address them and the crowd went off home without any bother. Some of the police have brothers down the pit.'

'Aye, but they might start bringing polis in from outside.'

'That would be a different matter altogether, but it hasn't happened yet.' He snipped a flower from the allotment for a buttonhole and gave her a kiss. 'I'll be all right.'

'Come home in one piece,' she said.

People thronged the Bigg Market, pushing and jostling in the free for all. The Salvation Army peddled the 'War Cry' as knots of people gathered round this speaker and that. Finally they gave the paper away as there was no-one had spare money. The girls wore ribboned bonnets. One of them came up to Ben and Wilf but they showed her their empty pockets and she gave them a copy.

'Thank you kindly,' Wilf said. 'Now that's what I call loving your neighbour. If you want any practice, hinny, you can start practising on me.' The girl blushed and disappeared into the crowd.

'Leave her alone, Wilf,' Ben said.

'Just a bit of fun, man. What's going on over there? There's a fair crowd.'

'Looks like a tub thumper.'

They jolted against a man passing out the 'British Worker'. He smelt of old clothes, sweat and cheap cigarettes.

'Sorry,' Ben said as they broke apart, 'but I'll have a Union paper, if you don't mind, lad.' He turned Wilf round to read the headline against his back in the crush. 'I gave mine away to John Hargraves. Yes ...*Peace Call Silenced*. It's the Archbishop's appeal. I think that's what our soap box special's on about.' They were wedged by the press of people behind them but he saw Wilf skewer his head round, creasing his eyes to skim the crowd. 'What's the matter with you, Wilf? Keep your feet still.'

'Just checkin' if it's goin' ter be lively. Lookin' for the usual hecklers.' He turned to his right again,

'Where are ye from, mate? I don't recognise ye.'

'Why should you?'

'You get to know the faces. Just a friendly question.'

'Me an' me mate's up from Sunderland. Seein' how the other half live!'

'Yer not supporters at Roker Park!'

''Course we are.' The man further along opened his coat, gave a cheeky grin and pulled the collar back to show a red and white Rosette pinned to his jumper.

'Well, ye want ter have a word with yerself, son. Comin' up here with that on!'

'We were just minding our own business. But since *ye* start the subject, it's my understandin' that there's nee such thing as loyalty at St. James' Park. So we thought we'd lend a hand.'

Ben laid an arm on Wilf's shoulder and moved him to his other side.

'They're little chickens an all,' the other red and white fan said.

'Mackems!'

'Geordie maggots!'

Ben stood firmly between them. 'Shut it, Wilf. I want to hear what's being said. That goes for you two as well.'

The speaker's voice carried over the hubbub. 'Do we live in a land of free speech? Friends, I tell you we do not! Only those supporting the right wing establishment and MONEY can have a voice,' People at the back started to clap. Further down the street, where another island of supporters was gathering, they heard a silver trumpet sound a note accompanied by Hallelujahs and the Salvation Army began to fight the good fight in song. Ben reached in his back pocket for the hip flask he'd smuggled out under Mary's nose. The speaker raised his voice above the melody lilting in the background. 'They want to gag the likes of you and me.' Ben passed his flask to Wilf, who shook his head and lifted a hand in warning. 'But it's not only us. The established Church itself has been seen off. The B.B.C.'s put the mockers on the Archbishop of Canterbury, would you believe it! The good Archbishop wants the three sides to take action together, nobody at the bottom of the pile having to kowtow.' Ben poised the pewter flask at his lips and shot whisky to the back of his throat. He closed his eyes and took another slug. 'Government continues the subsidy ... ' he half listened as he waited for the beam of heat to his stomach then forced his mind in gear again and heard the end of the sentence, ' ... owners to scrap the new wage scale. Miners return to work.' Ben relaxed as warm fingers smoothed wrinkles in his brain. 'But the BBC, friends ...'

A voice came from the back. 'Living in the clouds, the clergy! Miners won't have any jobs at all soon. They're trying to start a revolution.'

The speaker fixed a glare across the crowd. 'A living wage, that's all they ask.'

'Two and two have to add up and make four in any business. The coal industry's losing money hand over fist!'

The king of the soapbox stared the heckler down. 'Friend, it's sheer greed, to make the miners work longer for less.'

'Miners want to nationalise the whole bloody thing.'

'There's where your problem is ... little pits, inefficient. They need putting together together ... put some life ...'

'Paralyse it! Anyway, they're hooligans, the strikers.'

A rough voice croaked from beside the speaker, 'If I'm a hooligan, you're a hooligan!'

Howls started. 'I think this is getting dangerous, Ben.' Wilf edged out pulling his friend.

'Bill, take a pill.' The voice carried above the crowd. 'Anybody who looks at the misery of the miners gets muzzled like a mad dog!'

Someone moved, a pathway opened and Wilf dragged Ben out. The Sunderland supporters followed and the crowd closed behind them. They moved in a foursome to a clearing and Wilf forgot politics. He turned on the opposition.

'As I was sayin', it's a disgrace, turnin' up here in the heart of Magpie territory wearin' that!' He pointed to the red and white rosette now on show.

Ben took another swig.

'It's a free country. We can wear what we like! Anyway, next season ye'll see that Newcastle's right down in the shite.' Wilf grabbed the man's scarf and went for his collar. 'Where they belong!'

'Watch it, Wilf. There's trouble,' Ben said.

'There'll be trouble here in a minute,' Wilf growled.

'The law's comin' up from down yonder.'

'The only time Sunderland's beat the Magpies is when there's been a blind and deaf referee.' Wilf ignored his friend. 'He'd come from yor end, because the lot of ye are blind and deaf. No self-respecting human being would be a supporter of Roker Park'

Mounted police were pushing up from the lower end of the street.

A heat haze clouded Ben's eyes for a moment. 'Wilf, come away.' Wilf was deaf. 'And as for loyalty! Ah'll show ye what loyalty is. Any fool that speaks a foul word aboot the Black and Whites is likely to choke on 'e's own teeth! Ye want a knuckle sandwich?'

Wilf's clenched fist shot to the man's mouth as chestnut horses began their charge. Ben hurtled him sideways and the pair of them went down in a heap with one of the Sunderland men.

The crowd scattered but not fast enough. Batons came down on heads and shoulders. One man was knocked down and a horse's hoof glanced off his chest. The whisky haze hit Ben's brain and loosed a fury. He got up, ran after the mounted bobby and dragged him off his saddle to the ground. More police came to the rescue and laid about anyone nearby. Wilf wrestled Ben to the pavement, took his own hat off and rammed it on his friend's head pulling the peak down. A second lot of mounties advanced. Wilf protected Ben's head. The speaker continued in the chaos, attacking the BBC as cowards but a horse pressed up to him and a truncheon came down, missed the soapbox hero and cracked the skull of the person next to him. The young man collapsed and the police mount turned and charged part of the crowd running up into Grainger Street. Flat peaked caps gave some protection but the best protection was a swift pair of heels. In five minutes it was over. Ben got up, stunned. Wilf helped him and the Sunderland supporter to stand the man up, Wilf and the red and white fan with their arms round each other now. The young man by the speaker's tub was still. Ben was sober from shock, ice in his brain.

'Come over here, Wilf. I'll loosen his tie and collar. Can you check if he's breathing?'

The Sunderland supporter produced a small mirror he kept for his girlfriend and Wilf held it over the young man's mouth whose red hair lay damp and dark against the skull. 'He's breathing,' he said. 'There's a gash in his head, though, it's streaming. We'll have to get him up to Casualty at the Newcastle Royal. Careful how you lift him.'

'Staunch this blood first, Wilf,' Ben said.

The second Sunderland supporter took a clean handkerchief from his pocket and offered his white knitted silk scarf to tie it with. 'It doesn't matter,' he said. 'it'll just give us the white and red markings.'

Ben took the treasured scarf and fixed it over the battered head and under the chin. 'We could do more harm than good,' he said, 'blood's gushing. We've got to get him to the experts, quick.' They hoisted the injured man to his feet, moaning. 'Can ye hear us, lad? Can ye walk?'

Wilf and Ben took his arms round their necks and began to walk him. The Sunderland men took over when they could go no further. The Haymarket stretched a long way away. When they reached Casualty their charge was chalk white. A doctor saw to him immediately and they had to help as he bathed the wound and shaved hair to stitch the skin together. Ben held the skin.

'My God! He's been lucky. If this had been an inch further back it could have cracked the skull wide open or gone straight through to the brain. I'm afraid we can't keep him in tonight, though. Beds are scarce.'

'Don't worry,' said Ben, 'we'll take care of him. Is there a working telephone I can use?'

'One in the office at the end of the corridor on the left.'

Ben rang John Hargraves, disturbing his supper after evensong. 'Can you bring that old Austin of yours out, John? We've got a casualty at the Newcastle Royal needs moving.'

'Right away. Where do you want him taken to?'

'I'll bring him home.'

Ben went ahead to prepare the women while Wilf and the Reverend half carried the young man up the stairs, his mind almost out of it. They cleared the best couch and laid him on it.

'Stop staring, our Patricia,' Ben said. 'It's vittals are needed.'

'Yes, dad,' she said and went on staring.

*

Next morning Ben noticed a hand-written note pushed half way through his letter box. The brass flap shut with a snap as he pulled it through and recognised John Hargrave's writing. He'd been phoned by a friend to ask if he would read the Archbishop's banned speech from his pulpit. Priests all over the country were planning to do it.

Ben walked up and listened outside the church to the drifting sound of singing then powerful commanding notes of the organ as the congregation poured out. He shook Hargraves' hand.

'How did you get on at home? I didn't get to ask you last night in all the commotion.'

'Not well. There's a rift with my father.' He nodded and shook a pensioner's hand. 'Wouldn't have it that miners were being broken to get the country back on the Gold Standard, convinced we have to get back to prewar levels of prosperity no matter what.' A child ran up and grabbed hold of his legs. The vicar picked the child up, bounced him and returned him to his mother as women in hats stopped under the trees to talk. He waited for the last of the congregation to trickle out then turned to Ben. 'And he said I shouldn't confuse a soft bleeding-heart response with real principles.'

'Something wrong if we stop feeling.'

Hargraves waved to the last of the parishioners, stepped into the church and shook hands with the organist. 'He thinks you're making me into a Communist up here. Or at least into a Methodist. Maybe that's worse!' Ben slapped his friend on the back. 'And I left without eating the Victoria sponge.'

'Capital!'

5

Andrew Taylor moved and moaned. He'd lain stock still since he arrived. As if by an invisible cord, Patricia was drawn to him. That white face. She'd given him Sal Volatile to revive him. He sat up, ate two spoonsful of the porridge she fed him and went back to sleep. There was a large shaven patch on the crown and his reddish hair stuck against his brow. He hadn't stirred since breakfast. When he woke a pan of soup was on.

Diane burst in from looking after the shop. 'Some lads are upsetting us.'

'Sssh! Keep your voice down.'

'Where's mam?' The stage whisper didn't wake the sleeper.

'Mam's feeding the baby, and Katharine's asleep with her head in mam's lap, so she can't move. You'll have to tell me. What have they done?'

'They just came in, lots of them, one after another to ask if we had any sly cake. Then they told us to keep our eye on it, me and Louise.'

'If that's your only worry!'

'I'll bash them, me, if they don't stop.'

'You will not.'

'Anyway, why do we have to call it sly cake?' Diane screwed up her face. 'Then Mrs. Niff-Naff's been in to ask for tick ...' she rushed on, 'and Mr. Niff-Naff came in to tell us not to be rude to Mrs. Niff-Naff. I told him - We wouldn't be rude to Mrs. Niff-Naff, Mr. Niff-Naff.'

'Their name's Smith, Diane.'

'Then why does everybody call her Mrs. Niff-Naff?'

'Because of her cleft palate and the way she talks. She can't help it and people shouldn't call her that.'

'Oh.'

'Tell her we're sorry you upset her. And she'll have to see mam about tick. We can't take that on ourselves.'

'I never knew she wasn't called Mrs. Niff-Naff.'

'Say you made a mistake and you're sorry.'

'I didn't know anything about Smith. She's always just been Mrs. Niff-Naff.' She nodded towards the couch. 'Anyway, how long's he going to be here?'

'Till he's better.'

'I hope it's soon. I don't like him.'

'You don't know him. Now go back to the shop.'

'And mam says you're spending far too much time mooning over him. Are you mooning? How do you moon?'

Mary came in and passed the baby to Patricia. 'Back to the shop. I'll come and deal with the Niff-Naffs.'

'See! Mam said it. Only mam can tell me what to say.'

Andrew sighed. Mary shepherded the younger girl back downstairs and Patricia put the baby in his cot. She put a pillow under the sick man's head, saw the depths of red in sandy hair, then brought fresh water. He opened his eyes in a white face with white lips. But the eyes were mirror clear, a green fleck touching hazel.

'Is that better? Would you like to sit up?' Patricia pressed the flannel to his brow. The hints of green in the eyes were the most beautiful shade she had ever seen. *I'm going to marry you* chimed through her head.

'I ... don't know where I am.' He looked up as if at a vision, shut his eyes and looked again. She wrung out a cloth in the water and pressed the flannel to his brow.

'You were attacked, and my father brought you home. We've sent a message to your mother. We don't think you should be moved yet.' Mary trod heavily back up the stairs. 'I've made Scotch broth with that piece of meat, mam. I could give him some of the liquor. There are potatoes to go with the meat.' Her eyes bored into her mother. 'Could you watch them while I see to him?'

Mary sighed, 'Aye, I can watch taties. How long do you think you're going to be?'

Patricia hardly heard and put a hand under his head. 'You must try to eat ... just a little bit.' He did not open his mouth. 'Sup this,' she said. He took a mouthful, gazing at her. 'It's good.' He obeyed.

Suddenly he said, 'I'm going to be sick!'

She held the bowl of water for him supporting his shoulders as he retched and the soup came back up. Her youngest sister came into the room. 'Take this out for me, our Katharine.'

The nine year old obeyed, black eyes wide. Patricia heard her whispering to her mother, 'Is he all right?'

'Patricia's making him all right. Here, get some bowls and plates out for me while I mash these taties.'

Later Ben and Mary got him out of his clothes and into a pair of Ben's pyjamas. Patricia could see from the scullery his skin was milk white. She would wash his chest and arms next day as far as she could. Tenderness that hurt moved her to care for his flesh. '*God, if you are there*,' she prayed, '*let him get better. I'll do anything. Anything you ask ... even if I never see him again*,' she added. '*But let him get better.*'

'Go to bed Patricia,' her father said. 'Don't stand there like a calf that's lost its mother.'

She lay in bed, tense, and listened for the slightest sound of distress from the couch across the landing, slipping into a white sleep just alert, hearing the clock on the fire station sadly boom the hour. She surfaced on each hour and floated on the mourning of a foghorn from the river. No moan from Andrew. Did that mean he was dead? Her limbs would not move to get up.

Three o'clock. Boom, boom, boom quivered against the stillness. She turned and burrowed in her pillow hearing the quiet breathing of her sisters, all three snug in a double bed.

Then the sound of running feet, leather on pavement and pounding at the door. The knocking hammered her heart and she was up, shawl round her shoulders, feet counting the stairs in the darkness, hand on the latch.

'Wait, Patricia!' Ben shone a torch down the stairs.

The knocking was frantic. Her father was scraping the latch, opening the door a face width. 'For God's sake, let me in!'

'Wilf!'

'Bobbies could be after me!'

Ben pulled him in and shone the torch away from the door. 'You're shivering. Patricia, go and make a warm drink since you're up. We'll go in the scullery. That lad's on the couch.'

'An' divn't put the lights on, Ben.'

'Patricia! Find a candle. Put it down safe somewhere on the floor.'

'I'm doing it, dad.'

She rummaged for matches and had a candle lit before they'd stumbled up the stairs, dripped molten wax onto a saucer, stood the candle end up in the liquid wax, and put it on the floor in a biscuit tin. Ben held the torch for her as she brought the kettle from the range and made a cup of Bovril. Beef overcame the bitter smell of poured wax in the little room.

'Sorry we haven't got spare milk for cocoa, Mr. Robson.'

'Thank ye kindly, lass.' Wilf was heaving, sweating. She handed him a towel and Ben pushed him down onto the kitchen stool.

'Now what's it about?'

'I've just run from Cramlington, most of the way.' Wilf collapsed onto a chair.

'Cramlington? Are you mad?'

He heaved for breath, 'we've derailed the Flying Scotsman!'

'I didn't tell ye the plan. Fewer that knew the better.' Sweat was pouring down Wilf's face. 'We broke the line and moved it.'

'Bloody reckless, Wilf!'

'Neebody's hurt, Ah'm sure of it. Damn volunteers drivin' a pullman train. Don't know one end of an engine from the other. Ah'm tellin' ye, Ben, there's engines'll have ter be written off the way they've dunched and battered them, playin' at engine drivers.'

'That doesn't give *you* the right to derail the Scotsman.'

'We're all rail men. We knew what we were doin'.'

'Damn risky.'

'They were lettin' bloody blackleg coals through on it. **You** should understand that! On a Pullman an' all!'

'Hell, Wilf!

'It was an accident. I'm sure neebody was hurt. It wasn't actually the Scotsman we were after. Damned Pullman came through first and ran off the line.'

'Shut up, Wilf. We've got to think.'

'Coppers were on the scene almost immediately, shoutin' somebody'll gan to jail for this.'

'We have to make sure it isn't you. Sup your drink up. Go back to bed, pet,' he looked at Patricia. 'This isn't for you.'

'I just thought, dad, Mr. Robson might need to stay.'

'Aye, if you don't mind.'

'The couch's in use, but you can have a blanket on the settle.'

'That'll do, pet.'

She tiptoed into the living room and eased the lid of the settle up. There were two blankets and she found a cushion. The lid thudded as she tried to close it gently and Andrew stirred.

'What's happening?'

'It's all right. Mr. Robson's staying as well. Nothing to worry about. Just go back to sleep.' He obeyed her and lay down.

'Alibi ...' she heard from the kitchen. Ben turned to her. 'I'm going to have to involve you after all, lass. First, Wilf needs my spare pair of pyjamas.'

'I'll get them.'

'Then I want you to slip into bed with your mam in case she wakes up.' She opened her mouth. 'No, just listen. I'm walking over to the cree where Jim - you know Jim? our bowling friend – he's got racing pigeons. I have a key and I'm going to tie a carrier message on one and set it free. I'm sure he has the little cylinders somewhere around. It'll home to him. The birds are his bairns so he'll probably hear it.'

'Be careful, man, Ben. Bobbies are about.' Wilf clutched the cup of Bovril to his chest.

'That's why I'm walking. I daren't show a light on the bike. I'll have to use a torch at the pigeon lofts but I don't think they'll be down that way.' Ben rummaged in his coat pocket for a piece of paper to write a brief message. 'Jim lives near enough to Wilf's house and I just hope he wakes up in time to take a message to Mrs. Robson that Wilf's here. I daren't walk round to the houses.' He looked up to speak to Patricia. 'We're going to say he came back here last night after the concert for the Welfare Fund. We had a hand of cards and forgot the time. Then he had to stay the night with there being no public transport. Can you remember all that?'

'Yes, dad.'

'Put your mam in the picture and see to the young brood. We need to be up breakfasting early. Bread and dripping. We've plenty of bread, I suppose?'

'There's bread.'

He kissed her. 'See Wilf safe onto the settle and try to get some sleep.'

Andrew stirred and sat up as she showed Wilf into the room. 'What time is it?' he asked.

'Eleven o'clock,' Patricia lied. 'Mr. Robson's spending the night. Plenty of time to go back to sleep.'

He lay down again.

The table was decked with plain white crockery as Patricia clinkered out the range to get a fire going. Wilf sat bleary in borrowed pyjamas, Ben put an arm round his wife's shoulder and they sat down to yesterday's bread from the bakery. Patricia filled the big urn three quarters full with tea and brought a jar of dripping to the table. Dark brown sediment lay at the bottom, they plunged their knives in to drag it up and smear the beef goodness on bread, grainy against the doughy centre of the rolls. Andrew was awake and took half a slice, sitting up on the couch. He looked at Patricia as if she owned him and ate. His stomach kept it down.

'I don't know where this is going to end,' Mary said. 'They'll lock us all up for helping. I heard the Scrimshaw women managed to turn a tram by shaking it till it crashed over. And Herbie Scrimshaw's let down tyres on buses.'

'Don't talk, Mary.' Ben patted her hand. 'We're just going to be planning another Welfare concert.' His eyes met Patricia's. 'Can you see to the young ones? Let them have their breakfast in bed.'

Squeals were just starting in the girls' bedroom as Patricia spread dripping for them and took it in on the big blue and white plate. Ben put the seven o'clock news on as they heard pounding at the door and went downstairs himself. They listened over the voices of the wireless as he opened up.

'Can I help you, officer?'

'Is a Wilf Robson here?'

'Yes. Anything the matter?'

'I'd like to see him. His wife said I'd find him here.'

Heavy steps trod the stairs and a red-faced bobby took his helmet off. Katharine's brown face looked in.

'Have you come to arrest me and my sisters, mister?' she said, eyes wide.

The bobby looked at her and his eyes relaxed, though the mouth stayed firm. 'No, I haven't come for you. Not yet. But you'd better not be naughty.'

Patricia pushed a chair forward. 'Would you like a cup of tea, officer?'

'No, thanks. I was just checking the whereabouts of one Wilf Robson.'

Wilf put his bread and dripping down. 'That's me.'

'How long have you been here, sir?'

'The whole night.'

'And why are you not at home with your wife?' He took a notebook out.

Katharine sidled out and stood beside Wilf gazing up at the policeman. 'I got marooned here with the buses off. Too good a night after the Welfare concert. We got to planning the next one and I played cards with Ben here. My wife'd know where I'd be.'

'We thought it was getting a bit late for him to walk home,' Patricia put in. 'I gave Mr. Robson some blankets, and he managed to sleep on the settle.'

'And what time was this when he decided to stay?'

'Eleven o'clock.' A thin voice from the couch. They'd almost forgotten Andrew. 'He came in here to sleep about eleven. I can remember it.'

'And you are?'

'Andrew Taylor.' The bobby wrote it down.

'We're looking after Andrew,' Patricia said. 'He's been ill.'

'Everybody here when Mr. Robson called?'

'Yes.' Nods.

'All of us.'

'Well, I think that wraps it up.' He put the notebook in his inside pocket. 'Sorry to disturb your breakfast.'

Wilf crammed bread and dripping into his mouth and Katharine looked up showing the eggshell blue of the eye whites. 'So, you're not going to arrest us, mister?'

The officer smirked down at her. 'Not today.'

'I'll show you out if you won't have a cup of tea.' Ben walked downstairs chatting about the concerts, inviting the bobby to come to the next one. Wilf sat with his head between his hands and Mary hugged her little girl.

Patricia was gazing at Andrew who had some slight colour in his cheeks. '*Thank you, God,*' she prayed.

Next night it was her parents who watched Andrew till he settled. Patricia got up to pour a glass of water from the big jug and watched them through a crack in the door. They sat in flickering light, in the fire dances.

'She's too young,' she heard her father say.

'Aye, she is,' her mother looked at him. 'But what are you going to do about it?'

'We'll get John Hargraves to move him as soon as he's fit.'

'First love's the sweetest. Don't you like him, Ben?'

Patricia held her breath and tiptoed on the lino back to bed.

'Aye, I like him, it was me brought him home. But I don't want our Patricia throwing herself away. Even aside from this blow on the head he took, he doesn't look strong. She needs a man who can look after her.'

She tucked back under the covers, tears stabbing her eyes.

A few days later, Patricia had to help out at the Central Strike Committee taking the minutes, as Bessy stayed at home with a sick child. It was late morning to avoid a clash with a concert. Concerts and football matches raised morale as well as funds. Her father joined in these free-for-all mad sessions, one caser, once on the Town Moor and fifty a side. She wondered how nobody was killed.

Patricia took notes but kept quiet, shy in this world of her father's - essential transport, food supply, defence of men who were arrested. Footsteps echoed on the knotty pine when anyone came in. She wrote neatly with a pointed H.B. pencil. They were in an upstairs room at the Co-op with a working telephone. A knock but nobody stirred. The discussion was heated, over legal defence costs. Another timid knock and the errand boy put his head round. Ben motioned him in. The boy's eyes were starting.

Ben held a hand up and they stopped talking. 'Have you been sent with a message, lad?'

'Yes ... there's been a telephone call. The manager said I had to come and tell you.'

'What is it, then?' ... 'You can spit it out.'

'Strike's off. That's the message.'

A confused babble of voices broke out.

Patricia watched her father stand up red in the face, voice rising. 'What d'you mean, the strike's off? Are you sure that's what the manager said? Who called?'

'A call from London. The manager said you had to be told straight off. The organisers there've called it a day.'

'I'll come down and see him.'

Ben breathed heavily as he went out and the others sat dazed. Patricia put her pencil down. The sound echoed. The air seemed heavy. When Ben came back, his footsteps jarred against the unreal silence. He sat down and everyone looked at him. Patricia willed him to speak.

'Well?'

'It's true,' he said.

'What the hell?' Wilf was on his feet.

'T.U.C. decision. Said they were afraid the strike was crumbling.'

'Damned lies!'

'It's solid.'

'Another two weeks and the government would have had to do something.'

'It was the damned B.B.C.'s said it was crumbling!'

'Government putting lies out on the airwaves!'

'T.U.C. in London's believed the propaganda!'

Voices stabbed at each other, shouted over each other.

'They should come up here... See for themselves.'

Ben made himself heard. 'Herbert Samuel's put his oar in – he's drawn up some sort of peace memorandum. T.U.C's accepted it.'

'In London!' Wilf spat.

Ben slumped into his chair. 'And what's it worth? A government move. You know what that means?'

'They'll sell us down the river. 'All this ... sacrifice!' Wilf collapsed in tears.

They sat on for minutes then without another word stood up and left one by one. Patricia followed her father and took his arm before Wilf caught them up.

'The rail men didn't betray you. It's Central Committee's betrayed you this time.

'There'll be nothing to show.' Ben was white. 'Believed the government propaganda at the end … there was … *so much fight left in us!'* He paced on. 'All over. Since the lockout in …?

'Nine days, lad,' Wilf said.

'Feels like a … *lifetime!* Miners'll be on their own again.'

Patricia struggled to keep up with them.

'Nowt we can do now. If it was up to me we'd stay out with ye! - "Not a penny off the pay, not a minute on the day!" - How long d'ye think the lockout'll last now?'

'As long as it takes, Wilf. Just as long as it takes, man, to starve the men back on their bellies. Families to be fed. It's a bitter pill.' Ben stopped and leant against a wall. ' … And I think Mary's secretly giving tick.'

Patricia stood still.

'I'd stop that if I were you, or she'll never get out of it herself.'

'Too soft hearted, that's the trouble.' Ben held on to his friend's shoulder. 'This could go on for months … the pub'll have to go for a start … And will it be worth it? The privation?'

Patricia stood back as Wilf held him. 'It's always worth it in the long run, man. That's what ye've got to keep hold of.' He turned to Patricia. 'For children's children. Keep the dreams alive, Ben. The workin' class'll show them yet.'

'If we can get education.'

They held each other like estranged brothers, then walked their different directions without looking back.

Patricia took her father's arm again but he was hardly aware of her. Walking into a desert.

*

The day Andrew was to go was cold again. He'd been out to help Ben forage for firewood and tended a small fire. Patricia picked the baby up for the afternoon walk. There were still coals left from the last pitman's allowance, but they had to be eked out for autumn, and Mary's oven had to be fed.

Thoughts of Andrew and her mother battled for place as she pushed the pram through gusts of wind, not noticing where she was. Mary was drawn and had confided to her she'd given credit all over the place. Nothing was coming in. Patricia gazed in a shop window at a red calico dress for nine shillings and sixpence. Perhaps she could begin making clothes and selling them.

Christopher started to cry and she pushed a dummy into his mouth. How would they ever pay Mary's debt? The red calico dress seemed to invite her and she imagined herself dressed in it, swirled in Andrew's arms. He'd accepted her nursing as a dumb, grateful beast, looked at her with adoration and obeyed as if she owned him. Would he say anything? She put the debt out of her mind and walked home quickly. Christopher was asleep. No-one else in. She carried the baby upstairs and laid him in his cot.

'I ... was just waiting.' Andrew turned his back to the fireplace.

'Nobody's going to hurry you.' Her voice seemed distant.

'I've written my address down for you.' He handed a scrap of paper and she put it in a drawer.

Words she wanted to say stayed locked.

'I ... I'll never forget what you've done for me.'

'Dad couldn't just leave you there.' She waited, straining towards the silence.

'Patricia!'

'Yes.'

'Thank you.' She still waited. 'Would you do this for anybody?"

'For a dumb animal.' He looked desperate then she lowered her voice. 'You're more than a dumb animal to me, Andrew Taylor.'

The hazel green eyes shone. 'Will you have me?' he blurted.

She let him wait then smiled. 'Only one thing. Are you a drinking man?'

'I never touch it.'

'It's all right then. Don't tell dad.' She nodded. 'Yet.'

Without moving she knew they'd yielded to each other.

6

Throughout the next months of the lockout Andrew made the pilgrimage from Jarrow to the East End of Newcastle, often on foot, being careful not to arrive at mealtime at a pitman's house. Ben had introduced the young man to his home, but not for this. He grew less and less pleased. The gash on the head healed, but the lad had a fragile look.

Fresh back from the allotment, he scrubbed his hands to be presentable at mealtime. Potatoes, cabbage, sprouts, turnip and onions were in a sack on the scullery floor. He didn't notice Mary was sitting quietly gazing into space.

The tap was full on to splash the green household soap off his hands. 'I think there's enough veg there to last the week. If not, I'll dig some more up. I'm getting the leek trench nicely dug. Has Andrew Taylor been here?'

'Not today.'

'Looks like a puff of wind would blow him over,' he said. 'How he holds down a job in the shipyard I'll never tell.' He sat down and noticed her vacant look. 'What's the matter, Mary?'

'Oh, go back to your allotment and worship your leeks, Ben. I've got other things on my mind.'

'Like what?'

'Like putting food on the table.'

'We're coping, lass. I'm putting in the work at the allotment, supplying our own vegetables. Herring's cheap. I like herring, and you're a wonderful cook. We've got by so far.' He looked across at the cheerless grate. 'Here, I'll light the fire.'

Christopher woke and Mary picked him up, cradling his head on her shoulder. 'Maybe we'd have been less pleased about another baby if we'd known this lockout was coming,' she said.

His own words echoed. He turned and noticed how listless she was. 'Aye. There's some have regretted marrying. They'd have waited if they'd known.' He left the fire, went over and knelt beside her. 'But we can't regret our little boy.' He kissed her cheek and Christopher's. 'Especially since we lost the other one. He's the light of your life.' Tears fell. 'Come on, our lass. This isn't the way. If you give way, I don't know what'll happen to the rest of us.' He cast round for something else to say as she quietly wept. 'And those leeks you say I've been worshipping, they've been worth quite a bit. I did well at the show. Second prize and a bit of cash. If I can get first next year it'll make a big difference. Help us back on our feet.' He took Christopher from her and put him gently in the wooden playpen he'd made and handed in a toy horse, just carved and waxed. The toddler sniffed it and started to chew the mane. He saw the boy settled and went back to sit beside his wife.

She put her arms round his neck and cried on his shoulder. 'The leeks! The leeks will save us.'

Ben stroked her hair till she was quiet. 'What's the matter, our lass?'

'Money,' she snuffled against him.

'Everybody's worried about money. It's been the worst do in a long time.' He felt her shaking. 'But what's wrong? Have you been borrowing from somebody?' He held her gently away. 'You haven't got into a loan shark's hands, have you?'

'Worse than that, Ben.'

'What could be worse ...' he saw the grey at her temple, noticed it in unkempt hair, '... what could be worse,' and deep shadows beneath her eyes, '... than that?' Sweat broke on his brow.

She looked up and he saw red thread veins in her eyes. 'I did it after all.'

'What, for heaven's sake?'

'Gave credit. Let people run up dozens and dozens of tabs.'

The bolt hit him. 'Now you can't pay your bills!' Silence. 'How much, Mary?' His voice was low. 'Fifty?'

She shook her head.

'More than that?'

'Nearly a hundred.'

He was not hearing this. 'It takes me about a year to earn that amount of money.'

Her voice strangled. 'I'm sorry.'

'My God! What a hole!' He got up and paced the room. 'We'll never get it back.'

'One or two've tried, but there's rent and fuel first. Some are just keeping out of my way, walking further to another bakery.'

'You've lost their business for ever.' She crumpled up against a cushion. 'Think, think!' He paced.

'What's done's done. You'll just have to stall for a bit. It's going to be difficult to raise a loan from anywhere, though. Damn nigh impossible.' A loud knock at the door. He looked out of the window, saw Wilf and walked down the steps slowly to open up a hand's breadth. 'I'm sorry, you've caught us at a bad time.'

Wilf's face was red with excitement. 'Have ye not heard?'

'What?'

'Where've ye been, man?'

'At the allotment. I grow most of our food.'

'Aye, ye live down there.'

Ben opened the door fully and led Wilf into the empty bakery.

'Rumour has it your lot's goin' back.'

'The lockout's over?'

'Aye, man!'

Ben looked round at bare shelves. 'Thank God for that!' It was cold.

'But the terms have been accepted. An eight-hour day for less.' He held his arms out and embraced his friend. 'Pay's going to be on a district basis, not national, so God help us all. I'm sorry, kidda. I'm sorry.'

And it was cold the day they went back, dark days of winter, starting the shift before daylight. Ben locked his bike up and walked across to the entrance. Looking round he saw the men straggling in. It was as he predicted. Starved back on their bellies. The defeat was bitter. He wondered how some of them would stand a longer day.

But he was looking forward to getting back to work for company and purpose. The great wheels would soon be in motion, the iron cage rattling to take them to the bowels of the earth. He walked past the great chimneystacks and the pumping pond and felt like whistling. Whistling was bad luck. He walked inside.

'Hey, you! Where d' you think you're going?' Fingers jabbed roughly between the shoulders blades as he took his coat off. 'Hawthorne!' He swung round. 'This is no place for you!' The manager of the colliery stood over him.

'I've come to report for work.'

'Get lost! We don't want to see the likes of you here again.'

'I'm Safety Officer..'

'Not any more, you're not. We've got another man in.'

'What the hell's this about?'

'You were one of the strike organisers. That's what it's about. Anyway, the boss saw what happened in the Bigg Market!'

'What?'

'Draggin' the polis off a horse!'

'I don't know what you're talking about.'

'He seen ye, man!'

Ben stood dumb.

'See what your precious Union can do for you now! Doors'll slam in ya face. We've seen to that. You'll not find work in any other pit or factory.' He counted them off on his fingers. 'Not at Hawthorne's, not at Reyroll's, not at Parson's, not at Swan's.'

'Blacklisted!

'Aye, ye'll come to know the meaning of that word, lad. Now get your coat on and GIT!'

Ben stumbled out past the thin faces arriving and swung automatically on his bike. Hot and cold shivers trembled down his back. He got off and pushed the bike. Three daughters at school, one at home and Christopher a baby. He'd dug his grave. Forty-two years old. His life was behind him. He looked round dazed, not knowing where he was or how to get home.

He rode on instinct through a fog till he found a place he recognised, peddled up the bank and was there. The back door was unlocked, he stood his bicycle up, closed the door and sat down on the steps staring at the back yard, hardly feeling the cold outside his body.

Mary's voice finally reached him and he got up, stiff as an old man and jolted back to the concrete world at the sight of her grey face. 'What's wrong, Ben?'

'I've been turned back from work. They've blacklisted me.'

She folded her arms over her stomach. 'You'd better come inside, Ben. There's more.'

She took his hand, led him up the steps, through the scullery, into the living room and a dead grate.

Without speaking she passed him a letter. The words danced before his eyes. She had seven days to settle her bills or become a public debtor. All goods and chattels would be forfeit. Ben read with a dead weight of despair. There was no way they could get their debts in in a week. Mining families owed everywhere. A debt of honour for some but it would take time. Others would take the easy way and default.

A spurt of energy came back. 'Mary, lass, we're going to have to get a few things out of this house. Wilf might take some stuff.' He began to pace the floor. 'But Wilf was on the Strike Committee. That might not be a good idea. I'll give him what extra cash I've got, though, from the leeks.'

'Alice Scrimshaw might help.' She looked round at her furniture. 'But big stuff, we can't move that out.'

'It's difficult. People might be watching. Somebody shopped me as strike organiser. They made another excuse but that's what it was. They might shop us over this.'

'It was Niff-Naffs shopped you.'

'Good God! And how big is her tab with you?'

'One of the biggest. She hasn't paid a penny. I'm sorry Ben.'

'Judas!' He put a hand on her shoulder and breathed deeply. 'It's useless to blame. We have to think! Send the lasses round with bits and pieces when it's dark. They could just be going round to see the Scrimshaw crowd.' He sat down. 'We'll make a list. Bits and pieces of jewellery'll have to be got out.'

'I haven't that much, but what there is is precious. Memories ...'

'We want that out, then. The bits of Wedgewood and Maling will have to go round as well. Wedding presents and such like.'

'My apostle spoons! My mother gave me them.'

'Bits of silverware.' He wrote. 'What about clothes?'

'They could allow us what we stand up in and one change. We'd better get anything good out.' Mary's brow creased as she tried to think. 'Good coats and shoes. Keep the working ones here. We're not going to afford to replace them. Just keep one old shirt of yours in the wardrobe. ... Good shirts and cuff links. Your suit! We couldn't replace that.'

'I hope Scrimshaws don't pawn the clothes,' he said. 'You know what they're like.'

'At least we could get them out of hock. And there's the bairn's toys! I don't know if they'll have the room.'

'Speak to Alice. It'll take a few nights. Could the girls take the wireless safely? I don't want to lose that.'

'Patricia could carry it. Keep the Cat's Whisker here so it doesn't look suspicious. Will it be in the newspapers, Ben?'

'Yes. We'll have to live it down, that's all.' He looked at the unlit fire. 'And you won't be able to run the bakery.' They didn't hear Patricia come up the back stairs into the scullery.

'Why not?'

'You can't run a business till you clear your whole debt.'

Mary's face crumpled and she collapsed onto a chair. 'I'm sorry, Ben.'

'It's me that's sorry. I've failed you. I'm sick with shame.' He knelt and laid his head in her lap. 'I should be back at work. The politics have been the death of me. And the drink.'

Patricia came in, cold clinging to her clothes. 'I'll go out to work.'

Ben looked at her fresh face that had been radiant the last few months and hauled his heart together.

'We'll see, pet. One step at a time.'

Daily he tramped the town looking for work. Daily he worked his allotment to bring food home for the table. Daily they smuggled more goods out of the house.

And in the end he wasn't there.

No one knew exactly what would happen. Patricia had little time to see her young man, she looked after Christopher and the three girls, the serious eldest child as a third parent. Her mother was declared bankrupt in the newspapers but nobody said anything to them. The bakery closed.

Another week and they heard a tap at the door. Ben had walked into town to buy cheaply at the market. Mary was nervous of answering to anyone and picked the baby up. He struggled, preferring the feel of his own feet. Patricia opened the door the width of her face. It was a woman with her face half shielded by a scarf against the cold.

'Yes?'

'I've come to pay something off me tab, pet. Is ya mam in?'

'Oh. Come on in. Don't stand on the step.' There was no warm smell of baking but Mary offered a cup of tea.

'That's all right, missus. I'm sorry it isn't more but you'll get it in dribs and drabs.' The woman held out a worn ten shilling note. 'I'll pay you ten shillings when I can. I'll keep him out of the bookie's if it kills me! Ten shillings will go further for you than just half a crown at a time. That's four pounds I owe you now. It's a lot and I apologise I haven't been before.' Patricia took the dingy red note as her mother seemed frozen to the spot. She wondered what to say to the woman when they heard a very loud bang on the door. 'Let's hope that's more money,' the woman said. Patricia stuffed the note down her blouse. The knock was a hammering. 'They're set to bray the door down, missus.'

Christopher cried. Patricia picked him up and carried him like a shield in front of her to the front door. He clung to her hair as she reached for the sneck. Four men were outside.

'Bailiffs.'

She stepped back and was forced up the stairs as one man snapped the stair rods up and another began rolling the carpet. She jumped past the little woman with the scarf, made for the scullery where the big blue and white serving dish was still on a bench, rushed into the bedroom she shared with the girls and slid it deep under the mattress of the double bed. Then she put Christopher on her own bed and started to change him.

The little woman was standing with her mouth open. 'What are they doing, missus?'

'Stripping the place, I think,' Mary said. 'It's the tabs. I couldn't pay my own bills. You'll have seen it in the paper.'

'We can't afford newspapers.'

The man pushed past them both, two into the bedroom, ignoring Patricia. Two started moving the settle with the blue velvet upholstery inside the lid. It was empty of blankets. Christopher kept up a wail.

'You're never takin' her bits of furniture!' The woman tried to bar their way, first at the top of the stairs and then at the bedroom where Patricia was. The men were distracted and made for the parents' bedroom.

'It's our job, missus. Now get out of the road!' Two of them heaved the settle down the stairs and into the back of a van. The two from the bedroom edged out carrying an oak wardrobe, going slowly because of the weight and for fear the mirrored door would swing open.

Patricia came to watch and saw the little woman give one of them a clout. 'That's their wardrobe! Where de ye expect them to hang their clothes?'

'Divn't dunch us, missus! This is heavy. They can hang their clothes on the back of the door. What wrong with a nail?'

Christopher howled as the woman shrilled at the men each time they picked up a piece of furniture. They emptied drawers in the bedroom onto the floor and took the chest out. Patricia's heart lurched when they lifted the piano Ben had found second hand. She was learning to play. The leather couch from the living room went, the Scotch chest with its polished red wood and concealed drawer. She had to hop into the scullery as the good Wilton rug was dragged up from under their feet. They took the marble topped washstand from Ben and Mary's room and the china jug and bowl that stood on top. Mary looked dazed.

The little woman with the scarf tugged the arm of the man carrying the jug and bowl. 'Stop it! What are they to wash in?'

'The kitchen sink, missus!'

They pushed Patricia aside in the scullery and went through drawers taking chopping knives and scissors, things her mother had thought would not be touched. They counted pans and took two, the copper bottomed ones. They'd not been quick enough getting everything out.

The woman in the scarf was white, tears in her eyes. 'Do you know how this happened to her? Through helping people! Helping them to eat through that long lockout.'

'I cannot help it, missus. If it was up to me I'd feed every raggy bleedin' tramp in the whole wide world.'

'I just hope this happens ter yor wife one day. Surely that's the lot! Ye cannot take any more! You're leaving her with what she stands up in!'

'Check the bedrooms again. Aye. They can go.'

They rolled gold satin eiderdowns from the beds and slid them down the stairs. They lifted the cat's whisker then put it back. Christopher kept up a loud keening as Patricia hugged him and the little woman hit the men as they passed with another eiderdown. It had been her job to get the eiderdowns out that night.

'Them's warm! They need them.'

They ignored her as if she was a fly in summer. 'Outside now,' the foremen said. 'Check the cistern. People think we don't know about these hidey-holes.'

Her mother couldn't watch but Patricia and the little woman peered out of the scullery window. One man roughly forced the lavatory door open, then he paused and Patricia smiled. He stumbled back shielding his eyes then ran across the yard. A bantam cockerel flew at his face. The second man tried to pass but it turned its attention to attack him.

'Eeeh! Your little bantam's guarding the lav,' the woman laughed. 'It's flying at them. Serve them right. They're giving up. Them two's fleeing for their lives.'

The foreman took a last check round. 'That'll dee.' He nodded to Mary. 'It's just wa job, missus.'

They heard the van start up and rumble over cobblestones. All that was left in the living room was the table and chairs and bare boards.

'If they could have taken the wallpaper off the wall they'd have taken that. I'm sorry the ten shillings was too late.' The woman put her arms round Mary's waist. 'Eeeh, hinny, I never knew this would happen to you! I'll see you're not forgotten by your own now some of us have a man bringing a wage in.'

Patricia saw her out, put Christopher down, rummaged under a mattress and brought the willow pattern serving plate to her mother who took it and clutched it tight

Ben came home to find Christopher crying and the younger girls sitting quiet and white on the floor. Mary was cooking barley broth with a ham bone someone brought her, using the utensils that were

71

left in the scullery. He looked round at what had been his wife's home and went into the bedroom.

For the first and only time since the lockout he wept.

7

Young men standing on street corners, Ben noticed their hangdog look walking with the hunched shoulders of caged animals. Dangerous. He would have been afraid for his possessions, if he had any. Nothing worth stealing now. Their furniture had been quality second hand. He remembered hunting out good pieces in the early days. It had been exciting, their adventure setting up home.

A shadow passed over him. Mary stripped of everything! And no complaint from her. Everyone went without but life would have had some comfort if she'd had her bits and pieces to polish. No brasses reflected from the black lead stove. No red wood or honey grains. They were down to a trestle table and a darned cloth. The girls were using tea chests for their clothes. They'd brought nothing back from Scrimshaws' and squabbled trying to find things.

'Have ye got a tab, mister?' One of the youths stopped him.

'Sorry, lad. I've had to give up the baccy myself.'

'We're all in the same boat.'

He looked after the lad who was living for today, his horizons bounded by one cigarette. It made you less hungry. No pride, no sparkle in the eyes. No hope or arrogance of youth. If a young lad like that had no hope, what was there for him?

He caught sight of a reflection in a shop window and thought this might be an old geezer to avoid, the sort to touch you for a shilling. It was a shock to realise it was himself. He had never slouched. Next week would be his birthday. Forty-three. He felt he stood on a smaller and smaller space. He looked in a shop window full of household goods and knew he couldn't even buy Mary a cup and saucer. Lines were cutting deep round his mouth as his cheeks hollowed. He'd look like a ferret soon. Must bear up for Mary's sake. Keep busy. But there were brick walls wherever he looked, might as well go home and stare at his own brick walls.

Loneliness was cruel, Wilf at work, other men back down the pit, starved back on their bellies or not. He'd cursed the pit at times, vowed he wouldn't send a dog down there but he missed the work, the purpose, companionship. Men died for each other down there in that dark. No medals or remembrance plaques unless they died by the hundred. He'd left the pit but the pit hadn't left him. Mary said the good thing was she didn't have to think daily he might not come back after the shift, that the earth would swallow him. The pit swallowed his mind, though, stretched through his dreams.

Ben waited in line for unemployment benefit but found blacklisted men could not apply. They'd lost their jobs through their own fault. There was nothing for him. No coal allowance from the colliery. Savings were exhausted, except for a gift from his father, one gold sovereign hidden in the lavatory cistern for absolute emergency. The bantam had guarded it. There was no bakery to take their bread from for free. Vegetables from the allotment were staple and herring bought for a penny a pint jug full with the odd pence repaid by mining families. Louise was thin but pushed herring to the side of her plate. She said she was going to look like one. Mary still baked their bread and they had to look out for the man on his bike selling cakes of yeast from a basket. He didn't stop automatically at Mary's as he had when she had the business.

The woman who fought with the bailiffs brought them another ten shillings. With relief Ben cycled into town late on Saturday afternoon to buy at the covered market when stalls were clearing their goods. Butchers sold the last joints off in the final hour. Only the well-off bought meat before Wednesday. He bought as much as he could to store in the meat safe, a wire mesh contraption outside of the house. On a good week if a shilling or two had come in they might have breast of lamb for Sunday or scrag end for part of the week. Today he found a piece of fatty brisket reduced to rock bottom in the last half hour. Mary could roll it herself and preserve dripping for their breakfast bread. Bread and dripping was a luxury now. He found cracked eggs and cheap loose flour. He'd done well.

Sundays he was a stranger to the pub. That had been his day after trudging alone by the light of a Geordie lamp for the Sunday inspection of the seams. Gas and moving strata took no weekends off. The meal had had to be held up for the breadwinner, the lord and master to decide to come back, king of an hour. He loaded everything carefully onto his bicycle.

Patricia'd wanted to come with him but walking into town wasted shoe leather. She helped him unpack. Andrew was here, she said, and his mother had sent a nice pie for supper.

'That's thoughtful.' He nodded to Andrew and sat beside the fire without speaking to him again.

There were still plenty of potatoes and Mary was making chips in dripping rendered in the stove from a piece of fat picked up for nothing in the market last time. The fire burned bright. Another family repaid in kind from their free deliveries from the pit. Ben foraged for wood. At least it was cheerful. Food and a game of cards with the family and Patricia's young man.

When the cards were put away Patricia helped her mother clear up in the scullery and Andrew sat quietly opposite Ben. There was a babble as the younger girls got ready for bed. Patricia took the black kettle from the hob into the scullery and the window steamed pearl as she poured it into the sink. The girls giggled and prattled to each other. Plates clattered and coal glowed on the red fire. Ben made no conversation.

Andrew coughed. 'Can I speak to you, Mr. Hawthorne?"

'Speaking's free.'

'I would like to marry Patricia.' Silence. ' ... I mean ... we would like to start saving up.'

'You're in a position to save up, are you?' Ben didn't stir.

'It'll take time ... I know.'

Pride in his daughter wrestled with cold anger that this pale young man should ask for her. He stirred the fire rattling the poker.

'Saving's good. I'm glad you can manage it. But not for my daughter. She's not for a wedding yet. She's far too young. And we couldn't afford that sort of do!'

'I didn't mean just yet, Mr. Hawthorne. And we wouldn't expect a 'do'.'

'It's just as well.' Andrew had gone even paler. 'I'm sorry to set you back, lad. I can see you care for her. But frankly, you don't look strong enough to take on a wife. I'll not have her in want all her life.'

The lad swallowed. 'But I can still see her?'

'Perhaps less often. I appreciate your thoughtfulness when you come. But perhaps less often.'

Patricia came out of the kitchen and walked into a wall of silence. Ben watched tightlipped as she saw Andrew out and heard her determined step on the stairs before she burst back in.

'Well,' she said, 'I shall leave home in any case, married or not!'

'And where do you think you'll go to?'

'Out to work. That's where.' Her face was flushed, her hands on her hips. 'There's an advert in the paper the meat was wrapped in.'

'What advert's that?' Ben lowered his voice. She had never faced him in defiance.

'It's a place in Hexham. They want someone to look after their three children. I looked after Christopher while mam still had the bakery. I can look after three and be paid!'

'And how much is this ... pay?' Mary was standing in the door from the scullery.

'Ten shillings a week and my board and keep, paid monthly.'

'Aye, and they'll make you a slave for it,' Ben said.

'I'll try and send it all home. That'll mean I won't be able to get back myself! That should please you, dad. Then I won't be able to see Andrew either. If I'm going to be an old maid, I'd better have some means of support!'

'Patricia!' He got up to put his arms round her but she flounced into the scullery to wash and went to bed without a word.

Mary turned the gas lamp off, watched the silver light fade then looked at him across the hearth, her face illumined by the fluttering flame in the grate.

'We're going to lose her, Ben. One way or another we're going to lose her. And there's nothing we can do about it. I was about her age when we met. Do you remember? Waiting on at the colliery cricket club tea?'

'Aye, there was never anyone serious after that, my lass. But it's different when it's your daughter.'

'You had to fight my parents as well. I was brought up Catholic and you … an unbeliever.'

He listened in silence to the sound of gusting coals as wind played in their chimney. 'I think my quarrel's more with the Church than with God. You can't prove or disprove that kind of thing.' he said. The fire flared and crackled in its eerie song. 'But the world makes me think there isn't a God – and I wouldn't have my children brought up papists, that's for sure.'

Mary huffed. 'You're just particular about the churches you'll stay away from the most!' She leant forward in the gold light and shadow. 'But if they want each other, they'll have each other. One way or another.'

He sat back and studied her in fire glow witchery that gave her back the beauty of youth. 'Aye. We don't want her expecting out of defiance. Maybe it'll be a good thing to let her go now. If we keep her here they'll be together to spite us. If there's nothing really in it, it'll die a death. Perhaps she'll meet somebody else. He's not a bad lad, I'm not saying that. Just he's never going to be strong, you can see it.' He couldn't read Mary now in the shifting shadows.

'The money would help. It's good money for a lass. We've nothing coming in. We're through the leek prize. I get the odd shilling or half crown from people who owe us but I never know when that'll come. We can manage through this week, then I may have to start selling things I hid at Scrimshaws'. We could be starving soon. Let her work a while. It's not what you wanted for your daughters but it'll be one less mouth to feed here even if she can only send a bit back ... I don't want it all ... just till things look up.'

His hands clenched into fists as the flames sank and he watched the embers. 'Just till things look up,' he said.

Patricia came back from her interview with the job and with clothes for Christopher. His daughter would start duties at six thirty in the morning till eight at night. One weekend off in three, a half-day every week. No followers. It was kind of them to send the clothes but he found it hard to need them. He reached for his coat to escape from the house.

The first two postal orders for nine shillings and sixpence were used to pay rent owing. Their landlord had come to see them personally and had given them time. The only thing left apart from a few things in another house was the sovereign lying in the lavatory cistern. Ben's talisman. No question of presents for Christmas.

He turned up regularly to be considered for unemployment benefit, to be pointed in the direction of a job. Any job.

The young man in thick glasses looked at him. 'I think your only course is to go to the Guardians. They administer the Poor Law locally.'

'I'm not going to the Workhouse, if that's what you want! I'd rather starve to death!'

The young man shook his head. 'No, Mr Hawthorne, it's possible to get Outside Relief - for people who're not in the Workhouse. The government's trying to restrict this ... so I can't make promises. I'm bound by the rules.' He leant forward. 'But you just may be able to get a grant, a sum to tide you over.' He wrote something down. 'Here's the address. It's worth thinking about if only for the sake of your family.'

He took the paper, went home and showed it to Mary.

'What should I do?'

'You've always been a man of pride, Ben. It'd take a lot of courage. I'll not tell you what to do.'

With fear in his heart he made the appointment and turned up at the dark office in the Town Hall the Guardians used. A man and a woman were sitting behind a desk that seemed a mile wide. The third Guardian was unable to attend. No seat was offered. Ben stood as tall as he could. The man with greying hair and pince nez glasses was in a pin striped suit, impossible to tell his age. The woman's hair was fastened up and she wore a tailored navy blue coat. He thought that Bessy in her home-turned navy coat was handsomer and wondered how long it would take them to speak to him. Without looking up the man commented on the notes in front of him.

'You've been sent to us by the unemployment officials, Mr. Hawthorne, who say that you're destitute.' The voice was clipped, nasal. 'Is that so?' The man looked up at last.

'We have no money,' he said, 'and I have no job. I've tried the whole of Tyneside.'

'And why can't you find employment, Mr. Hawthorne?' The well-bred voice of the woman seemed to him to have a sneer in it.

'Do you want the truth?' Rage boiled. He said neither 'sir' nor 'madam'.

'Of course. What else?'

'The truth is I've been blacklisted. No-one'll take me on,' he blurted. 'because I helped co-ordinate the General Strike at local level. I'm a well-known Trades Unionist.' An invisible string pulled him taller. 'I believe in collective labour, and I believe in the working man.'

'Indeed, Mr. Hawthorne?' Again he thought he heard the sneer.

'Have you no savings, Mr. Hawthorne?' the man asked, looking over his glasses.

The door clattered and a young woman burst in. She apologised for lateness and sat down in a flurry, looking for a pen.

'This is Miss Stevenson,' the woman in navy said. 'she's a pupil teacher. We sometimes allow these younger people on the panel to gain experience.'

Ben nodded. The girl's black hair was scraped back severely but she reminded him of Patricia.

The man took over trying to be businesslike again. 'We were asking Mr. Hawthorne here if he had no savings. He's just told us he's a Trade Union agitator and has been ... blacklisted.' It sounded as though he'd murdered someone. The girl nodded. 'And the savings are gone?'

'Yes.'

' The other thing is, do you have a war pension? Were you left disabled through war service? That would count as income.'

Ben shook his head. 'I'm a miner. The pit was my war service.'

' Yes, yes ... nothing you can sell?'

Ben had to force his voice out. 'My wife went bankrupt with her bakery because she gave credit during the strike and the lockout. The bailiff's men have been in our house. They've stripped my wife's home down to bare boards. Sorry, we still have linoleum in our main room.'

'How many children do you have?' the older woman asked.

'Five.'

'Are they all at home? Are none of them working?'

'My eldest daughter's left home and is keeping herself. My other three daughters are still at school and my son's a baby.'

The pupil teacher wrote something.

'And you would take any job that was offered?'

'Anything.'

'Give us a moment, Mr. Hawthorne,' the man said rustling his papers. They dropped their voices and discussed him while he waited. The girl's back was almost to him but he could see her hands gesturing as if they were making a plea. Finally they turned to him and the man spoke. 'I think we can do something for you on this occasion, Mr. Hawthorne,' the man said, 'without bending the rules.

There's been trouble with the Guardians in Chester-le-Street about that. It'll be necessary for someone to visit your home to check that what you've told us is correct. Then we should be able to make you a grant of thirty shillings.' The girl's eyes crinkled at the corners. 'Repayable.'

'This seems a necessary case,' the woman said. She leaned forward and smiled benignly at him as though she were giving him something of her own.

He bowed formally and left. Outside he felt the cold sweat that had broken out. He would rather die than go through that scene again. He thought they'd stripped him naked and poured scorn on his nakedness, that is till the lass came in.

He was white with cold when he reached home. Mary kissed him.

The Scrimshaws had warned her what would happen if the Guardians of the Poor came to look over their home. Means testing meant more than money, income from anywhere or savings they might have. The Guardians could finish what the bailiffs had begun, though the young lass spoke up for them. The family couldn't take back any of the small things they'd got out of the house or any extra clothes. They'd have to sell anything the Guardians thought surplus to need before they could claim poor relief. Patricia's mattress would be considered surplus as she was working away from home, even if she intended to visit. An extra mattress was an extra mattress. They'd have to sell it, officially. Other people might be watching if they tried to take it out of the house. Ben carried it down to the shop. With a heave a single mattress fitted just inside the counter, covered with sacking it might not be noticed. Found, it might blow their case. Mercifully he was out when the spies arrived to judge whether they were in genuine need and no one started an argument with the superior beings. At the end of it the mattress stayed hidden and they were not considered to be the undeserving poor.

Patricia's next postal order saved them while it took time for forms to be filled out and the claim filed.

Three weeks went by before they had the thirty shillings.

Patricia brought nuts and a small Christmas pudding slipped to her by the cook on her two days' holiday. Cook had carved slices of ham for them as well from an old gammon as there was a whole one hanging in the kitchen for Christmas Day. The cook was entitled to left overs as their employers did not believe in waste. Vegetables with ham and the pudding for tea were a feast.

*

Spring. No work for Ben. Patricia and Andrew walked together on a free Saturday afternoon. From a distance they looked like a tranquil couple walking in step with each other, he with his arm round her waist.

'How long are we going to have to wait?' he asked.

'We've not been going with each other that long, Andrew.'

'Are you saying you're not sure anymore?'

'I was sure,' she said looking down, 'the moment I saw you.' When she looked up a shower of pleasure struck his face. 'Can we go somewhere a bit secluded?' he asked.

'We can walk in the grounds of the parish church. Nobody minds. The caretaker's used to courting couples. They sit on the bench of his little hut there.'

Andrew squeezed her arm. 'Hallowed ground,' he said.

They laughed as they walked down the path shaded with trees, plucking at delicate curled leaves. The caretaker was nowhere in sight.

Andrew took her left hand, kissed each finger and came back to the third. 'I've got something for you,' he said and brought a small box from his pocket. 'This is my grandmother's ring. She gave me it before she died. For the girl I'd marry.'

A gold ring studded with garnets nestled against the worn black velvet. Patricia's fingers opened to pick it up but she closed them and sat still. He drew the ring out and began to ease it onto the ring finger of her left hand.

'I can't, Andrew.' He held the hand while he kissed her mouth but she broke free. 'Andrew, I can't get married yet. I can't give up my work and Dad won't give his consent, so we have to wait till I'm twenty-one.' He stroked her hair. 'In any case I can only work if I live in. I send ten shillings a week home now they've given me a rise for helping cook. The rent's always paid and one or two other things.'

'You're working yourself into the ground.' He reached for her hand again. 'That family's just saving themselves money. How much do they pay you squeezing more work out of you?'

'An extra two shillings a week.' She held up her hand. 'I know it saves them having to take an extra hand on for the kitchen, but I get on with cook. I don't mind it. And it makes a difference.' She held back tears. 'Mam can buy fresh herring three times a week and pay the milk bill with the extra sixpence I send now. She needs six shillings for the rent and two shillings for household bills. That's before any food. She's still short. Many a time she doesn't know what she'll do near the end of the week.'

'It's too much for you to carry all this.'

'But they can't do without that money. It'll take a miracle for my dad to be set on at work.' She drew the ring off her finger. 'I can still pay for stamps and bus fares and I buy the odd remnant of cloth and do some sewing on my afternoon off.' She held the ring out to him. 'You would do the same for your mother, Andrew.'

He buried his face against her hands. 'Wear it on your right hand.' The words were muffled. ' ... if you won't wear an engagement ring.' He pushed it gently on the third finger of her right hand. 'Let's go into the church a minute,' he said.

They sat on a pew, watching the rays of the sun cut a kaleidoscope of stained glass in the nave and cast diamond patterns in the aisle. He took the ring from her right hand, kissed her left and placed it again on the wedding finger.

'With this ring I thee wed,' he whispered.

She received his vow in prayerful silence but in the green scented air outside she placed the jeweled band back on her right hand. 'I'm nineteen,' she said when they found the bench again. 'It's young to be marrying.'

He kissed her left hand and kissed her throat, touching her thigh over her skirt, over petticoats. She tried to move his hand. 'I love you, Patricia. That makes it all right.'

She tried to warn him with her eyes but he moved his hand up to her waist then suddenly, passionately kissed her breast over the ruched bodice.

'Say you'll marry me. Please.'

She spoke over the hardness in her throat. 'I'll marry you, Andrew Taylor ... when I can.'

A year after Patricia began her employment at Hexham, Mrs. Routledge decided to have a supper party. They'd been asked to a supper and cards party in the run up to Christmas and decided to test how much of a social asset cook really was.

The first entertainment was in mid-November with five couples invited. Patricia helped prepare ahead and managed to have the children in bed for half past seven so she could serve on the night. She wore a crisp white apron and a lace collar. Everything was polished to mirror brilliance against a roaring fire. After supper she served coffee and brandy in the drawing room where tables were laid out for cribbage and bridge.

The guests came to the card tables after enjoying the company and showed the mellow happiness of a peaceful digestion. Mr. Routledge kept the stakes low so no one lost too much and the party kept going till midnight. Drinks and small savouries had to be circulated. Each couple left a tip of a shilling for the cook who passed on sixpence to Patricia. Mrs. Routledge added her own sweetener of two shillings to cook and a shilling to Patricia. The gentlemen had been pleased by the sight of a pretty girl and the ladies were not outshone by her wearing plain black and white.

The Routledges decided to repeat the experiment and invited eight couples for the following Saturday. After supper there was coffee and brandy in the drawing room where tables were laid out again for cribbage and bridge. They bought a smart, fitted black dress for Patricia, which she could keep, in any case the lady of the house was bigger. Everything had to be perfect. Success brought success brought success. Five couples, then eight, then ten. Then a baroness!

'I'll give her baroness!' stormed the cook. 'I'm absolutely worn out. It takes me all week to plan this properly and I have to start to get ahead for Christmas.'

'They're very excited. A baroness puts them up in the social stakes.'

'I know all about Baroness Joyce Fitz Gibbons. She comes from round here and made a good catch because of her looks. It was a coal baron she caught, not a real one.'

'But she has the title.'

'We'd all have a title if we had enough money. You could be Princess Candy Floss and I'd be Queen of Sheba.'

Patricia giggled. 'You can't just make up titles!'

Cook stacked copper bowls on her soap bleached table. 'Today you can. Lloyd George has decided to sell off baronetcies like toffee apples. You just have to be big headed enough and rich enough. This is a bought title. I know the difference.'

'You're a snob, cook.'

'With my cooking I can afford to be a snob. Baroness Fancy-Pants is around because she's staying with her cousin for a family wedding. The wedding's not important enough for his lordship Coalmuck to attend but the cousin's a friend of our employer so we are landed with her. I'm going to put a stop to this, one way or another. But I'll need help.'

Patricia was getting the children through breakfast when cook came in to sort out the menu with the lady of the house. She stood professionally with her notebook and pen, crackling with starch. They discussed the merits of beef or lamb and she wrote swiftly.

'And would you like a special sherry trifle, madam?'

'Oh, yes. But make sure there's enough, cook. The gentlemen may like to come back for seconds.'

'I'll make two large bowls, madam. Perhaps we could use the punch bowl and the old punch bowl you use at New Year for the staff?'

'That would be fine. I wonder if it's the right sort of dessert for the baroness?'

'Oh, yes, madam. Everyone loves sherry trifle. I'll decorate it and make it look so dainty that even the ladies will be tempted to a second helping. We could serve it with those very thin biscuits. They're a bit expensive. Does that matter?'

'Not on this occasion.'

'And, of course, the real secret to sherry trifle is not to be mean with the sherry, which should be good.'

'Of course. By all means, cook. Use your discretion.'

When she had a spare hour Patricia helped with the trifles, which were a labour of love. She liked being in the kitchen with its copper pans and smells that reminded her of home. Cook made her own sponges on Monday, four of them. There was to be a double layer of everything. Sponge and sherry would be mixed with a little raspberry jelly so the sponge would not collapse, then a layer of puréed apricots, peaches with brandy from a jar, more raspberry jelly, then egg custard with a trace of cornflour for firmness. The layers were to be repeated with fresh pears poached in syrup and the whole would be topped with thick whipped cream squeezed through a forcing bag and decorated with glazed cherries, angelica and almonds.

The children were taking a nap when Patricia came in to help.

'Now for my secret addition,' cook said. 'I'm going to doctor the Harvey's Bristol Cream. We'll make a real gut-rot.'

'Can you get away with this?' Patricia asked.

'Yes. I can get away with it. No-one'll know what we've done. It'll be the most carefully doctored jollop you've ever known. What we do is mix it in with the sherry.' She uncorked the precious liquid and a deep brown smell filled the kitchen. 'First we take syrup of figs.' Medicine from the nursery curled round their nostrils. 'Then prune juice and the liquor of the dried apricots I stewed. Then we add molasses left over from Christmas puddings,' she poured the thick goo in a steady stream into the earthenware bowl, 'and last that nearly black sugar.'

Patricia opened the packet of dark sugar that moved and sifted over itself and smelled a smell of Christmas. They stirred everything together and added a whole bottle of sherry. Cook tasted a minute quantity and added more sugar. They both tasted and added a whisk of white sugar.

'Perfect,' cook said. "Now, let's dip just a little sponge in it to see how well it blends. What do you think?'

'It's lovely,' said Patricia. 'They'll want to know what your special ingredients are.'

'I'll tell them it's a secret passed to me by my mother which I never disclose to anyone. I'll teach madam Routledge to give me so much work! Did she test you for honesty when you first started?'

'Not that I know of.'

'My first week they deliberately left a sovereign out in the kitchen.'

'Did you give it back?'

'No. That was what I was supposed to do. I took a nail to it through the kitchen floor so they couldn't pick it up again. When they finally loosened it, it could only be used for scrap gold!'

The baroness arrived, elegant and fresh though cook said she knew her real age. The hair was newly set and owed something to a bottle, cook said privately. But subtly rouged, in cream satin and pearls, the baroness was lovely in a soft light. Mr. Routledge had treated his wife to a new bespoke dress in peacock blue. He had not been so pleased with her in a long time. The tailoring had been completed that morning. Laughter filled the dining room and cook's meal was a triumph. Oxtail soup with port wine, fillet of beef cooked in pastry, a lemon sorbet to clear the palate, then the final joy of the sherry trifle. The sight alone was exquisite. Even the ladies did not restrain themselves. The second punch bowl was brought from the kitchen and everyone had at least another helping. The baroness seemed taken by Patricia's quiet good looks and pleasant manner. She complimented Mrs. Routledge on the meal and the presentation. In higher social circles she was only allowed to say. 'That was lovely!' - but here she was more relaxed. The Routledges exchanged a glance.

Patricia cleared the final dishes, balanced them on a tray and managed to walk without staggering to the kitchen. 'About an hour,' cook said.

In the second rubber of bridge disaster struck. The colonel excused himself and Patricia showed him to the lavatory in the cloakroom. Mr. Routledge was next, then a cousin of the baroness. The need became so urgent the ladies forgot all embarrassment. By the time the baroness admitted she too was mortal there was a queue and cook and Patricia brought buckets of water from the kitchen for the cistern.

Patricia noticed the baroness's distress. 'Would you like to use the outside lavatory of the servants, madam?'

The lady in her finery mouthed YES! Then followed her to the bare, whitewashed outhouse. When the titled lady emerged she said she understood how Handel could write the Hallelujah Chorus and gave Patricia a hug after washing her hands in the kitchen. Gentlemen gave priority to the ladies in the queue and came out to the servants' lavatory, even using the ancient midden with the double seat and long drop. Mr. Routledge had to rummage for a rusty key to open it up and hastily handed newspaper for the gentlemen, two at a time, to rip up for themselves.

Patricia quickly closed the pine kitchen door behind her as poor Mrs Routledge could not hold out the eternity of minutes, all her lady guests had to go first. She understood and filled another bucket of water as her employer managed to take off her drawers, happily not the open variety. Perhaps as well she'd not gone over to satin camiknickers. The guests left quickly in confusion and the hostess managed to keep her back to them as they said goodnight. The peacock blue dress would never be the same. Patricia watched from behind the dining room door as cook took refuge in slandering the greengrocer for the produce he sold her and the remains of the sherry trifle were thrown out. This was the last of the supper parties and she could prepare for Christmas,

Five days later a letter in a lady's fine copperplate came for Patricia. From the baroness. She asked whether she'd like to leave Mrs. Routledge's employ and come to work as her own personal maid.

Payment: three pounds a month.

Poaching of servants was a social crime even by a title but Mrs. Routledge could do nothing about it. Patricia sucked her breath. More money and an easier job, she felt she had no choice. Cook was not the only one who got away with it.

8

Ben had bargained for some shoemakers' lasts in the market with a trade knife and a length of shoe leather thrown in for the price, the best use he could make of the money Patricia sent home after the dinner parties. This was bankrupt stock. Other traders had been cleared out. He felt for the people who'd gone under but bought the stuff up. Wilf's mother gave him a sturdy little table and he set this up in the back yard in the space the girls used to perform their concerts.

Louise sat on the bottom step of the stairs that led from the scullery door, watching her father experiment with his new skill. He turned the foot shape of an iron last upside down and clamped it firmly to the table end. It was smooth, shiny and interesting. He drew round a shoe on the leather, hacked a sole out and eased the shoe onto the last. Next he was struggling to cover the sole with honey-coloured glue. It stretched into a spoon shape and pulled outward leaving a hole in the centre. Ben dabbed a little more on the new leather and tried spreading it quicker.

The smell was strong. Louise found it pleasant. Pungent, organic, made from hide and bones, a smell in cobbler's shops that would always take her back to childhood. The glue had not quite begun to dry before he had the sticky mixture evenly spread. Her dad tapped the sole down onto the upturned shoe with a hammer and began to battle with the sticky stuff on the other sole. The small hammer gleamed. The last had to hold very tight as he held the sharp knife and trimmed round the shoe so the sole fitted exactly. Yellowish leather shavings fell onto the stone floor of the yard. The younger girls longed to touch all the equipment but it was forbidden, especially the tiny box of needle fine nails he opened now. Louise watched as he worked quickly before the weather broke.

Ben motioned her to hold a clump of the silver needles in her palm like treasure. He needed a helper because he daren't do the cobbler's trick of holding the little nails in his mouth.

'In their gobs?' She laughed.

He tapped a neat double row an eighth of an inch inside the sole. They couldn't just go out and buy shoes, These had been his best pair. Louise waited patiently for him to mend her best shoes as well. They bent in harmony over the task.

She was old enough to remember the money her dad had squeezed from the Guardians and the children had all had new shoes. She knew they were lucky to have had that. Some of the boys at school went barefoot even in winter, hopping from one foot to another when it was freezing. But the problem came back when they grew out of them. She wished her feet wouldn't grow. They were still small but she would like them to stay like that.

Her older sister sent so much home, she felt jealous of her. After Easter she would leave school but didn't want to go away. They said she wasn't strong enough to go into service. She'd been a premature baby and had heard they'd fed her milk from a feather and mixed it with a drop of brandy when it seemed she couldn't suckle.

'Why was I premature?' she asked her father.

'That's a difficult one.' He tapped a second silver row inside the first carefully, the hammer gleaming.

'Was mam not well?'

'She must have been feeling tired, she was irritable and weary with herself. Women get like that when it's near their time. I think she'd had about enough at eight months.' He shook his head. 'I couldn't do anything right. Not a thing. If I breathed it was wrong. I smoked every pipe outside on the step so as not to make her sick. She'd had a bad night. I knew that because I hadn't slept either. Like a great walrus heaving round beside me.'

'Don't let Mam hear you say that,' Louise squeaked. 'Anyway?'

'She'd been busy. It was Saturday and I'd come home early from the fore-shift, took that early one so I could be there for her and I'd hardly had time for a cup of tea. Fix this, fix that! A man gets exhausted down the pit and I'd had it by three o' clock.' He took more of the sharp silver nails from her hand, threw one onto the sole, drove it home with the hammer. Bang, bang, throw, bang. He stopped speaking till he finished a row, shooting nails, beating his hammer on the last like a little anvil in a brilliant arc.

It was cold now but she sat still at her task. 'So what happened, dad?'

'I'd just put my coat on to go out and have an hour's peace over a pint when the pit lorry decided to arrive with my coal allowance. The men, of course, couldn't use their brains to knock on the door.' Louise giggled. 'They couldn't open the coalhouse door themselves and count the little beggars in, didn't stop to say "how's your father?". They had to dump two bags worth on the back lane. Then they upped and off. Your mother hit the roof. It was all my fault. I had to take my coat off and shovel it all in immediately and I'd had just about as much as could stand. "Mary, give me one hour," I said. "Then I'll come home and do as much as you like." I was true to my word. Back in an hour. But she'd gone out in temper, tried to move the coal herself and was in spasms of labour when I came in. I had to run quick and get the midwife. It took a long time, but you were born alive. The neighbours blamed me, of course, leastwise the women did.' He put the hammer down. 'That's how you were born a month premature. And against the odds, you're still here. When you got eczema I cycled all the way to the coast with a barrel on the back of the bike and brought sea water back to bathe you in. You wouldn't eat.'

'I was the tiddler.'

'You got rickets. But you're still here.' He smiled and dazzled her with his blue eyes. 'Thank God!'

She gave him the nails and nestled against him when he finished.

Louise looked at herself in a small mirror her parents had risked bringing back into their bedroom. She pushed her fringe to one side and tried to curl kiss-curls round her fingers at her temples then pulled her jersey tight over her ribcage and thought there was the slightest roundness under the nipples. Her mother came in and she went back to brushing her hair.

'Can I have a lipstick, mam?

'You haven't left school yet.'

'But I nearly have.'

'Your dad would go mad.'

'I have to grow up some time.'

'Not yet. And we can't afford rubbish like that.'

She waited till Mary had finished baking, found a little bottle of cochineal on a shelf and poured a few drops into a small jar then reached down a bottle of real vanilla essence left over from better times, unscrewed the top and sniffed. Like Phulnana scent. She put a drop on a finger and dabbed behind her ears then took the trace of food colouring and darted back into the girls' bedroom to the tiny stand-up mirror. With cochineal on her little finger she rubbed hesitantly on her lips and sucked them in on each other. She stood back and studied her new face, smiled at herself and walked out to the kitchen balancing on the balls of her feet, pretending to be on high heels.

'What's that stink?' Ben asked. He looked up from the paper over his glasses. 'Go and wash your face, Louise. Then come back to eat. You look like Little Nell trying to be Cleopatra.'

She flounced out. 'I'll show you! I'll be leaving school soon.'

'That doesn't mean you have to take leave of your senses.'

She came back to the table and he ladled potatoes for her, steam curling from them. She wished it would smear his glasses.

'Anyway,' he said, 'we don't know what you're going to do when you leave school. Your mam could do with a bit of help with the odd bit of baking she does.'

'I'm not baking bread then sneaking it out so we can pay for our own flour.'

'Aren't you? What are you going to do, then?' He sloshed potato mounds out for the rest of the family. 'Perform pantomimes in the backyard?'

'I do that,' Katharine squeaked. 'Because I'm the bestest.'

'Not when you tip your brother out of his pram, you're not,' Ben said.

'Well, he shouldn't cry.'

'I don't know what I'm going to do yet. But it's going to be good. And I'm going to earn a lot of money. And I'll buy my own lipstick. Proper lipstick.'

'Fast women and royalty wear that muck. I'll not have a daughter of mine looking like a tart.'

'I'm better than the Queen,' Katharine said.

'You ruined that dress with the white sash Patricia made for you.'

'I couldn't help falling with the cochineal.'

'You shouldn't have opened it.'

'I shouldn't have been sent for cochineal.'

'What's a tart?' Diane asked, blue eyes looking back into her father's.

'You're too young to know,' Louise said. 'You're still at school.'

'So are you!'

Louise felt a stamp on her foot and deliberately crunched her face up.

'That's it!' Ben stood up. 'Diane into the scullery, and the rest of you behave!'

Diane put her knife and fork onto her plate.

'If she's going, I'm going,' Louise said, gathering up her things.

'So am I,' Katharine piped. 'Because I'm the bestest.'

Christopher sat gaping at them

'Now see what you've done!' Mary glared at their father.

'Just for once, I'd like to have my meal in peace!'

The girls huddled together on the scullery step and ate herring and potatoes between giggles.

Louise dreamed. But it would be necessary to find work before she found her prince. In the last two weeks at school she started looking in shop windows at cards that advertised services, second hand goods and jobs. Cleaning and gardening. She couldn't garden. She wouldn't clean. Anyway, she was too small for it. She still measured an inch less than five feet. She found nothing. They didn't buy newspapers any more. She would have to go into town to read the job adverts in the library or somewhere, though the Labour Exchange frightened her. She had to find something, but her clothes! Patricia might make her something. They didn't see a lot of her now she'd gone off with Baroness Snotnose. Katharine was going to sew, she said, but Katharine couldn't be trusted with anything yet.

When she got home, after dallying all the way from school Wilf was in sharing his baccy with her dad. And he was hugging the fire. Wilf, though, had news. He leant forward speaking quietly to Ben but she sat stubbornly on the three legged stool to listen cupping her chin in her palm.

'There's a lass leaving at the dog track.' Wilf said. 'The one that takes the bets in the little office. Getting married. How about taking your lass down,' he looked at Louise, 'who's leaving school?'

'She's a bit young, don't you think, for that sort of thing?'

Wilf turned to her and saw her. She felt he wasn't looking at a little girl. 'You could dress up a bit, couldn't you, lass? Do your hair differently?'

She uncupped her chin and sat up. 'I'm dying to.'

Ben shook his head. 'In any case I don't think I'd like her in that sort of atmosphere.'

She was interested. 'What kind of atmosphere?'

Wilf cut in. 'You could take her down yourself. Collect her. Stay and keep an eye on her in the evening. It would get you out anyway, man. You're getting to be a right stony faced so-and-so. I like a cheerful marrer. It'd take you out of yourself, man Ben. What's done's done. You'd maybe be more cheerful company for Mary an all.'

'Maybe's you're right. But would you put a daughter of yours down there?'

'If I kept an eye on her.'

Louise washed her hair with rainwater and the dirty looking soft green soap Andrew brought from the shipyard. It didn't look as if it would ease a ship into the water. It didn't look as if it could make your hair seem twice as thick. She rinsed till she could hear squeaking between her fingers then crimped it with the crimping irons from Scrimshaws. She watched in the mirror as the irons hissed. Scrimshaws never had a penny but they could turn themselves out. Nobody looked better. Their mother was good looking. If they could do it she could do it. The hair dried to honey brown not as dark as Patricia, Katharine and their mam. Diane looked like dad, blue eyes and gold hair. He said the rest of them could have had a gypsy for a father. She was just beginning to understand remarks like that. She moved her head to shake the hair and saw that in the light her eyes turned golden.

There was a navy skirt and jacket Patricia had just made for her from an off-cut she'd found in the market. She tried it on with a pink blouse. It almost made her look as if she had a figure. Ben objected but she'd borrowed a little powder and an end of lipstick from an older girl. She coaxed the colour from the brass holder onto her little finger, rubbed the blood red onto her mouth then softened it with a clean finger. The first thing she'd do when she had sixpence of her own would be to buy a lipstick. With the second sixpence she'd buy a little tin of Snowfire powder. Air spun. A proper shoe with a heel would have to wait forever.

The man at the dog track was not sure. 'She's a bit young.' He turned to his wife. 'What do you think?'

'The face is pretty. It's the face they'll see over the office counter.'

'I can add up and keep tally of everything as well as anybody,' Louise said.

'There's a bit more to it than that, dear,' the wife said. 'You have to make the men feel like spending their money. Encourage them to place another bet, put a little more down.'

'I can smile,' Louise said, 'if that's what you want.'

'What do you think?' the man asked his wife again.

'She'll do,' she said and turned to Louise. 'Now the hours can be quite long for a young one but you'll be in a little office not standing. Two in the afternoon till eight at night every day except Sunday. Wednesday's a big night. You'll be on till at least nine then, longer sometimes if a race gets held up. Same on a Saturday till at least nine but you start at half past twelve then. For a very big day it may even be earlier. The pay's five shillings a week. If we have you in before noon on a Saturday you'll have an extra shilling.'

Ben cut in. 'I want no bother from the punters for my daughter and I'll collect her every evening myself. Winter nights I'll be here a couple of hours before the end.'

'You can keep warm in the office,' the man said. 'We want no trouble ourselves.'

Her father was still unhappy but Louise enjoyed being out in the world. It was exciting at the racetrack and she started to recognise different dogs and their owners. Some days were slack. Saturdays left her wrung out but she enjoyed Fridays. There was a sense of holiday. The smell of the men's tobacco, sleekly brushed dogs' hair and the lavender brilliantine of their owners plus a whiff of beer on their breath at the weekend made her feel alive. If one of the customers had a good win he might tip her sixpence, even a shilling. There was bustle, noise, concentration on a race, cheers or yells at the end of it.

Mary let her keep sixpence out of her wage and she spent it on her little store of beauty products but hid the perfume from Ben who still 'borrowed' from his daughters to scent the handkerchief for his top pocket. She saved the tips up for a pair of high heeled shoes that cost thirty shillings. It might take a year and a half to save it up. She despaired of the flat shoes she'd worn at school.

Dog racing was big business, one of the few hopes of making money for people who did grinding work. But Race Week was different. Holiday time and horses, the festival for men and women who never travelled beyond the Tyne. From the odd sixpence she'd saved, Louise could stake her father a shilling for the Northumberland Plate, the Pitman's Derby. A punter had had an excellent night and too much from his hip flask, tipped her a shilling for her smile and came back with another sixpence, forgetting he'd already left a coin. This gave sufficient for the stake, a newspaper for form and the bus fare from her wage. After a year at work she felt she was a young woman not a child and a day out with her father was worth it if they didn't fight. The dog track was shut because nobody competed with the Plate.

The fair was on at the Town Moor so buses were crowded. Women struggled with young children impatient for their rides while the menfolk went to the race course. Gosforth Park was packed even though they'd come early. Men away from work, kings for the day. They deserved it, she thought. As she did. Ben carried his haversack from pit days with jam and cheese sandwiches in it, his favourite for quick energy at the pit. Wilf's wife had sent the bramble jelly round that she made from town brambles grown by the railway side. The bread was fresh from the bakery and they had a flask of tea.

'Don't go to the Gosforth Park bookies, dad,' Louise said. 'Their odds are bound to be the steepest.'

'I know, pet,' he said. 'We want to find a runner for an independent bookie, a small one. I didn't tell you but I had a tip at the dog track when I was waiting for you. A filly for the first race not fancied by the bookies. I've worked out a triple accumulator to end with the favourite for the Plate.'

'That's risky, dad.'

'Well, it's your money. What do you think?'

She squeezed his arm. 'Let's do it. It was only a tip. I'll get another one. If you're down on the first race that's our day out finished, though.'

'Only if we want it to be. We can still enjoy being out, nosing at what other people are up to.'

She took his arm and they wandered round trying to follow the sign language of the tick tack men standing on small tubs or steps they carried round with them, gesturing in white gloves. Ben went up to two or three to ask the odds. They had to invest the precious shilling well. Louise wore a straw hat against the sun that was frying in a cloudless sky on the day of the Plate. The hat was a bargain and she'd tied a pink ribbon round the crown, clipped little enamel scarabs and hieroglyphics in the style of Tutenkhamen's tomb onto the pink satin and kept her secret she'd almost begged for them in a clear-out sale in town. The floppy brim framed her face. Fashionable women in soft, bright-coloured cloche hats pulled down over their ears and shingled short hair styles glanced her way. Over powdered noses they looked down at the old fashioned, decorated wide hat and minced by in tee barred shoes, drifting exclusive perfume in their wake. But men turned in her direction and looked slowly as she walked past. She smiled up at her father and saw his eyes were crinkled with pride. He beamed when he met Wilf, who gave her a compliment. She waited patiently while they talked and looked round. She liked the excitement at the dog track but this was like a king's court.

'If you want good odds, Ben, try over yonder, the feller with his back to us.

'I'll try it, we'll have to get this on soon.'

'Good luck!'

They edged through the crowd to a young man in a charcoal grey suit, smarter by far than the usual brown the working man kept for Sunday. He was bare headed with thick dark hair brushed in waves back from his brow. He continued to 'tick tack' while talking to a punter, his face never still. Well-heeled women with their husbands never placed bets through a bookie of the flat cap brigade but Louise saw they noticed him and followed him with their eyes as they sidled into the smart bar in a marquee. Ben went up to him and fell into serious conversation. He could get ten to one for the first race, then five to one for the second but no one would give more than two to one for the favourite in the Plate. An accumulator? Yes. That would give him five pounds if they all came up. Louise watched as the young man filled in a betting slip and her father parted with the shilling. Sun shone like a spotlight on the hair that was falling in a stray curl on his brow though she could see it had been firmly brushed back with Brylcreem. He finished the serious business and only then looked at the girl on her father's arm. In spite of the brim of her hat, light dazzled her for a moment. She gazed up, more than a foot difference in their height, shaded her eyes and smiled.

He made a bow. 'If I had my topper on, I would doff it.' Even the crease at the corner of his eyes was secret with invitation. 'As it is, I can only shake your hand.'

They touched briefly and her heart set on a man that women would die for. Ben put an arm protectively round her shoulder and led her to a place where she would see the race better.

The first race looked like being a loser. The filly started badly and they stood tense in silence but half way round the course she began to cover ground and gained on two yearlings out in front. One was flagging and the filly, the first choice in the accumulator, overtook him on the home stretch. She drew level with the favourite, neck and neck for a century of seconds, both horses straining their heads forward, till the filly's jockey used his crop and brought her home by a nose over the finishing line. The swell of the crowd's voice dropped in disappointment as Ben threw his arms round his daughter.

A good beginning. The bookies were into pocket on the first race with the favourite losing. Louise felt she could reach out and touch a wall of excitement. Ben relaxed. His next bet was not till the fourth race. Gentlemen gave their ladies binoculars to follow the horses more closely and slid their hands round the women's waists, round their shoulders, responding to the mixed scent of crushed grass, sweat and speed, to the heady atmosphere, to a magnetic charge in the air. Louise looked for the man who'd taken their bet but he was not in sight. If the accumulator came in they'd have to go back for their winnings. The crowd began shouting again for the second race and transformed into a mass, not individuals, hoarse, thirsty, dripping with tension, then when it was over relaxing into friendliness with strangers. Ben produced tea and sandwiches during the third and fourth race. He met up with Wilf again and was having the best day out since the big lockout. His next horse came in and they were fifty shillings to the good. If the favourite wins the Plate,' he said to Louise, 'we'll have a party. I'm collecting a piano from the house where I'm doing a bit of decorating at the minute. They're throwing one out. Patricia could play. She'll be home this weekend.'

The bookies had had a good afternoon and could stand it if the favourite came in at two to one. Most of the pitmen had gone for the favourite but placed their money each way. Louise dabbed a little cologne at her throat. It was hot.

'You've taken a risk,' Wilf said, 'just going for a win.'

'Can't change it now.' Ben took a final swig of tea and packed the food away. For Louise the big race became a dream. Somewhere in the distance starter's orders were given, the gun fired and a blur, a noise came up from the earth itself. She became faint in her stomach and felt she was falling. As a cheer went up, she was lifted onto a cloud of dread and nausea.

Ben caught her round the waist. 'It's all right, lass! We've won.' Wilf produced a shooting stick he'd bought second hand and they took her aside to some soft earth, pierced the steel point in the ground and opened the small seat out for her. Ben coaxed a little more tea from the flask. 'Here,' he said, 'Drink this slowly. I thought you were used to the excitement of a race. Stay here while I collect the winnings.'

'No. Wait. I'll be better in a minute. It's just the heat.' She swallowed quickly and willed herself to stand up. 'I'm all right. Give me your arm.'

Joe Ellison was busy when they arrived. Ben waited to one side with his daughter away from the crush. The jockey was being presented with the trophy and he craned round to see the ceremony then came back to business. The punters, impatient for their winnings cleared. Collecting theirs felt like Christmas when she was little, when they'd had money and there'd been presents. But when Ellison looked up and saw her the lucky bet shrank to nothing in his gaze.

'I shouldn't say it, but I'm glad you've won. A triple's fantastic. What the hell! It's not my money.' He took a fine white five pound note from a wallet, unfolded the near transparent sheet written on in copper plate and held it up. 'You haven't seen many of these,' he said to Louise. She shook her head smiling.

'Put that away,' Ben said. 'I can't change that on the bus.'

Joe laughed and refolded it, counted out smaller notes with ten shillings in change and put the change into Louise's hand gently holding it. 'May I ask,' he said to Ben, 'whether I could have the privilege of escorting your daughter to the pictures?' He looked in her eyes as he spoke to her father, not needing her answer. She saw him take in the shape of her face and flawless skin. At work she'd picked up the spirit of gambling and decided then and there to chance her life on this uncertain love.

Ben took the change from his daughter's hand releasing it from Joe's. 'My daughters don't go out with men till they're sixteen,' he said. 'That won't be till September.'

'That's a long wait,' Joe said. 'I'll take care of her.'

Ben looked at the response in his daughter's face and pocketed the change. 'Or there'll be hell to pay, young man.' He stared a warning.

'I'll bring her straight back.'

'Aye. Well, you'll collect her from the house and I'll be up when you return. Time to go, Louise.'

'May I have your address then, sir?'

Ben wrote it grudgingly on the back of a betting slip and Louise saved the radiance of her smile for her father, took his arm in thanks and tried to show him that nobody took his place.

She had barely had tea and washed when he arrived and the younger girls hung over the bannister as he led her out, a giant from another country shrouded in mists and secrets. She stepped in a shiver of joy, a dancing illusion in a dream court, a fascinating charmed sphere. She feared to wake, to bump from the music to discord, to shear a glass bauble in pieces.

They walked over familiar pavements that looked different now, past shops to the picture house. Inside the cinema she trod into luxurious thick carpet and looked up at walls studded with portraits of the stars, angular Art Deco glass and lights. The luminous images on the screen were overshadowed by his presence, his shoulder, his hand that rested still and did not stray to hers. His smile that met hers when the lights brightened dimmed the glamour of celluloid stars. Reason froze in the sapphire of his eyes. Fixed and frozen on a beam of witchcraft.

Then she remembered, her father's party was really on. He and Wilf were going to collect the piano with a borrowed pony and trap on Saturday, they were going to fetch a cask of beer from Ben's allotment shed where he'd been secretly fermenting a home brew and every guest would bring food to share. Louise invited her prince.

'I don't exactly know how it'll turn out,' she said. 'It's a long time since we had a party.'

'We'll make our own party. It doesn't matter what anyone else is doing.' A spell in each word. 'I'm sorry I won't be able to see you before then. I have to see a man about a dog.'

The mist of a spell. 'You don't have to make little excuses.'

'It's true,' he said. 'I do have to see a man about a dog. I'll tell you on Saturday. Expect me when I arrive.'

Ben was waiting jealously when she came in. She slipped quickly into the second bedroom where she shared a double bed with the younger girls but they had put their bottoms together from spite, not to let her in, and pretended to be snoring. She gave up and slipped into Patricia's bed that was upstairs again for the weekend. It was cold but she hugged the memory of the evening to herself, the hope, the mirage of him, and was warm.

Young firemen from the station further down the street joined the party, drank beer with Ben and smoked a pipe with him if they didn't dance. Their lack of furniture had created space. The trestle table was pushed back against the wall and Andrew hung over Patricia at the piano. The girls cooled themselves with home-made lemonade and Katharine and Diane tried to dance together, awkward, though Katharine's ruddy cheeks and black eyes made men follow her movements already. The youngest firemen cut in and waltzed with the girls who made faces over their shoulders at Louise. She was wearing a full skirt and patent leather high heels from her share of the winnings, not allowed to dress like a flapper till she was eighteen but the beloved heels were enough, a talisman she was a woman. Young men waited to dance with her and she danced with every one, watching the door.

It was supper time, nine o' clock when he arrived. He stepped up beside her, shared a plate as there were not enough and stayed with her.

'Did you see that man about that dog?' she asked as they tucked into a corner.

'Yes. It was a carry on, that. You don't want to hear about it while you're eating.'

'I don't feel sick.'

'Well, I warned you. It's a bit grizzly.' She laughed. 'The owner of a racing dog sometimes wants to get rid of it, when it's past it.' He talked in their corner as though she was the only person there.

'I've heard about that at the dog track.'

'Of course. I don't know how we haven't met. I take the odd bet there sometimes. Anyway, my boss said I had to go round to this bloke's house and relieve him of his whippet. They can't afford to feed them if they're not bringing the money in. I hate it. You get paid sixpence but I hate it. I try to see if I can place the dog with someone else who wants a pet. Sometimes I'm lucky with that and I can usually sell it on for a shilling. Nobody wanted the dog this time, though, so it was the dirty work.'

'A piece of pie?' Diane tried to engage him but he did not glance up from her sister.

'I was never quite sure what they did with them,' Louise said.

'I'm afraid they're drowned in the Tyne. You walk them down, tie a brick round their neck and toss them in. I feel lousy when I have to do it. Anyway, when I walked back up and passed the bloke's house the whippet was sitting there on the step, soaking wet. I got out of it quick before he made me do it again. The boss was really annoyed but I said I wasn't going to take it to the water a second time. He could do it himself.'

'Err! Horrible!' Katharine had been listening. He turned round and smiled at her. 'Well, it didn't happen this time.'

Joe pulled Louise to her feet. He noticed the new shoes. 'What tiny feet you have.' She floated.

Ben had had too much of his home brew and was enraged by the story of the whippet. Katharine whispered it to him. He came over red faced to the dancing couples and thrust himself between them. So this is the dog killer?'

'Dad!'

'We had a dog and had to get rid of it because we couldn't feed it but we didn't *kill* it! We found it a home.' Other couples drew back and Louise died. 'In the Labour Movement we respect people. Aye, and I respect animals as well. The beast had worked. It deserved to live.'

Joe stood his ground. 'It was part of my job. But I've decided I *will* refuse it another time. The boss can do it himself. I'm not going to do away with any more.'

'A Labour man wouldn't do that!'

Joe stood quite still in the middle of the floor. 'I've seen more than one Labour man do it.'

'Lies! And in my own house. Keir Hardy wouldn't have sanctioned a thing like that!'

Joe folded his arms. 'I don't know what his attitude to animal welfare was.' Louise drew a deep breath and touched his elbow. He shrugged her off. 'But from what I've heard he was just an ignorant Scotsman who had no right at all to be in the House of Commons.'

Silence. Ben grabbed the taller man's elbow and bundled him to the door. Surprise put Joe off balance. Louise followed and, in horror, saw her father push him. He stepped out, missed the stair and fell over and over to the bottom.'

'Aye, cowp yer creels, lad. I'll not have that in my house!'

Louise slid past her father and clattered down to Joe. He'd landed on a thick clippy mat and a bundle of coats that had fallen down. She took his hand and touched his neck where there was supposed to be a pulse. It was beating, thumping.

'I'm all right.' He staggered up. 'It takes more than that to break *my* neck.' Ben was glowering at the top of the stairs but went in. 'I'll see you round, kidda. Maybe at the dogs.' He pulled her into a shadow, kissed her mouth and was gone.

Five days later, shopping in town in the morning, she caught sight of him with an expensively dressed woman.

Louise found she could attract other young men, made sure she kissed them, made sure he knew. He was sometimes at the dog track setting his own odds, ignoring her often but then at times he approached her with such delicacy and charm that her heart lifted, a bird in flight.

Walking one time near woodland he scooped her in his arms to save her feet over rough ground. Moments she knew he loved her. Moments of tenderness. She treasured a small green powder compact he gave her. At night she dreamt he carried her.

Then he would withdraw, be rough, assertive, keep her at a distance, keeping love's power at bay. Poison or wine. Louise shut out that the bitter poison was real. Her only truth was when a shaft of love broke through.

What did it matter if he had offended her father? And it was because Ben had been drinking, he never could hold it, her mam said. What did it matter ... her dad's politics? ... the newspapers he pored over, muttering as he looked over his little glasses to John Hargraves who'd passed the papers on. Pictures in newspapers of places near or far. What did it matter if her father was drunk in his own house? Except that did matter.

The rest was unreal. Only Joe was real. The inclination of a head, waiting for his approach, listening for the sound of his good shoes, the tap of his heels, the touch of fingertips, the beat of the universe.

After the party they'd made it up.

He took her to the official opening of the new Tyne Bridge. The Quayside was packed and they jostled for a place, standing on other people's feet. The whole of the town seemed to be out, young and old. The smell of brilliantine mixed with the mud and dust smell of old clothes and bitterness of fags. It was like a fair but she could see nothing. Joe made a pathway for her using his elbows and weight then lifted her like a child and sat her on his shoulder so she could see the king. The bridge with its arch of curved girders painted green was magnificent, strong, drawn clear against a bright sky. Her father said it was a feat of engineering and would be famous. He was right and he was probably here somewhere. The king and queen looked small and stiff but everybody cheered. She joined them, waving a scarf, then felt herself sliding to the ground in Joe's sure grip. The posh black car of the royals crossed the bridge. He kissed her in the middle of the crowd.

The following week he took her to a dance hall in town with a perfectly sprung floor and she rested in his arms to the rhythm of the band or watched the kaleidoscope lights from a spinning glass ball hung from the ceiling, coloured lights falling on his head as he walked across in the break with a drink for her. They tangoed and she caught the spirit of the dance, jerking through its urgent passion, back bent in an arch, face turned jaggedly away then pulled in close. She was on the edge of something new.

Then he vanished for weeks. And as suddenly was there again. He was sent on work out of town, he said. It might have been true. No one else seemed to have seen him. He didn't discuss it. She wondered where he stayed and with whom.

She kept quiet about Joe when she was in the house and the other girls said nothing to her father. They met outside, in town, at the picture house, the dance hall. When she arrived early for a dance she might see him standing with another girl, his arm round her waist and she'd turn to leave but if he saw her he would catch and pull her back. It was his neighbour or his cousin and he was going to introduce her to someone, always something. She'd allow him to take her inside again, then be brittle and stumble in the dance. After one spoiled evening he saw her home and disappeared again for weeks.

But when he returned he wanted to take her to a reception in a big house that had deep patterned wallpaper in all the rooms, socialising with his boss's friends, he said. The women looked expensive. They looked over bare shoulders at him and joked. Louise wondered what she was doing there, why he needed her. The boss began to eye her up and she looked uneasily for her coat then felt his arm round her waist where it stayed, whoever he was talking to. There was salmon and cucumber for supper with wine. She'd not seen wine before except in the movies. The bottles were in silver ice buckets, the glass filmed with cold. Joe nodded when the host held one up and brought her a fine goblet half filled. The wine was green and clear. She sniffed it. It had a scent of fresh herbs someone grew at the allotments for a fancy shop, it was sweet and sharp and tasted faintly of sherbet.

'Do you like it?' a voice behind her asked. She turned to a man in a silver grey suit. He raised his glass to her and she noticed his nails were buffed, his thin moustache carefully trimmed and the linen of his white shirt finer than she'd seen any woman wear. An earthy, grassy scent came from his hair.

'Not really.' She put her drink down.

'Anything wrong, darling?' The silver grey suit leant over her.

'It's just getting late for me.'

Joe's arm was round her shoulder. 'I'll take you home.'

'Come back. The party's just getting going. Here,' the elegantly dressed man flung a car key down carelessly. 'You needn't be long.'

Outside Joe faced her angrily. 'What do you think you're playing at? Those are important people.'

'Then you'd better get back to them, Joe.'

'The wine's upset you. You didn't like the taste?'

'I don't like the smell of a spiv.'

He drove her in silence and parked a little way from her home. 'You have to learn to mix with people, Louise. It's how you get on.' He leaned over and opened the door for her. 'I'll smooth it over. You're young, you can get away with it. For now.'

'I'd be glad to get away from that crowd. For good'

'Then I'll see you round, kidda.'

She knew that meant she might not see him again but felt him watching her till she got to the door.

At eighteen she began work at a golf club, a thirteen-hour day as waitress and assistant cook. It felt important though she missed the buzz and excitement of the dog track at the weekend. She walked to work, caught the bus home then put on her face for the two or three hours that were hers. 'Air spun' powder. Dark red lipstick in a cupid's bow like the movie stars. *Evening in Paris* perfume in a dark blue bottle. Stockings with a seam. Her legs were slim and she could keep the seam straight.

Her friends held simple gatherings at the weekend in people's homes, making their own entertainment, though she never offered their house now. Everyone brought something to eat or to make the evening go. Someone usually brought a pack of cards. When he stooped to join them, Joe might bring his precious possession, his gramophone with a lovely wide horn, polished lovingly for the evening. Music meant they could dance. If he was not there they would find someone to play piano, if there was a battered piano, if things weren't in hock - or they had the latest hits from a squeeze box, from a mouth organ, or enjoyed the wireless if dance music was playing. Scrimshaws needed no backing. They sang together, in close harmony, brothers and sisters. It was like the music hall. Then they'd descended like wolves on the food.

Word went round where they would all meet up and Louise dressed after a day on her feet, dressed with both excitement and dread. She washed her hair at work with a raw egg from the kitchen during lunch hour and dried it by the stove, crimping it into place. She arrived late and knew by the sound of the gramophone whether he was there, caught his voice through the babble, caught her breath. Light was in the room where Joe stood, it followed him to a corner or a chair. She walked in with a smile to shatter glass and might find him dancing with another close in his arms, or speaking softly to a girl on a couch. Louise was brilliant. If he danced, she danced, partners waiting for her. When he'd danced all night with someone else he might boldly ask to take her home.

She wanted to touch the curl on his brow. 'Not on your life!' The growl was like a cat disturbed at meat.

'Suit yourself.' And he staked out another prey as he was speaking. 'Others are easier.'

'You suit yourself!' And she turned on her heel to choose an escort, walked home with someone else, kissed him or left him and stalked in.

If she arrived prepared for battle, to fence and parry, show no feeling, he was waiting hungrily and allowed no one else near. To dance against him was to step off the earth. It was he who flinched and turned from the light.

He'd taught her to smoke, to hold the vapour in then slowly blow it out. She hid cigarettes from her father and mother, hid that she still saw Joe, though they knew. Her father would never like him she decided but he apologised for making a scene in his own home, for using his fists, for showing her up. And she loved him again like a little girl, the dad who was one man sober and another drunk. She wouldn't make that mistake, to marry a drinking man.

But Joe taught her to drink. He poured her a whisky with only a little lemonade and she drank to match him, expected the floor to come up and meet her but felt nothing, only warmth. She decided she would not touch spirits again. It looked bad if women could drink men under the table. And if she could drink like that no man could afford to buy for her. Not where she came from.

But Joe drank. The light would go out in his corner where it followed him when Joe drank. When Joe drank parties turned sour. When Joe drank some of the girls left. Other men tried to calm him. Louise left.

It would have to change. That was not her Joe. Where was he? Come back, Joe. Please.

9

The night of the party for the win at the Pitman's Derby Ben had settled on the back steps with Peter, his brother-in-law and they drank the remains of his home brew. Peter slept over on the floor on a clippy mat and woke up next day to a hangover. They mixed a cure of raw egg and Peter's brandy together and managed to get it down. With Peter being a badly paid farm worker and Labour supporter they saw eye to eye. Bacon for breakfast to line their stomachs and they went down to the allotment to compare notes on leeks, long since friends after the fight in the backyard.

'You haven't got rid of your own hangover yet,' Peter said. 'You look bad.'

'I'm not in a good fettle,' Ben replied. 'Anticlimax after a good night, I expect.' They sat and smoked. He was trying to grow his own tobacco but it was not successful. 'I only hope Labour can make a real difference if they get in. Two years I've been on this scrap heap. I feel thirty years older than I was.'

Peter packed his pipe and pressed it down. 'That's no way to talk.'

'You're still in work, man. I know it doesn't pay much but you meet your bills. You have your pride.'

'There'll be work some day, lad.'

'Maybe, when I'm too old to profit from it. We've just had a great night but there it is again. I feel like an old man.'

'Those leeks could be good. You might have prize winners there if you look after them. It's always something.'

'I couldn't afford to pay a round in the pub so I don't go.'

'You can make up for it with your own brew. Your marras can come round and drink with you at home. Or out here if you're under Mary's feet.'

'Aye, we do that. Sometimes. Then if I get a bit rowdy they don't come back.'

'Sorry to say it, Ben, but you're poor at holding your drink.'

'You want me even to give up my home brew?'

'Didn't say that. Your home brew's good. Anyway, there's your family. You have fine daughters and that son of yours is coming on.' He dug his brother-in-law in the ribs. 'Proved you were a man before you quit.' Ben didn't smile. 'That's what's wrong, is it?'

'It's not too good, Peter. It's not too good.'

'Mary's a fine woman.'

'She is, but I'm no longer a man for her.' Ben dropped his brow into his hands. 'I haven't touched my wife for over a year, except a passing kiss. I can't do it, Peter. I've been a lover since I was seventeen and I can't do it any more.' His shoulders shook.

Peter put his arm round him. 'There's nothing to be ashamed of.' And gave him a shake. 'We can all have our ups and downs. I was Jack the lad when I was young. Truth be told, I've had two wives, one legal. Yes, I still visit that other one. But I've my ups and downs as well. John Thomas can get moody. He's just gone to sleep for a bit because he's down in the dumps. Does Mary mind?'

'Never says. Probably doesn't want to make me feel worse. My wife's being kind to me.'

'It's this work business, lad. You take it too much to heart. When you're cheered up he'll cheer up as well. Here, have a look at this. This is my sweetheart.' He drew a sepia photograph from the inside pocket of his worn tweed jacket. 'Isn't she lovely?' A nude woman with bobbed hair had one foot on a stool pulling on a black stocking. Ben smiled. 'John Thomas needs a little fun sometimes, you know. Maybe he's sulking because you don't give him any fun. If I feel too low to do anything I go and see the other one. Aye, and sometimes a third.'

'You get away with anything, Peter. I couldn't do that to Mary. We've had a good life and had children together. I couldn't play about behind her back.'

'She needn't know. Then if John Thomas decides to come out and play again she might be glad of it.' He put his photograph away. 'You're too serious, I know. Forget I said that. D'you remember the time I knocked you flying in the backyard?

'Only because I let you.'

They laughed and smoked another pipe, making their breath bitter.

The following week Ben heard of another fatality at the pit. If pitmen weren't out of work or on short weeks it was this. Death after death. He'd always been first down if there was any commotion when he was safety man, though he'd been sick with fear. And it had taken him weeks to get over it if they'd not got everybody out. Wilf was right, he'd sometimes said he wouldn't send a dog down the pit. But you couldn't put a price on the courage of those men. He knew that once when the strata'd fallen in on a group of hewers in a thin seam a man with a broken thumb held a block of stone up till help came, to save a young lad's life flattened beneath it.

This young lad hadn't been so lucky. Fifteen and crushed to bits. The family lived only a few streets away, he knew them and went to the funeral out of respect. Mary'd retrieved his suit and sent an onion and tatie plate pie and an apple tart for the spread, the send off. She wasn't up to coming with him. He sold some of his produce from the allotment to put in to a silver collection when the women came round with a tin to help pay for the funeral. The poor help the poor. Heaven help them all if that stopped.

There were black horses with their manes tied up in plumes to pull a simple carriage. Fancy horses weren't needed but it brought some kind of comfort to the mother. Miners walked in front of the procession, holding up the colliery banner draped in black satin. People watched, men doffed their caps and bowed their heads. From the corner of his eye Ben thought he saw his two younger girls among the women. They shouldn't be here. He went into the church to show respect but found nothing in the ringing words, then on to the burial. Six feet of earth for those who worked the earth, one fathom deep.

At the reception he ate but took no beer, afraid his control might break. Someone had boiled a ham for the family, the two pies Mary sent were served with the other offerings, all very decent. The pit had closed for a day after the fatality and pitmen jostled in the little house with family and neighbours. Ben could pick out a miner he didn't know by blue marks on hands or wrists, arms were not on show. Others were pockmarked blue on their faces where shrapnel of rock or coal hit them. Coal dust seeped into wounds before they healed leaving uneven tattoos. Badges of honour. Ben had his own. He nodded to them and went over to talk. Word was they might be on short time again but it might not be for every team. Those with money in their pockets were generous before they left. In spite of the grief in the gathering, and without touching alcohol, Ben was warmed by the instant fellowship of the miners. They knew why he was out of work and feared the spells themselves when they might be 'left in the basin' for a temporary lay-off when the group cast lots by putting names in a basin. Ben had seen it - if a name was left in after the twisted papers picked out reached the number of required men, that man was out and it was time to tighten his belt. But it didn't last for ever, not like Ben's exile. He lingered with the last of the visitors then decently left the family alone.

He'd have given all he had to be joining a team in the pit, even wielding a pick and shovel again with an empty tub behind him. That night in bed he felt he was falling fathoms deep. But the shaft was loneliness.

It was nearly Armistice Day when Ben bumped into Bessy Parker selling poppies outside a shop. 'Buy a poppy, Ben?'

He turned his hands in his pockets but there was no chink. 'I haven't much money, Bess. I can only give you a ha'penny. I'm sorry.'

'It's the thought,' she said pinning a poppy on his lapel. 'I haven't seen you at Party meetings for a bit.'

'Been feeling too low, Bess. It gets to me, this unemployed business. Never been used to it. Some days I'm better but I haven't felt up to meetings.'

'You know, if I feel we're getting nowhere and think about giving up, I can take a bus over to Heworth.'

'Why Heworth?'

'To lay a few flowers for Thomas Hepburn in the graveyard.'

Ben smiled. 'Founder of our Union a hundred years ago.'

'I picture what they went through then,' she shook her head loosening carefully crimped waves, ' ...and even hard as it is now, where we are today.'

'I know,' Ben shuffled, 'I know. Families out on the streets for the man being in a union or striking. I know.'

'At least you've not been evicted, Ben.'

'But I can't pay the rent. We've been all right so far because the landlord's not a bad bugger ... he gives a bit of grace. But it's our Patricia who's paying rent now. Gone into service to do it. How do you think that makes me feel? I should be keeping my girls, not the other way round. I'm useless. I'm ashamed.'

'Days gone by were harder. Don't give up, Ben. You're not useless.' She straightened the poppy on his worn lapel. 'It'll get better – it will.'

He felt warmed. 'Nice sermon, pet. Wilf chivvies me. But I've been guarding my leeks.

'Whatever for?'

'Because I think I've got prize winners this year. Might get first. You couldn't get me any cream cheap at the Co-op, could you?'

'If there's any going off,' she shrugged, 'if we have any at all.'

116

'No problem with it being sour. It's for the leeks. I'll need to polish them for the show and cream's the best thing.'

'I'll see what I can do, Ben.'

'Then I'll bring you a little sack of potatoes. I had a good crop and could spare some. I don't want to keep them so long they'd go soft. When's your half day?'

'Wednesday. That's why I'm out selling poppies today.'

'Be in next Wednesday afternoon and I'll bring you some spuds. See if you can have a spot of cream by then.'

'It's a fair exchange.'

Ben could tell from Bessy's face that the door was still ajar for him and thought of what Peter said. They'd thrown him on the scrapheap. But not being able to make it with a woman ... it was the light going out. Some mornings when he woke up he wondered if he could get out of bed to face another day. His heart stabbed. He'd see Bess next week as a matter of course and keep his word. But cross that threshold? If he crossed it once, would he cross it again?

It was months since that funeral when he'd had the touch of the closeness of pitmen. Now there was another slump in the coal trade and a lot of them were left in the basin. Without hope of employment he followed what was happening in the industry. Things improved here and there but only where little pits amalgamated, more mechanization was coming in though pit ponies were still used. He wandered down the shaft of memory to the whitewashed stalls underground where ponies were kept. People thought they were sweet put-upon docile creatures, and some of them were. Others had the devil in them and would suffer no other hand than the one that always managed them. He'd had more than one kick from an iron-shod hoof. A quiet one he might feed with a bit of carrot or an apple.

Some of the lads were on the streets begging or busking. He avoided them because he had nothing to give and couldn't bring himself to do what they were doing. If he caught sight of them, though, his dream came back – falling, always falling down and down a shaft. This time there were pit ponies at the bottom. They'd gone wild and were waiting to trample him the instant before he woke up, sick and shaken.

On Sunday he brushed his suit down, put on a white shirt, fraying at the neck and cuffs, then fixed a decent collar on with a stud. He heard the band for the Remembrance Day march getting near, they must be approaching the bottom of the street. He knotted his one remaining tie, spat on his shoes again for a quick polish, pulled his jacket on and looked in the wardrobe mirror. He'd shaved while the girls were asleep and the reflection was respectable, not like an old bloke ready to touch you for a few coppers. It would do. His only buttonhole would be the remembrance poppy. He rummaged in a drawer among tarnished collar and cuff studs, retrieved from the neighbour's house and his fingers closed on it. He felt a warmth of affection as he drew out the fabric poppy Bessy had sold him. The squeal of the band was louder. He pulled the poppy carefully through his button hole, peered in the mirror again and was satisfied. You could be poor but you could be decent. He saluted his mirror image and walked through the living room.

'You off out, Ben?' Mary looked up from cleaning taties in the scullery.

'I thought I'd follow the parade up.'

'To church? John Hargraves'll get you yet.'

'I can enjoy marching and I can listen outside.'

'Go on, then.'

The procession was a third of the way up the street, band at the front, followed by ex-military men. He'd been too old, too valuable at the pit, doing his duty there. He pushed to the front of the pavement, stood on the kerbstone and started clapping to the rhythm of the march. Folk round about joined in, smiling. Rows of men with a line of medals on their breast stepped in time. He leaned forward and smiled at faces he knew. The Boys' Brigade was bringing up the rear after the ex-soldiers. Men with only one arm marched in time with the empty sleeve tucked into a pocket. But the last line of veterans wore no medals. Ben craned forward. They had tickets pinned on their jackets. He stood in the cobbled edge of the road and walked a few paces beside one he knew.

'What's that for on your chest, Jim?'

'Pawnbroker's ticket.'

'Medals in hock?'

'All of them.'

'You had a bravery one.'

'It's with the rest.'

'Ye bugger! A country fit for heroes!'

'Unemployed ones. Lend us a shilling, Ben?'

'Haven't got one to my name, or I would. You're the best, Jim.' He hopped onto the kerb. 'Best of luck, lad.'

'You an' all.'

They marched on. Ben watched and dropped back to the rag tag of civilians at the end then turned and tramped back to the house

'Back soon,' Mary called out.

'I am!'

'Thought better of it?'

'I did.' He placed his poppy on the mantelpiece, went into the bedroom and threw the suit, clean shirt and collar on the bed.

Mary looked in. 'You're a moody man, Ben.'

'Aye well, I'll take my mood to the allotment.'

'Taties are in the range.'

'Leave them there. I'll have them when I get back.'

'We'll not wait, then. If you're hours they'll be done to death.'

'Just like me.' He pulled on rough trousers and overalls and slammed out. 'Fit for heroes, be damned!'

Wednesday, he put the sack on his bicycle remembering the way and the last time when he'd not gone in. Bessy had a fire lit and a kettle boiled on the hob. She made tea and they sat opposite each other.

'Your cream's here, Ben, it's in the scullery. The manager gave me it because someone spiked the bottle top with a screwdriver. Senseless!'

'Thanks, Bess. I'm sure you could get your way with any man if you really wanted to.' They were sitting in the firelight, not to waste gas.

'Not ... any man.'

'Still lonely?'

'It doesn't get any easier. Some days are better than others, like you and your work,'

'Company might make the loneliness worse when it's over.'

'That's a risk I'd have to take.'

He put his tea down and kissed her by the fire as he'd kissed another when young. Bessy's mouth was sweet and her arms round him were hungry. They lay and loved one another on the mat, he uncovering her slowly to be sure he had power, then pierced her with joy, years falling from him as a surge took over and he rode her pleasure, almost with tears, knowing he was alive.

He hesitated but visited Bessy's house again the following Wednesday, this time with a few strings of onions. No-one asked where he was when he was out during the day. Mostly at his allotment, better he was out of the house, even wandering the streets. He rode his bicycle and hoped he didn't look like a French onion man with the string of them draped from the handlebars.

The door was open and he brought his bike into the passageway. Bessy was ready for him, the fire glowing, reflecting back from her brasses, tea leaves in the pot, a kettle on the hob simmering and scones hot out of the oven. They warmed through from the fire and steaming tea she made. Bessy's lace curtains, white as snow, were a shield from her neighbours' prying. She left the heavy curtains undrawn as she loosened her hair and opened her blouse to show white lace over the creamy breasts, linen that had been folded away since her husband's death, smelling faintly of lavender. A whiff of guilt.

She smiled at him in the shadows then took off her skirt and two layers of petticoats to her white drawers and lace bodice. Women of her age still wore the old underwear. It was beautiful. Ben pulled the bodice open to bury his face in her and breathe her incense then turned her round suddenly and undid the buttons on the waistband that held the flap of the drawers. The starched cotton fell away to show a rump rounded and pink in the firelight.

'You've got a lovely arse, Bessy,' he said and rose in quick excitement. She laughed with pleasure and lay by the flames with him in what seemed to be cool delight. Ben stroked the back of her neck leaving the prison trough of despair that had held him, felt vigour in his blood like a young man. Chilled creaking bones could wait till love was over. Damned well wait.

But he attended few of the party meetings. Best not appear in public with Bessy. People were not mugs, they could read your face. That was the joy of Bess, he could share that side of himself with her and the hopes they had of the next election. She'd had to stand up for herself, bringing up bairns alone and been a mainstay of the women's Movement. And by God, they needed them. Those women could rattle money out of trees.

With Bess he went to another country

Diane worked at home while Louise was out at the Golf Club and the ex-breadwinner spent his time at the allotment or with Bess. He had to get out. Too risky for him to go on visiting Bessy at her home. Love might be blind but the neigbours weren't. Finding a place was difficult but she could catch a bus on her afternoon off to his allotment. For the sake of appearances she weeded the soil for half an hour before he got there, a headscarf round her head, then they slipped into his shed to drink tea from a thermos flask. He smiled at her surprise when she first came in. A paraffin stove, a spare from the greenhouse, an old carver chair and cracket stool placed round a clippy mat. The sweet smell of drying tobacco leaves from the few he'd managed to raise mingled with onionskins from strings hung from the ceiling. There was light from two windows and a hurricane lamp. They cleaned their hands on a damp cloth.

'You've got yourself a nice little den here,' she said.

He lit the hurricane lamp and turned it down to a yellowish light. 'It needs to be cosy, Bess. I sit up nights here to watch my leeks before the show.'

'You never do!' She settled into the carver while he looked up at her from the stool.

'I've been too successful, lass. More than one's tried to sabotage those leeks.'

'I like a leek soup,' she said, 'when you're looking for somewhere to get rid of them afterwards.'

'The big ones are difficult to cut but you shall have some. I've got a more interesting one for you today.' He grinned.

'No need to be vulgar, Ben Hawthorne.' She produced their usual home-made scones.

'And I'll have more than that, my Bess!' He stroked her leg, shapely though she wore Lisle not silk.

'Can't you wait five minutes? I'll choke. You'd have to dispose of a body.'

'I'd put you in the leek trench to fertilise them. I'd be certain to win prizes then.'

They laughed, carefree lovers in mid-life. When she put her tea aside and closed her eyes, white petticoats crackled from starch over grey satin camiknickers. The Co-op stocked everything now.

'How beautiful, Bess,' he said, 'how beautiful.' She had washed in lavender soap that morning but her own scent was warm and deep.

Ben lay awake quietly at night listening to Mary breathe, the shadow of guilt holding sleep at the margins of his mind.

One Saturday she came back from the pork shop loaded with sandwiches, gravy and bits of crackling. She'd made an arrangement with the people who ran that shop that if she baked the buns for them she could collect a pork supper for the family at the weekend. No money changed hands. She dropped everything down into the scullery with a face like flint.

After supper they played cards but she sat alone by the fire. Joe was beside Louise and the circle glowed with fun. They laughed in a game of 'Chasey the Ace' and Ben pretended not to notice the silence by the fire. Aces were a long time coming to the surface. Everyone passed a card to the neighbour on the left and Katharine squealed as she turned the Ace of Hearts over.'

'That means I'll get married first, because I'm the bestest.' She scooped the kitty of farthings, still lisping as if she were the youngest.

Ben laughed. 'That'll be the day.'

'I'm leaving school soon.'

'It doesn't sound as if you are, speaking like that. And no boyfriends till you're sixteen, madam, so you've a long way to go.'

Joe and Louise left for a friend's house and a quieter card game began. Mary went into the scullery to wash a few plates. He followed her as she was opening the cutlery drawer and light fell on her carving knife. She picked it up and ran her forefinger along it.

'You look dangerous with that, Mary, lass.'

She looked up. 'You'll find out how dangerous, Ben Hawthorne.' Laughter came from the other room.

'What do you mean?' He closed the door and stepped near.

'Deceiving me now are you, Ben?' Her knife touched the soft skin under the jaw and she drew it down to the Adam's apple. 'Half living at your allotment ... how long?' She was white. The point of the blade circled the Adam's apple. 'I asked you how long, Ben.' Her voice was soft 'I've gutted chickens. I can gut you!' she pressed the sharp point through his skin.

'Twelve months. About.'

She drew the knife out and he felt a tear of blood run down the throat's valley then she smashed her hand across his cheek. 'And I had to hear it in the pork shop. Bessy Parker! Her knife followed the trickle to the soft V between the bones. He didn't move.

'Yes, it's Bessy.'

She stepped back. 'So help me, if you'd lied to me, I'd have finished you.' She threw a white, aired dish clout at him. 'Clean yourself up! You know where the medicine chest is.'

When the company had gone they undressed in silence for bed,

'Do you love her, Ben?'

'No.'

'Did you tell her you did?'

'No. Bessy knows it's liking not love.'

'Then why?'

'I was no longer a man,' his voice broke, 'I'd lost the power.'

'Couldn't you find it again with me? Did you have to go to *her*? Do you think I haven't missed you all this time? Do you think I'm a woman of stone?'

'I was ashamed before you. I couldn't talk about it.' She sat on the bed and looked up at him, eyes glittering, jewels of anger. 'I've failed you. Your home's been stripped and I'm not the breadwinner any more. We rely on our daughters. A father should keep his daughters, not the other way round. I'm not a proper husband.' He turned away. 'And I couldn't do that any more.'

'But you could do it with Bessy?'

'It was an escape.' He hung his head in misery. 'An escape from everything. A worthless life. And she lifted that away from me. John Hargraves tried to help but it was Bessy took it away. If you turn against me now I don't know how I'll go on.'

She swung under the covers. 'So. Just like that - you expect me to forgive you.'

'She always knew it wasn't for keeps. I won't see her again.'

'You can't just rewind the clock. To where it was.'

'Can a man not make one mistake?' He turned the tap and waited for the silver light in the gas mantle to fade. 'It's the first time. It'll be the only time.' He slid into bed and touched her shoulder. She moved away.

'Don't destroy me all over again, Mary! The rest of the world has done a good job at that first time round.'

She turned her back and he lay dry eyed and sleepless. Bessy had warmed him but if Mary threw him out ... he'd throw himself in the Tyne and be done with it.

Next morning she said she was going to see her sister over in Durham. He could look after Christopher and see to him after tea. Diane would run the house. She took three shillings from a tea caddy, saved to pay the rent and left. It was worse than when she set about him.

Next Saturday evening was when she came back. She walked in, took her coat off and he gasped. She'd had her hair cut in a bob. It curled into the nape of her neck and fell in a kiss curl on her brow and on both cheeks. She wore a styled pink dress he hadn't seen.

'Joined the flappers, Mary?'

She turned and went into the scullery, put her pinafore on and got her knives out to cook. He came in, closed the door and watched her.

'I hope those knives are for the onions, not for me.'

'Is that all you have to say?'

'You look lovely, Mary. I'm always proud to be at your side.'

'Something Patricia made for me.' Christopher ran in and flung his arms round her waist. There was an end to conversation.

After tea the girls went out, she bathed Christopher, read him a story, cuddled him and let him play on top of his bed covers with wooden toys his father made. She closed the door on the tiny box room and when she came in Ben was stropping his razor to shave in peace. He wouldn't risk slitting his gizzard when the girls were round with their high jinks.

'Who cut your hair?'

'Sarah's friend. I thought you'd be mad.'

'It becomes you.'

She took her pinafore off as he dipped his brush into a basin and worked up a lather. 'You're not the only one to think so.'

'And what's that supposed to mean?' He began to slide the sharpened steel over the white film, leaving a clean strip of skin.

'What's sauce for the gander ...'

The razor slipped into a gash on his cheek. 'What's that you said?' Blood mixed with soap on his face.

'You heard me, Ben Hawthorne.' She put the trestle table between them. The razor was in his hand. He turned with lather and blood dripping down his shirt front.

'You've been with somebody else!'

She held on to the table. 'We can be even now, Ben. Now we can turn the clock back. I'm allowed one mistake as well.'

He stepped towards her and tightened his grip on the razor handle. 'Who was it? Tell me and I'll kill him.'

'Like I should kill Bessy Parker?'

'It's different.'

'Not in my book. There's no difference at all, Ben Hawthorne.' Her voice was a low rasp. 'You expect me to live with that for the rest of my life, that you laid a hand on her when you wouldn't come near me - and do nothing about it?'

He came round the table and she moved to the other side. He lunged across the narrow part and caught her wrist. 'Tell me who it was!'

'No!'

He held on cruelly. 'Not all men are as faithful as I've been, Mary - and I did a wrong thing - but my wife doesn't open her legs to anyone else.' He held the razor over her vein.

She stared him back. 'Where's your fine equality now? One day we'll have a woman Prime Minister! - we'll walk on the moon first! Can only a man break the wedding vow?'

The door opened downstairs and they heard the heels of one of the girls. Ben thudded into the bedroom and almost took the door off its hinges. He heard Louise come in from work.

'Are you all right, Mam?'

'I'm not very well, pet.'

'I'll make some tea. Go and lie down.' Heels clattered. 'I love the hair.'

Ben saw her feet when she dragged into the bedroom and closed the door. His head was in his hands. 'I was pushed to the bottom of the heap by everybody else,' he ground out. 'But you! What you've done's humiliated me to the depths of my soul. I'll never lift my head again.' She sat on the other side of the bed as he retched. Soap, blood, spittle and tears were on his hands. 'And I don't even know who it was.'

She waited a full minute. 'It was no-one, Ben.' He looked up. 'There wasn't anyone.' His eyes were sore and gritty. 'I wanted you to feel the pain that I felt. I wanted you to know.'

'The truth, Mary?'

'The truth, Ben.'

He turned into the pillow with its faded case and cried like a baby.

10

Patricia was home in glory for a weekend. She had voted in a general election! The first batch of women over twenty-one to have their say, used her 'Flapper's Vote' helping Ramsay MacDonald home to number ten Downing Street.

'How does it feel to be one of the fair sex voting?' Her father put his arm round her, proud.

'Terrific, dad.' She laughed up at him, a little shorter than he was in high heels the baroness had given her. 'And a Labour Government home and dry!'

'Only ones who can't vote are prisoners, peers and lunatics,' he twirled her round, 'the last two being hard to separate out.'

'Sssh, dad!'

'It's all right, my lass! You're not at the baroness's now.' His smile was like the sun coming out. They sat down. 'It's only a pity you're still working away. I want you home again. This is no way.'

'Don't fret on, dad. I'm all right.' She looked up and saw Andrew at the door.

He followed her glance. 'Your young man's waiting his turn. I'll give you space.'

After half an hour Patricia and the love of her heart walked up the street stopping in shadows between lamp posts. 'I never have you to myself,' Andrew said. 'We're not old but we don't have a wedding date in sight.' He kissed the ring he'd given her and slid it over to her left hand.

'Dad still isn't really happy about us getting married.'

'And when will he be? No-one's good enough for his lovely daughters. Haven't you noticed?'

'I know. Louise is having a hard time. But that's not just dad. Joe can be difficult.'

'I thought they made it up?'

128

'After he threw him down the stairs? Yes, but dad still doesn't like him. A bookie.'

'There you are. Certainly not good enough.'

'He loves us too much, that's the problem.'

'You don't need permission. You're twenty-one, Louise is helping with the money. Diane's left school and Katharine leaves in another year.'

'I know but Diane didn't find her feet with work. She was a housemaid to a woman in a big house but was in tears every night from the way the woman treated her. Dad went down there on his dignity and collected his daughter.' They smiled at the thought. 'Mam didn't have all her own housework to do when she had the shop and the washing used to be sent out then, so she needs a hand. She's not used to the poss tub on a Monday. Christopher's a live wire, you know. It's settled. Diane's the one who's going to help at home. She does all the heavy work. Louise does very well and puts most of her wage down but it's not enough – without my money.'

'But it's not as bad as it was.' He kissed her neck and they hugged tensely in silence before walking on hand in hand.

Patricia sighed. 'Rent and fuel have to be found.'

'And so on, and so on and - so it's still down to you.'

'I get paid well. Couldn't you get a job nearer to me, to where I work?'

'Cumberland's a long way.' He fell silent.

'But you could think about it?'

They stood in the entrance to the fire station and watched other couples wandering in the shadows giggling over private jokes.

'I can't just up and leave *my* mother.' He spoke quickly. 'When we do finally get married I think we're going to have to live in with her.'

'Oh!'

'I'd better see you back home. It's getting late. Let's talk about it tomorrow. Meet me at the park and we'll stroll down the Dene'

'It'll have to be early. I need be back for lunch. Dad used to keep us all waiting when he had money for the pub but <u>we</u> have to be on time.'

'Nine o' clock?'

They parted at the door and Patricia stepped lightly past Louise who was lost in Joe's arms. She helped wash up, went to her bed and slept in spite of the tug of war she felt going on for her life.

Up first in the morning, she prepared potatoes and vegetables from the allotment before changing into a better dress. Her father was smoking a pipe on the back steps and seemed to be muttering to himself. She smiled and slipped out the front way before anyone could stop her and hurried down the street that was slowly coming to life on Sunday. She passed the Reverend Hargraves walking the dog that had been theirs. He tipped his hat and the dog flounced up to her. She knelt and stroked his silky long ears, while the Reverend asked how she was, the usual things. The dog whined, nuzzled her and she felt torn by the animal as well. The spaniel started to slaver wagging the whole of his hindquarters.

'Do you want to take him for a while?'

She pushed the spaniel back. 'I'd better not.' She got up. 'It might confuse him and you'd not get him back into the vicarage.'

He laughed and pulled the dog back on his leash. The fire station clock showed twenty to nine. She felt a chill, pulled her coat close, half ran down the street to cross the main road, no traffic in sight, and hurried on past a railway line. She had to catch her breath when she came to the park.

Andrew was waiting on a bench with his arms spread out on the back, his hat tilted forward watching a pair of sparrows searching for worms. She sat beside him silently and took his hand. He kissed hers, kissed her mouth ferociously then sat back at a distance, pale.

'What is it? What's wrong?'

He pushed his hat further back from his face. 'There's something I've never made clear in all the time we've been together.'

'You'd better tell me then.'

He took her hand again and held it so hard it began to hurt. 'My mother's as dependent on me as your family is on you. That's what's the matter.'

She tried to read his eyes. 'But what's it really about?'

He stared away. 'She used to do cleaning and take in washing but she's got a heart condition now, called angina. You can live a long time with it but she can't do this heavy work any more.'

'Doesn't she have any pension as a widow. From the war?'

He didn't look back at her. 'This is what I've never said. We don't tell anyone about it. My mam has no pension because my dad was shot by his own side.'

The sparrows skittered busily round a puddle finding food. 'What do you mean? Was there an accident?'

'No.' She tried to touch him but he pulled away. 'They shot him as a coward. That's why she has no pension.'

Patricia was stunned. 'I don't believe it.'

'They punish the widows.'

'Let's walk.' She pulled him up and they wandered on barely noticing the clouds had parted and the lawn of the park flashed like crystal.

He talked without looking at her. 'A friend of my father's from the Tyneside Irish came back from the war and told us what happened. I knew dad was called up in 1916 when the conscription came in and he was thrown into the battle of the Somme. He survived that but became very very depressed.'

'I expect they all did.'

'They weren't allowed to say much in letters, though my father did write about the wounded being dragged on wooden sleighs over near freezing mud, like as not to have an amputation. He told his friend he wished *he* could have an ampution and get out. Then he started suffering from the most appalling headaches and we learned later he would fall to pieces when there was an explosion.'

'Shell shock?'

'That's what it's been called but his friend said there was another cause nobody had realised. There were horrible lice in the trenches. The men were all covered, you can imagine. The damned things could lay twelve eggs a day to feed on human skin. Troops would go through their shirt seams cracking them. If there were any candles around they'd move a flame along the seams to flush them out.'

'But how did the lice things affect them?'

'Skin disorders. It doesn't sound like much.'

'Itches can be maddening.'

'The little beasts produced something called trench fever.' Andrew spoke ahead to the trees. 'Men could have back pains, leg pains, desperate headaches. We think this may have been what he was really suffering from. He told his friend he couldn't stand a single more explosion then volunteered to go on a night time raid into No Man's Land, took off in the dark and made for some woodland.'

'But they found him?'

'Three months later, wandering in Rouen. So he was hauled in for cowardice and desertion.'

'Wouldn't they listen?'

'That sort of thing was dismissed. Courts Martial had no time for men claiming headaches. They said the man simply had no heart for fighting so he was worthless and a coward. There was no right of appeal.' He kicked a stone on the path and a blackbird scuttled into the undergrowth of bushes. 'Eighty-seven men from the North were shot like this. Manacled, blindfolded, tied to a stake. Shot at dawn - worse than dogs.' Patricia held him but he couldn't meet her eyes. 'My mam just got a letter to say he'd been shot as a coward.' He shook his head and tried to hide tears. 'So you see ... I can't leave her.'

She touched his wet cheeks. 'You should have told me earlier. We won't set a date yet.'

One more evening left. They walked into town and went round window shopping and ended up at the Speaker's Corner in the Bigg Market. Her father might be there but she didn't see him. The usual hecklers were round a tub-thumper. The Salvation Army was out with the *War Cry*. Their silver band tuned up and next to them a man was trying to sing for his supper. His voice was terrible and a group of youths stood laughing at him. When the song ended they applauded raucously. One of them threw a penny and one stood beside him while his friends clicked pretend cameras. Patricia felt Andrew's arm go round her as the group broke up and they came elbowing past, whistling.

In an area near one of the pavements a woman sat quietly behind a bench laid out with pamphlets and a placard propped against it:

ARE YOU PREPARED TO WAGE PEACE?

They walked over and she handed them pamphlets about Indian Independence and the Congress leader Gandhi. Patricia recognised a photograph of the little bald man challenging the British Empire. 'Are you interested in non-violence?' the campaigner asked.

'I'm certainly not interested in violence,' Andrew said.

She smiled. 'I meant as a political method.'

'I'm not deeply into politics,' he said, 'not after the General Strike. I know some people who are. I don't think anything was achieved so I'm not prepared to go into it all now. I don't feel it's up to me.' Patricia waited for him.

'It's up to all of us to try to influence things one way or another. And it's sometimes in the long run that you can judge achievement.' The woman touched the leaflets in front of her. 'Gandhi could have said the struggle in India wasn't up to him but his philosophy's stirring things up. He teaches civil disobedience, the Indian people stop working and nothing at all runs on specific days. It's inconvenient but it's non-violent.'

Andrew shuffled. 'I don't know as much about the man as I should.

'He's a Hindu. But he's taken Jesus' words literally and fused them with Hindu thought.'

'Which words do you mean?'

The youths with the imaginary camera bounced back and one of them stood beside the political agitator, if that's what she was. He pulled his mouth wide with his fingers and went cross eyed. 'Hold it!' they shouted and made clicking sounds through the air cameras. Andrew eyed them but the young woman laughed. The clown behind her bent down and popped a kiss on her cheek. Wolf whistles. She swatted the lad away and they stamped off.

'If someone slaps you on the right cheek, you turn the other.'

'Nothing about kissing?' Andrew laughed.

'I know people think the whole thing's impractical,' she was in full flow. 'They explain the passage away. It's taken someone from another continent, another culture to show how powerful it can be to take blows and not to give them back.'

'Perhaps that's practical in India,' Patricia said, 'but not here.'

The girl shrugged. 'There are people here who've tried to live in peace. Some did refuse to join the Great War, you know. With all its savagery.'

'My father died in that,' Andrew said. 'Killed by his own side. Deliberately.'

The campaigner stood up and touched his shoulder. 'I have a story about two men who refused to have any part in it.' She spoke quietly. 'Our movement started in a bond of friendship.' Patricia could see her sweetheart concentrating but tried to pull him away.

'I can see you want to go,' the girl said. 'Take one of our pamphlets. It'll tell you the story.' She gave a leaflet to both of them. Andrew lingered a moment then put it in his pocket and went with Patricia.

They wandered over to the knot of Salvationists and listened to them, tapping feet to the music till it was time for Andrew to see her home. They were less at ease with each other.

Later, in the bedroom she read the pamphlet by torchlight, not to disturb Katharine and Diane's sleep. She quickly took it in. A young Quaker fellow had been on a friendship exchange in Germany just before hostilities … had to return immediately when war was declared … it ended in a handshake and a friendship pact on a railway platform at Cologne before he left … *It didn't matter what the politicians might say, they could never be at war with each other. They were one in Christ and no government could make a difference to that.* Back home the Englishman started a movement not to fight.

She crumpled it and slipped into bed.

Back at work Patricia went about her normal routine, listening to whatever came into the baroness's head, replying, laughing at jokes but she felt numb. Something happened that weekend. Andrew had opened a hidden part of himself and they'd felt a deeper trust. Then he seemed to jolt away. Had they missed their moment to get married? He wrote to her but not as often. When she was home for a day or two she made sure she wore the little ring he gave her. She almost envied her mother. Mary had had a hard three years with Ben out of work but at least she had her children. It would have been nice to have stayed at home like Diane and have gone on bringing Christopher up. She missed his little arms round her neck. He still wasn't at school but every time she came back he'd changed. Even at the Routledge's she'd been busy with children. She touched her navel and longed for a child.

A few months later she was tidying up. Newspapers lay everywhere and she heard the baron raise his voice. Patricia read the headlines and looked at photographs showing crowds milling about in New York. Investors had thrown themselves off skyscrapers. It was on the wireless. The baron sold off a piece of land. Their only son might have to change schools. They might have to cut their staff. She overheard snippets of conversation when people came to the house, visitors were worried about their money. She sensed panic.

How could stocks and shares in America affect people so much here? At any rate this wouldn't affect her family. Her lips turned down. They'd already lost everything. Maybe it was better to be poor after all, they were used to getting by.

The baroness became less generous with time off and had less to spend on clothes. Patricia helped her employer make the most of her wardrobe, she restyled a dress or two and made others that could be worn in the house. Extra tasks filled her mind and time.

Next, on a day off she saw on a Pathé newsreel that the banks were in trouble, people were queuing down the streets and round corners in America demanding their money out, shouting, hammering on the doors to be let in, rushing each other to get first to the cashiers, thumping on the counters to have all their cash out. NOW. Her dad said it was foolish, increasing the trouble, fools creating their own problem.

After a tense telephone conversation the baron was white. That same week they cancelled an expensive holiday, his wife quietly sold a good ring and he was one of the first to start the run on the banks over here. He sent the chauffeur-cum-handyman out on a lengthy errand then drove himself into town, brought a couple of valises back into the house and raided the tool shed. Patricia noticed him saw a couple of light wood pieces and spend the morning in the nursery and she realised what was happening, though Joyce Fitz-Gibbons managed one way or another to have most of the staff away from the house for two hours or more. Her husband practising his woodwork skills - where had he learned these things in the past? No one spoke about his beginnings in life. Before one o' clock he'd made a screwed down false bottom in both an old desk of Rory's and in a scuffed and scratched toy box the boy now scorned, then stuffed the old toys and books back inside and stood both pieces carelessly in a corner. It was not difficult to work out where the money was stashed.

Patricia said nothing but watched her employers in terse conversations, heard her father's voice in her head, tried to stay calm and left her scraped up savings in a friendly society. Another hard up Christmas, but she was in work.

11

In spite of spats with Joe, Louise slept late and rose early, spats with her father, spats with her father over Joe. And gossip. Joe saw others. The whispers were loud enough for her to hear.

Joe said he loved her.

There was a flurry at the golf club. Famous people were coming to stay. A movie star and more than one. The stars kept up appearances with separate rooms for the man and woman, but no-one was deceived. He was dazzling, he'd played romantic leads in films, a most handsome man. Louise stood to attention with the rest of the staff, who were wide eyed when he came into the dining room. The woman was all make-up they said. Members' wives bitched behind her back but she tipped generously. As a rule only the men tipped.

The female star had rose pink lips and an eggshell complexion. Her lovely lashes were lengthened with eye black that only the fast or the very rich wore. The eyebrows were drawn into a shape and there was a hint of blue on her lids.

'The muck she's got on her face,' the wives gossiped. 'I could take a scrubbing brush to it!' They pulled her to pieces, expensively and badly dressed themselves, hair set in concrete with sharp peaks and gulleys, heavy floury powder showing their wrinkles and scarlet gashes of mouths. The men hardly dared look at the movie star when their wives were about but Louise could see they would have given their eye teeth to be with her, a privilege to sit opposite her at table, to look at her lovely face and hear a voice that didn't have to be dubbed for the talkies.

'Of course, *he's* a gentleman!' The wives hung round hoping he would speak to them. 'She's just a slut. An over made up slut.'

'But he's the married one.'

'Found somewhere quiet to have his bit on the side.' But the style of her. Louise yearned for that style. To make the eyes up as she did.

She went to an expensive department store, bought eyeblack and ended with it over her cheeks. The star did not wear glasses and could see where she was aiming. Louise peered at herself in the mirror. On leaving school she'd decided to make the most of herself. It was a man's world, a world where she could play the feminine card. To have the kind of power the film star had! She played up to the men at the golf club who gave her good tips and flattered her. But she was still the servant.

One night Joe collected her from work and caught sight of the film star. 'What do you think of her?' Louise asked.

'Beautiful.'

'I wish I could be like that,' she said.

He drove her to a park, they walked under a cloud barred moon inhaling a scent of closing flowers, and leant against each other. He turned to face her. 'You're more beautiful to me.' He held her close.

'My life's nothing without you.'

'Why do you go with the others?' She looked up in the half darkness. There was no bitterness in him tonight.

He gripped her. 'Because this is too much for me. It scares the hell out of me. I don't want chains hung round my neck. I can't,' he swallowed, 'give up my freedom. Am I making a fool of myself by that? If I'm with you completely I'll lose myself ... but it's what I want most of all,' he cradled her, 'to lose myself in you.'

'You seem angry with me half the time.'

He kissed her ear. 'It's the same thing. I get angry if I've hurt you.' Her eyes shone behind the glasses. 'I need a woman but you're too good just to use. Your pain brings me low ... only I can't say so.'

A storm broke inside her, it drove upward to her throat forcing a sob. 'I love you, Joe. I love you with my life!' She felt a stone shift within her. 'Now you know. I'll never love anyone again like this. Not so long as I live!'

Grass beneath them in the dusk was half acrid, half sweet. He kept his head against her shoulder but she felt a sob go through him and the jarring of their spirits release. Even the pain of him was a relief. Pain, semen and blood flowed from her in a rush and the dawning of hope.

Next time he was careful. There was no baby, though she would even have welcomed that. They met undisturbed in a friend's flat. The place was basic with battered furniture and worn oilcloth on the floor, the kitchen greasy and smelling of cabbage but they were alone in the world, alive, concealed in the temple of their love.

A ripple broke the surface. She felt a ghost of worry even when his fingers were feathers on her neck. He knew so well how to be a lover. Was he playing with her? Then her spine relaxed, she bathed in joy and almost slept, the eyelids of the evening closing against traces of a sunset.

No one knew. She'd say she was meeting friends after work. Sometimes it was true. They'd drop in somewhere but leave time for themselves, time to caress each others' faces, to hurl this earth from off their feet. She accepted his adoration, proud of her slim frame that he loved, the tiny foot he kissed, walking in a new country, with the dream that she was the first person to tread there, focused on her lover, then over the edge into free fall.

For months she shone with radiance no cosmetic could give. With a lover's passion he loved the pink flushed dawn on her cheek after the semi-death. He no longer held back from her. As he came into the flat he would sing the same bars of a love song, humming the same fragment of a tune, before he worshipped her with kisses.

But the word marriage was never spoken.

When the flat was not free night folded them, a grass mound their pillow. Fences of convention, walls of warning were broken. In the day there was work but life was in darkness. Moonlight, noontide, pitch and pinnacle.

He lay in his friend's room, a hand resting idly on her hip as she bent her head to light her cigarette from his, smoking like the movie stars. She smiled and sat up.

'What are you thinking?' The lover's question. 'You look wicked.'

She began an argument to make him laugh, be pert and clever. 'If you know so well how to make a woman happy ...' He blew a fragile curl of smoke to the ceiling. '... and you had to learn that somewhere ...'

'Not your business.'

'... why can't a woman teach a man ... if she's the one who knows how to give happiness?' She turned on her tummy and looked up through the floating white grey haze. 'Could I ...?'

He stubbed his cigarette out and got up. 'That's not how it works.' He pulled his clothes on roughly. 'Not when it's been like this.'

'Joe, it was a ...'

He shut the door without a word and left her to walk home alone. Naked on a rug, their couch, she felt cold to her bones. He would come back. Emptiness inside told her she'd gone past a fixed point off the edge of the map, fallen into outer space. She pushed the feeling away. The ground beneath her feet was solid. She could pull him back. There was a cord between them. They were duelling.

The following Saturday he was absent from their weekend gathering. A 'friend' stabbed a stiletto between her shoulders casually, jealously saying she'd seen Joe with someone else. The blade froze her veins. There was music from the wireless. She looked round the room, wore a party smile and danced with a young man, any young man, cheek to cheek. With surprise she found her partner trying to break free.

'Something wrong?'

'I can't dance so well,' he said. 'My feet give me jip after a few minutes.'

'That's all right. We'll sit out.' She noticed the ruddy cheeks, fair hair that curled and brilliant, sea blue eyes. She spoke to him as if he was the only person in the room while with one ear she listened for another voice. If Joe came in she would not turn round.

Nights were lonely.

For three months the sun obstinately rose and set as if nothing had happened. She worked extra hours and slept from fatigue, woke and walked as a robot to work, fully awake when she arrived, an automatic smile on her face when the club members came in. She remembered to eat and sleep, she agreed to meet her new young man on Sunday as she now worked Saturday. The club was short staffed because a woman left to get married and they hadn't filled her place. The opiate of work made her function, every moment filled, and there was the satisfaction of putting food on the table. Patricia paid the rent and other bills but it was she who made sure they were all fed. The club was glad she would turn up. She took on more in the kitchen and reproduced her mother's hotpot in bulk. Mary seldom made it now and Louise cooked at the club with more meat than they would ever use at home. She multiplied quantities exactly with half as much meat again as her mother had used and it became a favourite. Head cook took the praise. What the hell! She packed leftovers and took them back with her. If she could turn out something popular she'd never be sacked.

On Sundays she was glad of company. The boyfriend of the moment was pleasant, gentle, undemanding, he filled a few hours that would have ached. She was twenty, not an old maid. When she got up in the morning she quickly patted on powder and drew a dark cupid's bow of lipstick. She scanned her face. Were there lines on her brow? Not a sign.

At home she tried to hold her temper in check, not responding to Ben's raised eyebrow. Let him read his paper, not her. If she went out he looked at her over his half-moon glasses, his little lenses, and she was met by a stare if she kissed him then left. She shrugged. He would keep them all on a lead if he could. One of the Scrimshaw girls was unlucky and fell pregnant and for two whole weeks he forbade any of his daughters to go out except for work or household shopping. Louise was first to break the rule. She would not be held in a prison.

Christopher finally broke her control. He foraged into her make up, her precious little horde, smeared lipstick over his face, upset a new box of powder she hadn't had time to decant into the little compact Joe gave her and began drizzling her perfume down the sink. She shook her brother.

'For heaven's sake! He's only seven.' Mary shielded her son in her arms.

'Than he's old enough to know better!' She went through the scullery onto the back steps and wept then flounced off to that den of vice, the Scrimshaws' house.

Down at the shipyard there was a big launch due. Andrew came over, excited, hoping Patricia would be able to go to it. But she'd written to her parents that the baroness had a lot of social engagements and there was really no chance of a few days free. He turned to Louise, who was running a cloth over her patent leather shoes. 'Will you come?'

'Why not?'

'Can you get the time off work?'

'I should. I've worked overtime for months.'

It was something to do. The rain was holding off as she took Andrew's arm to walk into the shipyard. She hadn't been here before and felt the atmosphere was charged as if a match could set it alight, more than at the Hoppings, much more than at the race course, or even a football match. The workmen were filled with hilarious joy. She absorbed it and felt alive for the first time in months.

Up close the ship was so big. Photographs in the papers made them look like toys. This was a giantess, a military ship but she seemed elegant, finished, sleek, ready for her big entrance. Rivets and bolts had been hammered and welded to a polished smooth surface. More of the green lubricant was brushed along the iron tracks she'd glide down. Champagne would be at the ready to christen her, yellow foaming stuff Louise had only seen at that spiv's house, to drip down the glossy sides into the black Tyne. Monster metal chains held the new creation, enormous chocks kept her back from the river. It would be a disaster if she broke free and glided down too soon, crashing through etiquette, breaking up the party. How lovely to name a ship!

When the tension was unbearable the launch party came out in finery, councillors in black suits, one with a gold chain. Words were spoken that nobody could hear. A woman in a skimming blue dress and cloche hat smiled and accepted the champagne bottle. Even from a distance her skin looked enameled. How did they do that?

She held the bottle firmly, drew it back like an archer. 'I name this ship ...' The trained voice was lost on a wind that was lifting hair and tugging hems. She let the bottle fly. Glass smashed clean on metal and wine frothed like the spume of a wave, smoked down the curve of the ship's beautiful shell. First time. It was good luck. 'May God bless ... '

The chocks were pulled, chains released to coil like snakes and the queen of the sea slid gracefully down iron tracks into her element. Frantic cheers almost deafened Louise. Andrew kissed her cheek and she felt another hand on her shoulder.

'Hello, kidda.'

She thought she was going to fall.

'Hello, yourself.' Her voice cracked, covered by the racket all round them.

'Come and have a drink. Andrew?'

'No thanks.' Andrew dipped away. 'I need to see some of my mates. I expect there'll be plenty of that later.' He glanced at Louise. 'Thanks for the company.'

Joe's hand was on her back steering her through the crowd. 'We have to make it before they all pour out.'

She hardly felt her feet, almost lifted through the throng of people. Women were flushed. A few of the men in boiler suits wept. Joe hustled her into a pub where he seemed to have claimed two seats by the window. The long mahogany counter was set up with glistening shots of whisky along its length and pint glasses of beer, burnished amber, behind them. Joe followed her eyes. 'It's like this every morning to get the men warmed up for the cold on their way in.'

She settled in a bentwood chair. 'My dad would kill me for being in a pub.'

'Let's hope your dad's not here, then.'

'I daren't go in smelling of drink.'

'A lemonade? With a little port.' He didn't wait for her to agree and was at the bar. Louise admired the dimpled glasses hung above it, alive with light. The barman poured in seconds and Joe was on his way back as she watched the door, engraved inset panes in danger of cracking as they swung open. A wave of people rolled in and broke at the bar. She laughed.

'Cheers, kidda.' She drank, her vocal cords refusing to work. 'I hear you have a new boyfriend.'

The port was warming. 'You hear right.'

'Fancy two timing?' She shook her head. 'Think about it.'

They settled into their game of fencing.

That November the girls and the Scrimshaw clan decided to celebrate Ben and Mary's silver wedding. They'd all arranged contributions to the supper. Mary needn't do anything and it was something to look forward to in the short days and dark evenings. Diane cleaned the house from top to bottom and guests brought home-made gifts. Louise looked round and smiled. She'd saved tips so they could lay something on the table themselves. Ben had a cask of carefully nurtured beer, home brewed. Patricia and Andrew would be there, together for a few days, Katharine had a good looking boy and there'd be others who could dance with Diane. She'd invited Edward, the lad she'd been seen about with, who wore special boots and could hardly dance. She knew that Joe was invited.

Ben looked daggers at Katharine's young man. All of the boyfriends were going to have a hard time. Katharine was not yet fifteen, plump and bonny, without the flapper's figure but with eyes that made more than one man keel over. Her father seemed to know all about the lad she had in tow, from a different area, slumming it in the East End and making sure everybody knew his father was a vet. 'Mines's the Lord of the Quayside,' Ben said. 'Mine's the Duke of Jesmond Dene,' Louise giggled. 'Good looking nowt,' she heard her father mutter as he turned away. Whoever the fellow was he could not tear his eyes from Katharine.

Only Diane stood by herself. There was an invisible screen round her in spite of the fine gold hair and a china doll complexion, a coolness of cream and gold. Louise thought she looked worried. The world of work frightened her.

When the house was full, Mary was the centre of attention and Ben stood back so she could enjoy her night. People had brought hand created sweets, fine crocheted d'oyleys, a papier mâché vase covered in foil mosaic. From the Scrimshaws there was a blouse they'd measured her for and made up from a remnant of crepe de chine, palest pink, hand sewn, seams rolled and the front falling from pin tucks in folds. For Ben, baccy from Andrew in a leather pouch, the brand he used to smoke.

The trestle table was draped with a good white cloth, darned but laundered and spread with a home baked ham Louise had bought in the market and cooked at home. There were homegrown and pickled gherkins, green tomato chutney from the baroness's kitchen and masses of Ben's potatoes boiled earlier and fried up. Apple pies were in the oven, pastry Louise had made from bits of lard cadged from the butcher, so light it almost floated. Tonight another girl played a borrowed piano so Patricia could relax and they ate to a lilt of ragtime. Louise wore a straight dress with a shiny paisley pattern and five fringes Katharine had sewn on for her, rising from the hem. They shimmered as she walked. A hip-length string of fake black pearls Joe had given her gently shivered to her movements.

In Joe's absence she sat between her new boyfriend and someone he'd brought along. It was the middle of supper when Joe came in, alone. He'd been drinking. He brought half a bottle of whisky for

Ben and when he saw her he turned his back, spoke to no one and settled down to drink beer from the keg of home brew. Louise made an excuse to leave her two supper partners and went into the scullery where Katharine was busy tossing and frying sliced potatoes.

'Can I give you a hand?'

'I can manage this but there's some washing up to be done. You've got your good dress on, though.'

Louise put her mother's big pinafore on with a double wrap over at the front and filled the stone sink. 'You've left your new boyfriend all alone, the one who thinks he's the Prince of Wales' butler.'

'I wanted to.'

'He's nice looking. That wavy dark hair. What's the matter with him?'

'I shouldn't have let him come. He invited himself.' Katharine stirred the frying potatoes vigorously. 'Always flashing his wallet about. The only reason he's got a stuffed wallet is that his dad doesn't take anything off him for his keep. Not like the rest of us. Anyway, I told him no amount of money can buy me.'

'You could be miserable in comfort!' They laughed. 'Is that all that's wrong?'

'He's always trying to get at my stocking tops. Dad would kill him.'

'You're too young for that'

'And I don't want it.'

'He's got eyes for nobody else, mind. Where did you dredge him up?'

'Walking down the Dene.'

'Him and Lord Muck!' Louise bent over the sink to laugh.

'He wants to see all I've got.' Katharine turned the potatoes crisping them golden.

'Drop him, pet. What do you think will annoy him?'

'He's not very good at dancing and he likes to show off.'

'We'll have a dance. Edward's brought a nice friend along. I'll introduce you.'

Diane came in. 'Everything all right?'

'Yes,' Katharine said. 'Here, you can take these taties in. They're ready. I'll fetch the apple pies through in a minute.'

They went back into the room and Louise asked Katharine to cut one of the pies, bring a portion for herself and another one. They took two plates each and Louise led her over to a corner where she gave the desert to Edward and introduced Katharine to his friend.

'Katharine, this is Fred.'

'Do you like apple pie?' Katharine handed the plate.

'I like anything,' he said, 'when it's served by a bobby dazzler.' Her face lit up and she sat beside him.

The good looking boyfriend, Leslie, came over and took two new packs of cards from his pockets, not greased and marked like everyone else's. 'Shall we have a game?' he asked. 'I asked your dad to get a card table out. We could have a whist drive.'

'I don't fancy whist,' Katharine said.

'Then we could have a beetle drive.' He sat beside her and tried to slip his hand round her waist.

Katharine choked down the last of her pie. 'I want to dance.' She stood up.

Louise joined her. 'So do I. Who'll help push the chairs back?"

'That's no trouble.' Fred gave Katharine his plate.

From the corner of her eye Louise saw Diane hover, watching her younger sister with two boys hanging round her, looking at the handsome snob.

'Why don't we toss for it?' Leslie reached for his wallet and managed to show a wad of notes as he drew a coin out. Louise saw Diane's eyes follow his fingers. She winked at Katharine.

'No! Dancing for me.' Katharine walked away with the plates and Louise organised the young firemen to finish the furniture removal, old stuff their parents had put together. She spoke to the girl at the piano who changed her sheet music and began a quickstep. Leslie's face closed. Edward was happy to sit out and Joe did not look at her, so Louise smiled quickly at one of the firemen who offered his hand and led her to the middle of the floor, fringes shimmering. As Katharine came in from the scullery Fred bowed to her, she twirled into his arms and they danced looking in each others' eyes. Diane brought a plate of fried potatoes for Lord Handsome who had just lost Katharine. One young man after another danced with Louise then the pianist ran her fingers down the keys and changed to the fast upbeat rhythm of a Charleston. Katharine and Louise broke off from their partners, wrists, feet, knees, hips jerking, shaking, strapped shoes beating the bars in little kicks, hands upstretched, spreading, circling on an invisible wall. Louise spun the rope of pearls. They were one with the music in a mad cheeky joy. Everyone stood back.

Joe continued to drink. His eyes followed Louise's feet. The Charleston stopped suddenly and the girls bowed to a hail of applause. She waited for a look from him then joined the group in the corner to get her breath back, laughing and turned to gaze in Edward's eyes. As she sat seeming to be engrossed in another she saw Joe from the tail of her eye put his glass down, stand up and leave without a word. She excused herself, walked through the scullery, opened the door to the back steps and saw him stagger down the lane. A girl she knew, uninvited to the party, came towards him and linked arms with him. He stretched his arm out round her shoulder, walked her further down the lane, swung her round and pushed her against the wall. Louise held the bannister as she watched them like shadow play. No preliminary kiss. No caress. He lifted her skirts and emptied his anger into this stranger.

Louise died. She stumbled up the steps to the scullery, her feet like stones and found Patricia filling a bowl for washing up. The scent of apple pie lingered, mixed with the strong smell of carbolic softening in hot water. She wanted to push past but saw something sparkle in the palm of her sister's hand.

Patricia held it out. 'Andrew bought me a brooch, a Suffragette brand. It's got the three colours – green, white and purple. Green's for hope.'

Louise peered at the oval pin. 'Coloured glass!' she spat.

'No, the middle one's an amethyst for the purple. Look more closely.'

'It's mam's day, not yours.'

'I tried to give it to her but she said I must keep it. Dad said I should wear it with pride.'

'He would! I've got no time for all that. They'll never do you any good, those high class bitches. Women who've already got money parading themselves about!'

'I'd have paraded with them if I'd been born a few years earlier. And they have done good. I've been able to vote.'

'Much good it's done you. You've got the Tory turncoat, Ramsay MacDonald.'

Patricia smiled at her. 'Well, you seem to know all about it.'

Louise picked the brooch up and turned it to the light. 'Can't get away from it in this house. It's like a poison in the air – politics! It's a man's world.'

'Women will raise themselves.'

Louise snorted.

'Only if men are at their feet!' Her cheeks were red with rage. 'That's my route.'

'One beauty's replaced by another – self respect.'

Lousie ran a hand through her hair. 'Well, I'm going to be the It Girl and go places.'

'Everyone looks at your lovely face but…'

'But nothing! You should see the tips the men give me at the golf club.'

Patricia stirred the water and fished the now soft red soap out. 'You're still wearing an apron next day.' She slopped the soap down on the wooden draining board. 'You're not Clara Bow in front of the camera.'

'Go to hell! And you're not Emmeline bleeding Pankhurst!' She flung the brooch into the bowl, pushed past Patricia and ran for the bedroom, traitor tears falling as she slammed the door.

For the next few weeks Louise saw no one, pretending to be unwell on Sundays.

Katharine started looking for work after Christmas to have a job for when she'd finish school. She came in tired after trying to be taken on as a seamstress. 'I've had no luck.' She flopped into a chair. 'But I'll keep going. I'm not going to lounge round.'

'They'll work you to death in the rag trade.'

'I'm not frightened of work and I'll learn enough to make my own clothes.' She looked at Louise, big eyed.

'What's the matter?'

'Nothing. I'll make a cup of tea.' The youngest sister dived into the scullery.

Louise followed her. 'There is something.'

Katharine splashed water over some cups. 'I just met Lily Scrimshaw.'

'And?'

'It's just gossip.'

'What?'

'She said she saw Joe's girlfriend going into the doctor's.'

'Oh God!' Louise hung onto the door frame.

When Joe met her one night at the Golf Club she was jaunty and chimed out, 'Hi, stranger!' He walked beside her quietly and led her to the flat they'd used. He'd come back. Ragtime played in her head and she chattered. It was all right

Inside he took her hand and sat at her feet. 'I've got something to tell you, Louise.'

'Something good, I hope.' She leaned back and took her glasses off to look at him under her eyelashes. The ragtime stopped.

'I'm going to get married.' She didn't move. 'Have to.' He kissed her left ankle. 'I didn't want you to hear this from gossip.'

Time froze. 'When's the slut's wedding day?' She sat up cold as revenge.

'As soon as we can arrange it. I ... I have no feeling for her. It was after that party. I was very drunk. Now there's a baby coming. And I have to.'

'That's it then,' she said. The radiance at seeing him drained. 'Both of us finished in one go.' She stood up, put her glasses on, reached for her coat. 'I won't say "I'll be seeing you." '

He stopped her. 'Louise, I've never loved anyone else.'

'You have a funny way of showing it.'

'I don't want to go through with it.' He kissed the palm of her hand and searched her eyes.

'Well, I can't trust you now, Joe. And you've got to marry her.'

'It's the decent thing. I'm not sure I'm that much of a bastard - to walk away.'

'She's not the first to get a man that way.'

He kissed her hand again and she tugged free. 'But it's condemning us both to purgatory. Do you know what it's like to lie beside one person longing for another?'

'I may find out.' She hardened her face. 'I've loved you since before I was sixteen, Joe, and you've always been a bugger. Time's passing.' She looked at him cold and he let her go. 'So long, Joe. I hope you're happy with ... Mrs Ellison!' She spat the words and slammed out. He stared blankly at the pattern of the oilcloth as she left.

The streets were lonely as she walked back wondering how they would steer their parallel courses of misery, then knocked on the door of the Scrimshaws' house where she could break down. Her pride, his pride. The door opened and Lily took her in. Her heels rang on the bare floorboards. Friends cradled her and brought a ragged old towel for her to cry into.

'I'll get married,' she retched, 'but I'll never love anyone again.' Lily stroked her hair. 'I can't stay an old maid. Oh God! I wish I could go back a couple of months. Why couldn't I have played my hand right? I went for broke and lost.' She sobbed till her ribs ached.

Five weeks later Joe married quietly at a registry office.

The sward on the fairways at the golf club was thick, birds carried twigs for their nests, stark trees covered bare branches in threads of green. In cool bright days with a promise of summer the hardy earth pushed out fragile flowers to frosts of night. Louise was unmoved by signs of life.

There was a note from Joe at the club. He'd never written to her there - he wanted to meet her next day from work. She had to hide it. Joe, Joe! He might not even show up.

But he was waiting. She'd worn her high heels just in case. 'Louise! I have to talk to you.' There were lines of strain round the mouth.

'There's nothing more to say, Joe.'

'There's a lot more to say.' He caught her by the elbow. 'I have to tell you something.'

'Save it for your wife, Joe.'

He forced her to face him. 'Hear me this once. Then you can make your mind up.'

'What's the point?'

'Have something to eat. We'll have a drink.'

'You know dad'd kill me for going into a pub.'

'I'll get you home by eleven, even if we have to take a taxi. I've ordered fish and chips at the shop. They'll have them put up for us.'

She walked beside him but brushed his arm away. 'This had better be good, Joe.'

'I think of you all the time, Louise.' She stabbed fury in the pavement with her heels and didn't answer.

He led her into the warmth of the shop, to the overpowering smell of vinegar and batter while he paid for two packets kept warm and rolled in newspaper. They walked along to a public house and sat on a bench outside.

'The chips are good,' she said biting through the golden crunch of the potato to the soft steaming white centre. 'I hope you're not wasting my time.' He sat eating from his lap until she was irritated. 'I'm going to get the tram!'

'Evie's lost the baby.' His voice was so low she just caught the words.

'Well! - that was convenient. She trapped you nicely, didn't she?'

'She fell the length of the stairs from a stepladder, decorating. I'd told her not to do any such thing. Then the baby stirred, she went giddy and fell headlong.'

'Maybe she fell on purpose.'

He stared at her coldness. 'Have you no heart? She was five months, for God's sake! She's in hospital. She could have broken her neck.'

'What have you been doing to make her want to do that?' She crumpled the fish papers. 'You should be beside her, Joe.'

'Past visiting hours, and ... I had to see you. We'll go inside.' He tried to take her hand but she stood up, automatically put their papers in a bin then followed.

'Port and lemon?'

'Whisky tonight.'

He brought their drinks to the corner where she'd settled. Men were shouting and laughing, playing a game of darts on the other side of the room. He drained his glass at a gulp. 'She's ill. But they say she'll recover.' He took her left hand and kissed the ring finger. 'I'll leave her ... when she's well again. I only married her because she was pregnant, did the decent thing ... after I knocked her up after that party. Drunk because I thought you were turning me down.'

'You never asked me, Joe,' she said bleakly.

'You knew I loved you?'

'You never asked me.' Her voice was flat. 'I started seeing him because you were seeing her. He actually wants to marry me.'

'Have you said 'yes'?'

'Not yet.'

'I'll get a divorce.'

'Not with my help, you won't.' She ground her heel onto his shoe. 'I won't be co-respondent and drag the family name in the dirt.'

'These things can be arranged.'

'It would still be a disgrace.'

'We could go away together. I'll get a job somewhere else. My line of business, I could get another job. I might even start up on my own.'

She sipped the whisky inhaling the sour warm vapours. 'Too late, Joe. Everyone would know it was over me. I'd be gossiped about.' Her mouth turned down. The place would be alive with cats young and old, hissing in her direction. Death by inuendo. She shuddered. 'I won't bring that on my mam and dad either. The tittle tattle. Remarks behind a hand. No!'

'Your father wouldn't care. Don't marry, Louise. I beg of you.'

The whisky warmed her stomach, helped her play the scene. 'I intend to have a ring on my finger. You didn't offer me one.'

'I'll give you anything you like.'

'It's too late. Everything's spoiled'

'I love you, Louise.'

'Then you've got a problem, haven't you?' He took her left hand and kissed the tips of each finger.

'Save it for your wife, Joe,' she said.

'Don't you care?'

'What I'm concerned about is my future.'

'Either you never cared for me at all or you're a very good actress.' He let her hand drop.

'I need to get back,' she said. 'Thanks for the whisky, Joe. I don't normally drink it.'

'I'll order a taxi.'

'I can get the last tram.' She got up and put her coat on.

'Louise!'

'Sweet dreams, Joe. I have a tramcar to catch.' She left him lurching towards the bar.

12

Twelve months went by as if in a dream. Patricia wondered whether she was getting so old that time was speeding up, a full year since her parents' silver wedding and nothing to show for it except some grey hairs – still in service but with some savings put by.

A letter arrived for her at the baron's house. She recognised Andrew's writing from ten paces, took it off the little dresser in the hallway and tucked it into a pocket to read later, touching it as she continued with her work, a little tremor of excitement each time. The shock was devastating when she tore it open in her room. Orders were drying in the shipyard after the last big job and Andrew had lost his. He'd had bronchitis and had to miss work now and then, she knew. His job could not be kept. Other, fitter men were getting their cards, nobody knew what the future of the yard was. His little savings would soon be eaten up paying rent and he was down to his last. Patricia asked for a few days off.

When she turned the corner of their street she could see his outline watching outside her parents' home, every minute checking the clock face on the fire station tower she guessed. Low rays of winter sun picked out the black Roman numerals. Women were resting from work with pinafores on, headscarves tied round their heads, exchanging a word of support or gossip before scuttling in to their black leaded hearths and glowing brasses, if they still had them, to chores lasting till bedtime. Children played on hopscotch grids chalked on the pavement, jumping, shrieking with laughter, making faces at each other, pulling their mouths down at either side with their tongues out. Patricia smiled at them, saw Andrew wave and her axis steadied. They walked up hand in hand. As soon as they opened the door she could smell the warmth of a waiting apple pie, saliva starting and her taste buds sensed the sharp sweetness already. Cut meat first, her usual gift from the kitchen. Kisses, welcome. Everything stopped for her.

Next day Andrew was there again and they walked outside in the cold to avoid gossip. She took his arm.

'What am I going to do, Patricia?'

'I have an idea.'

Bits of paper caught up by the wind swirled in a dance. 'I hope it's a good one.'

'We have a shop doing nothing, it just stores my mattress. We could ask mam if she'd sublet it.'

Andrew watched the papers whirl higher. 'Your father might object.'

'It'd help pay their rent if the landlord's all right with it. Every month they worry whether they can keep a roof over their heads. Louise and I bring in enough between us and Katharine'll earn something soon … but, if the hammer fell on us all we could all be begging for a bed.'

'I'd hoped to save enough to pay my apprenticeship but it didn't happen. She squeezed his arm. 'A shop would be lighter. It's a man's world out there in the shipyard. He frowned, breath labored against the wind. 'I don't know what I'd sell, though.'

'Up to you.'

'Nothing fancy. People are out of work, making do.'

'A newsagents? It's hard hours.'

'No good. Who has money for papers?... I could sell tobacco. Maybe. People still have a smoke. It's cheap and puts off hunger pangs.' He turned to her and held her as leaves eddied round their feet. 'Children still have sweeties now and then. But I've got nothing now – because of a stupid sickness. Everything's gone.' He kicked at a stone. 'I can pay the rent for about another month.' He seemed to shrink. 'All that saving!'

'I don't spend much living in. I've got something left, after helping the family.' Her heart went to her boots as she spoke. 'It might be enough to start the stock off. What you put away from a shop if there's any profit could go back into the wedding fund.'

He tugged her in against the wind and kissed her head.

Her job was not as demanding as the one she'd had in Hexham, acting as personal maid and only one child who was not her sole responsibility. But Patricia worked hard. Though days off were limited, she had some time to herself in the house. Dressmaking became a passion and the baroness allowed her to use the little Singer machine in the sewing room to make clothes for herself and the family. Self-interest. Her employer needed to dress well for weekend parties and couldn't keep up with the usual changes of clothing. It meant more work but slowly Patricia became expert. Cook's sister was in a tailoring firm and for a fee taught her the skills. With a natural eye, eventually she could copy a couture style and make the paper pattern, with a bought pattern she could do almost anything. Ben complained his daughter did too much dress making for Baron Hardup's household, made a rod for her own back but she took no notice. The baron was pleased his wife could ring the changes and they were saving so much. Patricia earned more, the extra money helped stock the shop and she knew she'd keep her job. Slowly she began to put something away again. The little ring from Andrew's grandmother was on her right hand during the day but she slept with it on her left.

The baroness passed on good clothes she could no longer be seen in as part of the arrangement for the sewing and fashion design and Patricia restyled some then quietly sold them on to a department store. Others she cut down for clothes for the family or for herself.

Joyce Fitz-Gibbon came in to the whirr of the Singer machine, carrying a biscuit-coloured dress of glazed cotton with flashes of red at the collar and sleeves. The material looked like satin. She held it against herself in front of a mirror and shook her head. 'I don't think I can wear this again. The length's old fashioned.'

'It's still lovely, madam. It's a day dress, isn't it? I could do something with it. I think I could lengthen it with a piece to match the collar so you could wear it in the evening, add embroidery at the collar, perhaps a little lace at the bodice.'

'No, you have it. I think it might be recognised.'

She breezed out and Patricia fingered the material holding it to her face. The dress fell a way below the knee, bias cut. She could find a toning length so it would sweep the floor for a wedding dress. She folded it carefully and lived on the mist of a dream.

At weekends the baroness was focused on entertaining. One party organised at their own home could mean five or six invitations for them. Young people were always included and it was a discreet marriage market. Women arranged who might be invited and constantly discussed pairings and forthcoming weddings. The baroness worried about her looks. Patricia helped comb her hair into new styles and with the eye of an artist could advise on colours she should wear. With cream and black, cream should be near the face. Pale blues and shell pink rather than the vibrant colours she preferred in youth. Patricia wore no make-up but borrowed a booklet from Louise on how to use it, learned skills with rouge and pale powder applied beneath the eyebrow, mascara brushed on the lashes to make her mistress's eyes look large, a little lighter foundation smoothed gently underneath the eyes took out shadows. The baron knew nothing of these tricks or what she spent on face cream, delicate makeup giving a subtle bloom to her face or the hairdresser who skilfully dealt with grey. All he saw was his wife looking pretty and well dressed and he was pleased to show her off. What he did know was Patricia saved them money.

'We're going to the Fitzhughes' this weekend,' the baroness said. 'I have to try to look my best but I think they've seen all my dresses. Could you create some magic for me?'

Patricia held in a sigh and thought for a moment. 'I could remake the bodice of the pink with lace, madam. There are some good pieces in the market at the minute ... hmmm … alter the skirt to make it less flowing, maybe re-cut it on the bias. I'll do something with it anyway on the Singer and finish it with hand sewing.

The baroness smiled. 'I've used my clothing allowance but I can find money for lace from somewhere else. Buy good stuff, though.' She hugged her. 'You're worth your weight in gold, do you know that? Don't tell anyone it's been made over.'

'Not a word. A yard and a half of lace should do it. I can find a good off-cut for five shillings.'

'And a sovereign for you, Patricia, if you pull this off.' Patricia curtsied and the baroness found two florins and a shilling from her purse.

It meant an overnight coach to join her mistress in Lincolnshire. Travelling was tiring these weekends but the food, even for servants, was good. She helped the baroness dress for the most important dinner on Saturday evening and carefully touched in her makeup. A little more could be used for electric lighting. The pink dress was magnificent with the neckline scooped low and covered with Guipure lace.

'The sapphire necklace?'

'Pearls, I think, Madam, with lace. And the pearl ear drops.' Patricia stood back to admire the effect and adjusted the thick glowing hair. There were younger women in the party but the baroness looked beautiful. She handed the perfume from Paris that was kept for special occasions.

Joyce Fitz Gibbon smiled at herself in the mirror. 'It would be hard to face these weekends without you, you know. Choose something from the wardrobe when we get back.' She rose. 'Now, forget my appearance and sparkle.'

After a few minutes she came back. 'Patricia, there's a bit of a crisis. They've no one to wait at table. A maid's slipped. They think she's broken an ankle and they're short staffed because of other illness.'

'I'd do it, madam, but I haven't brought suitable clothes for that.'

'They'll lend you the uniform. There's one that should fit.' Patricia hesitated. It was never ending and her feet were sore. 'They'd pay you well for it. Two sovereigns.'

'All right,' Her mind was calculating what that would buy for the shop.

At dinner that evening the guests were all immaculately dressed. Patricia was proud of her mistress but someone more beautiful than the baroness was there, a girl with elfin features and dark hair, next to the host's only son. Her dark dress was severe but elegant. She wore no jewellery except a pendant, an unset, unfacetted emerald, slim as a wide based wine bottle that hung from one diamond and fell from her neck on a slender gold chain. Patricia noticed the women in the party glance at it while the men watched a lovely sculpted face, the fine etched chin under eyes that glowed when she laughed. The couple, though, seemed immune to currents round the dinner table inside an invisible shield. After supper they left to attend a private recital at the girl's home.

Lady Fitzhugh asked Patricia to look after the men in the other room to cover the missing member of staff. The baroness winked and Patricia walked into the kitchen with a straight back, in spite of weary feet in heels. A huge silver tray lay loaded with crystal decanters, port, brandy, whisky and claret, with silver labels round the necks. There were glasses for the different drinks, a plate with little savouries and cheeses, side plates, cigarettes, cigars, matches and lighters.

'Will you manage all that, my dear?'

'I'm not sure, madam. I'm not used to carrying so much and the glassware's so fine it would be terrible to break anything. I'd rather make two or three trips to take it all in safely,' she bobbed a little curtsy, 'if that's all right to go in and out a few times.'

'Yes, I expect so. Better than another broken ankle.'

The hostess had a quick word with her husband and came back. 'That's perfectly all right. And would you hang round for a little while to see if they want anything else? My husband will give you a nod when there's nothing more, then I'd be happy if you'd come through and help me serve the ladies. Perhaps you could run between the two if it's not asking too much? There are a few sweetmeats for the ladies.' She pointed to other trays laid out on a magnificent dresser. 'And could you bring in my little brass kettle? It's usually reserved for tea-time but I like the ceremony at the table. In fact, bring those things in first'

'Madam.' She bobbed again. 'And are there other trays I could use?'

The hostess pointed to a pile beyond the big stone sink and left her. It was the biggest kitchen Patricia had ever set foot in. Everything from the meal had been tidied away. She hadn't had time to stand and gaze when serving dinner but now she took in the big range and glowing copper pans, the slightly blurred blue and white pattern on large serving plates on the dresser. The baroness had nothing on this scale. She raided the stacked trays and began to rearrange everything, took the little pan lid off the burner under the kettle and sniffed it. Vapours hit her nostrils, there was enough methylated spirits there. Matches lay on the men's tray in a silver case with a ridged band to strike against. Jug, sugar bowl and cups she moved separately onto a tray patterned from different woods in marquetry. She worked swiftly as she arranged the crockery longing to finger it. The ladies were sitting by the fire when she went in to the withdrawing room, one or two with fine embroidery in their hands. The hostess nodded to her and she placed the kettle on a side table. 'Shall I light it, madam?'

'Please, my dear.' She went on with her conversation as Patricia struggled to strike the match. 'She's an accomplished pianist herself. Violin too, but Jewish families are often keen on music.' Her friend raised an eyebrow. 'We're actually quite worried about it but there's no talk of an engagement yet. Thank God.'

'She *is* very beautiful,' the friend said.

The match flared at last and Patricia dipped the flame onto the meths-soaked fabric. A tongue of blue fire curled and she placed the kettle over it and checked the flame was licking underneath before going to the kitchen again to bring in the tea set then a silver coffee pot, not appearing to hurry.

'Beauty's one thing,' the lady of the house was saying as she carried the second tray in 'but Jewish blood marrying into the aristocracy's another. The very highest they can rise to is a baronetcy and that's only because that awful man Lloyd George sold them to anyone with pockets deep enough.' Then she glanced at the baroness and looked away.

One more tray then through to the other room.

'What we need to do is to invite him to lots of house parties and balls,' one of the ladies was leaning forward over her embroidery frame, 'introduce him to the cream of this season's girls. I have a niece who's just coming out. She's quite stunning!'

'If all else fails we could maroon him on a desert island,' the hostess said. 'I hear they're going to build a luxury ocean-going liner. I wish they'd hurry up, then we'd send him away on a cruise.'

Patricia picked up the tray with the decanters, placed the matches case back on it, braced herself and carried it through to the smoking room. No one acknowledged her presence. His lordship had already handed cigarettes round. She stood by the wall but didn't dare lean against it, overhearing one of the men speaking to the baron. 'We all lost money in the Stock Market crash. There's no shame in that. It's possible to bounce back. Have you thought of the aircraft industry?'

'Too risky,' the baron said.

She slid out quietly to fetch glasses and cigars. When she came back they were in a full scale discussion.

'Aviation's the future, old man. Anyone can see that.'

'I couldn't afford to lose another pile.'

'It'll take off. Haven't you followed the Everest Flight? Actually over the Himalayas. Finest damn thing in a century. I hear rumours they're even going to try to make a film about it.'

'Make the skyways Britain's highways! Flying clubs springing up all over the place.'

'Armaments investment, that's the one.' A retired colonel with a red face joined the conversation. He spoke in a gravelled whisky-matured voice. 'I don't know how many Americans made their millions through that in the war. Guns, ammunition, the whole supply line of hardware.' Patricia went out to fetch the savouries, salted nuts, Gentlemen's Relish, cheese pastries and squares of cheese varieties. She took them in and placed them on a mahogany wine table.

'Aircraft will figure more and more.' The baron was listening. 'The bomber will always get through - so someone is saying. Unless I made that up.'

'Not just the bomber.'

'What was that, colonel?'

She dipped out for the final tray of glasses and Havana cigars, placed them near the baron who did not acknowledge her and stood beside the door. She may as well have been a tailor's dummy.

'Are you sure tanks are that important?' The argument seemed to have shifted.

'They were available in the Great War, problem was that we didn't use them as we should have.'

'The Germans have already built an air fleet.'

The colonel took his brandy and warmed the balloon glass in his hands. 'Maybe they have but ground forces will always be important. Anyway, we're not dealing with the Kaiser now.' He looked at the baron.

'Hardly a patriotic remark,' another voice chimed in. The baron was concentrating.

'As I said, we're not dealing with the Kaiser. The trick is to know who your real enemy is. The threat's from the Bolsheviks. And that chappy Hitler knows how to deal with Communists.'

'And Jews.' It was their host.

'Same thing? The point is we need a firewall in Europe against the Bolsheviks.'

The baron shifted about in his seat. 'Are you sure they're the real enemy?'

'They murdered the Tsar, didn't they? And his innocent family. What proof do you need? Do you want us all killed in our beds? A guillotine set up in Trafalgar Square? They're set to storm right over to the West.'

The air was filling with cigar smoke. Patricia tried not to inhale it. To those not already smoking, his lordship offered cigarettes tightly packed in a silver box. 'We have to resume normal business relations with Germany now. Coal's been shipped over to Hamburg for years. But invest in a good armaments firm. It's not your responsibility where things finally end up.' The colonel tapped his nose. 'Don't quote me on that, though.'

A young man with hair immaculately brilliantined and brushed back from a centre parting took a cigarette and one of the lighters. 'Airplanes are the excitement. Man against the elements. I want to get my own plane.' The older men smiled at each other. 'It's perfectly possible. Six or seven hundred smackers.'

'Playboy of our time!' His lordship took a handful of savouries, egging the conversation on. 'And what useful thing do you think you could do with a little plane of your own? Or is it just for fun?'

'You'd be surprised what could be done. I might not manage the lolly but I know someone who's starting a company in Croydon. Support could always be given where it's needed.'

'What do you have in mind?'

'Spain. If we're worried about a Communist take over that's the place to be worried about. A real struggle to restore law and order over there and who knows what might step out of it? The odd plane could be useful, you never know. It could aid, maybe rescue the right sort of chaps. I'm certainly going to try to get my wings.'

'More power to your elbow! To the right sort of chaps!' They drank and laughed

'Speaking of which,' his lordship said, 'the Prince of Wales is a man to rally round. Democracy just leads to chaos - I mean, look at Germany after the war. You need strong government, a strong person at the top and everyone giving their allegiance. Strength in unity and loyalty.'

'We'll drink to that!'

When they'd talked round and round as though she were deaf and dumb and had drunk till most of it would be forgotten in the morning Patricia dragged in and out of the kitchen laden with trays and stacked the plates and glasses. Someone else could see to washing them. She rubbed her back and climbed wearily up the back stairs to bed.

She was allowed a few weekends off as the baron and baroness were invited to other weekend parties, meeting even more important people where there would be plenty of staff and where they were discouraged from bringing their own.

Andrew struggled with the shop in her absence. She travelled home by bus to save money and it was hard carrying her luggage, changing buses. Then even two nights were not long and Andrew had to open on Saturday. She became his assistant and could watch and help as he started to build a business.

He would break a packet of cigarettes for people who were hard up and sell two or three Woodbines at a time. There were heavy twists of tobacco for miners to chew and he put up snuff in small packets of paper and sold them for a farthing. Women mainly took snuff, not liking to be seen with a fag in their mouths, though younger ones would copy the movie stars holding a cigarette between their fingers to be smart and a little fast. The snuff takers never seemed to suffer from head colds. He sold sweets an ounce at a time or even counted them out singly.

But it would take hundreds of ounces of sweets to cover the cost of his scales. The curved silver scoop shone in sunlight. The cash register had been the most expensive item of all. Ben offered to look round the market for one but Andrew felt a new one looked better for business, showed confidence. A dingy shop put people off. This thing was his darling. Patricia played with it like a toy the first time she saw it, pressing the keys to hear the bell and see the cash drawer jump.

She looked round and decided paint was needed to make the premises look inviting. It was years since Mary had shut the bakery down, they should have moved elsewhere but hadn't found anything and her mother cherished the thought she might start up again – when pigs flew! Ben had some whitewash, that would do, white walls made the shop look bigger. She found posters Andrew had put away in a cupboard and dragged them out. Healthy, glamorous people smoking elegantly, fit navy men cutting a dash with the girls handing them cigarettes; sunshine, clear skies, genial pipe smokers, sportsmen lighting up. She blew the dust off and smoothed them. They would be bright against the walls when the whitewash dried. She would have liked to stay.

13

Ben worried that from the previous summer Patricia had spent most of a year away and as the baroness's social life grew saw little of Andrew and less of her family. During this time, though, other worries loomed large as British Fascism tried to make an impression on the North East.

In June the weather had been good for Race Week. Children went off to the Town Moor for the Hoppings in sandals or sandshoes not wellies, coming back from the fair half asleep and happy or clutching a prize.

With no money in his pocket Ben avoided the races but went to the Moor with John Hargraves for the Speakers' Corner. They dropped Gwen off at the First Aid tents. Hargraves parked the Baby Austin and they decided to relax, have a ramble round and soak in the atmosphere of sweet trampled grass, fried onions, squeals of children on the rides. John bought a couple of toffee apples with a reddish coating but the sticky stuff was a challenge to his dentures and he threw half of it away, then he tried candy floss. Ben watched him, enchanted in the moment like a child by solidifying sugar turning like pink wisps of straw round a stick till it was an airy cloud of sickly sweet strands. They wandered on and watched the dodgems crash into each other, young men with an arm round a girlfriend

'Do you ever wish you had a family?' Ben asked.

'Yes.' John was silent a moment. 'I've come to terms with it. But it hits me now and then. Our little boy died at birth. Gwen doesn't talk about it any more.'

'Sorry, John. We had that with our first little lad. I know what it's like. Mary spoils Christopher enough for two.'

Blaring music from the rides and a little further on the gypsy caravans then sideshows with garishly painted women on the temporary structures, finally a marquee. A man on a soap box was addressing a small group. A cup of tea would be good after sweet things that left their tongues feeling like sandpaper. They paused. John shrugged and went into the revival meeting in progress. A young man with brylcreem slicked hair greeted him and handed a hymn sheet. Ben inhaled sawdust at the entrance and a faint smell of strawberries some of the crowd had been eating. He turned and sat down on the grass outside but tapped out the rhythm of a Moody and Sankey style song. '*When the roll is called up yonder ... when the roll is called up yonder ... when the roll is called up yonder, when the roll is called up yonder I'll be there!*'

There was a lengthy prayer then a rustle and upheaval and more singing:

At the Cross, at the Cross where I first saw the light
And the burden of my sins rolled away
It was there by grace I received my-y sight
And now I am happy all the day!

Several verses with the chorus and the speaker congratulated them on their collective singing voice then Ben heard a voice warble loudly outside from the other side of the tent:

At the cross, at the cross
where the Kaiser lost his hoss!

John came out with the Brylcreemed young man and he got up to join them. A youth of perhaps fifteen in a black shirt was the cause of the disturbance. 'People are worshipping in there,' the Brylcreem said reasonably.

Ben bore down on him trying to look threatening. 'Go on! Get out of it!' The youngster ran away, 'I'll stay here in case he comes back with his friends.' The Brylcreem smiled his thanks and went back.

John waited outside then wandered over to the group the youngster had joined. Someone was slowly backing a lorry onto the turf, helped by a military-looking man waving him in. As soon as the lorry crunched to a stop the blackshirts erected a light trestle table and began putting out leaflets and fascist insignia while the driver of the lorry jumped out and let the back down. A table was set up inside with a banner and loud hailer. Ben walked over and joined his friend, pretending to be interested in the leaflets and noticed a group was beginning to gather, badly dressed kids not long out of school and some smart middle-aged people who had drifted over from the race course. The women wore knee-length dresses and bright cloche hats pulled down on one side.

A brief test of the megaphone and the driver led straight into a speech about trade protection within the British Empire and dangers of a stranglehold by Jews on the media, Trades Unions and business. The crowd swelled.

'And banking, my friends, is another story!'

'He's not my friend,' a voice muttered behind John.

'Jewish bankers caused the crash that led to this depression. Jewish Trade Unionists have ruined business and they take their orders direct from Moscow. Yet Jewish firms survive. Why is that? They have a stranglehold on the newspapers, they tell you what to think and they're sending this Christian nation to hell!'

'Have ye seen the tache on him?' the voice muttered.

'Aye, it's just like that Hitler's.'

Hargraves, in civvies, shouted out, 'Jesus was a Jew!'

'Christ would have had nothing to do with Communist-led Trade Unionists.'

'And he'd have had nothing to do with the likes of YE!' They felt themselves jostled from behind. 'With a half tache like that bloody Hitler!'

'Who said that? Show yourself! Don't skulk at the back if you're a man. And I'll tell you something else! Hitler's solving the unemployment problem in Germany.'

'Oh, aye?' They were propelled forward from behind. 'Then why don't you go and bloody join him? Jump on a boat and get across to bloody Germany because ya not wanted here! Haway, kiddas, let's get them.' A dozen or more men flooded out to the makeshift podium, surrounded the lorry and jostled to get hold of it. 'We'll

make him do the cakewalk! One, two, heave! One two HEAVE!'
The lorry rocked. 'Get ya backs into it, lads. Dance, fella! Two three,
HEAVE!' The Führer look-alike jumped off his bench before the
lorry crashed over.

They saw, horrified, that the youth who'd sung outside the
marquee was trapped underneath. John ran over. 'Stop! Someone's
hurt. Give a hand. Lift it. Gently. His back might be hurt. Someone
run to the First Aid tent. I don't want to move him more than we
have to. Quick!' Ben was on his way. 'He's just a lad.' Gwen raced
over with two more First Aiders. 'I think his ankle may be smashed.'

'We'll take it from here,' she said raising her eyebrow at John.

Ben kept quiet at home about this first clash with fascism.

*

Mary started to wear a woollen cap when Christmas passed and they
shivered in the house. They'd used up their coal and she missed the
allowance Ben used to have from the pit. She looked in a mirror,
took the hat off and grumbled at Ben, 'I don't know why you hang
round with the vicar. A person of your beliefs or no beliefs.'

'For intelligent conversation.'

'Oh, here it comes!'

'OK. You don't want a lecture but you asked. It's a mark of a
civilised society when you can have different opinions. We watch
Pathé news and some of the flicks. Charlie Chaplin's the common
man, you know. You should give it a try.'

'Chance would be a fine thing. The only cockerel I ever see is our
little bantam. You're lucky to have a ticket bought.'

'It's for company, Mary. Even a vicar needs conversation. It
doesn't matter we take different positions. It sharpens us up. You
think I'm cadging and it bothers me as well. I'll try and make it up
to him some time. Anyway, what's this about?'

'I miss my bakery.'

He sat down and put his arm round her. 'I know. You ran a fine bakery. You should have let me manage the business side for you.'

She wept and he held her. 'I'm sorry about that. We'd have managed without the girls keeping us if I hadn't wrecked it.'

'You didn't wreck it, other people did. And I know how you feel, I miss the pit. I dream about it.' She caressed the blue lines where coal dust had left marks in gashes on his wrist, his tattoo.

'Well, I don't miss worrying every day if my man's coming back or not and that's a good thing. You never said you dreamt about it.'

'It doesn't go away, that dream. I try to step on the floor of the cage after it's started moving. I step into the gap and fall down the shaft. I fall and fall through the pitch black.'

'Have you told the vicar this dream?'

'Aye, John says I've fallen out of my world and haven't found a footing.'

Mary sat away. 'Then you'd better go on spending time with him. That's wisdom that is. I must say it's better than having you mooching round the house.'

The unlikely friends emerged into daylight from the silver screen.

'Have a cup of coffee, Ben?'

'I didn't think even a vicar could afford coffee, John.'

'I have a private income now my parents have died.' They turned their collars up. 'There, I've confessed it. Father must have forgiven me for becoming what he called a Methodist or a Communist up here.' The pavement was turning dark with rain. A barrow boy shouted his wares but covered the vegetables with a tarpaulin as a gust of wind tore up the street. 'Coffee's more respectable than going into the pub over there. Somebody would catch me out. Come on, it's getting cold.' They walked head down against the rain, dived into a shop with an old fashioned wooden front and settled near a burning fire. The vicar pushed his dark woollen coat onto the chair back. 'Something worrying happened a couple of days ago.'

'Oh, aye?'

A girl with a frilled white pinafore over a black dress came over, took the order and was back almost immediately. She put two steaming cups down with a metal milk jug. The bitter scent of coffee made Ben reach for a pleated dark paper case holding brown sugar. He played with it a moment to see it shift and creep onto itself waiting for his friend to open up.

John Hargraves threw his sugar and milk in quickly and stirred. 'Milk?'

'I don't touch it. If the girls have it somewhere else that's their choice but we drink tea black at home. The T.B. risk.'

'I take my chance,' John said, 'Gwen sees to all that sort of thing. Anyway, I didn't come in to talk about milk.' He lingered over his cup while they were settling down for the real conversation. 'I had a shock recently.'

'What was this, John?'

'I was walking up Westgate Road at the beginning of the week.' Hargraves relaxed once he'd started. 'I'd been to an ordination at the cathedral and had to collect something for Gwen round there. It was a bright day and I could still hear organ music in my head, probably not looking where I was going. This car flashed past. I thought vaguely something was wrong then realised a second later what it was. No number plate. Then it screeched to a halt and two men jumped out of the back with peaked caps pulled down. They ran to a shop and heaved a couple of bricks through the window. It was like watching a scene from the pictures. The window smashed to smithereens on the pavement.' Ben whistled. 'They ground their heels on the glass then one of them saw me and pulled something out of his pocket. I ducked automatically and a stone bounced off my bowler.'

'You were lucky, John.'

'I was more than lucky. They threatened me - "More where that came from, vicar, if you don't keep your nose out!" - Then they jumped back in the car shouting - "There's Communists in there!" - and were off.

173

'Which shop?'

'The Workers' Bookshop.'

'Ah! ... they'll not have money to replace a big window either.'

'That may be the least of their worries. Somebody could replace it for them.' Ben nodded. 'Nobody was hurt. They can board it up for now.'

'It would be the Fascists.'

'An assistant told me the blackshirts had torn left-wing posters down at the college and beaten some of the students up.'

Ben sipped the cooling coffee, not sure whether he liked the bitter taste. 'It's happening fast. Remember those newsreels of Germany, scenes of uniformed school children marching about, camping and such.' He leant forward. 'I can tell you, John, Trade Unionists are disappearing over there. If they're lucky they get sent over to Britain by friends and we look after them.'

'And the rest?'

'God knows. I think they go to some kind of prison.'

'Have you been asked to help?'

'Not personally. We've nowhere to put anybody up. But there are well heeled people who will.'

'Would you do it if you could?'

'I hope so. Times are hard and it's difficult to look past your family. But I hope I would.'

'Times are hard.' Hargraves ordered scones to buy more time by the fire. 'There was a placard by the door of that shop, - *Millions now Facing Benefit and Wage Cuts.* Probably why they broke the window. Or where it'll end.'

'Ask the bishop to buy you another bowler.'

John smiled 'It had to have first aid that day. Germany's leaving the League of Nations and the Bible's come under suspicion there. That's my news.'

'They're going to abolish the ten commandments now, are they?'

'A bit Jewish! He finished a scone and wiped crumbs away. 'Talking of employment, would you come and do some gardening for us?'

'I don't want charity, John.'

'Don't be so proud, man. I'm not much use in the garden and it's heavy for Gwen. She does a lot of other things.'

'I'll do the gardening but it'll be payment for these tickets to the picture house.' They shook hands.

*

Louise came in and showed off a little ring to her mother, a shining cluster on her left hand. Mary hugged her but said nothing.

'What's that huddle in the scullery?' Ben asked as Diane examined the ring. 'Come in here.'

Louise lifted her chin, stalked in and held her hand out. 'I'm engaged. That's what the huddle was.'

Ben's face darkened. 'To that new lad?'

'Yes!'

He threw the *Manchester Guardian* on the floor. 'You're getting married out of spite, Louise. And it's your whole life you're playing with!'

She turned on her high heel 'I can't wait forever. A woman has to marry and he's a nice man.'

'You don't have to tie the knot just because *he* has. Wait a while. What's another year or two? There'll be someone else. It *is* possible to love again. This isn't it.'

Diane and Mary stayed quiet in the kitchen.

'How would you know?'

'I know what love is and I have eyes in my head. I never thought you'd be happy with Joe.' Louise took her shoes off and clattered them into a corner. 'He's not the marrying kind.'

'He's done it, hasn't he?'

'How long will he stay with her? You haven't lost as much as you think you have there. You were a moth to Joe's flame. He'd always burn you. I think you're well out of it.'

'Did I ask your opinion?' She pulled a cigarette out, lit it and inhaled luxuriously with her head tilted back. Ben raised his eyebrows. She blew smoke out through her nose, challenging the rule that only he could light up in the house. 'It's my life! I'm the one who has to live it.'

'And the people who gave you birth suffer over you.'

She picked a piece of tobacco from her tongue. 'Don't give me that!'

'This man may not be a good provider.'

'He's decent.'

'That thing with his feet. It could get worse. You don't really know what you're taking on.'

'He'll be all right. They turned his feet round the right way at St Thomas' Hospital. Anyway, he says he works with his hands not his feet.' She spat the words out. 'People will always need shoes cobbled.'

Diane stood wide-eyed at the scullery door as her sister defied their father.

Ben held on to the arm of his chair, knuckles whitening and spoke very low. 'He's nice, he's not from these parts, he's gentle. These are attractive things in a man.' She glared down at him. 'But at least put off the date. Get over Joe. Then think about whether you're getting married.'

'We're fixing the date, dad. I'm over twenty-one! There'll be one less to worry about in this house. And if you won't give me away, I expect Uncle Peter will!' She pulled her shoes on again and stomped out in the patent leather three and a half-inch heeled T bars.

Her father trudged up to the vicarage, nodded to Gwen but didn't put on the pair of overalls he kept there for gardening. She held the door open to show he could go in for a chat first and take as long as he liked. He knocked at the study went in and stood while John Hargraves put his pen away and straightened his papers.

'What are you standing there for, Ben? Sit down. Is something the matter?'

'For me there is.'

'Spit it out.'

Ben looked round at the study as if he'd never seen it before; the desk of polished oak, green leather inlay, a tidy row of pens, a curved honey-coloured wireless on the mantelpiece, the kind he used to have himself. 'I've actually come to arrange a wedding.'

'But that's good news!' The vicar sat back in his chair smiling. The spaniel at his feet wagged its tail uncertainly, not coming over to Ben. 'Whose will it be? Patricia?'

'That would be good news.' He didn't beckon the dog. 'It's Louise. She's found somebody else. I expect you know Joe got married. I wish I could talk her out of it.'

John played with one of the pens. 'You might make things worse. Delay would be better.'

'I've tried that.'

'Or maybe it's not the mistake you think it is. It's difficult, Ben, but you're going to have to let your daughters go.'

'Don't start that.'

'Would she come and talk it through with me? She may just be doing the opposite of whatever you say. Let's have a cup of tea, anyway.'

'I'll go and see Gwen in the kitchen.' He got up. 'I think there's gossip that I'm having it off with your missus. And you don't seem to care.' Ben dawdled off to the kitchen and came back with dark home-made Yorkshire Parkin on a tray set with a china teapot and cups.

John Hargraves was speaking on the `phone, stopped talking and said a terse, 'I'll ring you back.' He hung the earpiece on its balance and looked down at his hand. It was shaking. The priest slumped into his seat as the earpiece clattered onto his desk.

Ben put the tray on a side table and hooked up the phone. 'You look worse than I feel. What's happened in five minutes? ... I'll pour the tea.' The vicar picked the cup up but it trembled in his hand. 'Wait a second.' Ben took it. 'We can't have you smashing the Crown Derby,' he inspected the russet and gold of the pattern, 'or whatever it is.'

Hargraves tried to recover himself. 'Only the second best tea service for you.'

Ben grinned. 'Who was that? Forgive the long nose.'

'A friend.' He held his hands tightly together. 'It's an hour of testing.' He looked down at his hands, unclasped them and they shook uncontrollably. Ben poured tea for himself and waited. 'I've been asked ... I've been asked ... whether I'll help someone come over from Germany. It's the Jewish thing. Teachers lost their jobs about a year ago ...'

'That's the Fascism for you. Racist, as well.'

'I know. But I'm not sure what to do. Some university people are trying to get out.'

Ben put his cup down, reached across and took Hargraves hand. Shivers were going through the man, his hand was clammy and beads of sweat broke out on his forehead. 'Why do they need you? What about the Jews in Gateshead?' Ben moved back giving his friend space. 'Won't they take fellow Jews who get out of the country?'

'Yes.' The reverend played with the moist dark crumbs of parkin on his plate. 'But it might be a bit chaotic. Some of them may need a temporary safe house here and there till it can be organised. Little boats from Hamburg can make their way across to the port here and slip in quietly.' Ben was silent. 'I should talk to Gwen.'

'Yes. Think of her.'

'We have the room.' Hargraves reached for the cup and held it steady. 'I'm ashamed at reacting like that. I've been asked to shelter a refugee and I should be up to it. It's just ... you don't know where it's going to lead. What if there'll be a whole string of them? What if we go to war with Germany? What sort of position would it put me in? And would I be making difficulties for the Church? – but some Jewish clergy may be getting out as well. There's that to think about. They may need help … and it could go on and on. And I have to think about Gwen. Would we have been harbouring enemy aliens?'

Ben looked gravely at his friend wrestling with the situation, thrown in at the deep end. He poured another cup for himself. 'Sup your tea, lad. You're a human being. War's not on the horizon but you have to think this through.'

Hargraves drank slowly and put his cup down. 'If Gwen's happy with it … I'll do it.'

'It's right to be careful.'

'I even speak some German.'

'Now that's what I call suspicious.' They grinned.

The allotment continued to provide vegetables and Ben was paid in kind from the vicarage garden. He was more or less a full time gardener. Once at the rectory he'd heard John Hargraves speaking what might have been German in the front room. Gwen had come in and slammed parsnips and a couple of cabbages on the kitchen table.

'Sorry there may be a few insects between the leaves.'

'A compliment to your cabbage and its freshness.' He packed them into a khaki haversack, cocked his ear to catch the sound of the foreign language and lowered his voice. 'You still have visitors, then?'

She nodded. 'Things are getting organised. We thought these would be the last but …' she leant across the scrubbed pine table and whispered, 'Jewish Christian clergy have been thrown out of their pulpits and manses.'

'Oh bugger! Excuse my French. John mentioned that as a possibility.'

She raised an eyebrow. 'It's been going on for a while but some of them may be getting out. Not all of them but - we may be busy.' She mimed zipping her mouth. He nodded.

A month later Ben was disturbed by photos that appeared in the local paper. He'd paid little attention to one the previous year showing Mosley dressed up in jodhpurs and boots and surrounded by lots of smart black jackets with silver buttons and silver buckled belts. Now the Italian community was pictured giving the fascist salute at a war memorial. Was that important? He decided probably not. They could have leanings to Mussolini through family connections. Not many real blackshirts round here yet, most of those lads were unemployed, attracted by a uniform, by sport and by a drum to beat. Beefy brawn not brain. But there'd been those bricks through the bookshop window.

Street fights started. Not rowdies after the pub. There was general argy-bargy at Fascist meetings then bloody confrontations outside for a couple of months. Mary wanted him to stay out of harm's way but he slipped out on Sunday evenings to go to the Bigg Market with John Hargraves after evensong, always something happening on a Sunday night at Speakers' Corner, a gathering of intellectuals, fools and those whose fists itched for a fight.

John had taken his dog collar off to blend in and get the feel of things. Stallholders at the top of the market were doing good business selling whelks or whillicks, as Geordies called them, in big newspaper cones. The smell of strong malt vinegar was cheerful.

A cluster of Christians were singing hymns. John nodded to them. The usual hecklers were about and a few drunks. A little man dressed up in Sunday best staggered round the groups, started to sing *Land of Hope and Glory*, saluted, shouted God Save the King in a loud voice and collapsed. A number of women stood round a powerful female speaker proclaiming that women had a long way to go, the vote was just the beginning. They should not be tied to the kitchen sink and be baby machines. She waved a copy of *Married Love*. 'Marie Stopes can show you how to stop having babies.' Not the vicar's problem. Ben listened but John moved on. He turned to follow.

There they were, blackshirts setting up. Belts with heavy buckles that could be used as weapons and a well-dressed man with military bearing and an army title on Civvy Street started the meeting speaking in a clipped commanding voice. 'We need a controlled State, run by a Leader, a Caesar-man who can get things done and give us law and order. That's what this country needs. Full employment by protecting our industries and trading with the Empire. And women who are faithful helpmeets working in the home.'

The emancipated woman shouted over, 'While you men do whatever you like! Slaves! That's what you want the women to be. Don't listen to them!'

'An we divn't want your Mussolini and his like ponsin' aboot in their white suits.' Another voice pierced over the racket. 'Fancy that doon the pit!'

'The fascist leaders are bringing order on the continent!'

'Hadaway, man! Bleach ya black shirts.'

'Order and employment, I'm telling you. That's something you need to listen to. Strengthen the police and the army and get unemployed youth off the street! Give them military training and make men of them.'

'No standing army in time of peace!' John Hargraves shouted.

'And that, sir, is the remark of a coward!'

'It's right. No call-up. Are ye callin' us cowards?'

The shellfish in the newspaper cones appeared for duty. As if at a starting gun, men and women threw their whelk and winkle shells at the podium. There was a roar and the entire market place seemed to join in. Tiny hard missiles showered at the soapbox podium like bullets and the speaker lost his nerve. He stumbled down. Youths who had stood round in uniform facing the crowd looked at each other but nobody gave a lead.

A fresh shower came from the back. 'And that's for women's rights! Come on, girls, let's tear those shirts off their backs!'

'Oh, God! The women are starting. We'd better get out.' Ben pushed his friend to the edge of the crowd. More hot whelks were swiftly bought from the stall. The blackshirts gave way and ran in a hail of shellfish, booed all the way, racing pellmell for their offices in Clayton Street. Ben held back from the hue and cry and steered John out of the way up Grainger Street where they sat on the steps of the monument to Earl Grey and sheltered beneath the great reformer.

John accepted the offer of a whelk. 'All those voting reforms, social progress,' he struggled for breath, 'the whole thing could be dismantled, wiped out.' They leaned up against the base of the pillar. 'Don't tell Gwen where I've been.'

Ben grunted. 'Then you'd better rinse your mouth out for the vinegar on those whillicks, or don't kiss her.'

The leeks kept Ben busy again at the allotment but he had no success this year. They had almost come to depend on at least a minor prize at the show but Mary cooked the leeks up, complaining about the size of them for the pot. He cut the big woody leaves off for her and chopped them down a bit one at a time, keeping the rest down at the allotment in a sack. He thought better of sending any to Bessy. Diane finished off the chopping and they ate soups and stews. Nothing could be wasted.

Then there was work helping Wilf rebuild his pigeon cree. Wilf asked the vicar to bless his birds and they began to win races. Hargraves had loud complaints from the other pigeon fanciers that there'd been an unfair advantage and ended up blessing them all. Ben advised him to steer clear of dousing the racing fraternity with holy influence after that.

A big May Day rally was planned for Gateshead and John offered a lift across the Tyne in the Baby Austin. He had a meeting to go to in the area. Ben and Wilf were both wearing grey shirts to show anti-fascist credentials. They argued in the car on the way.

'We've got to meet force with force,' Wilf said.

'I think violence will only breed violence,' John joined in at the wheel, 'and it won't be long before somebody's killed.'

Wilf could hardly contain himself in the back of the car. 'You don't understand, your Reverence. It's the only language they know and it's the only language they'll respond to. We have to give them what they dole out. They come prepared with rubber bludgeons and lumps of steel wrapped in a bit of cloth. I've seen it.'

'Aye, but there's another point, Wilf,' Ben said. 'Violence in the street actually gives them publicity, which is exactly what they want. Then they play the victim, saying we've shed their blood. And another thing - it brings the Communists to the fore and gives them publicity as well, which we don't want. The Labour Movement has to defeat fascists with the use of reason.'

'You'll never get anywhere with them by the use of reason!'

'We know what we do and we know why we do it. For a decent life for everybody.'

'I think this is where you want to be,' John said, 'the Labour Exchange. Looks as if your man's already there. I'll double back when I can. I don't know how many will turn up at my thing.'

They tumbled out. 'Thanks, your Reverence.'

The dole queue outside the Exchange reached right round the block and snaked into another street, hundreds of unemployed. Ben and Wilf stood at the back of the crowd for the open-air meeting in front of the building. The theme was money, the trade slump, international unity between workers.

'Stand shoulder to shoulder, brothers. Don't be deflected by these fascists. There's order on the German streets, you might hear. That's because the opposition's all in the clink!'

A cheer went up. When it died down someone started it up again. Then a line of Blackshirts appeared. Ben had no idea where they'd been hiding. They headed towards the rostrum chanting.

'M-O-S-L-E-Y. Mosley!'

They forced a way through the bystanders to try to surround the speaker. 'M-O-S-L-E-Y. Mosley!'

Men in the crowd jostled them and one-to-one skirmishes began. Ben looked round nervously. Wilf was on his high horse, spouting a stream of anti-fascist abuse. They needed to get out of there soon.

'M-O-S-L-E-Y.' the chant continued.

The men outside the Labour Exchange suddenly broke their rank, surged forward, losing their caps, and poured behind the speaker.

'That's enough!'

'They need hoyin' in the river!'.

Two men handled the protesting speaker off the platform to safety while the rest dived into the fray, pushing through the heaving mass to find Blackshirts. Some of the Mosleyites worked back to the edge of the scrum and pelted down the street followed by an outraged stream of May Day celebrators.

One Blackshirt lay on the ground, blood streaming from his mouth. Hargraves screeched to a halt in the Austin, slammed the door, raced over and protected the unlucky youth from a menace of surrounding feet till he was dragged away by a friend. Ben spotted him, ran across and pulled him by the shoulders in the direction of the car.

'Wait for Wilf.' They bundled in.

'Come on. Lock it.' The clergyman slid into gear. 'No sense in either of you being knocked unconscious.' He glanced at Wilf. 'I think you're going to have a shiner on that eye.'

'Trying to break up a May Day meeting!' Wilf spluttered. He peered out of the rear window 'We'll have to sort them out. Me an' me mates hoyed the Bishop of Durham in the Wear once at the gala.'

'My deafness just came on.' The reverend shook his head and concentrated on the road.

184

'Butler waiting on the other side with his Lordship's tipple on a tray.'

Hargraves snorted a laugh and gripped the wheel.

'We need to start an anti-fascist league,' Ben said grimly.

'What we need,' Wilf spat, 'is to break the buggers.'

*

The following year Ben and the Reverend Hargraves tried to follow events in Germany. The Versailles Treaty seemed to have flown out of the window as young men were given the call up to be soldiers again. But there was enough going on at home. The little man in the loincloth was back negotiating with the British government. And Louise? Ben didn't know if she was following her head or her heart, or either. Most folks, though, were just looking forward to having a shindig for King George Vth's Silver Jubilee.

As her father knew, Louise was engrossed in her own affairs. Time she was married. People might think she was on the shelf. She might suddenly have grey hairs.

The local high street was thronged mid-day on a busy Saturday. On a rare day off Louise had to find a few things for her mother. She wondered whether to go into town to look round but men were elbowing and jostling their way onto tramcars to spend precious shillings at St James' Park. She'd forgotten there was a match on. One of the football fans had a klaxon horn and was edged off the boarding platform by the conductor. She covered her ears as the man honked the blasted horn at the passengers and the tram began to glide off. His friends made faces at him as he ran after it. Long faces in the pub or tables full of pints would tell the tale of the match later. Not a day for the town.

She checked her mother's list. Needles, thread … she crossed boot black off … her dad would use spit and polish … suet, flour, a light bulb and fuse wire. She found a butcher's for the suet, flour further down the street and bought her mother some nice cooking apples from a stall. The rest she'd try for in the department store in the hardware section, then buy perfume for herself. Be smart, smell lovely, turn heads, no matter what seethed inside.

It was hot in the store. She bought everything as quickly as possible but had to queue at the counters. Waiting, she caught sight of herself in a mirror, frowning. Her hair was properly crimped in waves but her expression could sour milk. She raised her eyebrows, breathed deeply, smoothed her brow and managed a smile for the harassed assistant.

Coming out she almost ran into another woman. Evie. Her skin was sallow, dark circles under her eyes, wispy hair hung lankly and she wore a shapeless old gabardine coat. Fatigue was in every movement. She looked as if she should be in bed. Neither spoke till Louise stepped sideways with a tart 'Excuse me!' and stomped pitiless, dry eyed up the street.

She spent the rest of the afternoon washing and setting her hair and pressing her clothes to perfection, banging the iron down. - How could he have married somebody like that? Letting herself go, dragging about like that, she deserves all she gets! She hung her clothes on hangers from pegs on the bedroom door and decided which to keep clean for the street party.

Next day she lay in. Diane was seeing to the dinner and she could hear her chattering in the scullery to Katharine, full of herself with a new job she'd landed. She could earn more money there if she worked fast enough on piece rate. Nothing frightened Katharine. She'd found her prince, or he'd found her. Louise turned and burrowed into the pillow, playing with the little ring on her third finger. The door slammed. Katharine was out for a walk while the sun shone. Christopher was thudding a ball against the door in the backyard. She could kill him. Her breasts were sore and there were cramps in her navel. She got up and found the thick webbed bandage-like sanitary towels. Part of her face was red and swollen with needles of neuralgia piercing under the skin. Her head throbbed. She braved the scullery for a cup of tea and a hot water bottle. She might feel better once it came - get the bloody mess over.

Diane brought hot water in a basin for her to sponge herself down. There was a dark spot on her knickers. She hadn't got pregnant to trap Joe. She almost wished she had. Much good it had done Evie. She bathed her temples, finished sponging herself, hooked the pad in place from the elastic belt round her waist and got dressed. Her hair was shining though she felt like hell. Her dad looked up from his paper and nodded when she came out. Without noticing what was on her fork she ate but the hot food calmed her belly. Then she pushed half of it away. Katharine was looking at her from the other side of the table making little signals with her eyes. What now? They helped gather the plates up to stack by the sink and Katharine passed her an envelope. She knew the handwriting anywhere. 'From Joe,' Katharine whispered. 'I saw him down the Dene. He said to give you it.' Her name written in blue seemed to dance. 'He said he'd like to see you.'

'Oh, did he?' She stared at the envelope then ripped it into shreds, went into the room, threw them onto the empty grate and stumbled out through the scullery to sit on the back steps. Katharine brought her a cup of sweet tea and tiptoed back in again. No one spoke.

Trestle tables with paper Union Jacks as tablecloths sparkled in the sunshine. Everyone in the neighbourhood brought something for a street party. The children had mugs for the king's jubilee and waved little flags for George V and his queen. Louise tried a little of everything in reach. It was Andrew behind the big silvery tea urn, pouring for everyone. He sat beside Louise. Her young man was on her left. Joe Ellison was not there. Her small cluster ring glittered on the third finger of her left hand, delicate to suit her small hand. That day had been perfect. She had even believed in romance the day Edward bought the ring for her. The paste shone as brilliantly as diamonds. Her father watched her from the other side of the table. She looked away.

'Have some ginger cake, Andrew,' she said. 'It's mam's home baking.'

'I don't think I can eat any more. You know,' he swivelled round to talk, 'I feel this is kind of unreal, what we're doing.'

'What do you mean, unreal?' Long pious faces, she could smack them.

'Flags today, gasmasks tomorrow.'

'For God's sake don't talk rubbish! Let people enjoy themselves for once. More cake, dad?' She passed a plate with her left hand so her ring would catch the light.

'No thanks, pet. I've enough on my plate.' Her eyes blazed at him then she shrugged. Andrew handed him a twist of baccy and Ben began talking of rumours that the king had problems with the heir to the throne. 'Royalty doesn't protect you from everything,' he added and stabbed a glance at Louise.

She took Edward's hand. Cake, tea, special mugs with royal faces transferred on before firing. She hated the whole thing and her father knew there was something wrong. Flags, laughter, singing, an ache in her heart.

Joe I could kill you!

She stood in front of the mirror, eyes fixed on the wardrobe Ben had made for her mother, put together from a couple of old ones. There'd be no big white wedding. She wouldn't have to be a hypocrite, standing in white. She swivelled round. Would Joe have married her as he did the other if she'd fallen pregnant first time? Loved her too much to be careless, that was what he said. She turned and craned over her shoulder to see the back of the two-piece, the view people would have of her in the service. The powder blue straight skirt hung perfectly and her white lace blouse did not ride up. She plucked the long sleeve of crêpe de chine. Tips at work bought all her clothes. She'd lost count of the number of months she'd saved for this and still had to buy the high heels to match. The costume from Fenwick's was expensive but she'd be able to wear it again and again.

Everyone had new clothes for the wedding. Katharine and Patricia made theirs, Patricia's a re-make of a dress from the baroness, shortened. But Diane's outfit had been bought by her boyfriend and not from the Co-op, a deep green linen costume that fitted her figure and showed off the beautiful gold of her hair.

Katharine's lavender dress and tailored jacket she'd made looked quite as expensive, the colour brought up the depths of her brown eyes and she'd found a hat to match in Woolworth's. The girls had a fashion parade before the occasion. They were giggling but Louise noticed Leslie's eyes followed the lavender, not the green. Diane went over and sat on his lap.

Louise kept her costume hung up. Bad luck to show it when Edward was there.

Everyone else walked up to the church for the wedding but Ben had managed to hire a taxi to give his daughter away, from whatever odd jobs she had no idea. He was waiting, leaning against the mantelpiece when she came out of the bedroom. He helped her fix a white rose onto a lapel.

'You're beautiful.' She smiled then he kissed her brow. 'It's not too late.'

'What?'

'It's not too late to change your mind. It doesn't matter about all this.'

She picked up the spray of carnations laid for her on the table. 'You say this to me now? Mam's baked for days!'

'It simply doesn't matter. They can all go home again. Just be sure. Better to jilt him than have a broken life. For a woman it's everything, marriage.'

There was a knock at the door. 'That's my taxi, I believe.'

'One last time, you don't have to go through with it.'

'If we don't go down and get in that taxi, I'll brain you with these flowers!' She clattered down the stairs, not looking back to see if he was following.

In the church people next to the aisle turned to look at the bride. She saw the scene as if she did not belong, everything seemed distant; cold stone walls, white flowers, coloured light that glowed in patterns on the carpet, hats, ridiculous hats, shone shoes shuffling on the worn flags, a perfume of pollen and wax candles. It was someone else this was for. The impostor put her best smile on and saw from smiling faces she was radiant as she gave the performance of her life. Her father offered his arm and she walked slowly towards the gleaming white surplus at the other end of the church. It was a dream in slow motion. The family was near the front and she could see Leslie between her two younger sisters. Patricia was next to her mother in the wonderful biscuit-coloured dress. They seemed far away but as if through the wrong end of a telescope she saw Leslie pass a note to Katharine before triumphant chords from the organ pierced her ears and everyone stood. Perhaps she should brain *him* with the white carnations.

The vicar smiled and leant forward to her in welcome. Edward looked as if his heart would stop. He spoke clearly and placed the slender gold ring on her finger without fumbling. When all the words were said he turned, gave her his arm and shone with pride. She matched her step to his uneven one and smiled into a rain of confetti as they emerged into sunlight. Her husband helped her into the taxi and drew a handful of small change from his pocket for children who crowded the car shouting, 'Hoy oot! Hoy oot!' Then he scattered coins for luck as they drove back to her mother's house.

Louise held her smile as she gripped his arm. '*I've made my bed. I must lie on it.*'

14

Patricia clustered round the wireless with her employers to listen to news bulletins that the king's life was moving peacefully to its close, attended by his physician Lord Daws. The baron noted with satisfaction that he died before midnight and that the death would first be reported in the Times. He scurried out in the morning for a first edition.

'Good thing it's been broken in a decent paper,' he said. 'Properly done.'

'Or been managed.' The baroness winked. Patricia brought toast in a silver rack for Joyce Fitzgibbon and stayed to see if anything else would be needed. 'All eyes will be on the Prince of Wales now.'

'Let's have a decent funeral first.' Her husband munched on the toast, 'Proper respects. He's been revered, George the Fifth. No rumours about him.'

'The working man idolises the Prince, so I've been told. He's interested in their plight. Appears to care. Is that right, Patricia?'

'I think so, madam. It's different in our house. My father's not a royalist.'

The baron snorted. 'They wouldn't idolise him if they knew what he'd spent on jewellery for that American piece of his a week after he'd been visiting parlours in little pit villages. He's getting through a prince's ransom - she must know how to keep him interested. In fact, some members of the gentlemen's clubs wonder whether she learned something beguiling from the orient when she took herself off to Shanghai.'

The baroness raised her eyebrow and spread marmalade delicately on her toast. 'Now who's digging up rumours? Some people will say anything. D'you think we should go to London and try to get in at the Abbey? Every hotel bedroom might be booked already.'

'As a matter of fact I was thinking of renting a flat in London for six months or so. It could help me with business contacts. We're a bit out of the way up here.'

His wife sprang up. 'Jeremy, that would be marvellous! We could stay for the rest of the season. Can we really afford it?'

'Investment dividends have been excellent. Especially from Germany, I had a good tip on how to invest there. We couldn't go for a big apartment with full staff. How would _you_ feel about coming up to London, Patricia?'

'It's so far away.' Her stomach tightened 'I wouldn't get home, sir. Too expensive and it would take too long.'

'We'd give you adequate time off and pay your fares and give you a salary wage. How does that sound?'

It means I'd be doing everything, she thought. 'I'd need to think about it, sir.'

'Of course.' The baroness smiled reassuringly. 'Rory's safely in boarding school but I'd be doing a bit of travelling up and down myself. I could give you a lift in the Austin some of the time, part of the way.'

Patricia stacked the breakfast plates and carried them out. With Louise married, her money was more important than ever. Katharine wouldn't earn much yet and Andrew couldn't afford to come traipsing to London. He had his mother to think of. She ground her heel in the kitchen and clattered plates into the sink. At least she could save if they paid her extra.

For the funeral Joyce Fitz Gibbon had a smart black outfit, though she would shiver in January cold. Patricia made a dress over for herself and managed to stand outside the Abbey to watch dignitaries arrive. Bishops in gaiters, landed aristocracy, pomp and circumstance, then small fish like the baron, the world and his wife to see and be seen. The sound of a heavenly choir drifted out, coppery notes from an organ. A good funeral was a good show and she was at least seeing one of the sights.

But after the dust settled eyes turned elsewhere. Coronation mugs, egg cups, teapots began to fill shop windows. Eddie the Eighth's handsome mug everywhere. Good business for the pottery industry. Long live the king!

But rumours swirled that summer about Mrs. Simpson, the king's friend. Prime Minister Baldwin's bowler hat wasn't big enough to sit on his headache. The woman the king married should be queen and parliament would have to bring in a law to elevate this wife to that station. Would they fig! Patricia caught remarks but there was nothing in the papers. Not one of them went to print.

Tidying the London flat she found a copy of Time Magazine. She held it up and saw gaping holes in it. The baroness looked in. 'Madam, I didn't do this.'

The baroness gaily twitched the magazine away. 'Of course you didn't! They're being brought in from the States and a scissors job is done before they can go on sale.'

'Really?'

'The Americans are writing about Edward and Mrs. Simpson. We're not supposed to know anything.' She grinned at Patricia through one of the gaps.

'She's divorced, isn't she?'

'American and divorced. Twice!'

'Can't he find someone else?'

'He doesn't seem to want to. Unfortunately, I'm not available.'

Months after the old king died, a local paper in Bradford broke the story and a bugle cry sounded. London followed. Patricia had to go out and get armfuls of newspapers, squinting to read headlines on the way back. The Times and quality papers were against Mrs. Simpson. An adventuress! The Mail and the Express were on the side of the king. Friends dropped round to the flat to maul through it. In the small flat Patricia could hear it all.

Wasn't it love that mattered to the individual? - But the king was not simply an individual. - Who, after all, is completely free to follow their heart? Intellectuals said he should be free to choose. Why have the cloak and hypocrisy of adultery behind the front of a more suitable marriage?

Patricia plumped the cushions when they left and swept up cake crumbs. In her heart she sympathised with the king but her father had no time for him. The working class now felt he should do his duty. Couldn't he at least renounce some personal happiness? When their country called they were expected to die for their country. The king should stay at his post.

But her mother wrote in one of her frequent letters that Ben was not interested in tittle tattle about the Windsors, as they called themselves. He worried himself as usual about things he could do nothing about, especially in Europe. Hitler had walked armed men into the Rhineland to reoccupy it, bluffed it. Her mother wanted her eldest daughter back and Patricia longed for home.

Her heart turned when she saw Andrew's handwriting as she sorted the mail on the small mahogany table in the entrance corridor. She put it in her pocket, touched it as she worked through chores, sang through them. After preparing a light lunch for the baroness with plenty of salad to help her stay thin, she had half an hour to herself. The handwriting was clear, on cheap lined paper. He wanted to come for a visit, attend a peace rally in the capital and go to Dick Shepherd's church of St. Martin in the Fields. She scanned it quickly … a bit more about current affairs. Stuff about Spain now as well as Germany. He was beginning to sound like her father - but at least he didn't drink. She hid the letter under her pillow.

Next day she sat in the kitchen for her sandwich lunch. The little work place was bright with yellow and orange patterned wall tiles that looked sunny even on a dull day. She had Andrew's birthday gift with her, a book to drown in for half an hour, Vera Brittain's memories of the Great War. The butchery of the conflict 'to end all wars' came alive. Tears fell hot on her cheeks and she was unaware of the door opening till a hand touched her hair like the gentle brush of her mother's. She pressed her face into the warmth of a soft waist.

The baroness was gentle. 'What is it?' She shook her head. 'Have you had bad news?' Joyce Fitzgibbon knelt to her level. 'You can share it. You're part of this family.'

'*She* had bad news.' She pointed to the author's name on *Testament of Youth*. 'Do you know what they did when her fiancé was killed at the front?'

The baroness picked the book up. 'You're reading about the war!'

'They sent his uniform back and it was still caked hard with his blood. Can you imagine opening a thing like that?'

The baroness put the book firmly under her arm and stood up. 'I don't think you should be reading any more of this. You're young and you should be enjoying your life. What's the point of torturing yourself like that? You can't make history any different.'

'But we might blindly do the same things again!'

Her employer pulled her up. 'Come with me. I'll find you something more suitable. She rummaged along a bookshelf then tipped out a new volume with a bright harlequin on the dust jacket. 'Here, I haven't read this one yet, the latest Agatha Christie. That should cheer you up.'

'Andrew gave me the other one.'

The baroness smiled. 'I haven't confiscated your reading matter like at school. You'll have it back later but you can't be in floods of tears at lunch time. Or you could try *The Mysterious Mr Quin*. I haven't read this one either but I like the cover. Jeremy says it's good. It'll make you sleep better,'

'I thought they were murder stories.'

'Yes, but they're not real. You don't believe in the deaths, not really. It's just a puzzle, working out ... well ... who dunnit! You know?'

'I'll try it,'

'You'll sleep better, I'm sure. Imagine you're a better detective than the sleuth and lie thinking about clues. Oh, and motives. You mustn't forget motives.' She heard the door click. 'That's the baron, he's bought something, I believe. Come and help.' She put the books on a coffee table. 'Will you open the door? I think it's an antique, a spinet, like a harpsicord. They have to lift it in very, very carefully.'

Patrica slid along part of the parquet corridor. 'Should I lift the runner in case they stumble on it?'

'Yes, Jeremy'll kill me if there's an accident.'

She rolled the long red Afghan runner from Harrods into the cloakroom before opening the door. Two men were carefully carrying the instrument up the last of the stairs. They put it down gently, straightened, hefted it and walked without stopping into the living room. The baroness pointed to a cleared corner by the window and went over to examine the surface.

'No scratches, I guarantee,' the chief man looked her in the eye.

She smiled and reached in her purse for silver coins and they saw themselves out as Patricia looked at the warm sheen of rosewood with a lighter inlay. Her fingers caressed the pattern. 'What's the design made of?'

'Orange wood, I think. Jeremy'll know. I was terrified they'd damage it.' The baroness lifted the lid and Patricia gasped. On the inside of the three-cornered shape of the lovely instrument a reclining nude was painted, her chin and limbs angular, the expression of the upturned face disdainful.

She stepped back. 'I thought you said this was an antique.'

'Yes. Isn't it fun? Ancient and modern!'

'Won't this have ruined its value?'

'Jeremy thinks it will be a great talking point.' Patricia shook her head. 'We're having a small do next Sunday. Summer parties and excursions have been wonderful but we need to move indoors. If we start the ball rolling we'll get invitations through to Christmas. Will you be free to do a buffet for us?'

'Oh!' Her face fell. 'I was hoping to have the weekend off. Andrew's coming down on Friday.'

'What time?'

'Late. It'll be Saturday before I see him.'

'Then I think I could alter arrangements and make it Friday evening as that had been a possibility. Will you work later on Friday and have the whole of Saturday and Sunday free? Rory's not coming home from school till the following week.'

'Yes. That would work.'

'Cold cuts, sandwiches, salads, some pastries, savoury and sweet. Perhaps a trifle. Jeremy will see to drinks.' Patricia nodded. 'I'll buy the meats and savouries myself from Harrods. If you'd make a list for the trifle and anything else you think of I'd include that. But not like the one when we first met!' Patricia exchanged a smile with her. 'And ... one other thing. Our friends are into this naturist movement. Everyone will be in the nude. Would you be happy to be the same to serve ... but you could wear an apron?'

Patricia stood wide eyed. 'No, madam,' she said quietly, 'My father would come in person to collect me and take me home - even if we had to walk all the way.'

'Yes. Well, there's no need to be prudish.'

'He used to do amateur boxing.' Patricia held her face straight. 'I couldn't answer for what he might do.' She backed away.

'Mmmm. The workers are always more puritan. Stay in the kitchen, then. We'll use the serving hatch. I'll handle the teapot and open the door myself. Or we'll leave it unlocked.' The baroness smiled. 'Make sure your father doesn't accompany Andrew. We can't have a fistfight near this spinet. I don't know what we've paid for it ... I'll need a couple of small tables out, maybe three for that game of Monopoly. It's the rage at the minute.'

'Card tables as for bridge?' The baroness nodded and turned to contemplate the spinet. Patricia dashed for the kitchen and crashed onto a chair in silent laughter.

She had the whole of Friday to prepare for the evening's buffet. She cleaned the flat, pulled the leaves out on the dining table, stood the card tables out then dusted and polished the beautiful glowing horn of the gramophone. She carried spare chairs from the bedrooms, laid a cloth for the buffet and set out plates, cutlery and glasses. The baroness was arranging flowers to stand on it but the lid of the spinet lay chastely closed. The modern kitchen had eye-level cupboards and an extending table that folded out of sight, every inch of space used. Light flooded it in the morning and the tiles made it light when the sun lit the other rooms. She had a tiny vase with grasses and berries on the windowsill and a bright patterned Clarice Cliff teapot next to it. It didn't pour properly so Joyce Fitzgibbon had given it to her as an ornament.

The trifle was first. She built the sweet up in layers with her own egg custard and stewed fruit as the cook at Hexham had. Versions of her mother's apple tarts were popular, even though people who came here ate in good restaurants. Her pastry was almost as light as Mary's now. She was supposed to use pure butter but smuggled lard in from the butcher because it rubbed in quickly then she added a touch of butter for flavour.

Earlier she'd written out a timetable and concentrated on it to keep the evening's palaver at bay. The baroness, after all, was not going to open the door to the guests. Apparently it was not etiquette for one person to be naked while the others were clothed - and neighbours might be passing by. Patricia was to answer to the doorbell in her usual black uniform trimmed with white, show the gentlemen to the spare room and the ladies to the master bedroom to 'get ready'. Toiletries were laid out on the dressing table for the ladies. Even the baroness's favourite compact with a sunburst of crystals on the lid was for use. Their faces were not going to be nude. Patricia had to show them the new sun lamp in Rory's bedroom in case they wanted to use that for a few minutes. Clothes could also be left in there if the guests preferred. After that she was to stay in the kitchen in case anything was needed and push supplies quickly through the serving hatch. The cloakroom toilet could be used if necessary. Being simple and back to nature made life complicated! She had a portion of everything put by with a mini trifle and quietly packed something away for Andrew so they could have a picnic on his visit even if it was a cold October day.

With her polite servant's face she greeted everyone, showed them in and settled in her lair to listen to the slow rhythms of Duke Ellington's tones drifting through from the gramophone. She could hear the click when the record finished and the arm replaced on its hook. There was a sudden squeal of laughter then a tinny chord. Someone had discovered the secret of the spinet. Glasses clinked and a fair version of a few bars of Mozart wafted through in squeaky trills. The baron's novelties entertained his guests. She poured the glass of sherry madam had said she could have, sniffed the Christmassy vapour then put it down in case it went to her head. The chink of cutlery on china began and a song from another record blended with the voices.

Patricia ate her supper as the guests were eating and strained to listen through the music for instructions. Impossible not to eavesdrop on the conversation. She knew the voices of the fat colonel and his wife, madam and sir, of course, but most of them were disembodied, just like listening to the wireless.

'Are we ready to play?' the baron asked. 'O.K. just bring your drinks along. Go back for seconds of dessert if you want to.'

'Damn good trifle.' It sounded like the colonel.

'Anyone mind if I bring my yo-yo to the table? It helps me concentrate.'

'He's the winner of two competitions, you know.'

'Fine.'

'Two boards of Monopoly should be enough? The third table will do to put glasses and stuff on. Let's divide the markers. Do you want the top hat, colonel?

'Actually I've brought something special along. All this talk about a monster in Loch Ness - don't believe a word of it meself - but our blacksmith turned this little marker of him for me. There! Rather cute, isn't he?' Dragging of chairs across the floor and shrieks from the women. 'I see you all want him. Perhaps we should throw for him first?'

'Oh, yes! Personally, I believe in the monster. I've fallen for him hook, line and sinker.'

'Well, there's definitely something there, though we don't know what it is. Monks who live round the loch claim to have seen something but they didn't bother telling the rest of the world.'

'Trick of the light. Let's throw.'

There was the rattle of dice in a cup. 'There! A six and a four!'

'My turn.' Prolonged rattling in the cup. 'There's been a photo, you know, of its tail or spine. Two fives. That's just as good.'

'You women just like to be frightened, There, Double six! I think he's mine.'

'I'm sure you're cheating, darling.'

'Not as much as that photographer.'

'I'll put another record on. Would you like more swing?' Patricia heard the baroness operate the gramophone and head off disagreement. 'There. More drinks?' The mellow sound of alto sax filled the room then was turned down. 'Everyone got their marker?'

'Actually, I have another little fellow for the second table. I must say it's a nuisance sometimes not to have a pocket. I think I left him on the mantelpiece. Mind that damned yo-yo. You'll bash someone's shins.'

'Complete control, old boy. It soothes my nerves.'

'Prefer a cigar myself.' Patricia thought the throaty voice proved that. 'Anyway, here he is. The second mythical beast.'

'What is it?' Guests must be handling the thing.

'A mongoose!'

'What?' Female laughter and a few shrieks.

'Oh I know!' It sounded like the yo-yo man. 'Chap from the *Listener* went to the Isle of Wight to investigate a story. Farming family say they have a spiritual mongoose that comes and talks to them. Only, when the *Listener* editor turned up it had gone shy and wouldn't appear.'

'Stuff and nonsense.'

'It's fun, Jeremy. Anyway, let's roll the dice for him.'

Patricia heard a key in the lock. No one else had a key. She padded quietly along the hall as the door opened and saw Rory with a haversack and a small case. There was a rumpus in the front room and no one came out. 'What are you doing home early?' she whispered. 'There's a party going on.' The record changed to New Orleans jazz as she took his luggage and put it in the cloakroom.

'I've been sent home for being in a fight. They should have had a phone call.' He was almost as tall as Patricia and his voice was breaking. 'Can I go in?'

'No!' she hissed. 'They're all in the nude.' Rory kissed her on both cheeks, laughing. 'Can I come in the kitchen?'

'Shhh! If your're quiet. Have some supper. They're playing Monopoly.'

'Priceless.' Rory slipped through the kitchen door, spotted the sherry and downed the glassful before Patricia could stop him. 'I've got something I should take out of my haversack.'

'Don't clodhopper round,' she whispered.

'Just a few minutes, then,' he whispered back.

She gave him a slice of apple pie. 'Use your fingers.'

'Whitechapel!' came through the wall from the game. 'No one on that, so I'll buy it if I can have my two hundred pounds for passing GO.' Rory hovered listening. 'Buy up the East End and oust the Jew boys. Thank you very much, two hundred quid should do it nicely. Bet I make more than you do on Park Lane, old boy.'

'No chance.'

'I have another turn, I think.' They heard the dice shake. 'Perfect! I'll buy the Old Kent Road. Show the Kykes some trouble between us, eh?.' A stopper clinked and liquor glugged in a glass.

'All those refugees that have come through the East End!'

'Not just the East End. I tell you, if the colonies are to be given away to other nations we should make a start in Hampstead! Full of foreign emigrés, putting it politely.'

'They're going to be shown trouble, though. Mosley's going to have another march through the East End this weekend. He's had a lot of success recruiting blackshirts.'

'You see, you can't blame them.' It sounded like the colonel. 'Look at the wages the Jew boys pay.'

'Almost slave labour.'

'Exactly, my dear.'

'Then you should see the Jews themselves - swishing round in showy clothes.'

'Not an issue here!'

'Dripping diamonds, the women!'

'You're all so beautiful you don't need all that.'

'Hmm!'

'Well, I don't mind telling you I've put a bit of money Mosley's way to keep his British Union of Fascists going. They've lost ground up in the North but if he can win the battle of the streets in the capital he can get somewhere.' The dice rattled.

'It's been very violent, you know.'

'Just a means to an end, my dear. Look at Mussolini and Hitler. They've got law and order and they've got their economy going. Clean up the wastrels. Clean up the Jews. Keep the damn Bolshevics at bay or we'll have a revolution. I mean, look at what's happening in Spain. You can't let the Communists get control.'

'And those idiots – have you seen them? - going over there thinking they can help the damned Republicans ... I'll tell you what they are ... a load of so-called intellectuals pretending they've got bleeding hearts for the poor. Are they? No! They're acting as left-wing spies for foreign powers. Others are beachcombers or layabouts of every kind. A dose in the real army'd sort them out!'

Patricia shut her ears at the voices and looked up to see Rory sidle back into the kitchen with something wrapped in what looked like a Superman comic.

'Home Secretary and the Commissioner for the Met are sending mounted police and bobbies on foot to clear the Fascists' route, or so I heard.'

'I'm behind law and order.'

'You've landed on Mayfair, Colonel.'

'Drat! Not paying attention.'

Rory stole the sherry glass, filled it again and placed something from the comic on his shoulder.

'What's that?' Patricia whispered.

'Pet ferret,' he whispered back and drank the sherry. 'Marmaduke Superferret.'

Another voice from the other side of the serving hatch. 'Well, I must say your talking mongoose seems to have brought me luck, Colonel. I can put my second house on Park Lane. I'll take your £200 from you before you can claim it.'

'Watch out! Watch that damned yo-yo.'

'Come on, mongoose, bring me luck this throw.'

Rory eased the serving hatch open before Patricia could stop him and threw his ferret in among the guests.

'Something's on the yo-yo. Get it off!'

'It's the mongoose! The real one.'

'It's tangling me in it. Help! The string's round ...'

'It's a damn ferret! Grab the thing!'

'Get a shoe box, Patricia!' the baroness shrieked

Rory ran to the cloak room and came back with a cardboard box. 'I can get him, dad.'

'What are you...? Stay where you are.'

'It's run under that table.'

'Thank God it's off me.'

The serving hatch flew open and the baron's face appeared, blocking the scene of naked bodies running round. 'Rory! Get in here and get that damned animal under control. Then get out again!'

Rory slid into the lounge and held something in his hand to the ferret. It lunged forward, bit his hand but he caught it by the scruff of the neck. 'Out!'

The boy rushed into the kitchen. 'Can I have some milk? That'll settle him.' Patricia opened the refrigerator, poured the top cream into a saucer and put it on the floor.

Rory stroked his pet and put its nose in the cream. 'There now. Good Marmaduke, There's a good fellow.'

There was a scream from the other room. 'Be careful with the scissors!'

'It's all right. They're only nail scissors.' The baroness's voice sounded strangled. 'I'm not attacking your manhood. There, I think that's the ... blessed yo-yo string freed.'

'All that talk of Kykes, old chap. I thought she was going to circumcise you.'

Rory sat on the floor with the calmed ferret in his lap, tears coursing down his face. He shook his head 'Wait till I tell this one at school! Whatever dad does to me, it'll be worth it. I tell you, it'll be worth it!' Patricia cuffed him.

Next day she claimed her promised day off and met Andrew at Leicester Square just as everything was opening. It was fresh after rain, the streets and window panes sparkled. Hand in hand, free in the capital, they looked at the picture house hoarding, Charlie Chaplin with his white face, big kohl-rimmed eyes, top hat and flappy shoes but they could watch Chaplin at home. Further on they bought a paper and looked for a place to breakfast. Andrew had hardly eaten and was taken by the idea of a milk bar, straight from the States, shiny, new, neon lights outside even in day time, counters of stainless steel, quick, clean white-coated service, high stools like in the movies, open day and night. Health conscious men went to them instead of the pub. They walked till they found one and counted coins out for the price of milk and a sandwich. That would have to serve as lunch too, but Patricia had leftovers from the kitchen. In the paper she'd wrapped them up in was an advert for a Mystery Rail Trip and they started to plan Andrew's next visit. The sandwiches amazed them, three tiers with things they wouldn't normally mix, bacon, lettuce, tomatoes. It felt they were in another place, another time, another country as they watched the young man mix milk shakes in a machine then sipped them though straws or got milky moustaches over their lips. They'd have liked to stay longer but couldn't buy anything else.

Outside again Andrew stopped at a bookshop window to gaze at posters with emaciated versions of Madonna and child. Faces of the women had been shaded by artists to show bones almost breaking through the skin. 'Living skeletons,' he muttered and squeezed Patricia's hand tight. One of the backgrounds was red, emphasising the skull like face. 'This is what people are brought to in Spain … we think we're badly off. Civil war! Look,' he pressed her hand again and pointed to the wording. *They face famine in Spain.*'

There's nothing we can do.' Patricia resented this intrusion to their happiness.

'I think there are collection points where you can donate food or money. I'll have to find one. If I had medical training I'd go out there to help.'

'Andrew, I need you here.' She tugged him gently and they walked on.

Their mood had dampened but they went on by tube to Westminster and began to recover the feeling of holiday, then they wandered by the riverside looking at the Houses of Parliament and on to the statue of Boadicea. Andrew was distracted by graffiti round the base. Big letters spelled out:

Palmerston and Pitt guided the British Empire from

'Anti- League of Nations feeling. You'd think we'd learn to join the rest of the world. I'd like to go to a peace rally tonight.'

She nodded. 'I've seen a peace march by the youth branch of the Labour Party,'

'Good, but let's forget politics now.' He kissed her mouth and they laughed against each other's' shoulders. 'The world's ours today.'

Like tourists they took a boat trip down the river to Kew, looking at the reflected images of buildings and the trees with leaves already crisping. They talked about the nudist party the night before.

'Too much time on their hands, too much money, too little sense,' he said.

Patricia laughed and decided not to tell him about the painting on the spinet. 'Rory's losing his pocket money for three months, he's grounded over the school holiday and has to write a personal letter of apology to everyone who attended the party.' She shrugged. 'He says he really doesn't care. He'll have a whale of a time spinning this yarn back at school.'

It rained but Andrew had an umbrella. Gardens at Kew were fragrant, even in autumn and dappled light fell on the water as they rode back. It was the most perfect day since she was a child when her father circled life and her mother was happy. After the trip, tea at Lyons with neat clippies in white-trimmed black dresses - a bit like her own uniform - but with starched hats. They ate cream buns and would have to save up for another time.

At the Albert Hall Vera Brittain would be on the platform so Patricia was happy. She'd retrieve her book from the baroness to finish it. Once there she observed the people. It was Andrew's world, big gatherings, similar to her father's. Dick Shepherd was known from his spell at St Martin-in-the Fields, A. E. Housman was also on the platform but for her the star must be Vera Brittain. Seats filled up.

'What did they have on the banners?'

'Who?'

'The Youth League of the Labour Party you saw.'

'Oh, yes. Let me think a minute ... *"I MAY BE GASSED"; "WAR MEANS RATIONS AND QUEUES"; "I MAY LOSE MY BROTHER"'* Her hands clenched. 'Christopher's eleven. I hope life's settled by the time he leaves school.' Andrew took her hand. 'The baroness wants me to stay in tomorrow morning as Rory's grounded.'

'I'll attend morning service at St Martin-in-the Fields. Could be something of the spirit of Dick Shepherd there. Meet me there when you're free.'

She listened to the rustle of programmes, the fall and rise of voices, people waving to each other, dropping things, moving in and out of the rows , men clapping each others' shoulders, women kissing, low ripples of laughter. Andrew read a note he found on his seat:

Join the Peace Pledge Union.

'This is Dick Shepherd's baby,' he said and folded it into his breast pocket. 'The vicar I was talking about who was at St Martin-in-the-Fields.'

A burst of clapping as the speakers came out onto the stage. Andrew sat, rapt. Patricia watched the small, neat figure of Vera Brittain in a tailored dark coat. It was not her words that impressed Patricia when she spoke of the League of Nations. Young lives lost. The prosperity of entire countries destroyed. It was her suffering that gave depth to her words, that powered her passion.

Dick Shepherd stood up, quiet, in civvies except for his dog collar and spoke of the cruel conditions the troops endured in trenches without any escape in the misnamed 'Great War'.

'And what I'm often asked,' he said speaking into the microphone as if in conversation with a friend, is "What if foreign troops came, burst into your house and tried to rape your sister? Well, my answer is that I would physically put myself between the men and her to protect her and use all means to chase them from our home.' He paused, held his hand up, held the moment. 'What would not help my sister is if I were marching in a foreign land far away, armed to the teeth, a threat to other women's homes and safety and also to their children!' Sporadic applause. 'We don't preach *Peace at any price*'. No. *Love at all cost.*' Clapping swelled and broke round the hall. 'We all know the commandment to love our neighbour,' he went on, 'well, we should try it. If governments won't act first and foremost humanely, we have to do it ourselves - by refusing to kill one another.' He sat down.

Further applause, then silence for A. E. Housman who held the audience with his address. War led not to peace but to a vortex of more and more death. They were still.

When the speeches were made Andrew whispered. 'I'm going to join this.

'Join what?' She was dazed.

'The Peace Pledge Union.'

Patricia read the card that had been on her seat. *I renounce war and never again directly or indirectly will I support or sanction another.* Still moved by Housman she said, 'I'll sign as well.'

'We don't know what the cost might be one day.' He kissed her wet cheek.

'And we don't know the cost if we don't.'

They wrote signatures and went forward hand in hand.

Next day, after the heavy emotion of the previous evening they felt released, light hearted. Andrew wanted to explore the East End where his hostel was and they boarded a train and got out at Aldgate East holding hands, chattering. Then they heard the chanting and memory came back to Patricia.

'Perhaps we should go back. This is near Mosley's planned march. I'd forgotten.'

He tightened his hand in hers. 'Or maybe we should go and see what's going on. What are they shouting?' They burst into the light of the street into crowds, hammering voices. Police on foot were trying to hack their way through a line of men and women backed endlessly down the street by thousands more. Heads strained forward, arms linked.

'THEY SHALL ....'

Batons unsheathed. The chanters' heads held high.

'NOT ...'

A line of police charged.

'PASS!'

Horses' hooves crushing down either on the road or on human feet. Ranks of blackshirts waited, led in person by Mosley in fresh tailored black, shiny high boots and military-style cap, peak gleaming in the late rays of the October sun. Police fell back, ready to charge the line resisting the blackshirt procession. The line stiffened, arms locked. Every road seemed blocked with police, Fascists, or their opponents.

'THEY ...'

Andrew grabbed Patricia by the waist and pulled her back, trying to find a pavement.

'SHALL ...'

The mouth of the station was clogged.

'NOT ...'

Two policemen pushed them out of the way.

'Move! Get into Cable Street. Don't obstruct. We've got a job to do.'

'PASS!'

A roar from the Mosleyites.

Patricia felt herself pushed backwards, praying she wouldn't fall. She tried to look round. Andrew wasn't there. No end to the throng. Answering calls to the blackshirts. Her ears hurt, popped. The din made her dizzy, she was pressed back helpless. Andrew was cast on this sea of people. Panic clawed at the merciless hammering noise. She felt nauseous.

Louder and louder:

'THEY SHALL ...'

A coat was up against her face, rough threads shredding her nose, suffocating.

'... NOT ...'

Her brain was going to explode.

'... **PASS!**'

A hand pressed her buttocks and she couldn't scream. 'Oh God!' A sudden surge forward. She rocketed free, gulped air, knots behind her eyes.

'Patricia!' He was calling but she couldn't see. 'Here!'

'Where? Where?'

His hand reached across a shoulder. She strained. He pushed and heaved her through. 'You're crying. Come here.'

'We'll never get out.'

He pulled her near the front of the swirling clot of chaos. Police were hacking at a barricade of flung-together mess. Bill boards, paving flags, planks of wood, an overturned lorry and a heaving press of people refusing to move. Horses were whinnying, instincts reining them back against unseen forces, terrified, hag-ridden. Hatred in the air they breathed. She saw a glint of broken glass. Riders picked their way through it then children's marbles rolled, crunched under the hooves, the animals slipped, nostrils flared and they backed into beasts behind them, bucking, in blind funk trying to rear, the horses themselves became a barrier.

Hundreds of police. A charge was forced back by the East End protesters, batons falling on their shoulders, on any shoulders. Patricia looked away, her throat closed.

'Charge!'

A thud. Cursing. Scrambling.

'Charge!'

Battering against a wall of débris, of bodies.

'Charge!'

Deep groans. A cheer.

'Charge!'

She opened her eyes. Cudgels thwacked and bounced back, hurting the arms of the police.

'Charge!'

The line behind the barrier, men and women with clenched teeth, panting,

'Again! Charge!'

supported by the line behind,

'Charge!'

sweating,

'Charge!'

heaving,

'Charge!'

Arms round waists to hold the line. Shoulders together.

'Charge! There's a break! We're through!'

Men spun backward, wreckage flying, falling. Fresh hands, arms collected the débris, backs bent to salvage it, a strong voice directed and a new barricade rose up feet behind the first.

'THEY SHALL NOT PASS!'

Roars.

Patricia looked round and saw Mosley talking with a policeman in a similar peaked cap. She caught the word '... impossible.' Mosley tense, white. '... out of the East End ... stay out.'

The crowd seemed to catch the order they could not hear and the mood changed. They cheered, the racket fiercer than the chant of resistance, surging forward.

Andrew took her firmly by the hand. 'Out. We fight our way through.' The police turned to directing the crowd. Terrified beasts were eased out, calmed. The knot of people at the mouth of the railway station opened for them to stumble through. 'Don't trip over.' He held her waist as she struggled for breath, trampling through at the head of a herd of folk escaping. A stench of stale urine hit her nostrils as they pushed forward in the grim neglected old building. Her eyes were stinging as they reached the grubby platform. 'A piss hole!' Andrew muttered. She looked up at him. 'Public lavatory, to you.' He kissed her head.

They got off at Liverpool Street Station and walked till they found somewhere to sit and draw breath, ordered hot tea with sugar, crammed sweet things in their mouths.

'You have to get out of London.'

'As soon as I can.' Tremors were running up and down her spine. She breathed in steam from the tea. Andrew put sugar in for her, she drank it slowly and he sat silently sipping from a big earthenware cup with faint veins spidering beneath the glaze. 'Is anything else wrong?'

'Something I haven't mentioned.' She waited while a cold sweat gave way to warmth in her stomach. 'I didn't want to spoil the weekend.' He dried up.

'What is it? It's worse not to know.'

'I've been picked to go on the hunger march from Jarrow.'

'When?'

'Tomorrow.' Patricia's hand stopped half way to her mouth. 'You'll never make it back in time. You should have let me know. We could have cancelled.'

'We're always cancelling. I wonder we haven't cancelled our lives. I didn't expect them to pick my name out. Anyway, we had a perfect day yesterday. I can sleep on the bus and I've packed my supplies all ready.'

She felt like weeping. 'Andrew, you'll make yourself ill. You know what your chest is like ... and you'll let people down if you're not there for the off.'

'The supplies are at your dad's house, I'll go straight from the bus. The vicar said he'd call in to see if I'd made it and give me a lift - if not, he'll ask your dad to take my place.'

'Mam'll hit the roof.'

'It'll probably be all right. Don't worry. Anyway ... it means I'll see you again before long.'

15

Ben attended Labour and Union meetings again, came across Bessy and said sorry with his eyes. She made the slightest bow of her head and her eyes lingered on his for a second. She'd be the one if he was single, he was sure she knew, but not even Wilf was aware they had reached out to each other.

The same bare, clean upper room at the Co-op with the faint smell of sawdust where they met to plan the strike ten years earlier. Bessy still wore the smart navy coat she had made from a turned greatcoat from the war. She preserved it by steaming the heavy material with an iron through damp cloth.

Business. Three years since Palmer's' shipyard had gone under, but the town was in complete crisis now. Precise, Bessy was ready to take notes for the minutes. Ben was alive to the warmth from her.

'We're here to discuss Jarrow.' Wilf started the agenda. 'We all know a third of British shipbuilding's gone to the scrappers and Jarrow's a part of that, keeping the other two thirds profitable, they say.'

'But it's McGowan's ran Palmer's shipyard down completely,' Ben said bitterly. 'Jarrow sacrificed for the Clyde. You know what they're saying in Jarrow? - St. Bede founded it, Sir Charles Palmer built it and McGowan buggered it.'

'I know, Ben, I know, man. We all feel it.' Wilf shook his head. 'We have to look at facts, though. See if we can marshall something out of them.'

'Facts? The _fact_ is,' Ben butted in, 'ninety per cent of the community's been involved by the time everything's gone - with knock-on effects. And it _has_ gone. Gone to hell. To the knacker's yard.' His voice was rising.

Wilf gently tapped the table. 'O.K. But let's keep a hold for a minute. We have to look at this claim here from the government that things is improvin'. A government statement says,' he put his glasses on and peered importantly at a typed sheet, 'that unemployment's down by half.'

Ben needed to shout. 'Well, I've just been *down* there and I can tell you it's a workhouse without walls. They feel no difference at Jarrow! The criss-cross of cranes is down and you can see the last hope's gone. Their death rate's the highest in the whole damn country, man!'

'Ben, lower your voice,' Bessy wrote without looking up. 'We have to try to observe procedures.'

Wilf put his chewed pencil down. 'We're all with you, lad. But how can they claim to have done it? And, more to the point, how can we make something of it?'

Bessy looked up from the minutes. 'They've done it by joining Jarrow Labour Exchange with Hebburn's. Things are not so bad at Hebburn so they can roll the figures for them both together and say the unemployment's dropped.'

'Fiddling the books!' Ben burst out again. 'In a noble tradition! Meanwhile the death of a community stinks to high heaven and the government starves them of contracts.'

'I know, Ben.' Wilf was losing control of the meeting. 'You're not the only one that cares. Belgian shipyards got Palmer's machinery at scrap price. You're not the only one that's done some homework.'

'Aye, and we'll be buying things back from them in a few years. We should've achieved more through the General Strike.' He dropped his voice. 'We failed.'

'No point dwelling in the past,' Wilf said. 'We're here to look at what can be done. The main point at issue is other employment for the town. They've been on about a steelworks to take up the labour.'

'I'm afraid that's been scuppered,' Bessy said.

Ben looked her in the eyes for a second time. 'Do you have inside knowledge?'

'I've a nephew lives there and they've been told the plan's dead. It's just not going to happen. They're murdering the town for a second time. There's talk of organising a march from there to London.'

Another voice chimed in. 'And do what?'

She stared at the speaker. 'Get a mass petition up and present it in parliament. So I want to propose we give any support we can from this meeting.'

'There've been hunger marches before. And I know for a fact the Labour MP for Gateshead doesn't agree with it. Mounted police in London ran the lads from Blackburn down in the streets when they tried it a few year back. And they filched their petition that had a million signatures on it. They just don't want to know.'

Ben stamped his foot. 'How do we know they'll kill this one? The other points at issue,' he wagged a finger at the meeting, 'are the means test and long-term unemployed. They cut benefit off completely if you're out of work for long.'

Anger was sweeping round the table. 'And where are the jobs?'

'I'll march with them personally,' Ben said, 'if it gets off the ground. Men have to try to do something for their own self respect.' He glared round. 'Anyone else?'

'Aye.'

'I'm in.'

'Gan on.'

Bessy interrupted them. 'We'll see if they actually need you to march. Best left to men redundant from the yard.'

'Men from the pits and the yards should stand together – everybody should stand together.'

'But we need a formal motion that any help available for the hunger march will be given to Jarrow, and we'll help to organise the petition.'

'Seconded,' Wilf said.

'Show of hands?' Bessy had no need to count. 'Carried!'

Bessy went out and carried a tea urn in with milk. She'd brought little cakes made from some old margarine, a cracked egg and flour with damaged packaging the Co-op couldn't sell. The cakes were all cut in half. Ben took the urn from her for the weight and filled the cups himself.

'I heard something was actually happening about the employment,' Wilf said after he swilled the last crumbs down. 'There *is* some money being ploughed into the town. Somebody's raised cash in Surrey, quite generous. That must be doin' something. Do you have any more inside knowledge?'

'Yes,' Bessy handed the cakes round. 'And I know it's very kind of them. But it's taking too long. Jack, my nephew, got something.'

'There you are, then.'

Bessy put her cup down. 'Do you know what it was? ... a pot of paint and a pot of distemper. For to brighten his 'little house' with.' She put her fingers to her mouth but tears forced down her cheeks and a gutteral sob tore her throat.

Ben held himself back as Wilf took her hand. 'Come on, lass. *Yor* always strong. You hold us men together.'

She shook her head. 'A pot ... of paint!' She groaned into her hand.

Ben got up scraping his chair. 'Well, I'll march if they want me. I don't care what the family says to stop me.' He lurched down the steps and into the cold. 'Whatever it takes!' He shouted his defiance to the empty street. 'And, St Bede - if you were around - you could do something for me, you old goat! I just wish **somebody** would get me a drink!' He collapsed against the cold dark metal of a lamp post.

Andrew had mentioned that he was still going to London to see Patricia and joked they might be able to use another old timer if he didn't make it back. Only two hundred could go and Ben could have his place.

The old pitman was up early as usual on the Monday of the March, breakfasted by seven. He felt he was in touch with the world by keeping old habits and his internal alarm still woke him after ten years out of work. He'd never needed a knocker up. Every morning he was taut, ready to speed off to the mine. Every morning he had to step into a cold reality.

An hour later John Hargraves knocked at the door. 'What can I do for your reverence?

'Where's Andrew?'

'Haven't seen him or heard from him. He's probably gone straight to Jarrow. Come in.'

John Hargraves lowered his voice. 'If he's not here by now something's wrong. He said you were to take his place. I thought you knew.'

'Thought he was joking.'

'Get your things, you're to take his haversack of supplies. I'll run you in.'

Ben quietly tossed a few clothes together, wrote a note for Mary and stuck it on the mantelpiece.

'Hurry, Ben. I'll start the car. There's a spare jumper in the boot, you can have that.'

The dignitaries of Jarrow gathered. Ben's heart warmed when he saw the MP, little Ellen Wilkinson, fiery as her red hair, ready to lead them. She was going to be with them from the beginning in spite of her breathing problems. The mayor stood proud, the bishop in his purple vest was ready to give a blessing, one or two councillors fell in.

The mayor stepped forward, chain of office glinting, to give them a word. 'Remember,' they could just hear, 'you're going to London for Jarrow and we depend on you to maintain the credit of the town.'

Alcohol was banned.

Women and bairns were waving, trying not to shiver in the autumn day.

Andrew had left twists of baccy, so Ben went down the line giving them out. They were shuffling, waiting to start, hoisting embroidered banners of their trades on poles, jostling, laughing to get their balance and hold the flags against a buffeting wind. Excitement was like the fairground, and a cheer leapt from hundreds of throats as a bowler-hatted councilor led off, carrying the banner

Jarrow Crusade. Little Ellen Wilkinson walked with him, a crew from Movietone newsreels filmed them following four abreast, women joined their marching song and a stray black dog ran alongside.

Oh me lads, ye should have seen them gannin'
passin' along the Scotswood Road
just to see them stannin'
Aal the lads an' lasses there,
Aal wi' smilin' faces
Gannin' alang the Scotswood ROOAAD
To see the Blaydon Races!

Cheers almost drowned the singing and Ben stepped out among the family men making the column, half of them ex-service, wearing British Legion badges under their waterproofs. Was this what they'd gone through the trenches for? Ben would have spat in the gutter but it was bad form. Here and there obvious blokes from Special Branch monitored the marchers for Communist riffraff. He snorted. In Jarrow the number of Communists could be counted on the fingers of one hand.

When they got to Ferryhill the *Shields Gazette* cheered them up.

'Have a look at this, lad.' A fellow marcher waved the paper in Ben's face as they took a break. 'It's time somebody stood up for us. The Labour Party's done nowt – and the other papers ignore us or throw shit at us. Listen to this: *"... the tramp, tramp of Jarrow men, swinging onwards today to Ferryhill marching half the length of England carrying the woes and troubles of not only their town but of all the distressed areas to the capital, is beating out history as it wakens the echoes of the villages and towns on its route." '*

They passed the article from hand to hand. 'Good for little Shields! Nobody else wants to know.'

Women brought out fresh-baked bread for them, warm stottie cakes flat and easy to handle without plates.

Ben carried two rolled up blankets and hadn't had his clothes off his back. Mary'd want to burn them when he got back but they couldn't afford new. He might have to keep John's jumper. Sleeping was where they could, community halls, church halls, on the floor of the Mechanics Institute. Blisters were the worst. Andrew had packed a roll of sticking plaster and Ben swore afterwards that it saved his life. He'd packed a spare pair of socks but it was difficult to wash them out. He had to alternate them.

When they could get hold of a newspaper Ben scanned the columns for reports of their progress but they gave little space to the march, the odd few inches slighting in tone

Elegant grey-brown hands, fine fingers like a musician's or a bank teller's snatched the Mail from under his nose – Ali, third generation Yemeni, born on the windswept edge of England where breakers from Denmark smashed against its cliffs.

'How much of that do ye believe?' he asked, his North East accent thick as clarts. 'Ah'll tell ye what ter look for. The name and the date. And look at *them* twice. Waste of time, man.'

'Aye, you're right, Ali.'

'Doesn't stop the folk comin' to meet wer. Had a hot pie yesterday, fresh from the baker's oven. What ah'm waitin' for's a brass band.'

'I'll order one,' Ben said.

Blistered feet were eased in a village by a gift of warm thick socks knitted by members of the Women's Institute. Practical wifies. Every man jack of them could have kissed the ladies. Further on Ali had his wish but it was a silver band playing them in. Yorkshire welcomed them with crowds - Northallerton, Ripon, Harrogate. Anglican and Methodist clergymen came out and a few politicians. They were fed ham sandwiches. On the way they'd heard the Unemployment Assistance Board had announced that families in Jarrow whose men were on the march would receive no payment during the marchers' absence. Ben saw one man take the ham from his sandwich, put it in an envelope and post it back to his folk.

In Nottingham people turned out. Cobblers tore the shoes off their feet to mend while they waited. Ben had stopped under a sign, a battered board with a faded name that read *Tailors for three generations.* Two men with tape measures hung from their necks emerged from the shop, fell on him and Ali and told them to take their pick of ready-made suits. Ben let them turn him round and measure across his shoulders, allowed them to take off his old clothes that were shiny with wear but not throw them away. After they dressed him in trousers and jacket with the warm smell of smooth new wool he and Ali left the shop almost in tears.

Halls were found to sleep in where they ate soup and bread like kings, a collection of Geordie lads, second generation Irish, Scots who'd migrated over Hadrian's wall, Yemeni, bound by the secret weapon of friendship. The oldest man who marched had fought in the Boer War then the Great War, one of five brothers who lived to come back.

Songs carried them on against bright bitter wind and bright skies.
Keep your feet still, Geordie, hinny.
let's be happy through the neet,
for we may not be so happy through the day.
Oh-oh. give us that bit comfort,
Keep your feet still, Geordie lad
an' divn't drive me bonny dreams away!
When they had to rest their throats from singing a fierce debate raged about the civil war in Spain.

'We cannot have it, man. How can our government stand by and watch as a bloody general marches in to try to overthrow an elected government?'

'Aye but you could argue it's none of our business.'

'None of our business? What happens there today might happen here tomorrow. It's been a long fight ter try ter get a better society …'

'And d'ye think we've done it. Go back ter yer dreams. I mean, look at us now! Parliament doesn't want to know. These emotional outbursts! That's all we are to them.'

'We haven't got soldiers' boots in wa faces yet. That's what I'm talking about. It doesn't take very long to overturn everything!'

Another lad spoke up. 'What I heard was that some blokes from England that have a little plane – the rich man's toy – only went and picked Franco up and took him over to the mainland.'

'I don't believe that! Which rag did ye read that in? Or was it in the pub?'

'Anyway, the point is people are suffering, starving. And if our own government won't do anything about it …'

'Hard faced man, that Baldwin. I'd like to knock his bowler hat off.'

'… well, the likes of us are going over to try to fight against this take over. The Brigades, they're called.'

'They'll just get themselves killed an all. What good will that have done?'

A few of the youngest shut this out and still had the energy to dance about to improvised ragtime at the end of the day. The veteran of two wars would have joined the republicans if he'd been younger, he said. He and Ben sat back, too old, too weighed down with family lives. But a white heat of argument raged on whether it was the greatest battle of their time.

'Neutrality, lads,' Ben said. 'Not engaging on either side in a foreign state's affairs.'

'Well, it's despicable! There's atrocities.'

'It's war. Brother against brother's the worst kind.' He felt old in his bones, damping down hot-heads of youth. 'There's nothing to stop anybody volunteering. But it's another thing for a foreign state to intervene.'

In spite of weariness they argued into the night and in the morning almost needed a shovel to lift them from the bare planks they'd shared.

But a rush of energy buoyed them when they finally hit the capital, when they arrived at Marble Arch after trekking over two hundred and ninety miles. They hardly felt the sting of rain on their faces. The assembly point for a rally next day was Hyde Park, where they sat on cold-hardened grass to listen to Ellen Wilkinson, then the following afternoon it was to gather near the Houses of Parliament. Ben's heart stilled at the sight of the building, a hazy mirror of the river reflecting the warm tones of the gothic spire.

Then the hunger marchers were surprised by the approach of well-dressed men greeting them with smiles and the offer of a boat trip on the Thames.

'What's to lose, lads?'

Most of them took the free trip, being treated as important visitors. The younger firebrands about to take boats directly for Spain for the battle of their time, even they couldn't resist this treat. Ben thought it odd. Why offer this after ignoring them or blackening their names as they tramped the length of the country? Something smelt bad. He decided with a few others to have a look at the public gallery if they'd let him in.

From there he looked down on an almost empty chamber, one of the few to witness the longest serving MP of the Newcastle area present their petitions at the Bar of the House. Eleven thousand signatures from Jarrow itself, a second petition from other Tyneside towns. M.P Wilkinson asked a question. 'Prime Minister, will you meet with representatives of the march?' Ben leaned forward.

Hardly looking up Prime Minister Baldwin said, 'I'm sorry, Ellen. I don't have the time.' The hunger marchers sailed safely down the Thames creating no havoc.

Cheated.

When they got back a cup of tea was the sum of their glory. No trumpet call. No rolling triumph. A cup of tea.

Ben met Patricia at the baron's apartment when her employers were out and was glad to see where she worked. A few days later the marchers returned on a special train from King's Cross.

16

Louise had been married for over a year, sorry to give up work and leave the Golf Club. Motherhood was now supposed to be her future. Time hung. Empty time stirred up thoughts of Joe; the turn of his head as he glanced over his shoulder, deep blue eyes shining to greet her as he talked with someone else, the bend of his head as he lit her elegant cigarette and in a polished movement looked in her eyes the way they did in the movies, clean fingers unspoiled by harsh work that lightly traced the arc of her foot, how he lifted her, the brush of his lips on her throat.

But marriage was not such a void as she had thought it might be - signing away her life. Edward was a sweet and tender lover and though his demands were not great his affection, his tenderness could touch her. She hardly noticed how painful his feet seemed the day after they made love, feet set and reset half a dozen times in childhood to turn them round, the delicate matter between husband and wife not discussed. He did not explain.

She went over to help her mother but Diane had the housework in hand and resented interference, so she had a cup of tea with Ben or went with him into town to the market. Ben would ride his pushbike but between them father and daughter carried enough to make a bus fare worthwhile. Cracked eggs carefully wrapped in newspaper, tomatoes with skins beginning to crinkle that would fry, the end of a bacon joint, ham bones for soup, old carrots from the bottom of a box, pigs' trotters that made her shudder, cooking apples for Mary, plums with pitted skins, meat if it was turning too dark but they could steep in salt and Mary could stew. No money from the pawnshop because nobody could redeem their things but Ben tended his vegetables and none of them starved. Lentils or split peas and onions with allotment potatoes, beef fat rendered for dripping in the slow oven of the range when the fire was on and

Mary's bread dipped in the dark sediment. All the greens Ben could grow. They were never ill.

But Louise could see the age ten years of unemployment had put on her father. His skin puckered like the tomatoes they rescued. Her dad. He seemed shrunken in height, wounded in spirit, though he still argued politics with an intensity that could frighten her. The wireless said they were coming out of depression. Who believed stuff like that? The flicker of hope in her dad was snuffed out. He no longer expected work, no longer was the hero of their house, one of the thousands of the downtrodden. He looked at her and she saw him recognise a flash of restlessness, knew he thought she needed a baby in her arms, looked back and saw his hope to be a grandparent, his only immortality.

Now and then she saw Joe in their shopping centre with his wife, more often it was Evie alone, trailing, wan faced. She'd gone back to him, always showed up again like a bad penny. They never spoke. Evie was sad, with a sadness that didn't lift and Joe was not a man to understand. She still thought he'd been trapped and was bitterly glad the trap had brought no happiness. Now and then she caught sight of him alone and tensed. If he saw her he smiled but she turned her back, thinking it might be mockery in the smile. He had not set up house expensively, though he could have bought a property if he'd wanted to. It was his business what he did with his money. He drove a Baby Austin instead. She had no desire to discuss married life with him, the weather, what the papers said, whether his father knew Lloyd George as the little chant sang. They had each made their beds.

At weekends she and Edward kept up the gatherings in someone's house but more and more of her friends were married and the evenings had changed. Guests still brought something to eat, taking potluck with their supper, or they might take a turn at providing supper. It was often a hand of cards afterwards rather than dancing. If someone did start the dancing she sat out with Edward and leaned against him as he put his arm round her. From time to time Joe appeared, once in a blue moon with his wife. Once he was drunk. She was not there. December they met at the same house.

She and Edward had arrived with Fred and Katharine. Joe brought his gramophone but not his wife. Records waited. They played whist and concentration settled over the card table as the dealer shuffled, dealt, the players sorting their hands. Louise threw a farthing into the middle of the table and found Joe gazing at her. Four months since they'd met. She looked down at the neatly arranged suits, black then red. She could see his hands across the table, cards sorted, familiar hands she had kissed.

Against her will, against judgment, against common sense she looked up, his eyes predatory, waiting, a cat to its mouse. The hand she was dealt was good and she smiled at the group. He smiled openly at her, not caring what anyone might think. Katharine opened the hand and talked to Joe, diverting him. Louise was grateful. Talk dried, concentration in the very backs of the players as they played out the game of skill and chance. Louise took five of the seven tricks and laughter burst out as she scooped her winnings. An hour later, when they took a break, she was still winning.

Katharine disappeared into the tiny scullery to make sandwiches for the hostess. Louise carefully put on a pinafore to protect the wedding outfit she'd chosen to wear. Of all evenings he had to be there tonight. Edward had sliced the loaf for them before they came out. It was their turn to feed the hungry and they quickly smeared the slices with a mixture of margarine and a little butter and milk, shelled hard boiled eggs, chopped and beat them with salad cream, vinegar and pepper then filled and stacked the sandwiches. Using a flexible knife from his leatherwork shop, Edward had sliced knuckled pork from a trophy discovered at the market and boiled at home. Louise kept the broth for soup and now deftly layered bread with pork and pease pudding cooked in muslin with the meat. An apple pie was warming in the oven and their hostess made tea. In the living room Joe handed brown ale to the men and came into the scullery to look for glasses.

'Shooh!' Katharine elbowed him out. 'We'll bring them in with us. There isn't room for you in here.'

'No room at the inn,' Louise chimed.

'Not even for a starving man?'

'You break my heart,' she said as he plunged back into the hubbub.

She was careful not to serve Joe herself. He spoke to Katharine while looking beyond at her. Louise turned away picking up their game.

But the card table was a disaster at the second sitting. Joe disputed a deal, was overruled, the ball of concentration they'd bounced from one to another fell flat and at the end of the next hand they abandoned the game.

He started the dancing and asked Edward's permission to sweep his wife onto the floor. Till now the stakes had been low. People round them relaxed, chit-chatting, clinking drinks, murmuring gossip. One of the girls sat in a corner with a headscarf on and offered to read palms. A storm of laughter broke round her then a loud rap at the door disturbed the peace. Everyone fell silent as a policeman stepped in and asked for Edward.

'I'm afraid your shop has been broken into, sir. You'd better come.'

Fred came over reaching for his white silk scarf and coat. 'I'm coming with you.'

Edward looked round. "If I'm not back, will you take her home, Joe?' He seemed to have noticed nothing.

'And Katharine?' Fred asked.

'We'll look after the girls.' Joe dropped Louise's hand. 'I hope it's nothing serious.'

'It may not take long to investigate, sir, but it's a fair step.'

Edward talked over his shoulder to Louise as he put his coat on and the policeman led them out.

Joe produced a new record and lovingly took it from its buff-coloured paper cover to let light spill across its shining black. 'Lady

Day. She's made a terrific version of *Summertime*. That woman's got a voice to stop the world – then spit in the world's eye.'

As the needle chased the grooves Louise heard a woman's voice with fire in it singing a lullaby, a fierce beat behind the vocal. Joe held her close against the rhythm and she felt something drain from her, through her fingertips, weakening her.

'I'd better not be late home, Joe.'

'They'll be busy at the shop for a while. Do you have a key? ... You can dance for half an hour.' She relaxed in his arms. 'And how is married life, Louise?'

'Fine.'

'I couldn't come to the church. You understand?'

'I know.'

'Is that what you wore?'

'Yes.'

'You should have worn it for me.'

'You were taken, Joe.'

Katharine touched her shoulder. 'I'm going now, the crowd's walking back with me. See you tomorrow.'

'O.K, Kath.'

'You can stay a little longer,' he said to her. 'I have the car.'

He broke away to change the record and there was a twist inside at the familiar turn of his head, the flame licked round her heart at a movement, a gesture. But a bond of belonging tied her in the gentle hands of Edward. One love for living, one for dreams, a dream that could turn black, leave her terrified and sweating. He held her in, joked while they danced. The record wound down. 'I'll leave the gramophone for the others and take you home, darling.'

In the car at first she took no notice of the direction, aware only of his presence. 'This isn't the way,' she said at last.

'I know.' He stopped the car and took her face in his hands. 'How can I be without you?' And she was the only woman on earth. Resistance seeped out as he touched her mouth with his little finger.

'Come and sit in the pavilion. In the park.'

'It's too late, Joe,' she said, 'in every way.'

'Not for tonight. Please don't say it.'

He helped her out and put his arm round her shoulder, held her against the wind till they reached the pavilion. The park had always filled her with a sense of peace. In daylight the pavilion overlooked a bowling green and it would be to this sheltered park she imagined she might bring her children to play, to make little chains on a daisy-strewn lawn.

'You were always so fragile, Louise. I could pick you up in one arm, place you astride my lap and kiss you as easily as picking a buttercup and ....' She placed a hand over his mouth. He eased her back and they talked low in the confessional of each others' arms. She had not chosen to meet him tonight. 'One more time. Once, my darling.'

The pleasure of him rocked her, took her breath, left her becalmed. For one night, the world was made for them.

When Edward returned from form filling at the station she was back home. The robbers didn't get much. It was cash they were after and he kept little money at the shop. They went to bed exhausted, she feeling no great harm was done in spite of a threshold crossed.

There were rumours, counter rumours about the king. Patricia wrote in her letters of fevers of debate in London society. Hypocrisy was worse than adultery, they said. The words sent a shiver through her when Mary showed her the letter. Louise turned the conversation to how Andrew was managing his shop. In her heart she felt Edward VIII would be king in his lovers' arms. Who knew anything? Gossip! It should be a capital offence.

Up and down the country people sat, ears glued to their wirelesses, smart ones in honey-coloured wood or a crystal set as Edward, a prince again, made his confession.

'At long last I am finally able to say a few words of my own.

229

I have never wanted to withhold anything, but until now it has not been constitutionally possible for me to speak.'

The nation listened in disbelief.

'... But I want you to understand that in making up my mind I did not forget the country or the Empire, which as Prince of Wales and lately as King I have for twenty-five years tried to serve.'

The words gripped her.

'But you must believe me when I tell you that I have found it impossible to carry the burden of responsibility ... and to discharge my duties as King as I would like to do without the help and support of the woman I love.'

'The weak fool!' Ben broke out and glared at John Hargraves, who was sharing a pipe with him. Louise was thunderstruck. The king had defied the ban on divorce, not ashamed of his love.

'... This decision has been made less difficult to me by the sure knowledge that my brother with his long training in the public affairs of this country and with his fine qualities will be able to take my place forthwith without interruption or injury to the life and progress of the Empire. And he had one priceless blessing, shared with many of you and not bestowed on me – a happy home with his wife and children.'

Louise breathed sharply. Her father had this, she thought. He'd brought it together.

'I now quit altogether public affairs and lay down my burden ... God bless you all. God save the King.'

'The weak fool!' Ben repeated. 'The weak fool. I didn't expect it to come to this. He was looking for a way out. So, what do you think now of your precious king that you've prayed every week for in church?'

'I'm devastated.' John Hargraves knocked his pipe out against the grate and into the fire. 'If the monarchy's to survive, and I believe it ought to, the king must give a moral lead. He's no use without that.'

'What's he ever done for the country anyway?' Ben asked. 'They're no better than anybody else.'

'They embody the traditions of the country.' Hargraves, she could see was thinking as he spoke. 'If you're conscious of your past … and what's been good about the past … you're more able to carve a decent future.'

Ben looked up, eyes fierce. 'The monarchy's an institution that's used to keep people in their place. Except this king, **this** one gave people hope. Now look at him.'

'I still think you need a figurehead, Ben, something to help unite the people.'

'Stop sounding like a history book, man.'

'It does give them something for inspiration.'

'Or the book of Common Prayer.'

'But, look,' the vicar leant towards him, 'it's the working class who are the strongest royalists. They certainly are in my parish.'

'Just because they swallow the bilge,' Ben said. 'They're the very people he's betrayed - planning to abdicate the next week while speaking words of hope to miners in the Rhonnda. We'd be better without them. What do you think, Mary?'

Mary was hunched in her chair. 'He should have stayed at his post. Done his duty. Like us. Like our lads had to do in the trenches.'

Ben nodded. 'But who knows? Maybe the brother will fit the shoes better. Give a better lead - as you'd say.'

Louise stopped listening. The king had cut through this knot of convention. Did that mean it was all right? Or would he find himself in another prison?

Head spinning she decided she would see Joe again.

17

Marriage hadn't altered the inside of Louise's head, her obsession, her addiction. She looked out on lovely summer days and missed the golf club with its soothing green immaculate fairways. With no garden to sit in, she'd walk to the park nearby where her father played bowls. He might be playing and they'd spar for a while with each other. Every detail stood out as she leaned back on a bench, scrolling iron, black paint on the gates, daisy heads that escaped the park gardeners, proud against the green, players dressed in their whites, the smack of bowls. She focussed on sight and sound, turned her head up like the daisies to absorb sunlight, smiled at the caress of a breeze. All this was real. And it was not where she'd met Joe.

An inner reality played in her mind. Scenes she'd lived with Joe when he'd carried her in his arms, made her happy, scenes there might have been if they hadn't smashed their futures. The click of bowls and the banter of her father caught her outward eye, she spoke and nodded then went back to cook a meal, accompanied inside by Joe's nagging ghost.

The year passed. She had kept her clothes from before she was married then had a win on the football pools, six pennorth of hope. She gave something to her mother, saved something and renewed her wardrobe, bright colours in rayon that she could run through her fingers in warm water frothy from Lux soap flakes. Blues, pinks her favourites, green and gold when in fashion, machine-made lace on underwear, a satin sheen on camiknickers, lovingly preserved garters with hand-stitched embroidery. She softened her black patent leather shoes with Vaseline and took them to her father to repair the soles, the tips of three-and-a-half-inch heels. Edward had no eye for her clothes. It made no difference to him if she wore the same thing the year round. Joe noticed.

She could not constantly keep up with fashion but kept in step with seasons, apple green in spring, coral and gold in summer, soft plum in autumn, dark evergreen with accessories of berry red in winter and a floating cloud of cream silk round her neck. Ribbons, necklaces, scarves, fresh flowers from Ben's allotment if he would spare her a bloom or two, pale airspun powder, crimson cupid's bow mouth, a dab of Evening in Paris behind her ears or vanilla essence if there was nothing else. She remembered when she had stolen that from her mother's kitchen at fifteen before life was complex, layered with plans, involved deceits, stolen sweetness. Before Joe. Heavy weights on her feet when she could not see him, she stretched thin in opposing directions wondering if her face would crack in two, movie star lips and all.

She missed her job, missed the tips, the sly flirting of the men behind their wives' backs, being able to help her mother put something on the table mid-week, the excitement of finishing her shift to squeeze what richness she could from the hours that were hers. One day followed another with housework quickly done, time freed for the duties of a young wife, not overburdened, preparing to have a family. Except she wasn't. A complication too many. She pulled in her stomach. Joe would lose interest if she swelled up.

She would go out pretty, then hunch along with pent-up secrets through the soft light of urban spring that fell on brick walls, on broken tarmac in back lanes, on sparrows tweaking bills near puddles of collected grey rain. She hunched through sporadic warmth of an uncertain summer and when she straightened, instead of trees she saw bill boards inviting housewives to rinse whites in Reckitt's Blue, take Bile Beans to keep healthy, slim, bright eyed and follow the enticing smell of gravy with the Bisto kids. She hunched into autumn, feeling cold when she put off wearing a warm coat, pretending she'd feel the benefit later, wanting to show her fashionable boyish figure, and listened with pleasure to the tapping of her heels against the pavement.

When the days shortened she wrapped up in her good woollen coat, bought from her win on the pools, and, if she was meeting Joe, cowled her head in the cream silk scarf to brighten her face, wore her shiny black high heels, shivered in nylon stockings, put on a filmy rayon petticoat, no protection against the cold. If she was meeting Joe. Others saw the outer Louise. Joe was locked in her heart and mind becoming a fantasy Joe, tended and nurtured by imagination – a stack of precious moments. She carried the green powder compact he'd given her as a kind of talisman. Real meetings could be different from the man she loved, could have no magic at all. The dream had to be kept alive or reality stared back from the mirror. She was no longer Joe's fragile love. She knew what it was to meet secretly in a hotel. She was his other woman, their future already in the past.

The big event in the year was Katharine's wedding, the youngest daughter was marrying before Diane. They had put savings together to buy her a Singer sewing machine for a wedding present but she begged to have it early so she could sew her own dress. Working hard in the rag trade on piecework in the West End she learned quickly. Paper patterns were draped all over the house and Diane's face soured at the mess. How was she supposed to keep the place clean and tidy for her mother? One daughter must stay at home to help out. Katharine bustled about her own happy business, a pincushion on one wrist, a thimble on a finger, a smile on her face. When Leslie wanted to call Diane said the house was a pigsty and she couldn't invite him in. 'When I get married ...'

'Quiet, Diane,' Ben cut across. 'Not everyone can have an expensive bought dress from her lad, and Katharine'll look just as well.'

'Better!' Katharine chimed.

Diane flashed her real diamond cluster ring.

'At least my lad's actually marrying me,' Katharine flared.

Louise shook her head at her younger sister and Ben raised a warning finger. 'I'll have peace in this house.' Louise heard the rap at the door and ran downstairs to let the 'handsome horror' in. He seemed delighted at the mess Katharine had made. Diane looked like gangrene as he leaned over the couch to look at the progress then offered to buy real lace for the bodice.

'Ta very much!' Katharine said, then turned away to her beloved machine, bent over it, adjusted the thread in its cloven foot and set it whirring with a rhythmic tread on the treadle.

Louise put her coat on. Ben eyed her carefully. 'And where might you be going?'

'Just out. I might go to the pictures and I might not. Edward's tied up with cutting out his leather.'

'We could all go together,' Leslie suggested. Ben looked straight in her eyes, into regret, deceit, the emptiness of her soul. He knew. How could he? She made for the door.

'There are some flowers in the kitchen if you want a posy for your outfit. Can't have you go out without looking your best.' His eyes had not left her face. She flushed under the powder then escaped, walking as fast as she could. Away. Out. Their meeting was in half an hour. She looked at the time on the clock tower of the fire station and scuttled to catch a tram.

At the box office of the News Theatre she gave the false name Jenkins Joe sometimes used and collected the ticket he'd left for her, clattered upstairs to the balcony and slipped in beside him to the splitting cry of the cockerel that announced Pathé News.

'Thought you would miss the start,' he mumbled.

'Held up in dad's house with Diane,' she grimaced into the darkness and watched the news item. It was only sixpence here and it was nice. Her attention settled. The film showed posed stills from after the coronation. Three kings in about twelve months, must have been. George V, Eddie VIII as should have been but not crowned – and George VI. They were weighed down by ermine-edged crowns, except for old Queen Mary and the little princesses. Little coronets looked nicer. The rest of them stood there like ramrods. Not her father's cup of tea. *What clips*! she thought *The four of us would look as good ... better, all dolled up.* Young Katharine was at least as good looking as the new queen. They had to make a fuss of them, though. Joe's hand rested gently on her knee.

Next ... Prime Minister Baldwin bowing out. The shot faded and they saw the new one, thin with whitish hair slicked back, bushy brows and an old-fashioned bristly moustache. 'One old fart after another,' she whispered.

Joe took her hand and kissed it. 'This one's saved a lot of women from dying having their babies ... his work at the Health ministry.'

She squeezed his hand and shuddered. The newsreel ended and they were presented with an old country house, then a journey round Britain. It would be nice to see different places.

He read her thought, slipped his arm round her shoulder and spoke into her ear. 'We'll do our own tour one day.'

Fantasy. Their day had not come. What had she done wrong along the way? He was proud. They both were. It was that party when she danced with others, did the Charleston - as if something hurled a bolt in amongst them scattering couples in new directions. Nothing was ever the same. If she'd reached out to him then? Live in the moment. He was here.

Lights glowed into life from side lamps beside ornate seating boxes that housed equipment. She loved the red plush seats, the stage effect with room for an orchestra pit, posh red velvet curtains cranking up into scalloped curves instead of swishing apart. It was a favourite place if she was sure Ben wouldn't be here with his righteousness, the vicar.

'Have to get back.' He dropped her hand.

'So do I.'

'Bit tied up. Same time next week? Sometime soon?'

'Maybe.' Her heart tightened as she walked slowly downstairs looking at framed posters on the plastered walls, wanting him to say more. Lies would do. Another poster caught his eye at the exit.

JOIN THE MODERN ARMY

He stood and she waited as he studied lorries in silhouette, tanks, searchlights cutting through darkness illuminating athletic men. 'It's new, this recruiter.' He was speaking to himself. 'Modernising the army.' He turned to her, his eyes lingered and he was with her again. 'About time they got rid of the bow and arrow crew. Attract new men. I might like to join the forces one day. They must be building defences up.'

She tugged his elbow. 'Joe ... no.'

'Probably too old for it.' He shrugged and turned away. 'See you, baby.'

She felt a ridiculous surge of warmth at the American slang, like the movies.

The year moved on with hope at the new year that everything would be better and come right. But her dad drank and you never knew how that would end. Joe could disappear on business and as suddenly be back. She hoped he hadn't joined up.

The weather lightened and it was a while since she had seen him. A cronie of his would come into the shop when she was behind the counter, leave shoes for repair and the name and address on green note paper. It worried her that even one person knew about them but Joe assured her his friend wouldn't split on them. He could hardly send a carrier pigeon.

They met over the bridge in Gateshead where he had contacts. Friends and family rarely shopped there but it meant being careful, arranging the house, a meal, a reason for being out, bus fare, getting away. If time wasn't a problem she saved money by walking across the Tyne Bridge, under the great green girders holding up the arch, icon of the city. Today Ben had called, Diane had come over, stayed and stayed and she had to dress quickly. It was unthinkable, though, to meet her lover without lipstick and powder firmly fixed, without wearing something decent. Joe would have his car ready the other side of the river to whisk her away. She looked round to spot the little Austin when she stumbled out of the bus. A mean wind was tugging, flattening her skirt, whirling bits of newspapers, paper bags, sweet wrappers to dance four feet above the pavements. She smiled when he looked up, switched on her inner light but he was sulky.

'What kept you?' No kiss, no smile.

'Dad dropped in, talking politics as usual.'

'Your father thinks too much. If old Ben didn't think so much he might still have been in a job.'

Sudden fury, she slapped his face as he pulled on the choke and started the engine. The car jolted as he turned and caught her wrist. 'You'll get more than you bargain for if you strike me again! What else kept you?'

'Diane!' she blazed at him. 'She dawdled round flashing her engagement ring, fed up that Katharine's getting married before she is. I couldn't throw her out. I almost thought she was going to come with me.'

'That would make a change Two sisters!' He eased the clutch in. 'You know she's prettier than you, don't you?

'Thank you.'

'That glorious fair hair. Does she bring it up with anything?'

'It's God's gift. Shall I get out and you can go back and collect her?'

'Cold as ice. The worst combination.'

The room at the hotel was cool when they went in. He lit the gas fire, sat in front of it, took a hip flask from his pocket, leather with a silver top, took a nip of whisky and offered it to her. 'At least you're not the ice queen. Let's warm ourselves up. Then we can roll about on the floor together.'

'Joe, you make me feel dirty.'

'You make me feel alive, dirt or not.' He took a longer pull from the flask, looked round at the room and she could see it was beginning to bore him. 'We'll have to find somewhere else.' He stopped her as she stood up and pulled her down by the gas fire. 'Here. We'll do it here today. He was rough and greedy for her with no preliminaries. When the moment came he found he couldn't find his packet of sheaths. 'That's Evie's fault. She was rowing with me when I came out.' He searched his pockets. 'I haven't got them.'

'We'd better forget it.' She sat up.

'It'll be all right. Just this once. It's been all right before.'

He was on top of her before she could argue, taking no refusal, no romance, no tenderness. But they recaptured it, lying in each others' arms. For a brief sleep only they existed. When they got up they kissed and clung. 'I don't want to go back to Evie.' He kissed her again. 'If we could only keep it this way.'

'I must get ready, Joe.' She went over to the basin in the corner to wash between her legs, wash away the wetness, try to avoid the dead fish smell after sex. She needed to be home in time to change, be sure there was no sign. 'You'll have to run me to the bus stop.'

Harmony stayed with them though they scrambled against time, adding the sharpness of excitement. The glow of love was on her face when Edward came home. After their meal he pulled her to the horsehair stuffed couch, laughed and cuddled and made love to her in the cosiness of their own home. It had never happened on the same day before. He was affectionate, boyish and she felt a rush of tenderness for him.

The church was decked with flowers for Katharine, irises and carnations that Ben had loved and nurtured for the wedding. Louise had managed to say no to being matron of honour. Weddings upset her, though she couldn't share that. Patricia sat on the other side of Edward, hand in hand with her beloved. How did they manage this patient, calm love? Christopher was behind them, uncomfortable in an old suit of the baron's that they'd cleaned up and cut down for him, growing fast. Diane was bridesmaid. All of the sisters might be married soon. Their mother dried her eyes.

In spite of Edward's warmth next to her, she felt dizzy and cold in the stone building but smiled at the memory of when Christopher had been born. They were told nothing and suddenly, after a night of adults moving about the house, there he was, a baby in their mother's arms. Mothers were fat, they hadn't thought anything of it. When it was Katharine's turn to come in to see the baby she'd stared transfixed, then slapped him right across the face. No snotty baby would take her place.

Louise shut her eyes. The blue wedding suit brought out for special occasions felt tight at the waist and her satin brassiere was uncomfortable. She was overdue.

Fred balanced nervously from one polished shoe to the other at the front of the aisle, the organ crashed, the bride came in, lovelier than a queen, a posy of flowers twisted in her hair and they stood up. Louise looked. Joe wasn't here, not invited, but a church was free. Weddings and funerals, people turned up. He mustn't know. She sat down and tried to breathe deeply. She could be wrong. It might just go away. She should have eaten breakfast. How was it her affair hadn't turned out to be glamorous like Mrs Simpson's? Maybe Mrs Simpson was miserable as well, thin and miserable, with no title of Her Royal Highness.

Diane was beautiful in the new gold dress Leslie had bought, nothing home made. At least there were a few things in the shops again. But Katharine could have been offered a job in a Bridal House on the strength of the dress she'd created. She rubbed her hand across her belly. Always bloated before a period, always uncomfortable. She'd been late before, been panicked before, then the welcome cramp. Just wait.

Dear God, I won't ever see Joe again! I won't do it again.

John Hargraves in his shining white surplice, Katharine in a swirl of white, a haze of white blooms stacked. Edward carefully unwrapped a mint and passed it to her.

From the front 'I do! ... I do!'

She sucked the mint and rubbed her abdomen. Warmth of peppermint trickled down her throat, settled waves in her stomach. A brandy would be better. Just breathe.

They were coming out, Fred proud as Punch, confetti everywhere, kids waiting for the coins of the 'Hoy oot!' She gulped the keen air and cold settled in her temples, clear again. Edward must have her coat somewhere. The party stood for a photo. Katharine had threatened to wear Ben's longjohns underneath the dress. She didn't shiver. Good for her. Her father stood straight in his black suit from the Jarrow march. There'd have been no row when he asked this bride if she was sure. This one should be fine.

Everything should be fine.

Except an evil gossip had told her Evie might be leaving Joe … and this year a divorce could be had for desertion.

The rest of the day blurred. A reception at their parent's house, home cooking, eyes on Katharine. She made an excuse to go to her own house and change out of her best things in case she spilt anything, found one of her rayon dresses, looser but stylish, washed her face and pushed her hair back, drank cold water, breathed deeply. A fluff of powder, lips redrawn and she stepped out of the door, her absence hardly noticed. Mary was too busy looking after guests and watching Ben didn't manage to get a brown ale. She ate a little of the cold meat and salad, had a cup of her usual sweet black tea and the room focused, her stomach lay down, she nibbled quietly in a corner then felt well enough to help with the dishes. It was all right, all right.

Katharine left with Fred for a weekend honeymoon in Scarborough, no longer queen for a day on her return. They were going to live with Fred's mother, a good bus ride away. It would be strange without her.

Nothing happened. Ben ranted about politics. She felt better but there was no familiar flow of blood that could lay her low for a day or two. She should talk to her mother. Every night she went to bed, closed her eyes and expected it would be normal next day, have her monthlies, get over it, everything would be the same.

Joe was away on business he didn't talk about. She heard no more of Evie doing a runner - a relief, it would complicate things.

Ben was going on about Germany whenever she dropped in, a greater Germany, Czech Germans. She couldn't care less if Germany decided to splodge out this way or that, it was just a huge squashed fly on the map of Europe. The monocled Prime Minister was making news, though, her father shook his head. At least this one was better looking than Baldwin with the bowler, in a stiff toffy sort of way. She wondered if he saw the world clearly through his one-rimmed lense.

The Reverend John was there when she next sidled over to her mother's house. The men listened to the wireless, talking over it. Andrew was taking stock downstairs. Diane was out, her mother was pleased to have company as she peeled and sliced big apples for a pie. Fat chunks of bright green peel lay on the kitchen table, coiling round, shaven in long serpent curls. They looked fascinating and the sharp acid smell made her salivate. She picked them up and began to crunch them as she had as a child.

'I'm not sure,' Ben said. 'It may be harmless enough as you say if Chamberlain gets cosy with the Italians.'

The reverend grinned. 'I think he likes their style. Those tailored white uniforms.'

'Looks as if he knuckles under to the Ities, though.'

'Mussolini's the only one Herr Hitler listens to.'

'Maybe.'

Louise picked up a curl of peel.

'Did I tell you about Lord Londonderry and Ribbentrop?'

'I doubt I'll be interested in … the damned owner of the Durham coal field.' Louise took another and her mother glanced at her. The acid was churning in her stomach but she kept chewing. 'And we all know the German ambassador's been far and away too friendly at the palace. Good thing that Mrs Simpson's off the scene.'

'Well, he's thick with Lord Londonderry, stays up here quite a bit. A friend of mine was officiating at Durham Cathedral when they turned up for morning service. He'd chosen that hymn "Glorious things of thee are spoken" to end the service with.'

Louise felt nausea rise to her throat.

'And?'

'That's the one set to the tune of the German national anthem.'

Louise had spinning in her head. Mary scraped her knife against something and the disembodied voices from the wireless blared. Ben jabbed his pipe in the air as he saw what was coming.

'While the organist's still playing the tune over, Ribbentrop stands up and does a Nazi salute!' Ben choked. 'They're calling him the Londonderry Herr!'

Mary dropped her knife and exploded in laughter. Louise jumped to her feet, her ears ringing. 'Oh, shut up! Shut up! Shut up! Shut up! - the lot of you!'

Ben looked at her, wide blue eyes sparkling, came over and put his arm gently round her waist. 'I'll take you home, pet.' She let herself be led downstairs and across the road. He took the key from her and opened the door. 'Is Edward in?' She nodded. 'That's all right, then. Maybe you need to see the doctor, my darling.' She shook her head and he left.

After her day as queen Katharine settled into the ranks of married women unable to go out to work and without it was lonely.

'Hello, Mrs. Reid.'

'Hello, Mrs. Thomas.'

'What can I do for you?'

'A cup of tea, please. I have to get out of that big old house sometimes. It spooks me.' Louise raised an eyebrow. 'And old Ma Reid spooks me even more.'

'Sit down, pet, the kettle's nearly on the boil.' Louise was glad of the distraction and rattled her best Woolworth's cups out. 'What's she been doing? You were happy enough to be over there when you were courting.'

'I know. Let me have a drink first.'

The youngest sister, the bonniest, gulped down her tea, almost scalding her mouth. Louise stirred her sugar and listened with mounting horror to Katharine's story.

She'd been out at a church social with Fred and got caught out by her monthlies. It was so light outside she let him stay on to enjoy the company, came in quietly and when she'd fixed herself up dropped into the kitchen. Ma Reid was helping a neighbour. A girl was stretched out on the kitchen table with her clothes up and they were pumping something into her through a forcing bag meant for baking. A palette knife glittered on the table on top of the young woman's skirt. When they saw Katharine her mother-in-law barked at her to keep her stupid mouth shut and fetch towels and hot water. She heard a scream and when Katharine came back into the kitchen the palette knife was red and soapy water mixed with blood dripped out of the girl over the table and onto the floor. The girl lay still, waxy white. Katharine had to get on her knees to wash up the mess then fetch more towels as they bound the girl's legs together.

'What happened then?'

'I had to help carry their 'patient' next door then finish scrubbing the table and the floor.'

'Did you tell Fred?'

'No, he idolises his mother and she'd deny it. She keeps giving me looks. I'm terrified of her.'

'What happened to the girl?' They were talking in whispers.

'She died. They had her taken to hospital and she died five days later. It was the woman's own daughter and she didn't dare go to see her.'

'Do you think they'd done this before?'

'Oh, yes, there's a big funeral today. That's why I'm here. It's all paid for, the hospital bill as well. The woman's got money from what she does. So has Ma Reid sometimes, though Fred's dad hardly works and drinks himself silly. She uses what Fred gives her for the housekeeping.'

'You've got to get out of there.'

'I know. I'm terrified the police might come one day, and I'm terrified of Ma Reid so I haven't done anything about it.'

'Listen, you know you made your wedding dress?'

'I'm not going to sell that.'

'But you could start making dresses for other people with your little Singer. It's an advert for what you can do. You'd be a lot cheaper than a bought dress and the word'd get round.'

'But I haven't got the room.'

'Could you make room - in your bedroom?'

'No … there's a box room.'

'Convert it into a sewing room. Offer Ma Reid a cut from your earnings till you have enough to move out. She might jump at the money. She may even want to get out of it herself.' Katharine nodded, thinking. Louise made toast over the fire and changed the subject. 'Anyway, what do you think of old Chamberlain getting in an aeroplane and going to see Hitler in his lair?'

Katharine munched her toast looking relieved. 'I think it's bloody marvellous at his age … do you want to talk politics like dad?'

'No, dad says he's going the second mile. But I've got other news … I think I'm pregnant.'

Katharine's face lit up. 'That's marvellous!'

It would be, Louise thought, *if I was sure who the father was.*

On the way from the surgery Louise walked through back lanes instead of the main street as if her condition was written on her face. Small children kicked gravel chips on the road playing chasey, safe from cars. A black cat crossed her path as she kept her eyes on the road and looked at her with baleful green eyes, unafraid. Was that lucky or unlucky? She kept her eyes down looking out for dog turds and puddles. She didn't even see his feet.

'Louise!' A cold shock slid down her spine, 'What are you doing here?'

She looked at his shoes. 'I'm walking home. What are <u>you</u> doing?'

'You know me. Business on the side. Don't tell my boss. There are a few people I run a personal book for. Business in back lanes.'

She watched a couple of children swing each other round cross handed. 'Where've you been?'

'In London, an affair to sort out for the boss. They get cheeky down there and think they can take things over in the North. Bloody Cockneys, eh?' She shrugged. 'When can I see you?'

'I don't know.' She walked not looking him in the face.

'I must see you.'

'No more hotels, Joe.'

'OK.' He marched in step with her. 'Then meet me in town - by accident. Have a cup of tea?'

'The ice cream parlour.'

'Tomorrow?'

'The day after.'

'Eleven o' clock. You can get into town in the morning. I have to go ... may have a big bet here.'

'I won't ask what for.'

'Hush, hush.'

'You're so sharp you'll cut yourself.'

'Yes.' There was bitterness in his voice as he turned away.

So what? When was Joe sweetness and light? At times. But his moods only cast a shadow, never wiped out the trail of hours when he'd loved her. She couldn't show him she needed him. He wouldn't say it. *Joe's back. Joe's back.* Her feet tapped out a rhythm against the tarmac. To tell him or not? Send him away with a flea in his ear, as usual.

She turned the corner, rattled the key in the lock and went in to her little house. There was the acrid smell of slightly damp coal drying behind the fender, the fragrance of tea with a hint of dried grass, the heavier, fungus smell of old tea leaves kept for her father's allotment and there was the scent of her powder, air spun, held somewhere. From the scullery she inhaled the spice of an apple pie her mother had baked, the yeasty pungency of fresh bread and a faint lingering of wax on the oilcloth. The smell of home. She dropped onto the couch, drew a rug over her knees and fell asleep.

She could not put on her best clothes to go into town on an errand but arranged her hair carefully, pinning it behind her ears, persuading it to coil under on the nape of her neck A whirl of pink-tinted powder swirled off the puff and floated on a shaft of sunlight as she examined her complexion in a mirror by the window. A red cupid's bow of lipstick, *Evening in Paris* perfume from a blue bottle, a pair of old high heels that would draw no attention then her lightest coat on, left open, she smoothed her belly and walked out. No stage lighting, no applause, only a breeze tugging at her skirt as she hurried to catch a bus. A clock over the bank told her she'd be on time. As she walked down the main street a yellow trolley bus overtook her, she ran, jumped on the boarding square and smiled at the conductor. He took her elbow to help her onto the side seat. It wasn't showing yet. She should have at least a couple of months before looking at all heavy. Her father knew, she could tell, but said nothing. Edward was in blissful ignorance.

The tower clock on the blackened big church showed one minute to eleven, Joe was waiting, for once not looking at his wristwatch. He turned without a greeting. 'I've bagged a seat in the corner. Sit with your back to the window if you're happier.'

She smiled at the sight of the shiny ice cream parlour with a gleaming counter, stacks of biscuit-coloured cones and a scent of cream and vanilla, like a child's treat. She put her bag at her feet and flung her coat over the back of the chair. Without asking what she wanted he brought a sundae in a tall glass and long spoon. The fruit layer was as bright red as her mouth. She felt nothing had happened. Make believe, no baby, nothing. When Joe sat opposite she saw him full faced in the light. A red weal stretched from the left ear almost to the side of his nose, purple in the gully of a cut.

His mouth turned down as she stared. 'Twenty stitches. I thought you'd never notice.'

She wanted to touch it but kept her hands on the table either side of the gaudy sundae. 'How?'

'Doing business for the boss in London.'

'Keeping blokes there away from here?'

'A bit more complicated, I can't tell you what it was. You don't want to be an accomplice to anything. Anyway, they cut up rough at the deal.' She could see the machine like pattern of the stitches, still new. 'They come at you with cut-throat razors, these boys. A rough business, the betting world.'

She stared at the gash, stunned. 'They could have killed you.'

He shook his head. 'They're not out to kill. They just slash at your face. They can't get the big drop for that, even if you dared report it. And everybody else knows they've marked you.'

'Joe!'

He grinned. 'I lived. And the other guy knew he'd been hit.'

'A gang of them could have mangled you for life.'

'The Rozzers were around. I was lucky not to get arrested.' He touched the cut. 'It'll look interesting when it's faded. Eat your ice cream. It'll melt.'

'I'm not sure I can eat now. I'm feeling sick.'

He reached over, dug into the sweet mess and offered her the spoon. 'I'd like to feed you but I daren't do that in public. You'd better eat it or I'll forget where we are.'

She took the spoon automatically and hardly tasted the lovely confection. The reason he'd been away. Terrible tenderness welled up.

'Evie left me when I got home.' She spilt jelly and ice cream on her mouth and he handed her a handkerchief. 'Then came back. Her family can't keep her.'

She spooned the red fruit up and let jelly slide down her throat. 'Same old story.'

'We don't speak much.'

'Did you ever?'

He leaned on one elbow and watched her. 'You look lovely. Your cheeks have a blush and I don't think it's rouge.'

She clattered the spoon. 'I'm having a baby.'

He pursed his lips in a soundless whistle and sat back. His features froze. An eternity. Then he whispered. 'Mine?'

'Could be. I don't know.' The cold of the ice cream curled into her stomach.

His brow wrinkled as it did when he was calculating odds. 'Does Edward know?' She shook her head as he looked past her out at the street then met her eyes. 'I'll pay,' he said flatly.

'What?'

'To have it sorted.'

She wanted to move but was welded to the chair like a dummy. 'Do you know what you've just **SAID**? ... You'd put me through that? I ... could ... die!'

He took her wrist across the table. 'I don't mean a hole-in-the-corner back street affair. Of course I wouldn't put you through that.' He dropped the wrist. 'There are trained people who'll do it. Doctors, even.'

'You'd know about that!'

'It could mean a trip to London. I'd arrange it all. We could dream up some cover for you being away.'

Her limbs obeyed her again. She picked up her bag and the coat behind her. 'Good bye, Joe.' He was still sitting when she looked back through the window.

Her parents did a jig and Edward was overjoyed when she blurted out her news. Then for weeks she went from feeling shielded by love to bouts of uncontrollable weeping, face swollen, eyes almost closed, voice lost in a hiccupping croak. Edward's patience and her mother's tolerance both irritated her. Diane came to help with the house but disappeared if she had an outburst. Her always uncertain appetite disappeared.

Ben came with homemade leek and vegetable soup, produce from the allotment, and coaxed her as he had when she was tiny. 'Come on Tiddler, eat up,' he teased. 'One for Ben, one for Mary, one for the baby.' She pushed him away and saw him examine her ravaged red face. 'A spot of powder would help fix that,' he said.

'I don't want this baby, dad.'

'Wants don't come into it.' He put the soup bowl aside and stroked her streaked face. 'Playtime's over, my darling. Once you have children that's it.' He lifted her chin. 'What's done is done. The past doesn't matter. You put your child first.' She looked back at him. *He knew!* 'And it'll be all right. We're here. You can rely on us.'

They faced each other, held each others' gaze, gauged each other. She nodded.

'And I've good news.' He fumbled in his pocket for an envelope and shook a letter out. 'I'm called back to work.' Her eyes widened. 'I know. It seemed impossible. I've to report to the Labour Exchange, the Dole House your mother calls it. There'll be a place for me at the factory down yonder if I'm prepared to take responsibility. It's not the pit.' She shook her head. 'But I don't think they can afford to waste skills any longer and nor can I. Mr Chamberlain's playing a two-handed game, trying for peace but getting ready in case.' He held a finger to his nose and winked. 'It's O.K. I'm not going to rant. Whatever happens, you'll be looked after. And so will the bairn be. My family's my family. Children's children.'

Hope of a spring baby took them all through cold winter months.

Thirty years old and with greying hair, Patricia visited from the Cumberland house her employers fled back to. They left fashionable nudism when clashes with the blackshirts burst onto the streets of London, left it behind for the green fields, mountains and rain of Cumberland. Fascists had done the fashionable that favour.

Louise sometimes walked into a family conference to be annoyed at lowered voices and wrinkled brows turning to smiles when she appeared. Christopher, aged thirteen told her what was said. They were thrilled at the thought of a babby. ...Yes? ... But worried because she was so small.

She crossed her fingers and decided to cross that bridge when she had to. Cross fingers. Cross eyes. Cross everything. She'd cross Joe's eyes for him but he kept away.

With Ben in work, money strains easing and the spectre of debt slain, her parents, white on top, were enjoying a second honeymoon or entering second childhood. They could be cuddled on the sofa when she walked in. She shook her head. Anything was better than the politics.

A man from the council came to see if there was much space in the back yard. She was flurried and needed to catch up on chores, dusting, sweeping, shopping, changing the bed, getting everything together for the laundry collection before starting to prepare a hot meal. What did this twirp want with the back yard?

'I won't keep you long, missus,' he said. She disliked being called missus. She disliked the chores but hoped she still looked like Greta Garbo in a pinafore, Cinderella just before the transformation, even with a swollen belly. 'Missus' was for old married frumps. She disliked his long bristly moustache, like a scrubbing brush lost from its mother. 'If I can just come through your scullery and measure what space you've got. I should be able to pace it out.'

'What's this in aid of? A war effort? My dad's always going on about so-called dictators in Europe. Silly old fool!'

The man from the council took important steps down the back yard. 'He's not such a silly old fool, pet. Mr. Chamberlain's starting the task of building a war machine - just in case, you understand.' He turned round and gave an excruciating grin. 'And I shouldn't be telling you but you'll have heard of bombing from the air in bits of Spain and Africa? Well, it's our duty to build air raid shelters for the population.' He grimaced again. 'If you do those things you can be sure you'll not need them. Like an insurance policy. You have it but you hope you'll never have to call on it.'

'It seems like a waste of time to me and I have to get on, if you don't mind.'

'Carry on with your work, missus.' She stood meaningfully at the back door, hands on hips. He began talking more to himself. 'There's not room for a full on shelter here, not one of the Andersons. But what we *could* do, ...' he tapped his teeth with a pencil, yellowing walrus teeth that smelt of stale tobacco, '... is put up a smaller brick construction - just here, do you see? A surface shelter as we call them. Concrete then a brick cladding, near the house, in front of your coal shed and the lav. A double layer of bricks, space between them and it could be quite secure. Even if the outer wall was damaged the inner wall should hold. All there's room for but it should do the trick.'

She came down to see the square he was pacing out. 'There'll not be room there to swing a cat.'

'Nobody'll be wanting to swing any cats. There's just you and your husband. And later on?'

'None of your business. Who's going to pay for this anyway? I'm not laying out a penny.'

The walrus teeth tried to flash. 'No need, no need. It'll come out of the rates.'

'What a waste!'

'Well, they are trying to negotiate ...' he lingered over the long word, '... negotiate' he rolled the syllables round his tongue '... for extra finance from central government.'

'Scaremongering. Have you finished?'

'Just about.' He took out a note pad from his inner pocket and reached for a chewed pencil from behind his ear, licked it and scribbled something for a few minutes dragging out his moment of glory. 'You'll hear from us in due course, my dear. In due course.'

The ridged rubber soles of his boots made marks on her lino as she saw him out. Another job to do! What next? Wasting money. Maybe as he said, her dad wasn't such an old fool! She wished she didn't have to listen to him ranting about the world. But that was him, her dad all over. Clever in his way. It clogged her brain up, all that stuff. He said that in the House Labour accused Mr.

Chamberlain of bringing in a war budget and Toffy Chamberlain took them on - get your fire fighting ready now, not when the fire's blazing. Such stuff she carried round in her head. But they were going to have to have an air raid shelter. The workmen would clart muck through the house, bound to. She sighed, better if women ran the world. A poster she'd seen came back to her mind, a tatty old thing left up, tearing and lifting at the corner. A Labour election poster. A baby with a gas mask on. She'd make a better job of it herself. She reached for a cigarette.

Her own doctor Garstang was in attendance when the pains finally came. The maternity hospital with its grand façade somehow frightened her, dark red sandstone built within reach of the city centre. Her G.P. was a gynaecologist but warned he might not be able to do everything in her case.

She squinted up at him. 'What you don't know somebody else will.'

'I can always ask the midwives', he laughed.

'They'll keep you right.' They continued a banter.

'Maybe you shouldn't have another, you're so small.'

'The spirit's willing,' she said, 'but the flesh is weak.'

Better to laugh than to cry.

Now was the moment. Wave after wave of knives in her belly, panting for breath. Could anything go on for so long? Women in nurses' uniforms round her and a stench of antiseptic.

'Where's Garstang?' she croaked.

'He's coming in and out. He's got more than one patient, you know.' She saw two midwives glance at each other and one left the room.

'Can nobody get this thing out of me?' The doctor came in, white-clad, and inserted his fingers into her. 'Don't bother to ask!'

He turned to one of the midwives. 'It's only four inches. How long has it been at that dilation?'

'Over an hour, doctor.'

He turned to Louise and stood looking at her. *What was the matter with her? What was the matter with him?* He turned back to the midwife. 'I don't want to move her.'

'This isn't sterile, doctor.'

'I know.' To her, 'Can you bear it if we move you on a trolley? A knife spasm again whose blade seemed aiming for her heart. She groaned and shook her head. He pulled a chair round and sat with his face close to her. 'Louise, do you want this baby alive?'

With all her strength she shouted, 'What do you think, you bloody bastard?'

A midwife tutted, 'Mrs Thomas!'

The doctor glanced at her. 'I've been called worse than that.' To Louise, 'You're going to need some help. We need to take you along to an operating theatre,' She shut her eyes. 'Ideally it should be a Caesarean.' He paused. 'But there's no one in the hospital at the minute with that skill. I'd have to call somebody from another and I don't think we should wait.'

'You do it, you old fool!'

'I haven't done a Caesarean delivery before. I'd need another doctor beside me. You've stopped dilating, Louise. Stopped opening up. The baby can't get through. I could use something to help you open up. But I'll have to move you and I'll have to have permission. Can you sign?'

She shook her head and wheezed, 'For what?' Her voice was receding.

'We'll give you an anaesthetic.' To a midwife. 'See if the husband's near.' To Louise. 'I can insert a metal ring to widen your cervix and hold it open so we can deliver this baby.' His eyes were moist. 'I can't do it against your will.'

'The baby'll die otherwise?'

'There's a serious risk. If I do this you'll be in pain afterwards. But we should get you both alive.'

A midwife's head round the door. 'The husband will sign.' Louise nodded.

'We'll make a sling and move you as quickly as possible.'

Nightmare as her body was trussed and swung hammock style, jangled along green nightmare corridors. Lights. Masks. Something clamped across her nose and mouth. Hard to breathe. Lights going out.

Coughing. Green slime. An enamel kidney bowl filling. Binding. Numbness between her legs. Garstang unfocussed, miles away. 'The neck of your womb's damaged and you've been bleeding very heavily but we've stopped it. I've had to stitch you. You've been darned, my dear, inside and out. You'll be unwell for quite a time but instead of dying you'll merely be ill. We're going to give you blood.' He smiled. 'You have a little boy.'

The family put savings together to pay for her stay in hospital. Patricia put in most but Ben would pay her back from his work. Louise mustn't worry about any of that. After her fever, after the agony of fingernails coming out from blood poisoning, appetite by degrees returned. She was allowed to hold her baby longer. He slept, his head covered in fair golden down that looked as if it might curl, like Edward's. A halo.

When she could sit up to hold him she would talk to the baby when she thought no one was there. 'Whose baby are you, my sweetheart?' Then she held him in. 'You're mine!'

She was letting him curl a little fist round a finger, speaking sweetness he could recognise by her tone when someone came in quietly and stood watching. Her eye travelled from the good shoes, well-made jacket to a smart tie, to curling dark hair.

'Joe!'

'May I?' He sat on the bed without waiting for a reply. He touched her cheek. 'My darling, what have they put you through?'

'Don't you "darling" me.' But her voice carried no force.

His hand hovered over the baby's head but he withdrew it. 'I know I haven't to tire you. Listen. Evie's left me.' He shook his head as she opened her mouth. 'Hear me out. I know it's happened before. This time I'm sure she's not coming back. Anyway, this time

I'm not going on with it. I felt guilty after her miscarriage. I didn't feel I was the one who could walk out when she was ill and low.'

'But you can walk out of here now.' She began to cough with the effort of speaking.

His hand stretched automatically to hers but she drew back into the pillows clutching the baby as a defence. 'I know this baby could be mine. I'm willing to take a blood test. Offer you a new start, Louise. I have business connections in Leeds. I could start on my own there. People always gamble, no matter what.' She shook her head but he continued in a rush. 'I'd take you right away so you wouldn't have to put up with gossip and back biting. At the same time we wouldn't be at the other end of the country. Your folk could keep up with you if they wanted to. I've saved. And I've had a big win. Enough to cover divorce costs. Even pay Evie maintenance, I should manage it. If you ever loved me,' he leant towards her, 'go away with me now. When you're strong. You're all I've ever cared about. Give me something to live for.'

'Words are cheap, Joe. If I'm so precious why didn't you marry me in the first place?'

'Afraid to ask in case you turned me down.' He got up and looked out of the window as though he couldn't look her in the face. 'Afraid our dream of love wouldn't survive normal life, through drudgery. Afraid you'd treat me the way my mother treated my father, humiliate me. I wanted to keep the dream of you perfect.'

'So keep the dream, Joe.' Her lip trembled.

'I beg you, Louise,' he turned back, 'come away with me when you're well. I've made an unholy mess ... but can I hold him?'

'Just for a second.'

He cradled the child who looked up at him steadily. 'And I think this one could put a chain round me like nothing else.'

Louise was pale with effort. 'It would be a terrible thing to bring a divorce on the family. They'd be the ones living with it. They've supported me through all this. Paying the bills, though God knows, they've had nothing for years.' She struggled up against her pillows.

'My mam sold the garnet and pearls her mother handed down to her, her very last good thing.' She watched him play with the baby's hand then went on. 'Dad sold a sovereign his dad gave to him. I've no idea where that came from but he kept it in the cistern of the lav, his final safety net.'

'I'd settle the hospital bill,' he said not looking up. 'I'd put my last in for you.'

'And I have to choose a father for my baby … for his future.' She played with the coverlet. 'He's called Benjie. Benjamin Edward.'

He put the baby back into her arms. 'You have the right to choose that. You have the right.' He held her gaze. 'But life will never have meaning for me. You know where to find me, Louise.' He got up and left.

Ben came in and found his daughter weeping. He kissed her. 'I passed him in the corridor. Forget him, my darling,' he whispered and gently lifted the baby from her.

As Louise recovered … slowly recovered … before the edges of the leaves crisped, before the sleeping Benjie cut a tooth, Mr Chamberlain declared war on Germany.

18

Patricia helped the family pack a few cases. The baron had made up his mind, they were going to the United States, he and his wife owed it to Rory. No point in taking too much. It would be for six months, less. If they needed more they'd buy clothes there. By Christmas they'd be together. Patricia had six weeks' pay, a contact address, a promised reference if needed and they went off in a whirl leaving her to close up the house. The gardener and a cleaner were to come in one day a week. The gardener would have one set of keys, the baron hung on to a second, Patricia was to keep a third. She overheard part of a discussion about investments, armaments, a now familiar word.

She wrote a letter home, oversaw a thorough cleaning of the house, found dustsheets and threw them over the furniture like shrouds, pressed her belongings into two cases, heaved them onto the curved red sandstone steps outside and let the oak door thud shut behind her. Fourteen years since she went into service. She patted her greying hair and saw Andrew waiting at the end of the drive.

The family was waiting. Her mother smelt of lavender when they hugged, Ben's pipe tobacco bitter on his breath. She stood back, looked at her father and saw how deep the lines on his face were, but creased with love.

Some of their things stowed by friends in the bad times were back, Ben's wireless with a yellow wood surround, silver spoons with apostles at the top of the stems and the crystal necklace hung round her mother's neck. A new clippy mat welcomed her in front of a fire, half hidden by the light. A pan of broth fragranced the room. Mary'd made sausage and sage rolls, an apple pie was heating in the second oven of the range and the blackened kettle spat on its tripod beside the grate.

The sisters were gathered. She took Louise's baby, shut her eyes and gently held him in. He rested his head on her shoulder then nestled down relaxed against the plump cushion of her breast.

'Is this it?' Louise asked. 'Home for good?' Her face was pinched and drawn but the voice strong and challenging. Patricia kissed the baby's head and handed him back holding the impulse to cradle Louise herself and stroke away deep blue shadows under her eyes.

'I don't know. The baron said they expected to be back by Christmas, it would be all over by then. So ...'

'Same as last time!' Ben sat in his captain's chair running his hands over the smoothness of the arms. 'It was all going to be over in the blink of an eye.' His middle finger had worn away the dark wood stain to a white channel over the years. 'Anyway, you're not going back. Let them look after themselves. You've done enough - for all of us. I'll not hear talk of you going away again.' No one contradicted him as he sat on his throne.

'Are you going to go to the country with the baby? - join the evacuees?' Patricia sat down and looked longingly at little Benjie 'That's started already.'

'I am not!' Louise almost spat. 'I'm not going to strangers with this bairn.'

'She's not strong enough to face all that', Ben said. 'And there's been no bombing, in spite of all the gas masks and such they made us have, before declaring war.'

Diane ladled the soup, smart in a dark green costume that showed her figure. The light of the fire glanced off the diamonds of her ring and shone the pale gold of her hair. She poured carefully not wearing an apron. Patricia took a bowl and passed it to Katherine, who was flushed. 'Too near the fire,' she said and moved. Fred helped her to another seat, fussing over her. Patricia saw she was putting on weight.

She felt old near her sisters, growing plump, but with no good news, the only one with grey hair. It was a relief her father had said she mustn't go back. Domestic service had eaten her youth.

From his corner Christopher sprang up at a rap at the door and hurtled down the stairs three at a time. Patricia could hardly believe he'd left school. 'Wilf for you, dad!' The voice wavered uncertainly on a high note then dropped to a foghorn.

'Tell him to come in!' Ben clapped his friend on the shoulder and Patricia tried not to smile at the sight of Christopher trailing behind him, shoulders bony, wide over a skinny body for all the world like a stretched-out coathanger. He hovered anxiously near the stock pan as if on starvation rations and tore off a huge chunk from a fresh loaf. Diane sighed and gave him a pudding basin of broth.

Wilf took a bowl and settled on an old three-legged stool. 'So, you've left school now, lad?' Christopher nodded, dunking his heel of bread and reached quickly for another piece. Diane slapped his hand and deliberately cut a slice with the bread knife, keeping the crumbs on the round breadboard, letting them fall into the little runnel of an inner circle. Wilf grinned at him. 'Any ideas for a job?'

'Actually,' Christopher replied with his mouth full, 'yes.' He looked up from the golden liquid, rich with carrot. 'I'm going to join up.'

Diane stopped sawing and let the knife clatter. 'You're fourteen.'

'I'll be fifteen in a few months. Any road,' he made an effort and swallowed, 'the navy'll take cadets.'

'They won't take idiots,' Ben growled.

Wilf frowned at his friend. 'Let the lad speak, man.' Patricia saw colour drain from her mother's face.

The boy looked round steadily. 'There's a war on. I'm joining up. It's not enough to parade about with gas masks on like we did at school – the way you see people dangling them from their faces like elephant trunks even to go to the pictures. Nasty, smelly things ponging of rubber and horrible disinfectant, nearly suffocating you.' He grinned. 'The lads at school used to make farting noises through them to make the girls laugh.' No one in the room laughed. 'Anyway, I've always fancied the sea.'

'First we've heard of it!' Ben snorted. 'They'll not be wanting you before seventeen or eighteen.'

'God help us,' Mary muttered. 'It'll surely be over by then.'

'The <u>Merchant</u> Navy would take him now,' Wilf said quietly.

'Who asked <u>you</u> to put your oar in, Wilf Robson?'

'Sorry, Ben. Just a suggestion. Anyway, it'd be safer ... don't you think? If he's got his heart set on it.'

Ben stamped his foot. 'He doesn't know what he's talking about. And it might be just as dangerous at a time like this.'

Christopher looked at his father and put the empty bowl down. 'More dangerous than going down the pit at fourteen?' His father shook his head. 'They're going to need plenty of coal as well.'

'King Coal be damned!'

'That might be the other option.' Wilf risked his luck again.

Patricia opened the oven door. 'Time we had these sausage rolls, I think.' She touched the dish and jumped back with burned fingers. Diane handed her a cloth. 'Let's enjoy the party. I've just come home.' Her father glared at Wilf who shrugged and took a roll. She offered the plate to Christopher who took two and settled to eating, not talking. The baby of the family she'd looked after when he was in nappies. In her heart she knew he was going to do it. *Please God, let the baron be right, let it be over by Christmas.*

When she woke next day there was a pile of pound notes in a saucer next to her bed. She screwed her face in bewilderment then relaxed. Ben was repaying her for the hospital bill. She patted the notes into a tidy stack and slowly counted the money. If she put her other savings with this they should have enough to buy extra stock. Supplies could dry. It wasn't only Christopher who needed to think of finding a job. There was the shop. Sighing she found her wallet.

Andrew had put sixty-five pounds by from the tobacconist shop, a fortune saved over six years at four shillings a week. She thought of the baron and baroness in London, keeping up with the Bright Young Things. In careless days they could get through a lot more than that in six weeks. Andrew said no to Patricia investing her savings. They'd need that for when they could get married - soon if she'd only live with him and his mother. The money he'd scrimped together, shilling by shilling, would go into supplies. He agreed it could be their last chance to stock up. Patricia chose not to think of sharing a flat with Mrs. Taylor. It would be transferring from one domestic service to another. To work together, though, would be a joy.

She cleaned the walls, took down the old posters and put up fresh showing men in uniform, strong, ready for action with packs of cigarettes natural in their hands. The navy was everywhere. Navy Cut, Capstan, Senior Service. No special brands for women who preferred the same as the men. A smoke was serious. She refused the pleasure herself but stood back to look at the effect.

They moved the counter to make storage space and had a new cupboard put in. Cigarette cartons, jars of black bullets, mint imperials, jelly babies, twisted sticks of liquorice, striped walking sticks of rock, fudge, fruit gums, wine gums, gob stoppers, boxes of chocolates, a sweet smell of earthy cocoa and sugar tinged with vanilla escaping through the glossy painted card. Toffee tins had sentimental masterpieces imprinted on the tops. She packed cigars, loose tobacco, snuff filling every shelf, every cupboard and unused space, spilled into Mary's scullery and the girls' bedroom. Diane complained.

Ben asked tartly when she was going to get married and she flounced - 'When we can afford it!'

'Buying Buckingham Palace are you?' She put her coat on and strutted out. 'Speaking of which,' he turned to Patricia, 'when are you two planning to get marrried?'

Patricia caught her breath. 'When we can, dad. You know the situation with Andrew's mam.'

'How is she then?'

'Not very well.'

'A creaking gate.'

She flushed. 'I can't wish somebody dead, can I? Do you want that badly to get rid of me? I know it's cramped with me back again.'

'I do not!' He looked at her over his reading glasses. 'I just want you to be happy, my bonny lass. Don't sacrifice any more for any of us. You're not getting any younger.'

'I know, dad. Look at me.' She touched the silvering hair. 'I have my dreams as well. I'd like my own home like everybody else, my own family. Don't rub it in but I'd find it hard to live in with Mrs. Taylor.'

He put down his library book, *The Grapes of Wrath*. 'Well, at least get out and enjoy yourself a bit. *Gone with the Wind*'s on at the Apollo. Spend something on yourself for a change.'

'Is that an order?'

'It is.'

'Do you want to come with us, dad?'

'Go with your sweetheart. I'm reading this.'

Mary had come in behind him. 'And I could do with going out, Ben Hawthorn. You've got your nose stuck in a book whenever you're not at the allotment.'

He reached round and pulled her onto his lap. 'We can't play gooseberry.'

'Then you can take me to the Regal, whatever's on.'

'That's an order, dad,' Patricia called over her shoulder and plunged down to the shop.

It was Andrew who helped Christopher realise his dream, helped with forms, an interview, helped him get his kit together. Patricia lent money when needed but had no heart to hurry the proceedings. It seemed like losing her child. But she saw him off. Neither father nor mother would do anything to help the process, his first destination South Africa. Mary was distraught.

'It's better than sending him down the pit,' Patricia said to comfort herself as much as to calm her parents. 'The bairn was right.'

'True enough. They'll want more and more young lads to dig the seams.'

'As much risk of the pit props giving way, dad, and a rock collapse as him being lost at sea.'

'At least I'd have his body,' Mary muttered bitterly,

'If they could find him under it all.' Ben was intent on arguing. 'Many a man's had the pit for a tomb. Miners say they've heard ghosts.

'You never said that.'

'Not one for superstition. I was convinced it was the timbers shifting, but it's weird when you're checking the tunnels in the pitch black, with a thin light to see by and you hear a sound that could be a creak or it could be a groan.'

'Come back, Ben. Your mind's wandered off. You're not at the pit now, just as well if it was spooking you.'

That was the last either she or Ben would say about Christopher's flight from home. The first postcard they received was from Australia.

Christmas passed and at last a note from the baron in a Christmas card. He'd found an opening in the U.S. in the motor trade. It could be a while before they'd be back. Rory was settling in. They might stay if he was doing well. Fair weather birds.

*

The hospital bill had been heavy for his little namesake and Ben avoided the pub even for a game of dominoes but he found sixpence for himself to go to the News Theatre in town. *Pathé News - something to crow about.* He remembered camera men from their rival with the magic spools turning, lenses trained on them during

264

the Jarrow March, in the rain with them, catching their moment for history.

Stepping into a cinema was stepping into another world. People flocked to the latest newsreel, the rescue of soldiers marooned on a beach in France at Dunkirk. Cheers were raised from the back of the hall for the fishing boats that crossed the Channel, for troops wading out to sea to meet them and for the men who hauled the Tommies to safety, smiles and a cigarette for them all, proving their mettle in an epic adventure, music over the action.

The crowd spilled out into the street, into the light, speaking to strangers, women reaching for handkerchiefs to dab their eyes.

'Lad! What a miracle!'

'The weather was.'

'The nick of time.'

'Bloody heroes.'

'Every one.'

Ben separated out, heading for his bus stop then decided to walk home. His stomach churned when he thought how near they'd been to disaster. There could have been slaughter on that beach. What had held the Germans up? That was the miracle and the mystery. Pushed right back to the sea and cornered. He went cold. They'd come out from the News Theatre with a sense of victory but the whole damn thing was a defeat. Desperate. What more lay ahead? He paced home with a feeling of dread.

Katharine's labour was not difficult and Ben felt a sigh of relief from the soles of his feet through his belly and lungs up to his thinning grey hair. He let the pain of anxiety out in a long releasing breath. Katharine was strong, thank God or whatever forces there were, her baby was healthy, a sturdy bellowing little boy who made his world sit up and notice and brought a jerk of joy in Ben's heart. Louise was looking better. Damn the war. Damn everything. There were bairns again, the completion of grandchildren, another stake in the future. Katharine's little Freddie, he was sure that one'd live.

*

A lad with a blackened face pedalled up the street and skidded to a stop. The eyes in white circles in coal dust were friendly. 'Hello, Mr Hawthorn.'

'Hello, lad,' he grinned, 'I don't know who are but you're obviously fresh from the pit. I hope they're going on improving safety down there. I hammered on for that year on year. Better lighting goes a long way."

'Aye, it's a bit better. The old 'uns say we don't know we're born. There's a rumour we could have a lot of greenhorns foisted on us some time.' Ben nodded and laughed at the experienced pitman in front of him. 'I'm Ronnie Charlton, your Christopher's friend. We were in the same class.'

'Oh aye, the Charlton lads. How's your brother, the older one?'

'Joined the navy, the proper one, not like your Chris.' The boy ducked as a friendly cuff almost clipped his ear. 'He's home on leave just now. In a bad fettle, our Chris.' He lowered his voice so Ben could just hear. 'He doesn't want to go back after what they made him do.'

'What was that, then?'

Ronnie leant forward in a conspiracy. 'Having the British sailors take over the French Fleet.'

'I read about it. A difficult one, and I wouldn't have liked to make that decision. But they must have been frightened Jerry would get hold of the whole damn fleet and use it against us. Wartime, lad. Wartime. He shouldn't take it so hard.'

'There's a bit more to it than that. 'E's spending most of the time at the pub. Me mam's frantic. That's him, I can hear him coming.' Ben looked down the street and saw a young man staggering, standing up to punch an invisible enemy and stopping to holler something. Ronnie pushed off, his language slipping broader into dialect with fright. 'Divn't say ah tel ye anything or `e'll bash us.'

266

The drunk on the other side came nearer throwing a right hook in the air. 'What are ye lookin' at, mister?'

'Nowt, lad, just seeing a man who's had one too many. We've all been there, though. I'll give you a hand.' He crossed the road.

'Divn't need nee hand. Oot the way.'

Ben's boxing skills were back as he ducked and danced to safety. He surprised himself at how light he still was. 'I'll help you home.' He came nearer and the drunk sprawled an arm round his shoulder. 'What ails ye lad?'

'Fuckin' navy, that's what ails me.'

'Steady there. Women and children could hear. That's language for the men.'

'Blast their eyes, all of them, that what I say. Where de ye work, mister?'

'The factory down yonder.'

'Ye must be makin' the munitions an' stuff.'

'I'm with the heating engineering, keeping the country going.'

'I'll let ye off,' the drunk slurred, 'but just this once.' They zig-zagged along together. 'Ah joined up ter fight the Jerries, the Krauts, not the Frogs.'

'We're not fighting the French, just taking charge of boats that could be used by the enemy. It's not the same.'

'Wish ye were right, mister, wish ye were right.'

'That's the beer talking, son.' The young man was beginning to sweat and a brewery seemed to leak out of his pores.

'French Captain wouldn't surrender the ship to us.' It was darkening for a rainstorm and people were blacking their windows out. Ben guided his charge away from the road. The house was on the opposite side on the top of the street. 'Frenchies were still on it. We set fire to the bugger and sent it to the bottom. It takes a lot of beers, mister ter get rid of the screams.' They slewed to a halt. Ben stared at his sozzled companion. The eyes were bloodshot. 'An' the worst of it was ... we never picked neebody up.'

Ben heaved his sailor further on, crossed the road, knocked at the door and tried it. It gave. The young man fell in and crashed against the first steps giving a salute. Ronnie was waiting at the top of the staircase.

Pacing the house when he couldn't sleep Ben felt a cry of pain deep below his throat, from the recesses of his ribs, the base of his belly. It was a whistle of air, a groan, a howl of misery in the depths of the night when dawn might not break, a cry for pity.

Judas cut. Slicing an ally down. And imagination was his enemy.

He wandered through the living room and scullery and heard the unnerving mourn of a foghorn through the streets that sloped to the Tyne. He was like the young drunk he'd helped earlier. Whether his eyes were open or shut he saw torpedoes launch straight through water to their prey, tear steel, gush foam into the gut of a ship. Imagination tortured him. Moans and shouts invaded his brain, terrified screams of men jumping from flames into a sea where none would rescue them, shocked, gaping fish-like so water entered their lungs, dragging them under to a young, surprised burial at sea. Worst, flaring flames on water with no escape, their breakout blocked by a burning wall.

His breath caught as he saw a mirage of a beautiful ship split, rend and splinter to its grave and he pitied those who had to obey and fire on friends, freeing nightmares to invade their reason night and day.

And there was his work. They worked with other factories, part of a bigger picture. Shiny metals paraded as torpedoes in his head, clicking to a fine finish. Shells, torpedoes, bullets melted from one form to another, gleaming, polished, curved to a point in perfect symmetry, upright for duty. Beautiful.

Bread and butter.

'God forgive us,' the atheist prayed.

He had a son at sea.

Next day he was ashen but went to work. When he came home he propped Christopher's photo next to their bed and saw or imagined its outline though the blackout-filtered moonlight. He lay listening to Mary's breath, a stranger to sleep. Whirling thoughts and his mind's eye had cursed him.

Flesh now seemed to melt beneath the skin of his spare frame. He ate nothing but hot porridge or soup. No word from Christopher. Mary said it was impossible for letters to come regularly. Two or three could be delivered soon after each other. They were never sure where he was. Dipping to Australia to collect food? Delivering it to where? The Pacific? Crossing the Atlantic? U boats hunted beneath with torpedoes.

Ben's eyes were shadowed black but he'd stay alert, not doze over the machines. On his shift there were no mistakes. The men respected him. It didn't matter whether they liked him. Mary smiled when he took money home. She raised her eyebrows when he handed his pay packet unopened on a Friday but his pride in it soured.

The fire was bright, the kettle spat on the hearth. Mary had his ration coupons for butter, sugar, bacon and ham and even if there was little meat to be had she made a hearty soup. Time off, he went to his allotment digging for his own victory. Even there freezing clods of earth he turned failed to blot the water covering French sons or their charred remains from his mind. Tears he held inside grew cold.

Ben unburdened himself at the rectory after a visit to the News Theatre.

John Hargraves sat him down. 'You can't take the word of a drunken young man over a thing like this – however sincere he seems, he's talking through the drink.' He peered in Ben's face. 'And look after yourself, man. Look at you! No point in running yourself into the ground. That'll achieve nothing.'

'But I know that lad, him and his brother and I don't believe that was a drunken fantasy. Beer can loosen the tongue.'

'"In vino veritas", yes. But it could just be the stress of war on his mind. War can destroy both sides at once.' Gwen came in with tea and placed a cup in Ben's hands. 'Did you hear anything of that, Gwen?' She nodded and sliced home-made bread. Ben's hands shook. 'Anyway, look, I'll see what I can find out. A couple of men I trained with are Forces chaplains. They might have inside knowledge.'

Gwen finished slicing her bread. 'And my father might know what's going on. The civil service could be more reliable. No offence, John.'

'Of course! Your father always knows everything but he might not squeak. Official whatsits.'

'It's probably not classified, just not for general consumption, especially not the papers.'

'Well, we'll both do our best to set your mind at ease.'

There was no easement. The sailor's account was confirmed. Ben ate better but prowled and seethed round the house till Mary seemed ready to scream.

Wilf came to take him to the pub.

Mary looked at him hard. 'No trouble, mind.'

'He needs to get out a bit, Mary.'

Ben kissed her cheek. 'They're selling off home baked hams.' He held his hand up. 'I don't know how they came by them. Maybe they keep pigs. But it'll help the larder and you can give some to the girls.'

'If it finds its way here.'

Wilf put his arm on his friend's shoulder. 'Just a game of dominoes, lass.'

'You know how little it takes to set him off.'

'I'll watch him.'

In the pub Ben did his under-the-counter business and relaxed in the surroundings: the red mahogany of the bar, glasses gleaming faint iris in the few lights that burned, a scent of pipe tobacco and haze of smoke shifting in frail blue spirals, men too old for the front bent towards each other in earnest, irrelevant conversation, friendship and calm.

Wilf fetched him a pint and he looked at the creamy head over deep amber ale. They took dominoes and began to lay them out, white dots on dignified black. He could beat anyone at this.

Earnest talkers came over and drew up chairs. Ben concentrated. The beer was still at his elbow. Heads went on nattering over the game and talk turned to the war progress. There'd been some funny business in the Mediterranean. Ben bit his lip.

'Course you could never trust the French.'

'Entente ... thing ... though.' Natter, natter.

'To pot! Churchill gave every ship's captain an ultimatum to hand over. It's coming out on the news now, on the wireless, if you listen carefully. Gave then forty-eight hours, that's what I heard - on the news.' The serious talkers were raising voices and Ben placed a hand over his ear.

'You must have been listening to the Third programme or something weird. I've never heard that.'

'Their ships, though, man!'

Ben tried to focus on the game to keep these things out of his mind.

'To keep them out of Gerry's hands, ye fat head! Don't think Gerry would keep his filthy mitts off those ships.' Ben saw his way on the matching patterns. 'Our Prime Minister couldn't risk it.'

He slotted his last pieces onto the table and his hand was out. He took a swig from his glass, smooth aromatic hops passing warmth to his stomach and picked up the ha'penny they'd played for.

'Of course Winston's got form for mowing people down!' he said

'Watch yer mouth, man!' The second serious head turned.

'Thou's got a short memory. Remember Tonypany? Sending troops in against the miners!' Another slug of the beer and anger fizzed through his veins. 'This time it was our allies.'

'No, No! That couldn't be true. I'm not having that. Rubbish! They wouldn't let them burn.' A finger wagged.

'True as I'm here.' Another slug. Ben's fingers clenched. The fist crunched on the table. 'There's always another way!' Chairs scraped away.

'Are you lookin' for trouble?'

'It's time to go, Ben.'

'I'll finish my drink.'

'Get all your stuff, then it's out and away for us.'

Ben picked his jacket up seething, dots of red on his cheek bones, and reached for his glass.

'No need for heat, man. We were just sayin' ...'

'Murder. That's what it was. Mass murder!'

'Steady on.'

He drained the beer, watched a dribble of froth slide down the inside of the glass. Wilf's hand came down firm on his shoulder. 'Here's your ham, Ben. We're gone.'

They made for the door as his brain felt swollen inside his head, about to crack his skull. A gulp of air hit them outside.

'Don't get so worked up, Ben, man!'

'Worked up? We just take murder in our stride? Worked up?'

'You might have noticed there's a war gannin' on. Hitler commits murder every day.'

'Not against his own. French sailors were standing with us!'

'They'd have rolled over to Gerry. That fellow was right. Given the ship up - to them. They would have.'

'Only their commander made the decision. They could just have arrested *him*. And you don't know he didn't have something up his sleeve. Waiting for something.'

The night was cool, pleasant, even though street lamps were off and no light showed from a house. A breeze touched them but Ben felt only a dark fluttering of death's wings. He faced his friend, picked out his blurred outline, black against black. In a back lane a cat squawked and they heard a flurry of spitting, a squall of shrill rasping cries scraping up through an octave. Pain ground Ben's eardrums. He shuddered with closed eyes. Reason retreated and alcohol drew a blind over his brain.

Wilf jabbed him. 'And *you* don't know he *did* have anything up his sleeve!'

Fury popped through aching in his ears. A ham was in his left hand. Fingers of his right closed. He circled Wilf and felt he was in the boxing ring but there was no ref. The ham fell to the canvas beneath his feet.

'Ben, stop! Of course I don't want anybody murdered.'

'Ratting on our allies. I'll see Churchill's men in hell for this!' He jabbed with his right fist, hooked with the left. 'If you say yes to this you're no friend of mine. You're a bloody Judas!'

Wilf ducked. 'Don't be stupid, man, Ben. I didn't give the order. I'm not bloody Churchill!'

'Aye, but you stood behind him in a long line with all the others,' he stabbed the air with his fist, 'the others that'll rat on their friends.'

'This is the drink talking. I never should have given you a pint to get you started.' Wilf ducked again.

Like slow motion, Ben picked the ham up, Wilf was shouting something open mouthed. He took a swing, landed the leg of meat square to the stomach, and dropped the joint. Wilf gasped as blows rained down but Ben was back in the ring, brain clouded, on automatic reaction, a fight for the championship as he sweated, urged by an imagined roar, looking for weakness. Wilf gasped as blows pounded him. For a moment he straightened as Ben led with a right to the chest, hooked a left to the chin and his opponent staggered, fell. There was no canvas, only a kerbstone. The mist cleared and he saw Wilf on the ground, bleeding from his head.

Footsteps rang on the pavement. Ben saw a pair of shoes and without looking up breathed, 'Can you get some help? Run to the station. This man's out cold.'

'Right you are.' Footsteps retreated down the lane.

He took his jacket off and laid it tenderly under Wilf's head then sprinted to the back alley behind his house, hurled the ham over the wall into the yard, heard the thud, turned, sprinted back and was kneeling beside Wilf, a handkerchief pressed to his head to try to staunch the blood before a pair of boots pounded up. 'We need an ambulance. He's bleeding heavy.'

The policeman leant over. 'Did you see this?'

'No.' He hadn't really seen it. He'd been crazed, half blind.

'I think it'll be quicker to take him in the squad car. Stay with him. Keep pressing on. Ambulances might be out. There's been a bomb down by the shipyard.'

He pressed, checking the flow of Wilf's blood. 'Hold on Wilf! Hold on Wilf!'

A car sped to the kerbside. Three police fell out. One started on first aid, a bandage tight to the head and checking for broken bones before moving him. Two of them lifted Wilf and laid him on the backseat of the car, head in a copper's lap.

The third uniform had pen and notebook ready. 'We'll need your name and address, sir. You were at the scene. We'll have to have a statement. Just routine.'

'I ... I'll come clean.' Ben was shaking, stammering. 'We'd been at the pub. I drank too much, I'm not sure how this happened. I followed him out. I came cold sober again when I saw him on the bottom.'

'So, you didn't see anyone else?'

'No. Not till that other fellow came up and I sent him down to the station.'

The constable snapped his notebook shut. 'We'll be in touch then. Can you get home all right?'

'Yes, I can walk.'

Next day Mary found the ham in the backyard when she went outside to the lavatory. She was furious Ben dared come home in a state. 'What's this?'

'The ham I bought.'

'What's it doing here?'

'I was drunk, pet. I think I threw it over the wall.'

'I'll throw _you_ over the wall!' she picked it up, pressed the pink flesh. 'It's a good `un, though. It'll wash. I'd better get it inside and hide it.' She forgot her pressing need for the lavatory.

Truth.

All he knew for sure was he'd been drinking with Wilf in the pub and he'd bought a ham from under the counter. They'd had an argument but that was nothing fresh - like an old married couple. An argument a day keeps the blues away. Wilf would needle him, say something blind stupid, he would rise to it, they'd play a Laurel and Hardie scene and then be friends again. Someone might pour a glass of water on one of them at the pub if it got out of hand. If it got out of hand at home Mary would put them out, they'd obey her and giggle like kids outside.

He closed his eyes, pictured the pub, the mahogany bar with the brass foot rail, their corner with the table and dominoes out, relaxed male comfort. It came back to him. He'd been spitting nails about sinking part of the French fleet near Oran, the Mir El Khebir incident, firing on the Frogs. He'd probably slagged Churchill off. Nothing new there. The fire in the mix was that Wilf had bought him a pint, maybe two. He shouldn't have gone into the pub. He only went to play dominoes but he knew the sour enticing smell of beer and other men drinking would set him off. Atmosphere, comrades after work - the lucky ones not called up, but practically all of them were lucky now in reserved occupations with the war effort - free to tamp a pipe without a complaint even though the smoke got into the curtains, free to speak his mind, listen to the thud on the darts board, criticise the strategy of the game, criticise past management at St James' Park, though he preferred the boxing hall to the football pitch, free to listen to a friend's troubles, give advice or tell a joke to cheer the bugger up. Male company. Free to sweat.

He'd do better to go to the boxing ring and miss the pub afterwards. One foot across the threshold and gritted resolve faded. The creamy head against the old gold of a pint was a thing of beauty. Harmless. Then half an hour later it was different.

He might have taken Wilf for a punch bag. But he didn't know he had and wasn't sure. He didn't know he hadn't either. He'd been riled up. A drink could make him free with his fists, he knew reason could go to camp outside of his head. They'd sent coppers into the pub to ask what had happened but everyone was guarded because black market goods had changed hands.

The other witness who called the police was interviewed. There was nothing to incriminate him except his knuckles were sore next day. The officer in charge examined his hands but there was no skin broken, no graze, no bruise. He'd taken a bruise out with witchhazel from the chest Mary used as a dressing table. The act of dabbing that on and a familiar pain in his hands made him guilty as hell. He knew, no matter what memory said. It was true he didn't really know what happened. It could have been only one blow. But he'd be the one who'd landed it.

Wilf was in hospital unconscious and they let him in to visit. He went every night. Everyone was waiting for Wilf to surface. The bang on the kerbstone had knocked his friend out and Ben didn't know whether it had wiped the slate of his memory clean.

Ten days in limbo. Ten nights without sleep. Mary walked the house like a ghost and outside she avoided Mrs. Robson. She'd hung the ham up from a hook in the pantry and then taken it over to Louise without a word. Louise cooked it. They ate from it. Louise stored the cooked ham in the cool of her pantry.

On the eleventh day the rap came at the door. He had to go with the police to the station and then to the hospital. Wilf was awake.It was the policeman Ben knew.

'Don't know if he's exactly what you call compos mentis but he can speak now. I want you in the room when I quiz him about his statement.'

'So he's made one.'

'Aye, he's made one.'

'I'll get my coat.'

Ben's footsteps echoed endlessly along sterile smelling corridors of the charity hospital, green wall tiles shining clean from a disinfecting rub. He kept his eyes on the bobby walking in front, shoulders bobbing up and down in the dark blue uniform.

Wilf lay at the end of a long ward, head bound like a mummy, face the colour of ash, no movement. Ben hardly drew breath as he approached and a nurse dragged a chair up for the policeman.

'Can you hear me, Mr. Robson?' A growling in Wilf's throat. He wasn't dead, then. Ben sat cautiously at the end of the bed. The constable raised his voice as if the patient was deaf as a post.

'Can you hear me, Mr. Robson?'

Wilf's eyelids flickered. 'Aye, I hear you. Divn't try and raise the dead, lad.' Ben breathed and held back a grin.

'Please don't tire him, constable.' The nurse hovered. 'He mustn't be agitated.' She fetched another chair for Ben.

The P.C. lowered his voice. 'Just want to know if you remembered anything else about the ... incident.'

'I've remembered Ben Hawthorne's a fool,' Wilf grated, 'a fool that argues black's white.' The eyelids creased tight shut.

'Yes. There was an argument in the pub. Did Mr Hawthorne lay hold of you?'

'Only thing Ben Hawthorne laid hold of was his best bitter.'

'A witness said you left the pub together.'

'Didn't stay together.' Wilf seemed to make an effort and his eyes sliced open, he gave a scathing look past the bobby to his friend. They bored into each other. 'I don't keep the company of fools. If I want to listen to rubbish I can get that at home.'

'What was the argument about?'

'Prime Minister's actions. And I'm a patriot, not a traitor.'

The P.C.'s notebook was open but he hadn't written anything. 'So ... you parted company outside?'

'That's what I said.'

'And he didn't follow you?'

'No.'

'Certain?'

'I'd have heard him, staggering a bit after the drink, and I'd have smelt him.'

'There's not that much to drink these days.'

'It doesn't take much for him to be off his trolley. Not fond of a bath either.' Another scathing look. 'You don't have to be well off to be clean, Hawthorne. And if you've got no soap, I'll give you some carbolic.' He turned to the constable. 'I'd have smelt his breath a mile off.'

'Maybe he lay in wait for you?'

'Too far gone. He didn't have the wits he was born with. And that's not many.'

'You're certain of that?'

'He was tomfooling about but not near me. Couldn't keep his mouth shut or his feet straight when we were out of the pub. I crossed the road and went in another direction. I'd have heard him coming. No doubt at all.'

'And you say you were attacked from behind?' Silence. 'But nothing was taken. No money? Nothing?'

'Reckon they mistook me for that fool there at the end of the bed.' His voice was stronger. 'He nettled a lot of people in the pub by that outburst. It doesn't take long to make an enemy.' Wilf looked at him again through half closed eyes. 'Very nice of ye ter visit with the polis, Hawthorne, but ye needn't come back. Where *were* ye when I needed ye? A friend's nee use if he's not there when he's needed.'

Ben sat taut. The constable turned to him. 'Could the attacker have mistaken Mr. Robinson for you that night?'

'We're the same build.'

'And you might have given somebody reason to hit you?'

'I might have offended some people by my views on Winston Churchill.'

'Any other possible reason to follow you and try to attack you?'

He sat straight, looked the constable in the eyes. 'I was carrying a leg of ham.'

'Oh, so we're getting to it.'

'Where did you get the ham?'

'Man gave me it.'

'*Gave* you it? Now, look here, ham's a rationed commodity.'

Words came out, Ben didn't know how he was making sense of it, except the words kept flowing. 'A lot of people owed us money from way back. The wife gave credit in strike times and she went bankrupt from the unpaid bills. Some people still remember, at least the wives do. They make it up to us now and then. And, you see, this was a dried ham. It'd been curing for a year or so. It wasn't rationed when it was hung. These debtors, they reckoned we could have it but didn't want to bring it to the house.'

'So, where is it?'

'Eaten. Shared and eaten.'

The constable shook his head. 'Did anyone see this ... present of a ham?'

'We weren't exactly drawing attention to ourselves where we were playing dominoes. But somebody might have noticed. You can never be sure.'

'I saw it.' They looked at Wilf, eyes as slits watching them. 'Thought ye could hold out on me over that as well, Ben Hawthorne. Mean bugger.'

The constable interrupted. 'Do you know the man? - this fellow that passed a leg of ham that no longer exists?'

'Only by sight.'

The constable looked at his notebook, wrote something and crossed it out. 'Possibly he followed you out. But you're certain the assailant was not the man sitting here?'

'This mean so and so? Not him. He doesn't have the guts.'

'And you don't want to press charges against him?'

'Wouldn't waste the time. Or polis effort.'

'It's not satisfactory, I can tell you that, but we can't waste time and money on a case that wouldn't stand up in court.' The P.C. snapped his notebook shut. 'Unless you remember anything else, or another witness comes forward, we'll have to let the case rest.' He scraped his chair, got up and made a little bow to the nurse.

Ben leaned forward over his friend. 'Get better, man, Wilf.' He touched his shoulder gently. Wilf nodded his head a fraction.

Next Saturday Ben sat staring at the back of the bedroom door. There were three hooks along it where Mary's best clothes hung. Good bedroom furniture was sold long ago or taken by the bailiffs but he'd knocked a few things together, nothing to what they'd had. She didn't complain. Soon as the war was over he'd get her better stuff, when there was anything to buy. To the right of the door was another hook on the wall where his boxing gloves dangled from their laces, the only things he wouldn't part with through the worst days. Mary kept her crystal necklace, his wedding present to her. He kept his gloves. One of the pleasures of employment was that he afforded the subs for the boxing hall. He looked along the windowsill to his collection of paperbacks, pocket Penguins with the little logo and the orange bands, his own copies, his other pride. Mark Twain, H.G. Wells, Jack London. The boxing gloves were dark brown leather, faded, scarred and battered to a dirty fawn along the punching line.

He could have killed Wilf.

Mary came in and asked what was the matter.

'Wilf's the matter,' he said and dropped his head on his knuckles.

She sat beside him. 'I didn't want to tell you yet but Mrs Robson was round here yesterday when you were at work. She said your presence wasn't welcome at the hospital.' He looked up cowed. 'It could be worse. He's getting better. That's your good news.'

'And the bad?'

'She doesn't want you associating with him at the pub, at the politics - the Labour - or anywhere else.'

A spurt of fire through Ben's darkness. 'Aye, well - we're not little bairns to be told who we can play with. Wilf and I go back. He'll make his own mind up. One thing, though, I'll not be meeting him in the pub. I'm never going to drink that stuff again.

She took his hand. 'Will you sign the pledge?'

'If that's still goin', if it'll make you happy. I've done with it, though. I don't need to sign anything. I know I've said it before but I could have killed a man this time.'

'Aye, well, he can come round here and you can smoke your pipes.'

'Mary, will you do me a favour?'

'What?'

'Reach the boxing gloves down off the wall.'

She brought them over. 'Now you can put them in the bin. I won't wear them again. I won't raise my fist either in anger or in the ring. You can get rid of my old trophies as well.'

'I'll not bin the gloves. I'll see if there's a young lad could use them - maybe up at St James'.'

'If you like, but I'm not going back to the hall again.'

'I'll put the trophies away. Christopher might like to have them.'

'I don't want to encourage him to scrap at all.'

'Right. But I might like to keep them.'

'Give them to Louise. She can have them, you can see them over there if you like. But take the gloves away. I don't want to touch or smell them. They've got memories. I'm turning my back on the fighting.' She made to go out. 'And Mary?'

'What?'

'I'm sorry for what I did when we were young. I'm sorry I ever lifted a hand to you.' She nodded and made for the kitchen again. 'Mary!'

'What now?'

'You're still my bonny lass.'

19

Joe walked back to his lonely flat in Leeds. No wife, no lover, no son to bring up; all left behind in an ice cream parlour. He passed a pub and hesitated, deciding whether to go in. The smell of the brewery rose from the hatch where draught beer was loaded. Tomcat piss and yeast, a smell that promised a good time even though Newcastle Brown was hard to find. What the hell! He turned back, went in and ordered a whisky chaser. Then another. He talked to someone and had no memory ten minutes later of what they'd said but polished mahogany, glasses and brass made him feel at home. No word from Louise though he'd left his address in a bunch of flowers at the hospital. The pub was the only damned place where he did feel at home. Before time was called he lined up another two whisky chasers. Where the landlord was getting supplies did not concern him. He lifted a glass. Evie'd found factory work for the war effort. She wasn't coming back. An idea was pricking through the blur of his brain.

He passed posters day in and day out, a few of them put up by the government. One said: -

Your children may be the next to perish ...
Move them to the country ...NOW!

An artist's picture showed children standing in front of charred and bombed houses. He always turned away quickly but yesterday he stood in front of another. It merged in his head through the whisky with the one he'd gazed at near the news cinema when Louise almost dragged him away. He'd considered it then thought better of the modern army. Lorries caught in beams of white light, modern light, exciting light - reality wouldn't be as charged and electrifying as they made it look. This other one was stark but fired his interest:

Defend your children!

ENLIST NOW!
Join the Royal Air Force

How else could he defend that baby he held for a few minutes? Defenceless, tiny, called by Louise after her husband. He'd defend all children and stop them having to stand parentless in front of their bombed homes. He could patrol the skies. Defender of the weak, Superman in his whisky dream. No cape, but a blue uniform. The R.A.F. Women love a uniform.

Someone bent over him as he slid off his stool. The barmaid's voice came through a fog, 'What's that, love? You'll guard the children? - Help me with this one, Harry!'

He was over thirty but fit, alert. They accepted him. He paid his debts and went for training to Kent. The uniform made him look taller, look like a dark tall stranger in light blue. The women really did love a uniform. It was worth it.

And another mistress came into his life. He joined the rest of the pilots in training to be a slave to her, to dream of her, to live and breathe for her. A lady with no vices, damned near perfection. The Spitfire.

Joe doffed a drunken hat to Chamberlain for taking to the air for talks, for buying a breath of time, for boosting numbers of this darling with radar, her far sighted, X-ray eyed brother. The pilots dived till their eyes popped then climbed a mountain of cloud. So did their fellow combatants in the Messerschmitt but this beloved made neat tight turns so the bastards couldn't skewer them to the sky.

The 'fabulous Spitfire' with a bulletproof windscreen, liquid-cooled engine and elliptical wing was Joe's swallow wheeling to the horizon. To be an ace or die, a fighter ace like the Red Baron! Hellfire Corner over Kent was a dare, almost a refrain among the pilots - to 'grab the enemy and claw him down from the sky.' Living to the very edge of the moment, day by day they went out to die.

At the refectory tables, empty places when the Luftwaffe was supposed to bring Britain to her senses by the great offensive. *Bugger them!* Joe's heart pumped with fear then sang for joy at Churchill's speeches, at his adoration of the flying men. He trusted luck, Lady Luck, the gambler's friend. He needed her for the epic Eagle Day air battle, the climax.

A formation of four came towards him and his capricious lady of the cards turned her back on him. Joe could not see how many planes were coming. He flew for the lead Messerschmitt, bullets blazing at full speed for a direct hit at the engine to set it alight. The tank, bullet proof, held but the craft went into a downward spin. An age before it righted itself. Joe thought he'd shaken the enemy off when the sun blinded him and the leader's wingman flew directly for him. He tried outflying the beast but was no match for the speed of the Messerschmitt. The punch of its twenty millimetre cannon hit him, damaged his wing and the aircraft went into a spin.

The wingman sped after him but he nerved himself to steady the plane, to right her, get her home. He'd lost contact with his squadron when the machine gun hit him and his engine caught fire. Flames came back into the cockpit. He tried to eject but the parachute billowed, became trapped in the plane and he plunged into the sea in a ball of flame, unconscious before he hit the water, sorrows drowned by the restless waves of the English Channel.

August 20th in the House of Commons

'Never in the field of human conflict was so much owed by so many to so few.'

*

Bodies piled, lives snuffed out into history.
Sirens, bayonets, bombs,
bomber aircraft blasting homes, limbs,
dog fighting over the Tyne to drop poison cargo,
turning tail for Norway hoping fuel would last.
No Joe.

Ration books, dig for victory.
Land girls as men pick up rifles.
Sewing boxes, make do and mend.

Curb tongues that could talk careless talk.
Tanks, submarines, smoke, dust and fire.
White cliffs of Dover. No bluebirds.
No Joe.

Patricia found she didn't miss her former work. Her sister was still not strong so she helped Louise look after the baby or cooked dinner for her and Edward. Then there was Katharine's baby. She'd get on a bus to visit her at the other side of the town. But most of her energies poured into the business with Andrew. The shop was busy as they were well stocked. She enjoyed it but thought the two of them had missed their time, they were growing grey together. Passions they held in when young flowed into the deepened channel of affection. Their one entertainment was the cinema. Everyone went to the pictures and queued round the block in the cold if they had to, to get in to a big film.

In late February darkness they closed the shop, put up the lift-in shutters that Edward had made from stiff card and plywood for the blackout, emptied the till, checked up, stacked coins in their different columns, copied up the books and put everything into a strong leather bag before sharing a meal with Ben and Mary. Soup was on the menu every day, then a vegetable concoction like carrot croquettes. She could hardly open a paper without seeing 'Good news about carrots!' Their eyesight must be excellent by now. Just as well. To confuse the enemy if he should come upon them, street signposts were turned and hardly any of the street lamps lit. They found their way by peering at white-painted rings round the lampposts and white stripes on the kerbstones.

They laughed as they went out, going to the flicks, going to see Disney's feature *Fantasia*. Everyone wanted to see it except Ben who waited for Chaplin's *The Great Dictator*. Mickey Mouse was good enough for them.

The animation lifted them to a sphere of magic, ballet music creating a world of mad toadstools, glowing blossom, dancing petals rippling on water, a diamond web and frosted leaves, underwater caverns, fairies with lace tutus of snowflakes then crazy, Cossack thistles. They were open mouthed at Mickey Mouse in sorcerer's hat, wearing white gloves, in his dream conducting the stars and comets but letting manic water-bearing brooms loose.

Best of all was the Dance of the Hours. They creased with laughter at the sight of flatfooted ostriches in ballet shoes, luxurious feathers turning to fans, doubling as short frothy ballet skirts. Hippos pirouetted on delicate feet, flimsy ruffles round their waists followed by a joyous, comic parade of elephants dancing, tripping lightly in chorus blowing bubbles from their trunks. Then a threat from a crew of nasty crocodiles that menaced in rhythm right up to Queen Hippo. But their leader was in love with her. Slim and snappy, King Croc twirled, hid round pillars and spun her in a heroic courtship dance, lifting her vast weight like a feather.

They moved on a cloud of music as they came out, carrying the enchantment of charming outlandish cartoons, twirling each other, trying to find each others' faces though they could hardly make anything out in the darkness. At a complicated junction near the cinema a faint glimmer of light aimed downward from a single street lamp and travelling cars showed only thin beams that sliced through dimming devices, slits on the headlamps like hard half-closed yellow eyes.

White fillets of paint on kerbstones did not reach her brain to warn her as Patricia threw her head back giggling, roaring with laughter. She stumbled against the edge of the pavement not hearing an approaching engine and tripped into the rumbling path of a vehicle that pierced the night, threw her and damaged a bone in the ear before vanishing into the darkness.

When she woke there was a riot in her head and a swelling the size of the universe, drumming, bursting cymbals in her ear. Infection. Hot tears rolled onto the pillow. Compounds of bitter herbs in milk, in water or in alcohol were vile, nauseating. If she retched an explosion went off and lightning flashed round the edge of open or closed eyes. Waves of pain rolled up and down, tongues of pain licking at the temple, probing behind her eyes, fire needles in one ear, burning along a cheekbone, round an eye and back into the ear. '*Make it stop!*' But they could not hear her voice. Life was drowned by the symphony of knives slicing and stabbing, jabbing and rattling, rising in a cacophony of PAIN. When the waves sucked back and agony died to an ache she was on a quiet shore, half alive under a blanket of heavy half sleep.

An unseen ocean came to thud pressure in waves across her head. Fire flares then ice played over her body, sweat soaked the bed but she could not move. Despair that she was abandoned in deep black loneliness at the bottom of a well, unreached.

Then in the depths of night something gave way in an inner howl and liquid trickled from her ear. She moaned in the nightmare. A nurse touched the yellow on the pillow, ran for help. When the doctor came she opened her eyes. He felt her forehead. 'It's burst. The fever might go. She may be safe.' The nurse fetched a damp flannel for her forehead, a clean nightdress, put towels beneath her. 'Leave her half an hour. Change the sheets then if she can face being moved.'

Cool fingers delicately wiped her, the slime of sweat was lifted over her head, clean cotton covered her. She lay drifting on dizziness but sleep turned healer and rocked her.

As she slowly surfaced she was conscious of Ben sitting by the bed with Wilf for company. Her eyes were sealed shut but she could hear them talk.

'Aye, it's started. I heard from John, the vicar up the road, those chaps he gave shelter to from Germany they've all been interned.'

'Wouldn't like to be in their shoes.'

'The Church might get them out but I wouldn't bank on it right now. Same'll have happened to the Trade Unionists our guys took in.' Patricia tried to open her eyes but they stayed gummed. 'And there was a bomb dropped last night near the High Level Bridge.'

'I heard it on the wireless, Ben.'

'We could see the flare from our front window. Spillers' factory's been badly damaged, they say.'

'It'll maybe be a one off.'

'And pigs'll maybe fly. I feel sick.'

'Not as sick as me, dad.'

A rough hand caressed her brow and dry lips kissed her eyelids. 'Come back to us, my darling, my bonny lass.'

'I'm running up a bill.' Her voice was low and hoarse.

'Don't even think about it.'

'I'll go out to work.'

He stroked her hair back from her forehead. 'You're not to think about a hospital bill. And I forbid you to think of going out to work' He shook his head shaking tears. 'My daughter's alive.'

Ben could look out from his bedroom window to the terraced streets with lines of backyards sloping to the Tyne and see the war come to his doorstep. Messerschmidts flew in to bomb the shipping and in light summer nights, open mouthed, he could watch a dog fight, planes circling, wheeling above each other for mastery of the riverside, or there was a chase. A sigh of relief, sweating, if the German plane turned tail to growl off over the North Sea.

Whirling dust in the night and in the breath of morning he heard the entire chimney of the Co-op stores was gone, the stack fallen right through the roof. Outrage that they could touch the Co-op. Whirling dirt everywhere, ruins, dust like chaff before a wind.

Ben shook his fist at the sky when he saw photos of the Heaton Secondary School. Great iron gates at the girls' end were shattered off their holdings in a big raid, the caretaker's house wrecked. He moved like a robot, weary, wading through a sea of troubles.

Coats and gas masks were by the beds now and small bags packed so they could rush out with a blanket to cover them and a hunk of bread and flask of milk or water they'd share if others were without. Patricia'd not be able to move fast and his wife thanked God she was still in hospital. They preferred to go to one of the bigger shelters. There was a culvert down by the Ouseburn but it was too far and they made a dash for the yard of a little school near the church where there was a shelter for the children.

After a long raid they straggled back before dawn, stiff, freezing, shaken, the shock as great the tenth time as the first time. How long? How long? And when the end came would they be here to see it?

As they neared home the sky was suddenly ablaze. Ben pushed his wife to the ground and watched white light shoot up. A tremor passed underneath them. The deafening roar of the plane was overhead then passed as it swooped down to the Tyne. 'He's missed the target. Come on, the house is standing. We're safer inside. Stay downstairs in the shop. I'll pull that mattress out from under the counter.'

'No, I'll have my bed.'

A fire engine screamed.

A few minutes of quiet, then a second hit. They piled downstairs under the counter then crawled upstairs again. Ben saw his wife to bed. She moaned but fell instantly asleep. He pulled the covers up over her shoulder and went to watch at the window. Outside was lit up, he moved the blind a fraction. One window uncovered would make no difference. The fire was opposite at the top of a street dropping toward the Tyne. Firemen were frantically trying to uncover a hydrant. He wanted to go out to help but knew a civilian would be in the way. He took a torch, left the room and switched it on to try and rake embers up from the fire. They were warm. He'd chopped sticks earlier and fed them on as tinder with paper, struck a match, shielded the flame, fired the scrunched newsprint and blew carefully. Blue light travelled up and down the old Chronicle in an up draught and danced over fine chippings of wood onto the sticks. He gently dropped warm embers on top, filled his lungs, blew air through. The fire flared and he added more wood scavenged from bombsites in spite of falling masonry. Charred rafters, doors, bits of floorboard, everything was collected. The blaze got going and he sat watching tongues of red and orange lick up the chimney. The blind was drawn down but he could hear the cries of the firemen frantically working.

Watching flames, he could see a flare down Hebburn way. Bombs fell randomly or were jettisoned on the way back. Houses were burning regularly across there. Poor devils who lived near the shipyards.

From time to time he peered cautiously from the window to see if the burning building was under control but daren't stay long. The A.R.P. might still be out even if the sky was lit up. At least no one seemed to have been in the ruined house.

He sat in the firelight in his spoked captain's armchair the girls called the 'Big Liar's chair'. He sat on as if glued. Diane was asleep. Their house could have taken this hit. At least he could wake them fast if another one flew over. He boiled a kettle on the fire and took Mary a cup of tea when he heard her stirring and sat on the bed. 'I had to stay up on watch.'

'Silly sod!'

'You don't use language like that, Mary!'

'This morning I do.' She warmed her hands gratefully on the cup, silverstreaked hair falling on her shoulder, her face grey.

'I don't think anyone was there in that house.'

'They were in the shelter with us.' She drained the hot tea with eyes closed. 'I saw them. Thank God!'

'Do you want toast? The fire's red.'

'And dripping . It'll put a bit of heart in us.'

He cut a slice from a home baked loaf and threaded it onto the long toasting fork, held it over the red glow, fingers and face hot. When the bread began to curl he pulled it back before it could scorch, smelling the moment it was browning, turned it over. A scoop of dripping to sink into the hot slice and he rushed it through to her on a plate.

Mary opened her eyes again. 'This is nice.'

'Don't get used to it.' He touched a wisp of the thinning hair, thanking her in the touch for staying with him, for being alive. He browned a slice of toast for himself, smeared a little of the dripping and went to the window. It was past blackout hours. He opened the curtains and the homemade blind. One or two people were gathering to look at the devastation but he couldn't see the family. Firemen had finished. He swallowed his toast and went out. A stench of smoke hit his throat as he joined the others peering at what was left of a home. Blackened bricks, timber reduced to charcoal. The whole of the front wall had collapsed with most of the ceiling, beds fallen through, broken, burned. He leant against the wall of the next house that had stood against the blast and wept till his ribs ached.

A woman touched him. 'Did you lose somebody in there, pet?'

He shook his head, choked, 'We've *all* lost everything.' She reached to him, held him like a child and he sobbed in the arms of a stranger.

Mary said nothing when he came in with a tear streaked face and poured a bowl of hot water from the range. In the tiny mirror in the scullery he saw a madman with red eyes and filthy hair standing up. The only soap was the girls' green sludge Andrew managed to get from a shipyard to wash their hair in. He doused his head with it, cleaned hands and face. Eyes were cleaned by weeping not by sleep. He stripped off, stood in the bowl and splashed his body then walked naked to their room and fell on the bed.

Two hours and Mary shook him. There were clean clothes laid out that he stepped into like a man machine, porridge waiting on the table that she made him eat. Then he walked to work. Men at the factory swore and got on. He spat swear words out from the bottom of his lungs, put his glasses on and lifted a worksheet.

Routine saved them all. Along with the blackout blind he pulled a blind down on his mind, shuttered his heart. Though he felt his bones were glass he mustn't break. Day followed day and night awful night. Then Christopher was home on leave and brought a food parcel. He might not have been safe on his ship but he gave them hope. They ate and laughed. Mary's face relaxed and she went to church. He walked to his allotment and dug and dug. *We'll get through. We'll get through.* With each spadeful he said it, *We'll get through. Damn the world! But we'll get through.*

*

At the weekend Louise pattered up the stairs. Ben looked up from his newspaper, recognising her footfall even without the purposeful tap tap of the three inch heels she used to wear. 'Is the bairn all right?' he asked.

'Yes, dad. The bairn's asleep.'

'Edward there?'

'He's working in the shop. Diane's watching the bairn. She's tired of shopping. Nothing to buy,' she said. 'And there's no need to look at me over your little lenses.'

He took his reading glasses off. 'I see. You must be feeling a bit better, Miss.' He searched her pale, drawn face, the hazel eyes seemed darker, bigger.

She kicked her flat shoes off. 'No, I'm not. I'm feeling anything but well. Little Benjie's's sleeping at night but I'm not and I could scream inside those four walls.'

He folded his paper. 'Right. We'll get you out of these four walls. Come down to the allotment. You can help me or you can watch, or you can pick some flowers and take them home with you.'

'Flowers would be nice. Nobody fetches me flowers, not these days.'

'Nobody has money to spare.' He threw a pair of soiled orange overalls over his clothes and a tweed gardening jacket on top of that, grabbed an old coat of Diane's down from a peg, looked at the cloth and put it back. 'Here, have this one. Patricia won't mind.'

Louise took the gabardine and swirled it round above her ankles. 'I could camp in this.' She scurried after him. 'Much to do down there?'

'There's always work', he called over his shoulder and waited for her to catch up.

'Digging for victory!'

'Done that for years. It helped bring us through the thirties, bloody Depression years.'

She was panting as they walked up the gentle slope of the street. 'I wouldn't mind if we just sat in the park at the top.'

'I need to go to the allotment, pet. In any case it's all dug up in the park. We won't stay that long. Just an autumn tidy up. There are some chrysanths you can have.' He waited for her again. 'Not like you to be out of puff like that.' He put his arm round her shoulder when she drew level. 'You've not been right since you had the bairn and that's a while. You need fresh air.' She shook her head and fell into step. 'What with you and Patricia, it's been nothing but worry, worry, worry.'

He dragged an old chair out from the shed when they got to the allotment so she could sit in the late season sun, then picked up a spade and garden shears to tidy a corner and started digging.

'Whose grave is that, then?'

'You can bury me here when the time comes,' he grunted. He dug deep then fetched a sapling from the shed. 'This is a little apple tree. I'm going to see if it'll take. It'd be handy to fetch Mary apples for her pies - if it ever fruits.'

Louise opened a packet of ten Woodbines and offered one to her father. He sat on an old bit of tarpaulin and they smoked together. 'From Andrew. He can spare them,' she said.

'You'd be better to come off the fags, panting like that, clear your lungs out a bit.'

'Pot calling the kettle. Tabs never did anybody any harm.'

He blew a blue smoke ring and watched it float widening and dissolve. 'Did you hear about Heaton cemetery?'

'I heard a bomb dropped on it.'

'Aye, well, this bloke rings in to report it - must have been an A.R.P. or something - tells H.Q. there's a bomb fallen on the cemetery. They ask him - Any dead? - Why, there must be hundreds!' he says.

'Dad!' Louise choked on her cigarette.

'True as you're sitting there. Heard it from Wilf himself.'

They smiled. Louise took a last pull on her cigarette and twisted her heel on it. 'Edward's volunteered to drive an ambulance with St. John's.' Ben was silent. 'He can't fight, he can't do a lot of digging like you but he says he can drive, so he'll do that.'

'We've all got to do something. It's getting cold. Come inside. I've got a kettle on the Primus I keep here for a brew. Will an old mug do?'

She looked round and settled herself in a battered bentwood chair. 'This reeks of you, dad. Your own hidey hole.'

'I have to have a place somewhere.'

'Edward heard something on the grapevine. They're going to call unmarried women into the munitions factories.'

He poured steaming tea making a sweet fug with the onions strung up and bunches of sage hanging to dry for Christmas. She took a mug, his best blue striped mug. 'That business about the women might not be true.'

'Why shouldn't it be? They're working on the land. It came from a civil servant. I can't name him.'

'It could affect Diane.'

'She'll pee her pants.'

'As if I haven't got enough worries. It might be all women if you've picked it up on a rumour.'

'Patricia could help mam in the house - unless they want her as well.'

'She's been ill. I'll see the doctor and get a letter. I thought we were going to lose her. She couldn't possibly do it.'

'Diane'll get married. It'll suddenly be the moment, wait and see.'

'About time as well. Then it'll be Patricia's time, I hope.' He put his mug down and saw her crying into hers. 'Come on, pet.' He rummaged for an old handkerchief from his overalls, took the mug from her hands and patted her cheeks. He felt a spasm through her when he touched her and knew. 'That's not it, is it?' She shook. 'Joe?' He whispered it and folded her in his arms. 'I heard about it. He joined the R.A.F.' She muffled against him and he let her cry.

When she looked up from blind eyes he could just hear her. 'He's not coming back.' She choked and said it again. 'He's not coming back, dad. Not coming back.'

'Sshh!'

'Scrimshaw girls saw his wife. Missing, presumed dead. Shot down. I feel it in my bones. He's not coming back.'

He held her close and thought *At least that's an end to it.*

'There's nothing left, dad.'

He dampened a cloth and wiped her face. 'There's your child, your little boy.'

'God's punished me.'

'Joe punished himself. He let you go then ran away.' He poured her more tea. 'Children are the future. Children give meaning. Look after little Benjie. Don't let him play about with the bits of shrapnel kids pick up from the ground, in fields.' She drank and he waited for her hands to steady. 'And, Louise ... look at his eyes. Look at his hair.' He held her gaze. 'He's Edward's.'

She gazed back at him and blinked, with the slightest movement of her head.

They were walking back carrying potatoes and cabbage with the flowers when he heard it. It wasn't English. He couldn't explain how but he knew a Spitfire when he heard one. This noise was deafening. He turned round and saw a plane flying low down the street between two houses. Everything became very clear, in slow motion.

There was a coal wagon standing on the street, a little girl playing outside a front door. His body moved without him. He hurtled towards the girl, pushed her through the open door, dragged Louise with his other hand, flung her after the child and crouched on the doorstep, newly cleaned, fresh yellow ochre. He could see the pilot. He could see a swastika. On top of the roar of the engine there was a burst from a machine gun, a racket, a drumfire of hail, then it was gone. He'd hit the coal lorry, holes all over the coal bags. The driver climbed down swearing.

'Bloody hell! This is too much. I want a gun so I can get the bugger! Doon the street! Doon the bloody street! Have ye got a gun?'

Ben was surprised as he heard himself speak. 'Lost,' he said. 'Aiming for the shipyards. He's lost.' Louise was moaning behind him. The little girl was rocking herself.

'He'll be more than lost if Ah could get a howld of 'im!' The man danced in rage over a hopscotch grid chalked on the pavement. 'Look at me coal bags, man! Peppered, every one of them! Bloody holes! Bloody Fritz shootin' bloody holes in the bloody coal.'

Ben started to laugh and tears ran down his cheeks.

'Ah divn't knaa what yer laughin' at, ye silly old bugger!'

Ben pointed at the road. Cabbage, chrysanthemums and potatoes were strewn all over it. Potatoes began to roll down the tarmac.

The wireless gave grim news. The Blitz hit the South of England, industrial bases, ports. He followed the horrors and wreck of Coventry, then London, Liverpool, Birmingham, Glasgow, Belfast. Tyneside had a bitter taste of it flown in from Norway and the Battle of Britain screamed to a crescendo.

Next they heard bombs had scattered over High Heaton demolishing two houses, seriously damaging thirty more. A surface shelter stayed intact while the house was wrecked and an occupant killed, but miracles of survival happened. A man was shot through the window of his bedroom to the end of the garden, seriously injured. But he lived.

When bombers destroyed the cinema where she'd watched Shirley Temple singing *The Good Ship Lollipop* Patricia was hard to comfort. Personal memories. Wartime films helped their morale, actors stiffening upper lips, cinema goers identifying with the ship *In which We Serve,* stories and songs kindling hope there'd be another day.

Early in spring the following year Diane married, wearing a smart Utility suit. Photos, kisses, flowers. It seemed unreal.

A major goods yard was hit a stone's throw from the town centre. Ben watched from his window as intense white shot up then colour seethed across the sky in frantic red, green and yellow, assaulting the clouds, trailing a furious glow as the sky itself was eaten in fire. It felt like twilight of the gods. The explosion could be seen from miles away. Everything went up, a volcano of dry food supplies - sugar, flour, peas like bullets from a gun.

Ben walked over the Byker Bridge with Wilf to inspect the wreckage and stood round with dozens of others, breathing the stench of burned brickwork and scorched, blackened food. Long windows were blasted out but he was amazed to see part of the front façade still stood, a gaunt skeleton in the smoke. The supplies burned for days, sugar a mucky river like lava.

'Damn them!' he snorted to Wilf. 'They'll see their way clear to the Walker shipyards from the light of the fire of this lot.'

'And St Peter's. Poor devils in Walker'll have to be rehoused, God knows where. Whole communities broken up.'

'If it goes on we'll all be in tents on the Town Moor. Most of the lads are at the front. So who's going to build it all up again?'

'And with what?'

'We'll have to borrow more than the entire country's worth.'

'That'll not be much.' Wilf turned a bar of wood over with his toe and watched it collapse into soot. 'We could sell the crown jewels.'

'Or get a loan from the Yanks on the strength of them,' Ben said.

'We could never pay it off. You and me, we'd be six foot under before it was even touched.'

'Well, here's to that.'

'Fancy the pub, Ben?'

'Not after the last time. Sorry, lad.'

'It's me that's sorry. I shouldn't have encouraged you to take a drink. But we're both still here.'

They walked back. At least the bridge held under their feet.

Mary was uneasy when he went to the allotment alone but he shared the fatalism of the day and carried on. When the one with your name on fell, it wouldn't much matter where you were.

Ploughing through 1941 Ben opened the *Evening Chronicle* and flicked to the deaths page with less dread. *They're not peppering us the same* he thought - *fewer press photos of buildings in ruins, none recently. Is the worst over? Locally?*

But the broad canvas of things looked bleak. He took to marking reported victories and defeats on a big calendar, crosses and flags but Mary would not have such a thing in the living room so he carried it to the allotment.

Onions hung as usual in a string from the ceiling of his shed, taties, cabbages, turnips in sacks, the brussels sprouts were yet to come. His hands were gnarled but they did not starve. He was in work, things were better in their house than they had been in the depression years.

Winter came round with blackouts but his sense of hope grew. They sat up in the evenings, used to the lights-out routine and listened to the wireless, news was Ben's addiction, light entertainment a lifeline for Mary. Christmas should be a good one whether or not they had much on the table. He thought people on the street who'd never had two ha'pennies to rub together had put on a bit of flesh. Mary complained about rationing but it meant food was shared according to the little green books, not the size of your bank account. Except for the black market. All sorts of people got involved in that. Even Ben Hawthorne had had a stab at that. But if there was no more bombing they'd been through worse. Patricia was better this year and none of the girls was in the munitions factories. They lived with the hope Christopher might turn up to make their Christmas.

Mary went into the scullery to sponge herself down before bed. Ben knew there was not much soap and if they used the tin bath the water was supposed to be measured in inches. His wife could boil a kettle, though. The only light in the room was from the fire. Ben watched it die, reds and blues flickering, casting nets of shadows, thinking about a last pipe.

'Ben, them taties were no good today,' Mary called from the scullery, 'half of them rotten. I wouldn't feed them to a pig.'

'But you fed them to me.' He smiled. 'I went to the allotment this afternoon and dug some more out. I told you, you're getting forgetful, lass.'

'I'll forget <u>you</u>.' Tension came out in small irritations. 'Where are they anyway?'

'Under the stairs in a little sack. I haven't pulled them all. They last better in the ground.'

'You're not supposed to put things like that under the stairs. If we couldn't get out in an air raid that's the best place to go.'

'Haven't had an air raid in a long time, touch wood.' Then he shot out of his captain's chair, on his feet at a news flash. 'Bloody hell!'

Mary came to the scullery door with a towel in her hand. 'Do you have to shout like that and make me spill some of what little hot water I've got?'

'Ye bugger! There'll be hell to pay now. Japs have punched the American Fleet out.'

Mary turned back to her sink. 'Yanks'll punch <u>their</u> lights out if it's right. But I don't believe it, They won't be having a night raid over there.'

'It's morning in the Pacific - Hawaii islands ... I think. Shush, Mary. The B.B.C. must have got this wrong. I can't believe it either ... I must've missed something. They're not saying any more.'

'You'll have to wait till the morning then. They'll probably apologise for misleading the nation,' she yawned ' ... or something. I'm going to bed, Ben. Try to be quiet. Patricia's asleep.' She put his pyjamas over a chair and closed the door.

He knocked his pipe out behind the fire, remembered the commandment about noise, cupped it downward in his hand and gently tapped the ash out. Her voice drifted from the bedroom 'Put the wireless off, Ben.'

'I won't spoil your beauty sleep.' He took the worn leather tobacco pouch from the mantelpiece and pressed the hay-smelling shreds into his pipe bowl. *It can't be right*, he repeated to himself. But the Yanks had been edgy about the Japs ... a spider's web getting bigger, that spread out in the Pacific when they'd had to find other supplies for oil after the US put an embargo on them. But if this report was right, how the devil had the Japs managed to attack the fleet? Forces gossip from lads on leave had it they didn't rate the Japs for flying, not long distances. He snorted and sucked on the dead pipe. Slitty eyes! That was it. Thought their eyes couldn't stand it. By God, they'd have another think coming if this report was right. He clamped the polished stem of the pipe between his teeth and sucked on it till embers in the grate were grey.

Where the hell was Christopher?

A few weeks after Christmas a letter arrived in a thin fine envelope addressed to Patricia. Ben recognised a stamp from the United States. 'For you.' He handed it to her. She slit it open and her hands trembled as she read. 'What is it?' She handed him the blue near transparent sheet:

Dear Patricia,

I can hardly hold the pen steady but must write to you. Rory was killed in the attack on Pearl Harbour. He wanted to go back to Britain to join up but we wouldn't let him, so he chose the U.S. Navy to be ready to play his part. There's fervour here now in support of having joined the war. They say they can rebuild the Fleet as only part of it was in the Hawaiian islands when the attack came.

I curse the whole thing. I curse the navy. I curse the history between the U.S. and Japan, curse Uncle Sam for not supplying oil for the China/Japan war. Most of all, I curse the day we left England. And the money we've made here. What are dollars? The war followed us. We had happiness in Cumberland, drenching wet, beautiful Cumberland, and we couldn't see it when we were there.

I hope you've all survived.

With loving memories,

Joyce

Ben folded his daughter in his arms.

20

Patricia managed the shop in the new year when Andrew's mother was ill. Bombs had missed the little flat but pneumonia felled the old woman. The lad took it hard and kept the body in the house keeping vigil till the funeral.

Katharine made mourning clothes or black arm bands from blackout curtains. After the funeral Andrew was white and Louise ran to the off-licence to get a bottle of sherry. His little shop made enough money and they could at least warm themselves up.

'Patricia'll be able to get the gold ring on her finger,' she muttered to her dad.

'Don't mention that. It's high time. But let him get over this.'

'Nobody'll be talking about decent intervals.' She walked in with the sherry and popped the cork out. 'Born to be a bar maid,' she said and poured as they huddled round the fire.

A month later Ben talked to Andrew and they decided on a June wedding. He hadn't like the lad at first but this love had lasted. Come to that, he hadn't liked any of them at first, except maybe Katharine's lad. His girls were other loves in his life. John Hargraves would marry them, no-one else. They'd flown the coop one by one. He'd be glad when Christopher came home from the Merchant Navy. Luck or something was protecting him. You couldn't trust to luck.

On Sunday he bought a paper and took John's *Manchester Guardians* for the week down to the allotment. It irritated Mary when he wouldn't get his nose out of the news at home. He made an early start on digging, weeding, harvesting what was ready, then allowed himself a break while the light lasted. He scanned the international news and reached for a pen to make up his calendar chart. Last year's was on the wall with a huge cross for Pearl

Harbour. Now Greece, Crete and Singapore. A row of crosses was standing out. North Africa. He paused. A flag for the Seventh Armoured Division Eighth Army? Rommel at their heels, not clear whether it should be a cross or a flag. He left that one, lit a pipe and wondered how much of the truth came out to the public.

Hitler could be a clever bugger but the campaign in the East was overextended. He must know you don't fight on more than one front unless you have to. Till now he'd called the shots with forces in Europe and Africa. Britain had bitten his heel but Russia seemed to be the final goal. No quick victory over there. Might he have scored an own goal? Napoleon had limped back from those steppes. He doodled a toothbrush moustache and swastika in the margin then studied the row of crosses. It looked as though there was little hope. But would the Führer's supply line hold in the East? He tapped his teeth with the pipe then scrubbed over the swastika and moustache with the pen, wrote RUSSIA along the top edge of the calendar and drew a faint outline of a flag next to the word. He left the flag blank. It wasn't theirs.

Next day after work he called at Wilf's house and had to wait outside in the back yard for his friend to come out.

'Glad you could make it,' Wilf said. 'I've got something for you.' He opened the shed with great ceremony then Wilf wheeled out a gleaming red bicycle. 'What do you think of that?'

'It's a beaut. How did you come by this?'

'For you, lad.'

'How come?'

They sat on the stone steps leading down from the scullery. 'It's a sad story actually. One of the neighbours, her son's been killed out in North Africa. It was his and she wants to get rid of it. Just wants a few shillings.'

'I couldn't do that, Wilf, not for a treasured thing.'

'No. The money's not important. She can't bear to look at it, she wants it away.' Ben got up and ran his hand over the cross bar and the handle bars. 'You'd be doing her a favour by taking it.'

'Then I'll pay her something decent. Find out what it cost them and we'll negotiate from that.'

'Just take it, man. She really doesn't want to set eyes on it again. We'll sort a price by the end of the week. It'll be O.K. She trusts me.'

Ben rode off like a boy on his first bike and made a detour to try to pick up soap a chemist's shop was supposed to have. A lorry obstructed him on the way and he was pleased when it stopped beside a row of houses. The outside had a pointed railing and a couple of men in overalls wearing thick gloves and big boots stamped out putting on goggles and went round to the back of the lorry to a couple of cylinders four feet high that were strapped on the top. Ben skidded to a halt stopped and stood to watch as they carried leads from the cylinders that joined in a tube with a metal feed. One of the men turned a knob and a brownish orange flame flared out, iridescent blue shooting through the centre.

'What's in the cylinders?' he asked.

'Oxygen in one. Acetylene in the other. Why d'you want to know, anyway?'

'Just interest. Don't worry, I'm not a spy.'

'Makes a cutting flame.'

The first man adjusted the valve to control the torch and began to melt the paint on one of the railings. He held it steady till the iron glowed and the bright flame cut clean through the metal. Ben was surprised there were no fumes. He watched a few minutes as the whole of the railing came down and they put the burner down.

'I thought they'd got enough scrap metal by now.' he said.

They wiped their faces of sweat and turned to talk. 'Got to get the last available. We're still collecting any extra pots and pans as well. Has your missus got a few surplus? Any metal's needed.'

'I'll have to ask her. I don't poke my nose in at the kitchen. I might have an old hammer. I'm not sure. Tools are hard to replace.'

'Anything, mister. There's a collection point. You'll know about that.'

'Yes.' His nose was itching in imagined irritation as he watched the bright flame. 'Just surprised they needed more. He reached in his jacket pocket for a twist of Andrew's tobacco. 'Here, have some baccy.' They beamed.

'Something big's coming off.' The men smelt the tobacco through the paper. 'They don't tell us what. We just have to try and get the stuff in. But it's big, you can tell that.' They pocketed the baccy.

'Thanks, pal. And don't forget to quiz your missus.' They shut the levers off on the cylinders and loaded the railings onto the lorry.

'O.K.' He mounted his bike and found the shop just before it closed. Lavender soap. They would let him have only one cake. He jingled coins in his pocket for a half crown. Expensive, but it was little enough to give to Mary.

The pub was a miss on Sunday but he settled down, opened his paper and smoked a pipe before heading down to the allotment in the afternoon. Mary was looking after little Benjie. The girls were in the scullery, washing their hair in rainwater from a barrel in the yard, using the green soap from the shipyard that Andrew still collected for them. The shipyards were busy again and the girls had come over to use this stuff. It had to be in his scullery. He noticed Louise's hair was growing back more thickly.

When they trooped in to the room to dry each others' manes he was deep in his reading and groaned. 'Have you no place of your own?' Louise pulled a face at him. He passed the adverts on the front page, was taken by a headline in bold print and his hands began to shake.

Biggest Air attack of the War - 2,000 Tons of Bombs in 40 Minutes.

He pushed past his daughters and turned the wireless on. Louise pushed back. 'Watch what you're doing, dad.'

He hardly heard her voice. The news was coming over the airwaves. More than one thousand bombers had flown in the night over Cologne and smashed it. He clicked the wireless off, sat down with the paper again, tore it up into squares and handed them to Louise. 'Put them in the lavatory.'

'My hair's wet, dad. Put them in the lav yourself.'

He snatched them back. 'And nobody's to put that wireless on again!' Louise shrugged as he slammed out to the backyard.

Outside he opened the W.C. door and threaded the newspaper squares onto a nail driven into the white distempered brick. After bolting the door again he pulled the bike Wilf had found for him from the shed, reached for a lubricant and hunkered down to oil the chain, ran a cloth over the metal trim and checked for punctures. It was a beauty, a Raleigh. He touched the handlebars and swung up in the saddle. Time he had a cycle again. For work, for the allotment, getting into town to scour the market, he wasn't getting any younger. Music began to drift down from the house. They'd put the wireless on again to the Light Programme. It wasn't worth the argument.

He opened the back door and rode off then pedalled furiously and without thinking arrived at Bessy's street. Her door was opening. He wheeled into a side street, came to a halt and watched from the junction. It might be possible to have a word with her, she'd understand how he felt. It surprised him to see two smart young women come out. One of them turned and shouted something up the stairs as they shut the door then linked arms and trotted off down the street ... they were her daughters, all grown up! Lovely girls. Bessy had this. He watched them till they turned a corner, remounted the bike and pedalled off. What was he thinking? He mustn't disturb the life she'd put together, he couldn't do that to her again.

A chill wind was in his face as he rode automatically to the allotment to empty his fury, turning the hard ground with a spade till rain began to spatter. He'd not eaten much. He lit the Primus stove and paraffin heater to drink tea remembering guiltily, fondly, the times Bessy had come to him here. He mustn't disturb her. She deserved better. He made a brew, drank hot tea and began to pull himself together. Far too old for that sort of thing, losing his marbles. Finally he looked at the calendar with his chart of the war and last year's beside it. He drew out a pen and poised it over yesterday's date, Saturday May 30th 1942. It was declared a great event, the destruction of Cologne. He wasn't sure whether the newspaper headline was correct but details were coming through on the wireless. It had taken ninety minutes to destroy thirty-six factories. For the factories alone it should be a flag. They'd not announced how many civilians were killed, injured or made homeless. For a revenge for the destruction of Coventry it should be a flag. More detail would be raked over in the news. It was hailed as a great advance. He started to draw a flag then pulled the calendar off the wall and hurled it into a corner. What was the point if they were turning to terror themselves?

Rain had fallen while he'd been inside his shed. He let the door swing open and leant against the frame. Sun broke through in shafts from the rain clouds and lit the trumpets of a few remaining daffodils he'd coaxed in a corner of the soil, turning them to glowing yellow gold. Drops sparkled from the petals like tears. *The flowers are weeping* he thought *like when foul bloody bombs dropped from the air on Spain's little Guernica.* He trailed inside and stared at the wooden floor. *Tragedy is, we don't give it a second thought any more. Flames of hell on the streets … till they're blasted into heaps of red rubble from this … blasted evil seed.* He collapsed onto a stool and wept with the flowers. *It's become standard. We've learned nowt. Bloody nowt.*

Haunting imagination again became a curse. Haunting imagination howled.

The papers next day were triumphant. He glanced at a poster outside the newsagent's:

British Bombers Now Attack Germany a Thousand at a Time!

By the end of the week, he found if he read carefully, the effects were clearer; five hundred civilians were dead, five thousand injured. Forty-five thousand civilians were made homeless. He spat in the gutter outside the paper shop.

Pictures built in his mind of sleeping children and women hurled into the sleep of death, images cursed him in dreams. It took only another week for 'Bomber' Harris to be given a knighthood. Rubbish anyway, the honours. His mind was cold and numb by the time the U.S. and U.K. joined forces to bomb the enemy by night and by day.

At work he was called into the office.

'Sit down, Ben.' His boss was finishing a telephone call, smoking at the same time, breathing fumes into the shiny black bakelite. He waved a secretary away as he put the receiver down. 'Sorry about that, we're rushed off our feet. Right.' He drew a chair up and flipped a notebook open. 'Will you go over to Vickers', Ben?

'What for?'

'We've got to up production. The big firms are working together.'

'For how long?'

'Obviously, I couldn't say. But it might be a good spell, maybe to the end of the war.' He waved his cigarette around and started writing with the other hand.'

'Why me?'

'It won't just be you.'

'I don't want to go over there.'

'Listen, Hawthorne,' the boss squashed his cigarette out in an overflowing ash tray, 'labour's got to go where it's directed and that's an end of it. The factories have <u>got</u> to work together. I mean, our Director's over at Vickers' now, with a foot in this camp, aye, in Reyrolle's as well. He's all over the place - Director of Weapons Production at the Ministry of Supply. If he can spread himself, so can you. If you're needed there, you get over there.' He stared Ben straight in the eye.

Ben dug his feet into the thin carpet and set himself. 'It's just as important to keep the power stations going. I want to stay on the condensers.'

Eyebrows raised at the defiance. The boss drummed on the table. 'You're a good worker, Ben. I'll tell you what, we can use you in the Gun Assemblies Shop here. You can work on tank parts in there, on tank guns and field guns.'

'The gun room!'

'That's fair enough.'

'I don't ...'

'Shut up! Do you think you're running this war? Start on Monday.' He looked down and concentrated on writing notes.

Ben stood up feeling dizzy, wanting to vomit.

Friday night he came home and took his overalls off on the landing, marched through to the scullery to dump them, came back and lingered by the fire to sniff the ham bone and leek soup on the simmer, then without looking up slapped a pay packet on the table. He paused to check Mary's reaction, she smiled and he added another one neatly beside it.

'What's this,' she asked, 'a bonus? Have they given you double pay?'

'That's my week lying on,' he answered quietly.

'They've sacked you?' She put a ladle down.

'I gave my notice in.' Patricia came in from the scullery. 'They were putting me on munitions. It's been civilian stuff till now.'

'And?'

Their daughter put her arm round Mary. 'It's like pulling a trigger, firing on people myself. Only from a distance. They wanted me to work in the gunroom. We make tank guns in there, howitzers - mobile field guns - blow-your-head-off-with-shells bloody guns.'

'Now I've heard everything.' Mary sat down. 'What about what they've done to us?'

'Tit for tat. It killed the cat.' He started pacing back and forward. 'His brain's turned.'

Patricia knelt beside her mother and hugged her.

'We'll go on till nothing's left. Can't you see? Like a vendetta, till the last man's left standing.'

Mary's expression soured. 'What I see is a man who won't provide. For his own.'

Ben stood at the end of the mantelpiece with his head on his forearm. 'We're blowing up little bits of bairns.' She sat like stone. 'Women, grannies. What have <u>they</u> done to us?'

'What?' The soup over the fire was forgotten. 'They've only sent their men to do for us completely.'

'I don't think they've got any say. They're caught in a trap.'

'You're caught in a trap, Ben Hawthorne. You're like a blinkered horse and can't see what's around you.'

'Our own men can get injured by a shell or a bullet working at the factory. Have you thought of that?'

'I've never heard anything the like of this! Other men are doing it.'

He looked at her dry eyed. 'All <u>I</u> know is ... I <u>can't</u> do it.'

'Won't. Won't!' She shook Patricia away. 'Won't! As if we haven't been through enough.'

'I've got a bit of savings now,' he said.

'And when that's gone?'

Patricia stroked the wisps of hair falling over her mother's face. 'The shop's making some profit, mam. We've still got stock. We'll manage.'

'Keep out of this, Trish.'

'I'll get a job,' he said.

'And how long did it take you to get this one?' She stood up and seemed to grow in height. 'Twelve years!' Her face set. 'What you don't realise is <u>we </u>can't afford principles. Maybe the rich can.' Mary brought her hand up to her chin. 'I've had poverty up to here.'

'Don't give me that look. It's ...' Ben walked over a chasm and knelt before his wife, 'it's like this.' She drew back and slumped down in her chair again. Patricia moved away. 'A horse that's been raced for years can shy at a jump. And nothing the trainer can do'll make it go over.'

'So you've got spooked, like a horse?'

'I am that horse. I can't ... do it.'

'Right.' Mary was on her feet again. He sprawled on the hooky mat in front of the fireplace. 'You can get out and find another stable.' She strode into their bedroom. 'I'll chuck your things down the stairs.' She came out with jumpers and a blanket in her arms, opened the door and hurled them down the stairs. 'Out!'

'That's it?'

Patricia automatically picked up the unopened pay packets. 'Where will he go, mam?'

'To hell in a handcart,' Ben snorted.

'You can have your coat.' She threw it at his head as he clattered down. 'And don't bother any of the girls. Or I'll have your guts for garters. Diane's just lost her baby!'

He sat on the stone step outside with his head in his hands.

Next day he woke cold as stone with aches in his shoulders and knees. When he moved his head hurt, when he stretched his hips were agony and a sharp pain shot up his back. He sat back on the bench in the churchyard and threw the blanket round his shoulders. His feet were freezing but there was nothing else to cover them with, he was wearing all of his jumpers.

Leaves threaded green lace on the trees. He looked at them idly as if in a picture and listened to the tender throaty call of pigeons. It was a limpid morning with a clear washed sky. Sparrows were busily pecking at the path or digging for worms. A fluffy fledgling tried to fly from one branch to another and fell clumsily to the grass looking surprised and stunned. If it wasn't for the soreness of his body he'd have enjoyed the moment.

He heard footsteps and his senses focussed - it was Louise. She sat beside him and passed a piece of bread and margarine. 'What are you doing here?'

'What does it look like?'

'Is this the best you could do? You could have walked over to Wilf's, or are your legs not working now?'

'Wilf's wife wouldn't open the door to me after what I did. And I don't want to create trouble for him.' He chewed on the bread to create saliva. Hot tea would be the best.

'What about the vicarage? You're thick with the vicar.'

'John's been away and I couldn't go and stay there. You know what people are like.'

Louise grinned. 'It'd be worth a headline in the *News of the World*. - "Unemployed man sleeps with vicar's wife."' Underneath - "The vicar says – no comment." It'd be worth a bob or two.'

Ben choked on his bread and they laughed. His head began to clear as he heard another voice.

'What are you doing here?' He knew the caretaker's voice. 'You can't stay here.'

Louise stared straight ahead. 'We're waiting to see the vicar.'

'Getting married, are you? Hee, hee!' He laughed at his own joke.

Louise looked him in the eye. 'None of your business if we are.'

'None of my business, eh? We'll see about that.' He lumped off up the path. She sat smiling. 'You can stay at my house.'

'Your mother won't have it.'

'What's she going to do to me?'

'It'll end with people not speaking, it's not worth it.' He threw a crust to the birds. 'Is our Diane all right?'

'They've decided to let her stay at home, not hospital. I think she'll be O.K. She's pulling through.'

'Her first bairn.' He shook his head.

'I know. Look, old Tommy's coming back.' She screwed her eyes up. 'And somebody's with him.'

John Hargraves hurried down. 'What's all this?' He spoke to his caretaker. 'Will you open up, please, Tommy? We have a wedding at ten and they'll be coming in with flowers before long.' He waited a few moments. 'What's happened?'

'Dad's homeless.'

'Right. We'll hear the ins and outs later but we have to get you out of here. Why didn't you come across to us?'

'Thought you were away.'

'I'm just back. So come over now and we'll get you sorted.'

'Can't do that.'

The vicar took him under one arm and nodded to Louise. She took the other and they heaved. Suddenly it was too much to fight and he allowed himself to be led away. Gwen asked no questions but went out to her hens for a couple of eggs and brought another three in for Louise to take away. 'Boiled or fried, Ben?'

'Fried, please. But only if you've got some fat.'

'It'll have to be dripping and you can have fried bread with it. Louise?'

'I'm all right, thanks.' She had a quick word with John Hargraves, left then came back with more of her dad's clothes.

Gwen continued as if nothing odd had happened. 'Have a bath. The water's hot. You can have my five inches. And I'll put a hot water bottle in the spare room bed for you. Wear a pair of John's pyjamas. They'll be far too big but nobody'll be taking your photograph.' She was dishing up as John came back in then left them together.

'So, you've got a chicken farm now?'

'Gwen's doing it. A pair of good layers as well. I always say she should be in 10 Downing Street. She'd organise everything.'

He poured fresh tea and Ben allowed himself to be managed like a child. A comfortable bath, a clean bed, a little piece of heaven for a few hours.

Louise defied her mother and he was to stay there during the day and sleep at the vicarage at night. He knew his friend had whisky cellared but Gwen served Horlicks. Mary kept his ration book but they ate omelettes cooked in lard, courtesy of the thriving hens. Ben quietly accepted everything except the suggestion he should go to the Labour Exchange.

'Why, dad?'

'I'm not going to the Dole House.'

'I think mam might let you back if you do.'

'I've had enough of them at the Dole House and their like - the Guardians of the Poor, I remember them. I can't face it all again. They strip you naked for a few coppers. Some of them at the Dole are a lot worse than the Guardians ever were. A few of the Guardians might have had their hearts in the right place, though I didn't think so at the time with their La-de-da. I don't know what I'm going to do.'

'Well, something has to happen. Patricia's due to be married in just less than three weeks and she said she won't go down that aisle unless it's on your arm.'

'Leave me be.'

Late that afternoon Louise found her father in the backyard sitting on the stone steps staring at something in his hand with their little bantam cockerel perched on his shoulder.

'Dad, what are you doing here?' Before he could open his mouth she lifted a finger to hers, 'Sscchh! Mam'll kill you.' She spread her skirt out and sat beside him. 'You haven't been drinking?"

He shook his head. 'I've been breaking and entering the lav. I'm held hostage.' He stroked the bantam's foot and it spread its claws firmly in his coat. 'I was forgetting I'd spent my father's sovereign. Don't give me that guilty look, it's all right. It was just force of habit. The world hasn't ended.'

'It'll end if mam finds you here.' She took something out of her pocket. 'I've been thinking about the Dole House.' He looked away. 'It's wartime. It might be different. They can't waste labour.'

'That lot'll waste anybody.'

She passed a note to him and he laid it on top of the metal case the sovereign had rested in. Water began to seep through the edges of the scruffy scrap of paper. 'What's this?'

'Kipling, the fish man, said to give it to you. Open it, dad. It's going to fall to pieces.'

The bantam cockerel shifted its weight from one leg to another and dug in comfortably while Ben opened the pencil written note. "I might have a rabbit for you." What the hell does that mean?'

'Don't know. He said to get rid of the message and arrange a meeting.'

'Does he want me to eat it an' all?'

She took the note. 'I don't know what it's about.' She got up and opened the plank door to the lavatory, threw the paper into the pan and poured bleach on top of it. 'Do you want me to take a message or not? Here, I'll put that case back if you still want to hide it. You might have something else to put in it one day.'

He handed the case over to her. 'I keep it at the back of the cistern, useless now. I suppose I could meet him. But I don't know what he's up to.' He straightened up and dusted his trousers. 'You can't reach. I'll do it.' He struggled for a minute and got his sleeve wet. 'Tell him I'll see him in the back lane outside our yard at ten o' clock tonight. I'd like you to listen in on the other side of the door. Patricia could join you, and Andrew. But you'll be looking after the bairn, I suppose. If it's funny business I might need a witness or two.'

'I'll see if Edward can be in. He may be on an ambulance shift.' She leaned against the lavatory choking on silent laughter. 'This is like a John Buchan story.'

'Good film that. Yes, *The Thirty-nine Steps.*' He settled the cockerel back on top of the cistern. 'Better than a watch dog, this little feller.'

'Trish, is that you? Who are you talking to?'

She bundled her dad out through the back door. 'It's Louise. Talking to myself ... I know ... it's the first sign of madness.'

At ten o'clock Ben was in the backyard with Andrew and Patricia who were pretending to be courting. They stood silently with their arms round each other. Louise unexpectedly turned up and sat quietly on a little hooky rug on the back stairs. Footsteps crunched along the gravel and stopped outside their door, then they heard reedy whistling. Ben slipped out of the back door.

The whistling stopped. 'That you, Ben?'

'It's not Attilla the Hun. What's this about a rabbit?'

'Aye, well, you see ...' he dropped his voice. ' ... I'm raising a few rabbits and I've got some extra fish.'

'Poached?'

'Never you mind where they're from. I've got buyers in Heaton and thereabouts who want more than their points allow.' A pause. 'I need a runner. Are you up for it?

'Black market ... what's in it?'

'You'd get some pay, mebbeys ten bob a week - depends how much you do - and I'd keep your Mary happy with fish and rabbit for the table.'

'You mean you'd keep my missus in fish and rabbit while I did time for you? Not on. I'd carry the can if it came to light!'

A snort. 'It'd be worth your while.' The voice was tinny, squeezed, breathy.

'And you'd be open to blackmail for the rest of your life when I came out. Because I'd never work again.'

'Looks to me as if you're never going to get work anyway, son!'

'And I could turn you in.'

'Shop me,' the voice grated, 'and a couple of the lads'll be round.'

'Don't like threats.'

'Neither do I, bonny lad. Think it ower. You'll find I could be very good to you. Or very bad. Think of your family and look after them.' A cold hand touched Ben's heart. Rough hands might lay hold of his girls. 'Let's just say, my good side's very good.' His steps ground away on the gravel. 'See you Saturday, Ben. Call in.'

He knocked on the back door and they came out. He was shaking. Patricia put her arms round her father. Andrew whispered they could be witnesses. Louise stood back and watched everything. Ben stayed a moment in his daughter's embrace then withdrew.

Louise spoke for the first time. 'You can stay with us, dad. Edward's all right with it.'

'It'll make trouble.'

He walked away, feeling trembles up his spine. Darkness had held back. Now the sky was tinged with cobalt, clouds spilled across it in silken patterns at the end of the long northern day. He would have liked to go to Wilf's house but that was impossible. He started on his way to the main road but changed his mind … that would be passing Kipper's shop. He set off up the road again, walked down to the churchyard and sat on the bench, straining for any sound of being followed. A wind moaned in the trees and the branches shivered but birds had settled, no little sparrows or black crows or striped magpies. He waited till shadows of the young leaves drew a pattern across the path, tracery like scrolls on the church windows. When he was sure no one had come after him he got up, walked under the trees whose trunks were beginning to merge into velvet darkness, crossed the road and slipped into the vicarage.

Gwen Hargraves filled two mugs with Horlicks without asking where he'd been. He took one in to John in the study. A Bible looking book in an odd script like old English was spread out on his blotter.

'What are you reading?'

'It's the New Testament in German.'

'Oh, aye?'

'A gift from a friend.' He swivelled round to face Ben. 'I've been to London to try to help release one of the Germans we sheltered for a few weeks. They're all interned.'

'Difficult. I mean, they could be spies.' Ben was relaxing in the comfort of the booklined study. 'Mind if I smoke, John? Have some Virginia to share a pipe.' He got his worn pouch out. 'I'm not short of baccy now with the shop underneath.' He put the leather bag on the blotter next to the German writing. 'I'd rather Mary still had her bakery, though.'

'It's not been the first time I've tried to get this man out. I'm working on the possibility of him being an interpreter for the government, which he's willing to do.' They lit up, their ritual, drawing on the stem to get the tobacco to glow. 'He gave me this.' John pointed to the book. 'A symbol of friendship. In spite of all the bombing on both sides.'

'You know my story.'

'Yes.' John didn't question him.

'Can't the Church do anything? About this battering of the cities.'

'That's the other reason I've been in London.' He looked towards the door and lowered his voice. 'Not even Gwen knows. It was business for Bishop Bell. He's the one who's asked questions in the House of Lords and condemned this blanket bombing. He's very unpopular.' He shook his head. 'It's like a frenzy takes over. I'm not an outright pacifist. We have to defend ourselves.' Ben nodded. 'But reason goes out of the window. I would have gone with Bell to Sweden if he'd needed me. In the end they decided the fewer the better.' He sat for a moment examining the bowl of the pipe. 'He went to meet a churchman from Germany on neutral territory. As clergy they could always have matters to talk about. Bonhoeffer and Bell. In reality it was a contact from a German group to try to make peace'

'A back door effort?'

He nodded. 'The government isn't interested.'

'Churchill! A waste of time.'

'It's never a waste of time to try. And you don't know they won't come back to it.'

'You'd be taking a risk going on a mission like that.'

John put the small New Testament in his inside pocket. 'Maybe doing nothing risks everything.' He shook out a Swan Vesta match from a little metal case, stroked it along a roughened edge and relit his pipe. 'I think I understand what you've done at work.' He puffed and looked at Ben through a smoke haze.

'Your position's probably more of the mind than mine, more intellectual.'

'You're quite as clever as I am, Ben.'

'Maybe.' He smiled at the compliment. 'I just couldn't go on. It's as simple as that.'

'Your political roots. You've believed in internationalism – in the Brotherhood of Man. Your beliefs have come out and walked around.'

'Keir Hardy lives! Maybe you're right, I don't know.' He sucked on the pipe and inhaled. 'And now I've got another problem.' He paused. 'I've been offered money and food supplies if I'll do black market running.'

John spluttered and put his pipe down 'Run a thousand miles before you do that. We'll supply you with eggs.'

'This fellow has rabbits.'

'Gwen's thinking of raising them as well. <u>We'll</u> send you a bunny and eggs. You should report this to the police.'

'I'm not that daft. You don't know what these types might decide to do. He threatened me if I did. And ... I have to think. I have daughters. It's not straightforward.'

John got up. 'I'll go and put in an appearance in the kitchen. Just a minute.'

Ben looked round the study at the bookshelves. He'd have liked to have devoted himself to books – if – if – if .... He found he was sweating, rubbed his palms together and spread his hands out. They were steady.

The priest came back with more hot drinks and the dog followed him. 'Camomile tea, from a pre-war hoard. It won't keep us awake. Gwen's treasures.'

He took the cup. 'You shouldn't waste them on me.'

John sat down and patted the dog. 'I think you should stay here during the day rather than go over to Louise if you're worried about the girls, till we sort something out. You don't know what you'd be getting into. There may be more to it than he said.'

'Aye, I've thought of that. He could be into a few games. It might be more than just fish he's peddling. There's been something of a crime wave in the blackout.'

'Police keep that quiet so as not to cause panic.'

The spaniel lay at Ben's feet. 'But I don't want to be a burden or a nuisance.'

John touched the Testament in his inside pocket and grinned. 'We've had other refugees here. You can make us a rabbit hutch. I'm not very good at that sort of thing.'

'Done.'

'But you have to go to the Labour Exchange, Ben.'

Ben nudged the dog with his foot and took a minute to reply. 'I can't face the humiliation. I know what it'll be. I heard that one man leaned over the desk and shook the clerk by the lapels. Everybody cheered. This chap had nearly ruined his health working all hours all his life before he became unemployed.'

'Hard times.'

The spaniel whined and Ben put his drink down to stroke her head. She put her muzzle in his lap and Ben fondled her ears for a while. 'But I suppose,' he said, 'if you were willing to take a big risk, I can take a smaller one ... and force myself and go down to the Dole.'

'I'll put my dog collar on and come with you if you like. Look impressive.'

The spaniel followed Ben round for the next two days as he helped Gwen with the garden and started to build a rabbit hutch from bits of an old shed and chicken wire. The hen coop could be improved as well. The dog made him feel homesick and a quarrel with Mary was a stone on his heart. He missed the cosiness of their small home, the company of the girls dropping in and out interrupting his reading, interrupting his conversations, owning him.

Vegetables from his allotment were pooled with those from the vicarage garden and he laughed with Gwen at lunchtime over *Workers' Playtime* on the wireless. Mary would not give up his ration book so he would not supply vegetables for her kitchen. But he missed her breathing next to him at night, her singing as she cooked, the scent of her, the warmth, missed even the arguments. God knew, she was right, she'd suffered enough from unemployment. And there could have been money from the black market.

Louise came in while he was sawing, looking lost as she walked down the driveway. She stood beside him and passed a note on a scruffy piece of paper written in pencil:

Game's on
You're out
Silence is golden

'Kipper Kipling?' She nodded. 'I understand it.'
'Destroy it, dad.'
He threw it down beside the dog that sniffed and started to chew it. Louise vanished.

It was the end of the week when he finally walked alone to the Labour Exchange. The spaniel was the only company he would have liked but he couldn't explain to them how he could afford to keep a dog. He passed the door of the Labour Exchange, walked round outside, came back, crossed the road to the other side, took another detour, pounded the pavements for half an hour, took a deep draught of air and went in. The atmosphere seemed grey and thick, though no-one smoked. Only one man waited in front of him. He stood back at a distance when the worn comrade was called to the counter and tried not to listen in.

Soulless faded walls, hard to tell their colour, government posters up everywhere:

Careless talk costs lives
Keep Calm
and
Carry On

He'd seen them all before and felt insulted. He'd dug for victory - but lost the battle. The man bent over the bench, speaking low while the clerk edged back from his breath saying, 'Speak up, please!' every few sentences. Finally the poor devil signed a paper, was released and shuffled off stooping.

'Next!' Ben watched the man go. 'I said "Next!" ' He looked over to the clerk. 'Yes, you. Are you going to wait till Kingdom Come? I expect you'll be at the back then as well.' He tried to walk firmly to the counter. 'Yes?' The man's face was lined and yellowing. He looked like a smoker gasping for a fag. Ben shrugged. 'Yes?' - louder.

'Out of work.'

'I didn't think you were Santa Claus with his elves.'

'Here we go!'

'What did you say?'

'Nothing.'

'A long nothing.' The clerk looked him up and down. 'When did you last work?'

'Finished a week ago. Engineering.'

'So why did they finish you?'

'I left.'

'Why?' The clerk folded his arms.

'Because they wouldn't let me stay on the civilian side. And,' it came out in a rush, 'I don't want to be making ammunition and the like to mow people down.'

The clerk whistled through yellowing teeth. 'Bloody conchies! There's a war on!'

'Don't you swear at me.'

The clerk scratched his head making its corkscrews stand up higher. 'I don't suppose you've worked elsewhere?'

Ben leant on the counter to bring his face nearer the other man's. 'Nearly thirty years down the pit. Maintenance and safety at the end.'

The clerk's face relaxed. 'Why didn't you say so in the first place, man?' He dug in a drawer and slapped a sheet on the counter and pushed a pen over. 'Fill that in.'

Ben straightened. 'No good me filling that in, son.'

'Why the devil not? They're desperate for experienced men in the pits, what with the little Bevin boys sent down to graft and don't know one end of the pickaxe from another. You'll be welcome as the flowers in spring. Doesn't matter that you left your other thing. Surprised you were ever away from the mining.'

'Not my choice, and nobody's going to welcome me.' He leant on the rough wood again. 'They blacklisted me all over Tyneside, pits, shipyards as well for being involved in the Union at the General Strike. No owner'll let me back.'

The clerk's face creased. 'We'll see about that, then. I think you'll find your boss is the government. There's a war on! It's a reserved occupation. And your country needs you. Fill that in and you'll start next week. That do?'

Ben's hand trembled. He came out into the warm air, clothes sticking to him, leant against the wall to take a fag from his pocket, turned round to light it and bent over cupping the match to hide tears. When he straightened up a riot of ragtime exploded in his heart.

21

Patricia walked down the aisle on her father's arm in a dream, almost outside of herself, watching the scene. Flowers from the allotment, a plain gold ring Andrew found in an antique shop, the organ triumphantly heralded the bride, John Hargraves smiling, beautiful words ... *to love and to cherish.* Andrew gazed at her saying firmly, I do!' Sunlight through the trees as they came out and a haze of confetti.

The stock was holding up but there were people round about who begrudged them their business. Patricia stood behind the counter and Andrew was mending a broken hinge on a cupboard when a plump woman came in. She dithered about what she would have. 'You've still got those penny gob stoppers?'

'Yes. It's Mrs. Firbank, isn't it?'

'Freda. I'll have three of them and a packet of twenty filter tipped.' Patricia put the packet on the counter and scooped the garish sticky balls from a sweet jar into a newspaper cone. 'My nephew's expecting his call up papers,' Freda said. 'The younger ones round our way have all gone already. All in uniform.' She paid and checked her change. 'They say it's the over thirties next. That'll be you as well.' she turned to Andrew. 'You'll be in the same batch as our Jim.'

Patricia slammed the till shut and Andrew put his screwdriver down. 'I won't be going,' he said.

'Oh, why's that?' Freda stood by the door expecting to hear a tit bit of gossip.

'I'm not going to be part of the killing.'

'Oh, but you have to go if you get your papers.'

'I'll go to jail first.' He turned his back to her, tested the cupboard door and closed it. 'I'm not going to take a human life.'

'But there've always been wars and there always will be. It's in the nature of human beings. You can't just say that.'

Patricia heard them as if over waves from a long way off.

'It's surely possible to make progress. I mean, we're not living in the jungle. We don't eat each other now.'

'Well, there's not enough on you to be tasty. I'd have to feed you up a bit first, keep you in a cage.' She leered at Patricia. 'But then, is it worth feeding him up? Will he ever be any use to a woman? If not we'll put him in the pot. Only thing to do!' She went out laughing at her own wit. The door closed.

'You mean to go through with it?' Patricia asked.

'I vowed never to go to war. I signed it.' He took her hand. 'I signed it. I know it was different in the big crowd when so many were doing it. But what's the point if you just give way at the first hurdle? I mean it wasn't a game. Will you stand by me?' He kissed her fingers.

'Yes. … But it is different, Andrew. People will say you're just a peace crank. They'll say you're a coward.'

He dropped her hand. 'Will you say that? Will you think I'm less of a man?'

She put her arms round his neck and clung to him. 'No, Andrew Taylor. It doesn't make you any less of a man.'

Two weeks later he received his call-up papers and had two weeks to reply. It took him one week. Then they waited in dread for the response.

Patricia watched nervously every day for an official letter. When it arrived, Andrew had already left for the shop. She picked up the large envelope, feeling the weight of it, played with it, put it down then picked it up again. Should she take it with her to the shop? She placed it in the centre of the table, left it there and looked round for another task that would keep her from leaving.

There was sorting to do in the spare room, the room that used to be Andrew's when Mrs. Taylor was alive. She still thought of the flat as her dead mother-in-law's. Whenever she came in and pattered up the stairs she had the feeling of being a trespasser. Every stick of furniture had been Mrs. Taylor's, every ornament, except their wedding photo on the mantelpiece, Andrew in Ben's best suit, tailored on the Jarrow Crusade, she in the beautiful dress the baroness had tired of and she'd shortened for Katharine's wedding. She'd lengthened it again in a contrasting russet and tailored a fitted jacket from the russet worsted. She wished the photo had been in colour, but happiness showed in black and white.

She would have liked to have taken some posters from the shop to put up in the flat but Andrew liked things as they were, the sense that his mother had just gone out. It had taken persuasion even to give away her clothes. Everything in the flat was gloomy. Furniture, brown paint, wallpaper with a small diamond pattern that had darkened from beige to light brown, navy blue or black home made clippy mats. The only relief was in the scullery, painted in deep forest green.

The second bedroom was small and they'd stacked it half full with boxes of tobacconist's goods. All of the lollipops and sweeties had gone to the shop and most had been sold, only a few packets of bubble gum and lemon sherbet left, last of the treats. Liquorice twigs were all they could get hold of now. She sniffed the dry scent of tobacco. Stock was dwindling. It might last another year, maybe even two if they were lucky. She calculated quickly in her head. People weren't flush with money. If there'd been enough sugar she'd have made sweets for the bairns herself, children who'd been jealously kept at home from the evacuation or who'd been unhappy and brought back to the town. Mary went through practically all of their sugar rations with the little bit of baking that kept her sane. The tree Ben had planted at the allotment took root and bore sour fruit but apple pies still came out of the oven on the range, or fruity bread puddings sometimes sweetened with carrot. It was time to go. She closed down a box lid, grabbed her thick woollen coat and ran for the tramcar.

At the shop Mary was serving. Andrew had to buy something at the market and her mother sat irritably pulling out wool from a jumper, unhappy in the shop that had been hers. Patricia kissed her and let her go back to the house. No customers. She settled to do something useful, took out the accounts, neatly recorded in a clear hand and brought them up to date for that week, snapped the book shut and tapped her finger nails on the counter. Where was Andrew? Probably walking around. This last week he'd taken to pacing inside, outside, anywhere. The envelope waiting in the flat came back to mind and she brushed the floor to banish it, punishing any dirt.

He came in. 'What's the matter?'

'Nothing. Why do you ask?'

'You always look round and speak when I come in. Something's happened.' He took her shoulders and turned her to face him. 'What is it?'

'The post came before I caught the tram.'

'And?'

'There was a big envelope. It looked official.'

'For me?' She nodded. 'Why didn't you bring it?'

'I didn't want to lose it on the way.' He shook his head. 'I was frightened. I wanted one more day. With you.'

He kissed her eyes. 'I won't be able to wait the whole day. It's on my mind all the time. I've hardly slept.'

'I know. But I can't ask mam to watch the shop again.'

'If we're not busy I'll slip out early this afternoon, if you'll finish off. Go up and see your mother.'

She kissed him, trudged upstairs, helped Mary wind the wool and listened to her chatter without registering a word. What could they do to him? The word coward they'd attached to his father echoed in her head. People might reach for the word no matter what any authority said – or they'd say he was a parasite. She went back to serve a customer and counted the minutes, palms cold and clammy. Andrew left at three o' clock and she was glad when Diane, in need of something to do, came in to lend a hand. Patricia asked her to turn out a cupboard, clean the window if she had time before locking up. Time was what her sister had. And sadness.

On the tramcar she sat back on the wooden seat resting against the sloping pew like back and watched scenes outside; pale women with children, old people shuffling, shopkeepers hooking the awnings to roll them back, only the occasional young man. At the flat she clicked their front door open in a trance and slowly climbed the stairs.

Andrew was standing with his back to her, reading at the window. He shook the papers out. 'I've got to go to a hearing, some sort of tribunal.' He turned and spread the papers out on the table. 'It's going to be a great rigmarole.' His face was white. 'I've got to write a statement explaining my beliefs, explaining why I ... can't go.' He sat down. 'I have to go through this to register as a Conscientious Objector.'

She peered over his shoulder. 'The vicar might help you. And dad.' He propped his head on his hands. 'I expect we could stay at mam's tomorrow. It might help to ... say the things out loud.' She trailed into the scullery. 'I'll make more than we need tonight so I can take something. There are odds and ends left from Christopher's food parcel.' She knew she was speaking to herself. When she came back he was still staring at the papers.

They slept in each others' arms and woke early, washed and dressed carefully in fresh clothes as if today was the day of an appointment, arriving early to open up. Mary gave them bread and dripping and hot water to drink. Tea was low.

Patricia checked remaining stock and recorded it in a note book, helped her mother wring clothes through a mangle in the backyard, shredded vegetables for a soup, found a clean pair of old sheets to make up their bed and served a few customers in the afternoon. It was a relief when Ben came home. They shared their meal with the luxury of a bread pudding laced mainly with the sour apples and relaxed round the fire.

Trisha slid into the kitchen to wash up alert to hear what was said..

'Now before we start you've got to realize it'll be no picnic.' Her father's voice.

'Well, I know that.'

'And it could be worse than you've imagined. The judge seems to be an old bugger. His job's to be impartial but he's set on trying to get people like you to change their minds and join up. I hear tell he's even stated in public that when this war ends the Conscientious Objectors should be cold-shouldered. Your war could go on for a long time, lad.'

Patricia heard Andrew cough. 'I – I think I can be firm about it.'

'In his head this judge might think he's being fair. He's got to test whether your convictions are true. But he'll throw the book at you. People think that men like you join this register because they're shirkers.'

'Dad!' Patricia came to the door.

'Don't worry, pet. I'm preparing him for what lies ahead.' She shook her head. 'But at least this thing exists and people can record their moral standpoint.' He turned to Andrew again. 'The judge, like as not'll treat you like an idiot and a fool, lad, and needle you the whole time.'

'Right.'

'Remember, lad, the House of Parliament decision was that it's not a crime – or contemptible to be a Conscientious Objector – if you're genuine. Keep that in mind.' Ben grinned. 'I think I'm in my pulpit now.'

'On your soapbox, dad! What else is new?' She shrugged.

'Now, where'd you say these convictions started?'

In the scullery again Trisha listened to her father. 'Start at the beginning, lad.' Scraping of furniture as they moved the chairs. 'In your own heart ... where do these convictions start?'

More scraping, then Andrew's voice. 'With what they did to my dad. He was probably sick when they tied him up and shot him.

That's what war can do to people, make them do to their own. I've grown up with a father who was only a photo.'

She heard Ben sigh. 'They were a lot of blinkered fools. But I wouldn't write that down. They'd not accept it. Close your eyes. What else comes into your head?'

Stillness. Her clattering of plates in the scullery sounded like pistol cracks. 'I don't go to church all the time.' Andrew's voice. 'But I believe in all that.' She put the last plates down gently, washed the cloths and hung them up. 'I suppose ...' She sat down on the scullery step, 'I suppose it's something from the Bible - *Thou shalt not kill.*'

There was the scratching of a pen. Ben writing. 'Right. Anything else?'

'And ... I think also ... it has to be *Love your neighbour.*'

'Aye.' She heard Ben's chuckle. 'The old question *Who is my neighbour?* Some other fellow asked that.'

'You know this stuff better than I do,' Andrew said.

'Beside the point. It's where <u>you</u> stand that we have to get down.'

She heard someone get up. '*And your enemy.* Didn't he say *Love your enemy* as well?'

'They'll dispute that, exactly what it means, an enemy, probably say it just applies to our own private lives - like when I was blacklisted by the owners.'

The chair scraped again. 'I think ... I think in the end I'd have to ask whether the people I'd be sent to fight were human beings, like us. If so, the government's wrong to say different. They'd have us think they're all maniacs or something.'

More scratching. 'That might be your starting point, lad. What about the Peace Pledge?'

'Yes. It seems different from the days of the rallies, you know. Thousands back then in the Albert Hall, one in five of the nation were involved. Mostly under thirty-five.'

'But now you stand alone.' A heavy sigh. 'Maybe we lose our brains as we get older.'

'It's hard not to get drawn down into a whirlpool with everybody else, almost irresistible. What are my ideas, after all?'

'Nothing if they're swept away by the tide. Think deep, lad. Try to remember that stuff.'

She heard him mutter, 'War being murder. A sin against God and the Brotherhood of Man. The speakers had been involved in the horrors of the Great War one way or another.'

'And you could quote the words of the Peace Pledge. Have you still got it?'

'I think so.'

'Put that in your statement and take the card along with you. It usually helps to have a piece of paper of some sort. What about joining the Friends' Ambulance Unit? They go to the Front.'

Another silence. 'I've lain awake wrestling with that. I know it's a noble thing to do. But in the end I feel … I feel I'd still be taking part in the war effort, supporting it indirectly, giving it some kind of sanction … God help me.'

'If you do decide to go on with this John Hargraves would help you get all this down on the page, if you need help. These are only notes. He'd be able to phrase it. I might not do the same thing in your shoes. I might have looked for a different occupation, even though I quit work – this is a different kettle of fish from the first time. But stand by your convictions.'

'I'll try.'

'One other thing.' Ben's voice was stern. 'And I must warn you about this. If you live under a shadow when it's all over, trouble could be from the government as well as from people you come across.'

'What do you mean?'

'I mean the government could spy on you.'

'Come off it, Ben.'

'No, listen. After the Great War, people who stood out as pacifists, conscientious objectors, whatever you call them, they were monitored afterwards – the first lot to have our government keep an eye on them. Must have thought they were dangerous. I'm not saying it <u>will</u> happen again but it could do.'

'How would they keep an eye on me?'

'Informers you'd be unaware of. They could intercept your mail and you wouldn't even know they'd done it.'

'Well, I just won't write any letters. You can carry messages for me.'

'Aye, I'll be your go between. Or we'll borrow Wilf's racing pigeons and use them as carriers.' They laughed.

Patricia filled a hot water bottle. It was a relief not to have to go back to the flat and almost against their will they slept.

When they stepped off the bus and walked to the Moot Hall for the tribunal it was pelting down. In spite of the elegance of steps running full length at the front and columns at the entrance, the soot blackened building stood grim in the rain. Patricia had to jump back from the path of a car that sprayed her ankles. Andrew caught her. 'Can't have you in another accident. Come on.'

An official stopped Patricia, saying she couldn't go in with her husband. She was trying to persuade him when a woman in a black coat swept up and laid a hand on her shoulder.

'She's with me.'

'And who are you?'

'I'm here to observe proceedings. From the Society of Friends.' She smiled at him. 'The Quakers. We're reporting on each case.'

'Why?'

'To see that people are fairly treated – we're upholding their right to be placed on the register of objectors to military service.'

'Oh!'

'This lady is going to help me.'

The official looked round but no one was watching. 'I suppose that's all right.'

The woman smiled brightly at him and steered Patricia into the big room. She winked and held a finger against her lips as they sat at a small table and she handed Patricia a pen and a piece of paper. 'Write anything,' she whispered. 'They're on a recess but they'll be in soon. It's your husband who wants to be registered?'

'Yes.'

'And you're in agreement?'

'Yes. Thank you for getting me in. There's been a lot of discussion at home but my dad's supporting us.' She rushed on to this stranger. 'My dad thinks this is the second round of the Great War.'

'What else does he say?'

'He has a favourite. "We sowed the wind" – he means the Great War – "and we'll reap the whirlwind."' – says the second round could be worse … though I don't know.'

'Terror from above now – for women and children. Only a taste of that last time. Oh, here they come. That's the judge.'

Three others joined the dignified official. The chamber was a long room that was dark from walls that looked as if they hadn't seen soap and water for a long time. The arrangement was like a little court with a table on a raised dais at one end with four chairs and an area for the press reserved in front of it, other chairs in the body of the room. A coat of arms with the Lion and the Unicorn hung above four elderly men on the platform. Twenty or thirty other people were waiting to be called. Not Andrew's turn.

The Quaker pointed to two of the men behind the table. 'One of them's an Alderman and one on the other side a Trade Union representative. I'm not sure who the other one is.'

Patricia watched a young man lumber forward to take a seat in front of the main table.

The group listened closely as the candidate stood and read out his statement.

Rain was lashing at the windowpanes and she strained to hear him. He simply stated he believed he could not join the army and stumbled over his words. The judge sitting in the middle then asked questions. Patricia felt embarrassed for the man interviewed who shuffled his feet and mumbled. She thought he didn't understand. To every question he answered 'Yes' or 'No'.

The objector sat down as the three spoke quietly to each other at the table till the judge summed up. 'It seems to us,' the voice sounded clipped, 'that the person in front of us is devoid of any intelligence whatsoever. Anyone with any sense would have answered differently.' The Quaker lady wrote and Patricia pretended to do the same, then the judge leaned forward speaking directly to the young man, very slowly. 'We are putting your name on the register. You don't have to join the army or the navy or the air force. There are no conditions.' The young man sat on. 'You may go home. Go.' He got up and shambled off.

The Quaker wrote and commented to Patricia, 'Nothing else they could do here, though fewer than half of the people who apply are actually registered.

They looked through their list and called Andrew's name. Patricia twisted her wedding ring. The judge rustled his papers and gestured for him to sit, hardly looking up. 'So, why are you here?' he asked still reading what was in front of him.' Andrew rose but seemed unable to speak. Patricia's fingers froze over her paper and the judge finally looked up. 'Well?'

Then he spluttered out phrases she recognized. 'I have renounced war. I've pledged never directly or indirectly to support or sanction another.' Words from the Peace Pledge rolled out and the Quaker nodded as she wrote his reply.

The judge sighed and handed down a paper. 'This is your statement. Please read it.'

Andrew took it. 'I believe war is … murder,' his voice trembled, 'it's a sin against God as our Father. I was taught to obey the Ten Commandments. 'One of them says *Thou shalt not kill*. And Jesus said,' he made an effort to control the tremor, 'I must love my neighbour and my enemy as well.' The Quaker wrote vigorously. 'If we're all children of God, we're brothers and sisters, so taking human life is the crime of killing a brother … I can't take part in this system of destroying human beings.' He coughed, almost a sob in air. Patricia pressed her lips. 'The authorities organise this crime in wartime. War doesn't end war as our fathers were told. It just brings about another. So ...' his voice faltered again and the paper in his hand shook. ' ... I refuse the call up to any form of military service and accept whatever punishment I may be given if my statement is rejected.'

Patricia was cold as the tribunal listened in silence. Her husband stepped forward before they could question him and presented the card he'd signed for the Peace Pledge Union. The four stared at Andrew.

'So,' the judge sniffed at the card and looked at him, 'You won't die for your country?'

'No, sir. That isn't what I said.' Andrew drew himself up. 'I am prepared to die for my country.'

'Then I don't understand why you are you here' Another pause. Patricia's tongue was dry on the roof of her mouth as he cleared his throat. The judge put his spectacles down, red with irritation and glared at Andrew. His voice grated, 'Your record states that you've worked in a shipyard. That's a reserved occupation. You could go back to that.'

'I could, sir, if they were making civilian vessels. But it's all destroyers now ... like the Dreadnoughts in the Great War. I'd have a responsibility for the results of the thing I'd helped to make ... I mean, if hundreds of people were killed by it.

The judge frowned into his notes. 'So, you won't help to fight Hitler!'

Andrew seemed to have himself together now. 'It's just ... I wouldn't be killing Hitler, only other people who were ordered to pick up a rifle or a bayonet, like me. And civilians. I can't take part in a wholesale butchery.'

There was an aching silence then the judge leaned forward. 'I suppose you realise Hitler likes people like you? You're one of Hitler's friends, aren't you?'

'No. I don't consider myself to be that, sir.'

'Another thing you haven't thought of. If Hitler gets to this country the first thing he'll do will be to fill every town and village in England with German soldiers. They'll round up people like you. First they'll really rough you up - and I <u>mean</u> rough you up. Then they'll shoot you!'

'Why will they shoot me,' Andrew burst out, 'if I'm one of Hitler's friends?'

The judge leaned forward angrily. '<u>I</u> ask the questions!' Sitting in the centre, he was the only one to speak. 'So! You want to stand aside from all this?'

'Yes, sir.'

'How do you think anybody living in a country that's engaged in total war can cut himself off from the economy of that country?'

'I'm not sure, sir.'

'I'll tell you how. It's easy. You just go away and buy a plot of land.' The judge glared at him and leant forward. 'Then you fence it round, grow potatoes and live in it completely alone. Is that what you intend to do?'

'I can't afford to buy a plot of land, sir.'

'Then let me ask you another one. Would you eat food that the Royal Navy or the Merchant Navy had run the risk of a blockade and their own personal safety to bring you?'

Andrew swayed from foot to foot. 'I'd ... I'd try to give place to others first and exist on as little as possible.'

'You people,' the judge said. 'You don't think things through. What if this country was invaded? Would you still think it right not to join up?'

'I'd resist the invaders by any means I could without killing.'

'So, how then do you plan to deal with war?'

'I'm not a politician. Nor am I a king.'

'Answer me, please.'

Patricia watched as he racked his brain. The judge refused to help him by asking another question. At last he replied. 'The only way is to avoid it in the first place.'

'How do you do that?'

'I think, by not having enemies, only friends. Find peaceful solutions - trade with each other instead of killing each other.'

'And you're also an expert on theology, aren't you?' He leant forward. 'Let me tell you, young man, I'm as certain as I sit here that if Christ appeared today, he would approve of this war.' The Quaker lady gasped and put her pen down. 'And you're living in cloud cuckoo land, young man – make Hitler a friend!' He slapped the papers down. 'If you carry your argument to its logical conclusion you should eat nothing and starve yourself to death.' He looked up at the ceiling and muttered, 'And that might be the most useful thing you could do!'

The Quaker stood up. 'Shame!' Her voice carried.

The judge peered at her. 'Sit down please, or I'll have you evicted.' He glared till she sat down then turned to Andrew. 'So, young man, you want to be friends with everyone and you will not die for your country. How do you look young men or young women for that matter,' he peered at the Quaker. 'How do you look them in the eye, those who do go off to die for their country and for your protection?

'I have never asked them to do that for me.'

'Yet you enjoy their protection!' He sat back lips curled in a sneer. 'And let's return to your wonderful knowledge of scripture. I suppose you realize that Pontius Pilate was the first pacifist?'

The Quaker dropped her head in her hands.

'I don't understand what you're saying, sir.'

'Pontius Pilate was the first pacifist,' the judge leant over his elbow on the table, ' … because he did not resist evil! Neither do you. And people like you are trying to put a spoke in the wheel of the national effort. The fact remains that you refuse to die for your country.'

'Sir, that is not a fact. I have never been tested on that.'

'This court is testing you.'

'I have not refused to die for my country.' Andrew shut his eyes and swayed. He struggled for breath, closed his eyes, hands clenched into fists then straightened and looked ahead. He seemed to find a lightning rod through the whirlwind, see something. His brow cleared and he spoke firmly. 'Sir, I do not refuse to die for my country. But wherever I am, I am bound by the ten commandments. I am bound by the commandment, "Thou shalt not kill." What I refuse to do is to KILL for my country!'

The judge became red. 'THAT commandment, young man, is for civilian life. If a soldier kills the enemy on the field of battle he does NOT commit murder! He's obeying orders.'

Andrew looked the older man in the face. 'That's why I refuse to become a soldier. So no one can put a gun in my hand and give me the order to kill – for my duty.'

The judge looked up at the ceiling. 'How long, Lord, must I listen to this utter tripe?'

The Quaker clattered to her feet. 'Sir! Sir, I protest. These courts have a vital principle to uphold – the principle of liberty of conscience!'

The judge turned to the Alderman. 'These opinionated young women! Pure poison. One more word and she'll be evicted.' He spoke loud enough for everybody to hear. She remained standing but he continued. 'We'll adjourn to consider this matter.' He motioned the others and they stamped into a smaller room. Andrew shook his head and Patricia thought they were going to dismiss the appeal outright.

It took four minutes' consultation before they returned, till the judge took his seat in the middle. He motioned Andrew to stand then gazed at him as if he was a half-wit and said, 'The objection of Andrew Taylor to military service is upheld. However, we must record in our opinion that he is a young man with a very limited outlook on life and he will be registered,' he looked up at Andrew, 'on one condition. That is that he should work on the land.' Relief swept through Patricia and she trembled. 'Do you agree to that?' *No prison sentence. No firing squad.* 'I asked, do you agree to that?' The Quaker lady put an arm round Patricia.

'Yes, sir. I agree to work on the land.'

At home they danced round the flat like children. Patricia began to trill with her mouth and two fingers the way the 'Red Indians' in the films did while Andrew beat the dining room table for a drum. They were starting a two person hokey-cokey when they heard a furious banging underneath the floorboards. They stood still, collapsed giggling in each others' arms then tiptoed, shushing each other, into the bedroom to make love with a joy they hadn't yet experienced and floated into sleep.

Next morning the finger of reality touched them. No arrangements were made. Andrew had to find the work for himself. Patricia made breakfast, kissed her husband and pelted for a tramcar. She could run the shop herself.

When she got back that evening he was sitting quietly. He'd taken buses and walked to visit two farms not far from town asking for work. Both turned him down.

She put the kettle on. 'Don't they need help?'

'I'm sure they do. But not from a damned conchie.'

She picked up potatoes from the allotment that had earth clinging to them and began to wash them. 'Try again. It was the first day.' An opaque blind came down.

Next day it was the same, and the next, for two weeks. Andrew had an official letter asking if he'd found work on the land but there was no offer of help to find it. He went further and further on the buses, able only to visit one farm a day. It cost money. All doors were shut. When he got back he was white and strained. After a month both were at their wits'end. Andrew couldn't come back to the shop while he was supposed to be looking for other work. Days were long without him, even with her mother upstairs and Louise across the road. Business seemed to be falling off while bus fares mounted up. Their sleep was broken and they were tired next day.

Sundays he could take off like everyone else. Mary invited them to dinner to whatever she could put on the table and for company they slept over the night on Saturday when evenings were lively if Wilf came by to play dominoes with her father.

'No work on the farms?' he asked building a wall with the white pipped black blocks.

'It's not that there's no work but my face doesn't fit with the farmers.' Andrew stirred a poker in the fire till Patricia took it from him for destroying the solid glow of the coals. 'Though to be fair some of them are frightened they'll lose business on milk rounds if a conchie's working for them.'

They played in silence till Ben conceded the game, clattered his dominoes together and began to build a little tower. 'I know all about that, lad. Doors shut in your face. Destroys a man.'

'I'm wondering if I'm going to have to go down to Yorkshire or something. I've been to the Labour Exchange but they've been no use to me.'

'Probably no experience with this ... Cumberland?'

Patricia dropped a piece of toast onto a plate from the long toasting fork. 'We'd have to live apart like when I was in service there.'

'Cruel, after all that time waiting to get married. But they'll be on your bones, Andrew, before long.'

Wilf picked up the pile of farthings that were his winnings and reached for a pipe. 'I know where you could try.' He tamped the baccie down. 'Try the Forestry Commission. They're government, aren't they? And you've been through proper channels.'

Ben took his own pipe down from the mantelpiece to knock out on the top bricks of the fireplace. He smiled. 'Wilf of the big ideas!'

'Why aye, man!' He struck a match and drew on the stem of his pipe. 'Worth a try. 'There's something out past Gateshead way, forest in County Durham. You might find it in a library that's open if the Dole House draws a blank with it.'

'I seem to get Koko the clown there.'

They laughed and Ben cleared the dominoes away. Patricia helped her mother in the kitchen and listened to the chuckling. Her father'd had a spring in his step since he went back down the pit, even though the dark caverns still held fear. Finding a place where you fit!

On Monday they counted out bus fares and Andrew started again on his trek. Without telling him Patricia had dipped into savings. Please God this wouldn't go on much longer. Please God this war would end soon. Please God.

Mary came down into the shop with her and Louise finished up to let her get home.

She raked the fire out, regretting she hadn't had time for it in the morning, clinked cinders and rattled dirt out from the flue, shovelled muck from the grate onto a newspaper. Her hands were filthy when the door slammed and she heard the tread of his footsteps two at a time up the stairs.

He was down on his knees and knocked ash over the floor kissing her. 'They've taken me on.'

'Oh, thank God!'

'The Forestry Commission.' He stood up. 'I'm sorry, I've made a mess.' She stayed on her hands and knees automatically brushing the grey dust. 'The only thing is ... '

'What?'

'... hours are long.'

'Is that all?' She stood up with the dustpan still in her hands.

He rushed on. 'They start about seven and say I'll have to take digs out there to be sure to get in to work.'

'Couldn't you cycle?'

'I asked that. I told them I was used to cycling all weathers but they said they can't risk hold-ups on the roads, due to weather, anything. I'll have to live locally during the week.'

'Do they have a hostel?'

He took the ash pan from her. 'They say I have to find lodgings and I have the address of a farm. I went over there before coming back and the farmer's wife said she had a room.' He took the ashes to the bin in the yard and called up. 'I should be home at weekends.'

She stood at the top of the back stairs. 'We've just got settled in.'

'Let's hope it's not for long.'

Patricia could have stayed with her mother and father to make looking after the shop easier but she felt she held things together by living in the flat, cleaning, warming it, keeping it ready. Her parents often gave her tea before she went back and her breakfast in the morning. She just had a hot drink before running for the tram, settling on the wooden seat, answering if anyone spoke to her.

On Monday she'd finished dusting the shelves and polishing the counter when a customer came in, a broad woman with a flowered crossover pinafore under her coat. It was the same woman who'd made fun of the idea that Andrew could refuse the call-up.

Patricia smiled. 'Yes, Mrs. Firbank?'

Freda Firbank came forward and fidgeted with her shopping bag. 'Can you split a packet of Woodbines? I just want three.'

Patricia reached down a packet and tore it open. 'Five would be easier to split off,'

Freda banged her old leather purse down. 'Suit yourself, hinny. Three's what I came in for and three's what I'll have or I'll have nothing.'

'Right, Mrs. Firbank.'

'Or I can go elsewhere. There now!' The face reddened.

Patricia made a little cone from newspaper and poured three Woodbines into it. 'I'm always happy to serve you, Mrs. Firbank.'

Freda put the little cone in her battered shopper. 'So long as it's not that husband of yours. I'll not be served by a conchie. There's many a one not come back from the war round here, I can tell you.' She snapped her purse shut and flounced to the door. Patricia said nothing when Freda looked over her shoulder and slammed the door shut. The bell went on ringing.

Nobody had much to spare. Business was slow. Women drifted in and out for a twist of snuff or some baccie for a granddad or a liquorice twig for a bairn to chew on. She tried to forget Freda but by the afternoon the shop was dead.

She sat writing to Andrew or knitting from wool Mary had unraveled from an old jumper. Looking up she saw some of her customers cross the road when they got near the shop. One or two appeared to collide with each other and stood on the other side in meaningful conversation nodding heads, glancing across. Patricia felt cold as she sat. When she got up to clean the window outside the women moved on. Mary was furious but Ben said to take no notice. Like kids they'd get bored. Patricia was grateful her parents now refused rent for the shop. At the weekend no one said anything to Andrew about the cold shoulder.

On Saturday when he was back they hugged and kissed and Patricia felt her nerves unravel when she lay in his arms, staying in their own place. He had little to say about the work and she had little to say about the shop but he slept like a log and was hard to wake on Sunday morning.

Potatoes were their mainstay with parsnips, cabbage and little bits of meat from a ham shank Mary had cajoled from her butcher. Louise came in with Edward and little Benjie. They shared soup from the bone stock, vegetables fit for a king then a slightly sour apple pudding.

'So, how's tricks?' Louise asked settling to a cigarette after the washing up was cleared. No-one else had questioned Andrew about his week. She handed him the packet. 'They're yours,' and threw her head back blowing smoke gently from her nose. Ben handed him a box of matches. 'The cat's really got your tongue.' She turned to

Patricia who was cuddling Benjie away from his mammy's smoke. 'What are they doing to him out there? Has he taken a vow of silence?' Patricia shrugged. 'What are your digs like?'

'Well,' Andrew lit his cigarette, 'it's been the most miserable week of my life. And I'm going to have to get off soon to catch the bus back.'

Louise fixed him with her stare. 'You're not going out of here till you tell us what's what.'

'It seemed all right at first, pleasant enough,' he settled back in the chair. 'We were having a bit of supper on Sunday night after I'd given my landlady my ration book, bread and cheese with her own chutney which was very nice.' He took a drag. 'Then I had the first shock. She said there'd be no breakfast before I left next day, not even a hot drink because she wouldn't be getting up before six o' clock to see to me.'

'Can't you make a cup of tea for yourself?'

'Of course. But she wouldn't have it, said she wouldn't risk a fire in her kitchen from a lodger. It was the first time I'd ever gone to work without even a hot drink. And only cold water to splash myself awake.'

Louise tamped her fag out on a saucer. 'But she gave you some bait?'

'Oh yes! A tin box with breakfast and lunch caked together. I had some tea as well, a pint bottle that was clay cold - for the day. A thermos flask would be extravagant.'

'So, what had the old bat given you?' Louise uncoiled and sat up.

'The first break was at half past eight and I found she'd just given me six slabs of bread an inch thick, some spread with jam, some with paste of some sort and a little piece of limp lettuce. Lucky to have it at the time of year. That was for the whole day's work.'

Louise took her little boy as he came to her and scrambled onto her lap. 'I'd like to get a hold of that witch!'

'What's a witch, mammy?'

'Somebody nasty. And did you eat the muck?'

'I did. But it got worse because I left the tin box on a grass verge and didn't realise the lid was open a chink. My fault. When I looked inside ants were running all over the whole thing, the bread was completely infested.'

'You didn't eat it?' Patricia felt sick.

'I'm afraid I shook them off and ate it, all of it. It was the most horrible thing I'd ever had but I was starving. I'd already had a few swigs from the cold tea at eleven when they gave us a few minutes. That was utterly foul but I had to wash the doorsteps down with something. We had half an hour for lunch and there was nothing else. I asked for plain water next day.'

Ben had his pipe stem clamped angrily between his teeth. 'What about the work, lad?'

'Really hard, I found it harder than the shipyard. We had to squat in pairs all morning on a piece of sacking to pull weeds out by hand from tiny trees they were growing from seed. We weren't allowed to talk. You get stiff sitting like that in one position, it's murder.'

'You're unused to it,' Ben said.

Mary clattered off to the kitchen and banged about with a rolling pin.

Once started Andrew couldn't stop. 'The afternoon was even worse. We had to go from one o' clock to five thirty without any break at all and I was in hot water because I pulled some of the saplings instead of the weeds. They were only an inch high, you see, and it was hard to spot the difference. It was one of the longest days of my life.'

Louise had provided extra tea from a private hoard she'd stored before rationing. Mary made a fresh pot. 'Don't go back, son,' she said. 'At least you have hot tea here.'

'He'll have to, Mary.' Ben took his cup. 'But I'll set him to the bus stop. Can you get a fresh loaf out?'

'I can do that.'

Next weekend Trisha went to meet her husband and walked up with him from the tram. He was in the same digs and they were talking about their problems, nearly at her parents' home when she heard a scuffle behind them and a little chant began.

Ginger, you're barmy!
You should have joined the army!

Andrew stopped but she took his arm. 'Don't look round.' But he turned and jumped at the group of children. They ran off laughing. 'Come in.' She pulled him by the elbow and shut the door.

'They're just bairns.'

'Don't encourage them.'

'Should I look as if I'm frightened?'

'Just come in.'

Mary was waiting with a fire on and an apple and bread pudding in the lower oven, potato and lentil rissoles done in dripping and shredded cabbage on the hob. By the time they'd eaten her dessert they'd forgotten about naughty children. He stretched out and fell asleep in his chair. Nobody woke him and he was out for two hours.

'I'll need to go, mam.'

'Let the lad have his sleep out.'

'I know, but I need to get a fire going in the flat.'

'Have you enough coals?'

'Dad brought some round.'

'He'll see you tomorrow. He's at the allotment. Come for dinner. Mostly veg.'

Andrew snorted and opened his eyes. 'Anything you cook is lovely. Sorry I drifted off, thought I was in heaven here.'

They kissed her, left and ran for a tram at the bottom of the street. When they got home they spent an hour simply lying together, warming each other, shutting the world out. As the light faded Patricia sat up and went to the scullery to try to coax an omelette from dried egg. There was a rap at the door and footsteps running.

'I'll get that.' Andrew ran downstairs and Patricia tried to master the yellow powder. 'Who was it?'

'Nobody.'

'Andrew, we'll not make it if we have secrets.' She took a dirty note from his hand and spread it out.

'*Your name is Howard. Welcome back, Ginger Howard.* What on earth?'

'It rhymes with coward. That's a word I'll have to get used to.'

'If only they knew how hard you're working.'

He lit the kindling and held an iron blazer over the fireplace for an up-draught. 'I could have joined the Friends' Ambulance Service.'

'I know, you talked to dad about it.'

He took the blazer away and added more small coals. 'I felt it was still being part of the war. Maybe I'm wrong.'

'You made your decision and you're working your guts out behind the scenes.' She caught the dehydrated egg as it ballooned in the pan and tapped the sorry thing out onto a plate. 'We'll have supper and put the wireless on. We've each other.' He kissed her hand.

Over dinner next day they talked about the lodgings and Ben asked what was charged.

'Twenty-two shillings.'

Ben dropped his knife and fork. 'Not counting the weekend?'

'I may get a couple of bob back for that but I'll have to press her for it.'

Mary choked on a potato. 'I'd press her! Daylight robbery! That's nearly three times a normal rent. But you get a hot meal at night?'

'Three times a week,' Andrew mumbled.

'Did you know that, Trish?' She shook her head. 'What does she give you for your cold meal?'

A sigh. 'I don't want to talk about this'

'Best get it all out,' Patricia said.

349

'It's usually a hard boiled egg from the farm - so it's nice and fresh. And a piece of ham.' He sketched on the tablecloth. 'About an inch square. Maybe some salad, a tomato or something.'

Ben picked his knife and fork up. 'Eat all you can while you're here. But you need to get out of that place.'

'I'm listening out.'

'A pity you didn't present yourself for the medical. I doubt you'd have passed. And I don't think you'd have made it for much longer at the shipyard if it hadn't gone into receivership.'

'Dad!'

'Shut up!' Mary glared at him. 'So, what do they have in store for you next week?'

'I'm being transferred to the Forest itself.'

'Heaven help you.'

'It'll probably be better. Anything'll be better than that monotonous weeding.'

'Try and get back on Friday night.'

Andrew shook his head. 'I'm done in by then. I couldn't make it.'

Next week it was a different chant when he came up the street.

Howard, Howardy Custard!
You stole the baby's mustard!

Ben came out, caught the kids and sent them packing, Patricia dragged her husband inside and he flopped down. Then they dragged out of him what the new work was.

Andrew warmed his hands on the teacup. 'I've had to carry felled trees this week.'

'You were walking up the street like an old man,' Ben said.

'That's how I feel. We had to shift newly cut trees across ditches and over rough ground to the road by the side of the plantation. They give you a bit of rough sacking for your shoulders but that's all. I could hardly move on Tuesday when I got up.'

'You'll harden to it, lad.'

'If they don't kill him first.'

'It's tough down the pit first off but your body gets used to it. Stay here tonight, Patricia.' She nodded. 'In fact I think he should just get to bed. Can you fill him a hot water bottle, Mary?'

'I'll do it.' Patricia got up. At least she could do that.

Each week she prayed he'd find other lodgings. Only the newest workers stayed at this farm, they called it the 'palace'. Six weeks on and there was a vacancy on another farm. He moved. Then another scandal, the landlady wouldn't return his ration book saying the grocer still had it. The following week it was the same story. He decided to stay over on Saturday morning to see the man himself. Without ration coupons he couldn't stay on for long at his new digs.

Mary gave him hot soup in the afternoon when he arrived before giving his latest bulletin. Louise had come in to hear it.

The 'palace' landlady had gone on drawing his rations after he'd moved. But the grocer thought he could fix it. He supplied both women and held all of their books so he'd give her personal rations next week to the present landlady to make it up. They laughed. But Andrew's sugar ration for a month had been drawn.

'Cheek!' Mary was outraged. 'I could have made pies with that.'

Louise leant against the mantelpiece drawing on a cigarette. 'It needs somebody to go out there and sort her out.'

'I'll send you next time.'

'She's a little bantam,' Ben said.

For the rest of the weekend Patricia said nothing about her problems with the shop.

The business hardly ticked over. Women on the street passed without a word, some crossed the road a few yards away if they spotted her coming. She was being shunned. If she spoke the best reply was a nod. At first she thought she'd imagined it, then decided to ignore the behaviour. Surely they couldn't keep it up forever. But folk on the street became even frostier. Children no longer played

351

outside the shop and hopscotch grids were chalked out on other pavements, always the figure of Freda Firbank, her plump back turned, whispering in a little group, conducting this symphony of silence.

The hours stretched. If Ben had been taking rent for the sublet and they hadn't laid in stock already paid for everything would have folded. She wished Andrew was back but that might make things worse. The small clock ticking on the wall got on her nerves and she was startled when a neighbour from further up pushed the door open. The brass clapper bell rang through her head. The little woman was thin and dowdy. Everyone was dowdy. Most had lost weight, except Freda Fairbanks who seemed fatter than ever. She smiled. 'What can I do for you?'

The neighbour leaned on the counter. 'You can give me three packets of tabs.'

'Tens?'

'Twenties. And Senior Service, not your clarty little Woodbines. My lad's back home on leave and we've got some cash. These are for him. And baccie for the dad. Two ounces. And three little twists of snuff.'

Patricia turned to get the order and was about to start talking about the weather when the voice started again, nearer.

The woman was leaning over the counter. 'Ah think what they're doing to you's cruel, hinny. Ah think no ill of your man even though my lad's in the forces. Ah'd buy the whole shop if ah could.' Trisha's hand began to shake. 'Here.' The woman turned the paper round and took the pencil from her. 'Ah'll reckon it. And ah'll not diddle ye neither. There you are.' She placed a pound note on the counter. Ah'll tell ye what. Keep that bit change and open a tab. We'll buy nowhere else. Ah'll tell my lad to bring some pals down here when they're home. There'll be a few of them knockin' about. And ah'll get me sisters to walk a bit further and come in here. We'll show that Freda.'

Patricia wiped her eyes and gave the change. 'I'd rather keep the money straight than open a tab.'

'Right, pet.' The woman leaned over again and Patricia could see missing teeth. 'Have ye ever wondered how Fat Freda with them fat jowls keeps' gettin' fatter?'

'Maybe she's got a condition.'

The customer wheeled out laughing and the bell clattered again. 'Ah wouldn't mind that condition!'

Patricia shrugged, wiped her eyes again and smoothed the pound note out. Louise came in. She was pale and wore no make-up these days but her voice was perky. 'How's tricks?' Patricia held the note up. 'That's better. But you don't look pleased?'

'Something the customer said.' Patricia pressed the till to spring open and jammed a lever over the precious note. 'About Freda Firbank.'

'The stirrer? What did she say?'

'Something … about it being odd Mrs. Firbank was getting fatter while the rest of us were getting thinner.'

'Ha! There's a rabbit off. I'll keep my eyes open. Freda flaming Firbank! Love to mam. I have to go.'

That week a trickle of customers came to the shop. Patricia felt better and said nothing about the gossips when Andrew staggered back. Sunday came quickly. She stayed over at her mother's that night and when she took the shutters down in the shop window next morning thought she saw a shadow disappear. But there was no one outside. She wiped the counter and began to set the window. A couple of women had stopped to stare at the pavement. They scuttled away when she looked up then Louise bounced across and shouted after them. Patricia was unlocking the door.

'Don't come out, Trish. Stay there. I'm going to get a scrubbing brush.' She dived back through her own shop front and Patricia stepped out. Yellow chalking covered two paving stones.

'Oh, my God!'

Louise hurried back with a bowl of water, red carbolic soap and her brush. 'Go back in. I'll deal with this.' Her sister stood still. 'Go on!'

Patricia went in and leaned against the counter feeling faint. The door was ajar and she could hear frantic scraping of the scrubbing brush against the pavement then the swish of water. A minute later an arm was round her waist. 'Go upstairs. Diane's coming round this morning, she's lonely. Give me that key. I'll open up again when she can watch the bairn. I'm scared Benjie'll get in Edward's way and damage himself. Edward's in the shop working with sharp knives. Mam'll make you a cup of tea. Have a few days off. We'll manage things.'

Patricia went back to the flat and stayed there alone for a few days. She hardly slept the first night then she cleaned the place right through, scrubbed every lino floor, polished windows with a spot of paraffin, cleaned the scullery with white vinegar and washed vases and ornaments. Mats hung out in the yard, she took a loop patterned carpet beater and thrashed them till they were plump. Everything was tidy and sweet for the weekend and she felt better.

But the weekend seemed like a few hours. On Monday she took the early tram and walked up the street to do battle but the only people she saw were firemen at the station cleaning an engine. Nothing on the pavement outside the shop window. She was sweating. But business started quickly when two of the firemen came in to buy packets of twenty each and extra for their mates. Mary fetched her a cup of tea and Louise crossed the road to look in, nodded, walked down to have a word with the firemen and came back smiling. She'd drummed up custom.

Things seemed better but on Saturday Patricia heard the rap of the letterbox, hurried down to collect the post, picked up an envelope, turned it over and saw it wasn't stamped. She plodded upstairs to prod the bacon she had in the pan, part of her precious meat ration, turned the rashers, opened the envelope then went into the bedroom and sat down. Andrew'd been dozing. She passed him a short note. 'We're to leave the flat.'

He was on his feet. 'They can't do that. I've lived here all my life.'

'They probably can. The landlord says he needs it for himself. Who are _we_? We're nobody.'

'What'll we do?'

A smell of burning, she rushed into the scullery, threw the pan off the gas and opened the back door to clear the choking fug. The air was thick with blue smoke. Andrew was beside her and chiselled the rashers off the base of the pan. 'We'll eat it. I'll cut the bread. Go into the room.'

She sat on the old horsehair settee Mrs. Taylor had been so proud of. People who'd been bombed out were queuing up for housing. They might wait for ever for something else.

22

When she was alone and didn't have to put on a brave face Louise wept. When husband and son slept her pillow was wet with tears of silent loss. When sisters or mother took her child, when Edward was out she retched raw rib aching sobs. Cold water doused on her face then her glasses hid the ravages of a private vice. Ben said nothing but stroked her hair in passing. A touch could make her want to scream.

Then Patricia's world cracked, Patricia who helped raise them, went away to work to help the family, who'd put her life aside. Her high holiness Patricia cracked, no longer calm, unflappable. She had to leave Andrew's flat and come back to their parents' home as a married woman, after all this time – like a widow. Louise could see her sister struggle with the work, sitting head in hands in the shop while money had to be written up and tallied, no energy to clean the pavement if there'd been another chalked message. She felt a call to action.

With daylight and her first cup of tea the younger sister put the mountain of morning grief away and kept look out on the street, in the shadows of their shop, standing to catch whoever chalked these foul words on the pavement. She helped arrange the empty room at her parents' place for Andrew and Patricia, persuaded Diane to give up the spare room at her flat to store their furniture and organised the men; Leslie to borrow a van from the little engineering firm he worked at, her dad when he was back from the pit to lend a hand and Katharine's husband. Fred worked all hours serving the war machine at Vickers Armstong's but squeezed time at home to help with the removal. Thank God for reserved occupations. All three lifted, carried, stacked. Edward's foot made him a liability for the physical work but he directed them.

Then Andrew was felled with his old enemy, bronchitis. He could lose his job if no word was sent but they were afraid to trust the overstretched postal service in case the delivery took too long. Patricia had her hands full looking after her husband, trying to cope with the business as well, Diane couldn't take something like that on and no one else had time.

Louise organised like a machine– her mam to watch the bairn, Diane to watch the shop, Ben to lend money for the fare. The journey seemed long but the bus driver was friendly and put her out at the right stop. She straightened for battle, walked into the forecourt and found the foreman who turned his back. She asked for his superior, the foreman dropped his hacksaw with a thud and said she could have two minutes. But when he looked in her face she smiled with her eyes, coaxed and chatted small talk till the weather-beaten face cracked and he showed her where she must take the sick note. Andrew's absence from work was smoothed. Glances from other men gave the faintest flicker of warmth that she carried with her to the cold of the bus stop and the long wait to rattle back home.

The following week Diane had to run the tobacconist shop. Patricia had washed the floor, fallen on wet lino, struck her temple and the piercing headaches from her time in hospital were unleashed, drowning her in waves. Ben would not even allow her downstairs. The younger sisters alternated between the tobacconist and the leather shop while looking after little Benjie. Some days Louise knew where she was by her nose, the reek of tannic leather, the resin sharpness of glue and the flat cold metal of nails, or sweet earthy Virginia tobacco.

Edward's shop had shelves piled with shoes to be cobbled or waiting to be collected but they were still moving furniture and stock from Andrew's flat. When they got to the last few boxes and picked up the final packets of cigarettes, coarse cut shag for pipe baccie and a little snuff, they stumbled on big glass jars of sweets hidden in a corner. They collected them and moved them with everything else to the shop. Louise struggled with the top of one of the jars and rummaged out a dimpled clear lollipop.

'What are we going to do with these?'

Diane looked up from scrubbing the floor. ''We're going to sell them. What else? Lunatic!' She sopped the bubbled grey water into her bucket.

Louise found her breath caught as coughs of deep laughter bellowed up from the base of her ribs for the first time since she'd heard about Joe's death and she had to sit down. 'I mean, we've got to try to get the business back on its feet. Fat Freda's had it her own way. You'd better sit Benjie on the counter till this dries.' Diane wrung the floor cloth out. 'We don't want another one slipping.'

The child smelt sugar. 'Sweeties!'

'If you're good you can have a lolly after your tea. If you eat everything up.'

'Lollipops,' he squeaked.

Louise wiped her eyes, lifted him onto the counter then stacked the delicious treats into a wall cupboard. 'Maybe we could make an offer. A free lollipop with every five packets of twenty.'

'Six,' Diane said.

A beam of delight passed from one to the other. 'That'll bring them sniffing round. I'll help you with that bucket. You should still be careful.'

They made up their special packs and Louise tied smaller bundles of ten Woodbines with lengths of string salvaged from stock and stuck a twist of snuff in with them. 'Now we have to advertise,' she said. 'People have to know what they can get.'

'They could club together to get the offer.'

Ben levered the top off a pot of old brown paint with a chisel and Louise sniffed suspiciously at a solid leathery covering. Underneath there was liquid. Ben begged turpentine from Wilf and they thinned it. Backs of dog-eared old posters were clean enough to use so Louise trimmed them, Diane painted adverts and they stuck them in the shop window.

News went round in a day and business picked up, their hours eaten up. Then next day the words *Conchie Coward* reappeared on the pavement.

'This is war,' Louise rasped as she made a mental inventory of the closed shop. 'I'm going to catch that bugger.'

Again she got up early and took her breakfast bread and dripping through into the shop and stood in the darkness of a corner to watch. Dawn breathed through the window, shadows merging purple to charcoal, lightening grey to soft pearl on the pavement.

A shade moved and dropped to the kerb. She draped a coat round her shoulders and crept forward but the shade was away down the street the instant her key turned in the latch, small, nimble and quick. Tomorrow she'd have the door unlocked.

Edward gave her a tiny flashlight. When she crossed the threshold next day the thin beam showed the back of a young lad fleeing for his life. But the chalked message was there. She scrubbed it out. No one there the following day. On the third a lad came like a ghost from the shades and ran off down the street when he caught her footfall.

Allies were needed. Firemen at the station let her stand sentry at their entrance but the enemy was out even earlier and raced away next morning like a young demon. Louise tore after him but was left peering up and down the main road at the bottom of their street. Trams loomed through the mists like floating ships. The little devil must be laughing.

As she walked up and down the street on errands she checked doorways and entrances. He seemed to have folded himself into the background. Mornings she wore soft soled shoes but still didn't catch him. He must duck in somewhere on the opposite side of the street. Someone opened a door. One of the firemen decided to keep watch with her while another kept a look out from a window in the tower. He spotted the escape and pounded down stone flights of steps. 'Into the fish shop!'

It was a starting point.

Patricia and Andrew were recovering but Louise still spent part of the day in the tobacconist business. When Benjie had his afternoon nap and Diane was with them she'd come out to stand on her own front step for a fag or walk up and down one of the back lanes to enjoy a quiet smoke in peace. She wandered to the other side of the street, down a different lane to stretch her legs and leaned against a brick wall before stubbing the cigarette out. Pigeons on splayed claws were strutting along the brick wall tops of back yards in false safety. A cat uncurled, crouched and fixed a bird with venomous puss-green eyes. The bird took off frantically in a flap and flurry of feathers. Further down a door creaked open. Louise froze.

'Mind you get that cod delivered straight off to Heaton.' The lad dropped a parcel and a fish slithered out onto the cobbles. 'Idiot, I'll have to wash that.' It was Kipper Kipling's voice. 'Here, take another packet, and straight home after.'

The boy slid off over the uneven lane but she had a glimpse of his face. Something in the way he moved was familiar. Her mind clicked. The shadow chalking C by Andrew's shop, the shade disappearing halfway down the street - into the fishmonger's. *Freddie Firbank. That's him!! I'll get the little freak.* She dropped her cigarette and went to the fire station.

They set a watch, noted times and dates, noting when the youngster went in and out. Diane waited and slid out of the shop as Freddie passed. She started to sing the chorus of a Northumbrian song so he could hear and changed the words:

> *Thoo shalt have a fishy*
> *on a little dishy*
> *Thoo shalt have a fish*
> *when Freddie's boat comes in.*

He scurried off. Freda was seen in the street later and Diane was out again calling so ears listening behind a door could hear. 'When did your boat come in, Freda?'

'Don't know what you're talking about.'

'Did you enjoy your fish?'

Freddie disappeared in daylight but a bobbie they knew watched the back lane on his beat, saw movement, shade against shadow, clamped a hand on a shoulder and swung him in the darkness.

'Carrying something, lad?'

'Nothing ... nothing.'

'We'll check that nothing in the station.'

'You'll have to tell me mam!'

'I'll send someone to tell your mam just where you are.' He sent the youngest P.C. to Louise with the message for Freda.

But there was no news from the police station, not even through the firemen. Prejudicing a case, someone said to her - if they could make any case. The chalking stopped. She was sure then the lad who used the chalk was in a cell. They'd locked him up for a couple of nights till Freda made such a to-do they had to release or charge him. A charge would have to be illegal trading for Kipper, or of theft for the lad and it was one boy's word against Kipper's, a businessman's, against a whippersnapper not long from his school desk. They had to release him.

Next evening she called over to her parents' and found Andrew and Patricia up and about. 'Anyone got a shilling for the 'leccy?'

'Has the juice gone?' Ben opened his mouth to say something else but a rap at the door stopped him. 'I'll get it.'

Louise settled by the fire. Coals weren't a problem now her dad was back at the pit. She heard him talking with someone at the door then showing a man upstairs. One of the older ruddy faced bobbies from the station came in. They shuffled the seats round so her father and the policeman could sit at the table.

'How can we help?' Ben asked.

The policeman looked round and nodded to Mary. 'We're trying to investigate a matter of black marketeering, a serious thing, this. We have suspicions but can't make a move without evidence.' He looked round. 'Mrs. Hawthorne, have you ever had the offer of 'under the counter' goods from the fishmonger on this street?'

'No,' She handed him a cup of tea. 'I can honestly say I've never had the offer.'

'Right.' He scanned the faces. 'Anyone else?'

Louise stared her father in the eye. 'Our Patricia can tell you something about that.'

'Mrs. Taylor?'

Patricia inspected her nails. 'It was just a rumour from a customer about someone who might be getting extra.'

'But who did it concern?'

Patricia looked up. 'I feel it would be passing on gossip because that's all it was.'

'It might help me in my enquiries even if it's just off the record, might give us a lead. If it comes to nothing then it comes to nothing.'

'People say all sorts of things and I don't want to do somebody down on hearsay.'

'I'll tell you who it was!' Louise spat. 'It was Mrs. Firbank.'

'You didn't hear that yourself, you only heard it from me. That makes it third hand, I think. Anyway, it was just a hint.'

Louise pressed her lips together.

'Mrs. Taylor's right about that. But all I'm looking for's a starting place.'

'Dad could tell you something.'

'Louise!' She tossed her head.

'What can you tell us, Ben?'

'That I'm not going to court over this.'

'I'm surprised at that.' The officer stopped writing. 'But you do know something? You're in a difficult position if you withhold evidence.'

'It isn't evidence.'

'Stop pussyfooting about, man. What do you know - or what have you heard?'

'Don't write this down.' the policeman nodded and put his pencil behind his ear. 'Kipper made me an offer when I was out of work.' The constable waited. 'He wanted me to act as his runner, for the black market.'

'Did he offer you money?'

Ben nodded. 'And payment in kind.'

'You see, we might have the beginnings of something here because we found young Firbank loaded down with parcels of fish.'

'Kipper denies any knowledge, I'll bet.'

'Says young Freddie stole the fish from him. But with what both you and your daughter say,' he sat back, 'well, that throws doubt on his word. Did anyone else hear this offer?'

'I did,' Patricia said softly. 'From our back yard.'

'Would you testify to that?'

Ben cut in, 'She's my daughter and I don't think a family member's word would be enough to back mine up. In any case, I didn't see any real evidence of illegal goings on. A court of law might call it an intention. I refused the offer and after that have no knowledge he carried this intention out.'

'You're being slippery, Ben. Think you're a lawyer, do you?''

'A serious thing to put a man in jail.'

'And it's a serious thing to withhold evidence.'

'Since I didn't get involved I didn't actually see anything so it's difficult to call this hard evidence, just casting doubt on his character. Look at it this way,' Ben drew his pipe out, 'what good is it going to do to put a fishmonger away who's providing a service to the community? And if you arrested everybody who's had their fingers in the black market pie one way or another there wouldn't be room enough in the prisons for them, or the staff. It'd be a mess. I know you have more serious crimes to look into.'

'I'd thank you not to tell me my job, Ben. And what about young Freddie?'

'Yes, what about him, dad?' Louise glared at her father.

'He's a harum-scarum and can be a damned nuisance. But he's wet behind the ears and he could turn a corner. What I want to know is how he's got all this time on his hands. Is he in employment?'

The Bobbie shrugged. 'Not that I know of.'

'Then he should be, he's left school. We're short handed down the pit. We've had lads more clueless than Freddie sent to us as 'Bevin boys'. Why not give him a fright ...'

'I think we've done that,'

' ... then make the little blighter go down the Dole, have a word with them first and get him down the pit. At least he'd be putting an honest day's work in, not mixing with crooks.'

'Something to be said for that. It could keep him out of trouble.'

'Exactly. As for Kipper, I'm not going to put him away but if he's really up to something and you keep an eye on him, you'll get him.'

The constable sighed and got up. 'We'll leave it for now.' He looked at Louise. 'But let me know if you think of anything else. What you've said could help us build a case that might make other people think twice.'

Ben saw him out, came back and handed Louise her shilling. She took it sulkily. 'I don't know what you thought you were playing at there, dad.'

'Looking after you is what I was doing. I don't want any of Kipper's bad boys attacking my girls in a back lane. Now get home to your little lad. He needs his mother. In one piece. And keep your little mouth shut.'

Ben grinned the following week as he cycled up the street, already bathed and clean from the showers at the pithead. He slid off the bike and stopped to watch Benjie play with a top and whip he'd made for him and delivered the previous day, his peace offering.

Louise waited while her father saw him spinning it on the pavement then stood up. 'Aye, aye!'

'Aye! Aye, yourself!'

'You look pleased.'

'So'll you be.' He grinned. 'Young Freddie's been sent down our pit, terrified when he sees me. Past like greased lightning.' The corners of their eyes crinkled. Peace broke out. 'I'll paint that little top up properly if I can scavenge a colour from somewhere. I'll set Wilf, Mr. Fix-it, on the look out.' He picked his grandson up and swung him upside down by the heels. Benjie screeched, his granddad righted him, kissed him and put him down.

'You'll make him wild, dad.'

'No wilder than you are.' They laughed.

'How's Trisha?'

'She was up when I left this morning. A lot better.'

'I saw Andrew out walking.'

'Has to get his strength back. Another week at the most and they'll have him at the Forest business again.' Ben pushed his bike over the road. 'See you soon.'

'Not if I see you first!'

Ben went cross-eyed for the bairn. Benjie copied, nearly fell off the kerbstone then ran off along the kerb, waiting to be chased. She stood her ground, picked up the top and whip and put them on her step ignoring him, then spun back when she heard a little whinny. He raced up, gathered speed, hurled himself and flew into her arms.

Diane came round like a second mother, filling her loneliness. They were ready to double at the tobacconists' at a moment's notice if Patricia had a bad day. Louise checked pavements in the mornings for chalk but it was quiet on the Firbank front. Andrew went back to work, frail, but the fresh air did more for him than doctors and in a month or two he was putting on weight.

In their neighbourhood not all of the schools were open and Louise was glad, happy to have her child a while longer. He climbed into their bed in the morning and clung to her neck in a game when she kissed him goodnight. On waking her first thought was of him and the last before she slept.

The echo of Joe's presence was fainter, forgotten for days when she'd taken cudgels against Fat Freda. The small green compact, his first gift, brought a cloud of memory in a swirl of 'airspun' powder. She placed it at the back of a drawer and fluffed her fine-milled cosmetic straight from the perfumed box. Before the war had taken off she'd laid in a little hoard of beauty products but hardly touched them in years. Lipstick was greasy from lack of use but Diane had a supply and gave her one smooth as a bullet for a birthday. The face that looked at her from the mirror had fine lines under the eyes, between the brows, at corners of the mouth. But a whirl of powder gave her cheeks a pearly sheen and when she rouged from the temple following the plane of the bone under the eyes and gently blended colour then filled in her mouth, she recognised the person looking back from the glass.

Life was quieter for a few months except as usual Ben obsessed over the politics and spent a precious sixpence a week at the News Theatre, followed up in harrowed conversation with Wilf or the Reverend Hargaves. Louise avoided newsreels, her meeting place with Joe. Better not stir dead love by the aroma of the hall or touch of the seats, lush drapery, the shades of the lights, memory lurking in her senses. Her inner life was moving from that perfumed, poisoned past.

Suddenly the venom of gossip bit again. An article from a newspaper cut out and covered in cellophane was stuck on a lamppost, the bold headline:

Sunbathing Conchies

The article underneath began:

Lazy C.O.s find time to sunbathe while our boys fight.

Alongside the type a grainy photo, hard to make out, showed a couple of young men on a grass verge reading books. Diane read it on her way up, tore it down and gave it to Louise.

'Patricia mustn't see this.'

But Patricia went to early communion at the parish church and found a copy outside on the notice board with another hand-written note in capital letters:

NAZI LOVER

John Hargraves took them down and asked who was responsible. No answer. No one dared challenge the priest directly but the toxin spread through the street's artery. When Andrew came home people chatting in twos or three's stopped talking as he passed.

'What's going on?' he asked inside.

Louise passed him the cellophaned poison arrow from the paper and watched as, for the first time since they'd known him, Andrew flew into a rage.

'I'll tell you what this is! The foreman's got a grudge against us. He set us up and gave a damned interview to the press.' He kicked his boots off and flung them in a corner.

'Steady, lad. don't break up the happy home. Sit down and tell us. Where's that tea, Mary? – So, what was this bloke up to?'

'I got moved to the nursery on Monday with another chap who's a C.O. as well.' He took a steaming mug. 'A lot of weeding to be done and we had to plant some seeds. In fact we'd finished everything by the tea break at eleven. We waited round half an hour when the foreman looked in and asked if we should go back over to the main Forestry area. The foreman's always spiteful and seemed to think we were telling him his business.

'Touchy lot, foremen,' Ben said.

'You haven't to leave a job till I tell you – that was him, little Hitler. So we spent till lunch time looking for imaginary weeds and thought we'd be moved on after that. But he said we were to stay there for the afternoon. At five o' clock he said we had to come back to it next day and he'd decide our movements, not us. So, and it seems to have been a BIG mistake, we brought books in with us to pass the time.'

'I'd have done the same,' Ben said. 'He's making monkeys out of you.'

'That's what we thought. We had to report for the rest of the week for fake work in the nursery. Then there was a spell of bright weather so we took to sitting out for half an hour on a grass verge at lunch time to read.'

Ben reached for his pipe. 'And we've seen the rest.'

'The foreman gave an interview.'

'He's had his moment. It'll pass.'

Andrew looked pale. 'The problem is - it seemed so clear at the beginning - making a stand on conscience. And now we're away from the bombing and were safer than women and children while that went on.'

Ben rattled a newspaper. 'Understood. We get all that through the press. But don't get lost in the middle. If you have a conviction you should stick to it. Who knows what importance the stand has in the end?'

'It's brought trouble on you lot.'

'Are you saying you want to be on active service after all?'

'No. I'm not joining the armed forces.'

'So, you have to stick with the decision of the tribunal at this stage. We'll survive it, lad.'

'We damn well will.' Louise drew Benjie away from the fire.

'What's damn, mammy?'

John Hargraves preached on 'Careless talk costs lives'.

Patricia attended. He unrolled the poster with Hitler's ears coming out of the walls listening in to conversations. The congregation settled back to listen to a tame talk they'd heard before, the old chestnut of a fifth column everywhere. Then the vicar rattled them, saying that gossip was careless talk. Were we going to attack each other with vicious rumours, like poison gas, after the Nazis stopped dropping their bombs? One enemy was enough, without turning on each other.

She relayed it to the family.

Ben laughed. 'He's right.'

'They knew what he was talking about. Not many people spoke to him on the way out.'

'He should put that into print, get it out through the letter boxes. Get a letter into a local rag.'

Andrew went red. 'I don't want people to fight my battles.'

'It's not your say, son. It's his parish.'

The Reverend had a cut-down version of the talk printed in his parish newsletter and Louise helped distribute it and with satisfaction Ben read his letter that the local newspaper decided to publish.

But the freeze out went on. Business in the shop fell off again. Freda Firbank reappeared. Louise was with Diane looking after the shop. She slammed the door shut.

'Fatty's out there again.'

'Have you seen her?' Diane went on scrubbing the lino.

'Mumbler, telling tales, looking up here. Fat old bully. I'll settle her hash!' Louise burst into laughter. 'D'you remember when you took that safety pin to the Sally Army?' They giggled 'Have you finished with that pail of water?'

'Nearly.'

Louise looked out and saw the plump telltale move further down the street, nodding her head, talking twenty to the dozen to the women taking a moment's leisure on their door step. She wore a smart dress, patterned with hideous huge flowers, stretched tight over her majestic bust. Louise nodded to her sister.

'Together.'

They hauled the bucket from the front door, down the step and heaved dirty water in a wave. It swished down the pavement and slopped onto Freda.

'That's for the black market! Clean it up!'

Children watched open mouthed as fat Freda danced back on delicate feet and Diane started to sing her words of the folk song.

Thoo shalt have a fishy
on a little dishy
Thoo shalt have a haddock
When Freda's Boat comes in!

The women cottoned on and joined the chorus.

Dance to thee Freddie
Sing to his mammy
Dance to thee Freda
When the boat comes in.

The persecutor scurried down the street. Chanting children followed, picking up the song, and housewives watching started to laugh.

'About time!' Somebody shouted.

Clapping and cheering took off down the street. Louise put her arm round her sister then they bowed.

Next week Louise walked into the police station and asked to make a statement. Kipper was called in for questioning again.

'I'm on ambulance duty,' Edward kissed her, 'can you watch the shop? Just keep Benjie away from knives and anything dangerous on the work bench.'

'Andrew's coming over. You don't mind him fixing the back door, do you? He wants to be useful.'

'I don't mind. Tools are in the air raid shelter in the yard, definitely some screws and nails in there, and a torch. He'll find two on a shelf where Benjie can't touch them.' He kissed her again. 'Anyway, I know there's somebody around for you.'

'I'll be O.K. Dad's off as well, no Saturday shift for a change.'

She settled on a stool in the shop, thought of tidying the work bench with its sprawl of fine nails, cutting knives, hammers of various sizes then thought better of it with Benjie playing at her feet. The lathe Ben had bought years ago was fixed to the table, glistening in the light. She picked up an out of date newspaper and began to read. The bell tinkled and her boy rushed up to Andrew to be thrown about.

'Can I play outside with Uncle Andrew?'

'You'll be a nuisance.'

'He'll be all right.'

'Edward said there are tools in the shelter. Hammers here but he tries not to use them for other jobs.'

'I'll take one with me but see what I can find out there.'

'Look on the shelves. There's a torch as well.'

Little Ed took his uncle's hand and swung out happily to the back yard. 'Can we play hide and seek?'

'I expect so.'

She sniffed the scent of cut leather from some bags Edward was making, settled again to read and found her horoscope even though it was last week's. Ben said she shouldn't waste her time on such things, there didn't used to be this rubbish in the papers. She lifted her chin, shook the pages out, turned over and read a recipe. The bell clattered again and she looked up to see Kipper Kipling standing right up against the counter.

'What can I get you?' She'd not noticed earlier how big he was.

He leant over. 'You can get back down to that police station, miss ...'

'Mrs.' She got up from the stool.

'... and withdraw that statement.'

'Won't make any difference. I hear they've had young Freddie in again.'

'Solid as a rock,' he said.

'That little bugger'll crumble.' She was edging towards the workbench.

He grabbed her hand across the counter, pulled her back and was through the gate and onto her side. She glanced at the shop window. No one was in the street. He dragged her through to the living quarters. 'You'll take it back!'

'Go to hell.'

He leaned over her and she caught a whiff of stale beer on his breath. 'I shut your father up. I'll shut you up. What's it going to take? Mangle your face? Get down to that station!'

She moved her head a fraction. 'They'd not believe me now.'

'Oh, you'll be very convincing.' He pulled her head back by her hair, his other hand at her throat. 'Or shall I give you something you might enjoy?' He let his weight fall on her and began hauling at her clothes.

She tried to kick and a hand closed over her mouth, she struggled to breathe inside the dirt sweat of it. Panic rose in her throat. She wanted to bite but he had control of her jaw. He slammed her face down onto the table and horny fingernails caught at her thigh, ripping her skin, tearing her underwear.

'Get off her.' She could see another pair of feet. A hand. A hammer. The huge paws released her.

'Come on then, son!' Kipper's voice grated like a saw. 'I can take on two of the likes of you.' He lunged at Andrew. Louise coughed for breath, tears on her face, winded, collapsed on the table. She could see the feet scuffling against each other, the men turning. Andrew's feet came nearer, his back towards her. Her lungs filled and eyes streamed. She lifted her head and made out Kipper's red face, eyes creased. He swung Andrew round and paused to check the window to the back yard. *Benjie was out there.* She took another breath, tried to stand and saw the hammer swing. A crack and Kipper went down like a felled tree. Andrew stared at the tool in his hand. The shop bell rang. Someone coming. Ben's voice, his arm round her. 'Sweetheart!'

He squeezed her shoulder, knelt down, felt Kipper's pulse and looked up at Andrew. He checked the pulse again and let the hand drop. 'I think he's done for!'

Andrew crumpled. 'I've killed a man!' he wheezed letting the hammer go and sat on the floor rocking, head in hands.

The thud went through Louise's brain. Her breath came more easily, she straightened her clothes. 'Benjie?'

'He ran round to us. Got out the back way'

'Thank God,' she whispered then lifted a finger to her lips and stumbled into the shop holding on to the workbench. Her hand hovered, picked up the sharpest cutting knife and lurched back.

'Don't slit his gizzard.'

'Ssshhh!' She lifted Kipper's right hand, placed the knife in it, curled lifeless still-warm fingers round the handle and laid them back on the floor. 'Don't touch, dad.' The bell clattered again. 'Keep quiet.'

Ben nodded as John Hargraves appeared in the connecting doorway. 'What the blazes?'

'Stay here, John. I'd better get someone from the station.'

Louise stared wide-eyed at the vicar as he knelt down. She was shaking. 'I don't think you'd better touch him. Please don't touch anything.'

Hargraves pulled his hands back. 'What happened?'

'Kipper was threatening me, trying to rape me. He had a knife ... Andrew came in from the yard, they struggled and ... he brained him.'

The vicar stood up. 'Are you all right?'

She nodded. 'I will be ... but ... do you think you could put the kettle on?'

He moved to the scullery. Andrew moaned and sat up on the floor. He looked at the body and dropped his head in his hands. 'I've killed him. I've killed ... a man.' John Hargraves tramped back, helped him up and sat him in a chair. 'I've committed murder.'

Hargraves pulled another chair up and put a hand on Andrew's shoulder speaking quietly. 'You had no intention of killing him, did you?' A shake of the head. 'Protecting Louise? Struggling?' Andrew nodded. 'It was a reflex.'

The bell again. A policeman stood looking at the scene. Louise leaned against the table. 'Kipper was going to kill him,' she croaked, 'at least maim him for life. Kipper'd attacked me.'

The officer knelt and touched one of Kipper's hands. The knife stayed gripped. 'A doctor's on his way. We need a medical man to confirm death.' He stood up and took out a notebook. 'Will you give a statement as to what you found, vicar?'

'Yes. And I can testify to this man's character.'

'Ben?'

'Yes.'

He faced Andrew. 'I'll have to take you down to the station.' Andrew offered his wrists. 'I'll not bother with the cuffs. We'll read you your rights there.' He put the notebook away. 'It seems to be a clear case. Self defence.'

He left and Louise crumpled to the floor.

Andrew's job was suspended till he cleared his name. The case was to go to the Crown Court for a jury trial. Louise had to testify about the attack, the police had unravelled Kipper Kipling's books and the

Hawthorne family gave evidence about the background to the case. Freddie Firbank had made a statement. His boss was dealing in stolen ration books under cover of the fish business. Kipper had been furious that Louise ratted on him. He, Freddie, didn't know the boss was going to assault her.

Evidence was all one way. The jury brought in a verdict of manslaughter. Andrew must report to the police on a regular basis but there was no prison sentence. Freddie Firbank was not put away, treated leniently because of his age.

The drama of it all exhausted them.

When they came out of the court Ben got rid of the local press then turned round to the knot of the family as if conducting them. 'I think we could all do with a good feed. What do you say to fish and chips?' They burst out laughing almost in tears with relief.

Louise was white. 'Take us all to Fenwick's, dad. We'll eat whatever they've got.'

'Right you are!'

'And you can pay!' Her father nodded and put his arm round her.

Two days later Mary was frying bread in the kitchen with a precious rasher or two of bacon when the post clattered through their letterbox. She brought the pan in, blue smoke curling from it, served Andrew bread with half a rasher, scraped up crunchy rind for him then filled Patricia's plate. Andrew collected the post, came upstairs with an envelope, slit it open, read a letter and sat staring.

Trisha gratefully attacked the hot food. 'What is it? A love letter?'

He handed it to her. 'I wish it was. It's from the Forestry Commission. I'm not to go back.' Her knife and fork clattered down. 'My services are no longer required.'

Mary put the frying pan down on the breadboard and took the letter. 'They've judged you're guilty, son.'

'But he was acquitted, mam. It wasn't murder. It was ... self defence.' The voice trailed.

'They don't give a reason,' Andrew said. The bacon was going cold and hard. 'I was going to go in on Monday.'

Mary picked her pan up and heaved into the scullery. 'They're working on a no smoke without fire basis.'

'We've got the shop,' Patricia said, 'if we have any customers. But people around here have made their own minds up. It's been all right for a while after Freda shut up.'

'You're dad's in work, anyway. Mary forced them to finish their food and they almost slid down to the shop in silence.

A week later Andrew received another letter. This time the envelope looked familiar. Mary twitched it from him at the breakfast table. 'Eat first. You don't waste what's been put in front of you.' She hovered till their plates were clean then handed the letter back.

Patricia watched numb. He seemed unable to read the contents. Mary tried to see over his shoulder and he put it down.

'It's my papers. They've called me up again.'

'Oh God!'

'I'm not working on the land any more,' he said quietly. 'That was my condition.'

When he came home Ben tried to take charge. 'I don't like glum faces,' he said.

'You should have looked in the mirror over twelve years.'

'Thank you, Mary. I should leave the coal dust on. Can I have that kettle? We have a bite to eat and then think of a solution.' He banged into the scullery.

'We could do with that Wilf's famous brains,' Mary yelled after him..

'That's an idea. Have you got a carrier pigeon?'

'Only we don't want him coming up with a corker like he did for Christopher.'

'I'll ride over and see him.'

'If Mrs Robson'll let you in. And don't you go into a pub. Anyway, you'll break your neck in the blackout.' She opened the oven door on the range and prodded a baked cauliflower.

'This is not my fault, Mary, lass. I'm not the War Office. Now let's have a bit of peace.'

Trisha and Andrew were in bed when he came back. They dozed, impossible to sleep. She lay against his back and listened to her parents.

'Did she let you in?'

'We went out into his shed, if you must know.' She heard him laughing. 'I'm sure she doesn't go in there. He's got pinup pictures.' Stony silence. 'Right. Well, we thrashed it through.'

'And did he come up with something?'

'He did. But I don't know if Andrew'll touch it.'

Patricia lay tense.

'There's a way of joining up without in any way bearing arms. He probably knows about it. The Non-combatant corps.'

'And what do they do'

'It's as risky as anything else. They can help in digging out unexploded bombs. Stuff like that.'

'Oh, Lord! The bomb squad!'

'Wilf reckons it's not making war. It's clearing up the <u>mess</u> of war – if he's got the stomach for it.'

'I knew I shouldn't have sent you over there.'

Patricia had again the nightmare feeling of falling.

*

They parked the car of the Royal Engineers near the top of a terraced street where the bomb was buried. The car's khaki paint blended into a grey day but its red mudguards marked out that it was from the bomb disposal squad. They showed up bright and clear like a signal of hope.

377

Andrew battered feverishly on doors to clear people from the street, helped elderly out, carried a toddler then went round the corner to an infant school to see the children marched in a crocodile to a street further away. He carried the bag with the gear down to the sapper, who was hunkered down studying a spot where a bomb lay.

He mentally worked through layers of dirt to get to the casing that held a lethal device that had to be broken without setting the charge off – gaine, main charge, then started the work of clearing with a trowel. The sapper took it from him and moved the crumbled surface of the tarmac gently, delicately working round the metal shell. A baby cried in the distance. They had to try to shut out the outside world. Andrew had scissors, clippers and a blade ready, laid them out on the ground then moved back with his notebook as the sapper went into the bomb container that they'd found cracked open. It was like watching a surgeon.

'This one's nasty,' the sapper said. 'The wires are painted black so you can't see how to defuse it.'

'Do you want me to scrape them clean, sir?'

'Are your hands steady?'

They talked in whispers. 'Yes.' He could see the wires.

'Stay back just now. I'll tell you if I need you.' The sapper brushed dust away and began to scrape the black paint with a blade. 'Red and blue already.' Andrew wrote notes then the sapper stood up.

'Bloody cramp.'

'Let me finish it, sir.'

'Go carefully.' The officer walked a step away, stamping his foot while Andrew uncovered a green wire. 'We have to be sure where the positive is.' The sapper was back and watched him remove the paint, peeling back to the colours underneath. 'They might have switched the colours to confuse us.' He took the instruments again.

From the top of the street they heard running, a child had slipped through the loose cordon of police and anxious parents.

Andrew waved her back and raced up towards her. No one else moved. 'Stop!' He saw her brace her feet, check her speed, skid, stand still as in a game of statues before he felt the tremor, turned to the flash of bright green and white and saw the sapper thrown back and knew he must be injured. He ran to his officer in time for the second explosion, flared lights, dirt rising in a black cloud, ground collapsing and fell in a pool of blood, feeling no pain.

*

When it happened Ben was at work at the pithead. The words came over a loudspeaker.

Germany has surrendered. The war – is over!

They took a break and drank tea from blue-rimmed enamel mugs. Ben had to force himself to concentrate on the rest of his tasks his eyes hardly focusing.

Men at the coalface came off their shift into the light, into a burst of joy. At the end of his day Ben danced a jig before straddling his bike. He'd have liked to have balanced like a trick cyclist.

That's it! The atheist lifted his heart to whatever force might be there. *Please let it be real peace this time.*

Bankruptcy. The Depression. Unemployment. War. They'd survived. What he wouldn't give for a drink with his friends! Then eyes closed for a second, he pictured Wilf in hospital white and still, the image his defence against the demon. He took a deep breath and pushed on the pedals. One more time, he'd go home and make love to his wife. One more time. By Jove he would, if it killed him!

But the war with Japan wasn't finished.

Christopher was at sea. Ben comforted his wife that bad news travelled fast. He was sure himself that they'd all come through, against the odds, sure in his heart. Even Andrew'd come clear, just about, when his sapper lost a leg.

Every lad he saw who'd been demobbed, some not old enough to vote, hardly believing they were alive, Ben had a word for them. They were determined to remake the country, chuck out old restrictions. Ben clapped them on the back and went on to election meetings. This time they really had to make a country fit for heroes.

Cheer Churchill! Vote Labour! He joined the campaign. Yes, he'd cheer Churchill, even though the old man was threatening Britain would suffer the Gestapo if Labour got in.

When election results were coming through the wireless Louise sat up with her father to listen. Her face had more colour, and not from rouge. He looked at her and a shaft of tenderness rose for his child. 'Are you expecting, pet?'

She stamped in annoyance. 'Trust you! I was just going to tell you.'

He furtively found the apple cordial Mary'd made from his apple tree and toasted her with a few drops. They began to giggle. 'Neither of us should have this!' They ate hot potato scones and listened intently. At the next bulletin he slapped his thigh. Results weren't fully in. But it was clear. He poured a thimbleful more apple cordial. Looking at her, his face shone with love and hope. 'To the future,' they clinked glasses. 'Education. Medicine. A better future. Your bairns might even go to university!' They sipped the sweet-sour liquid. "To children's children!"'

*

Ben grinned over to the conductor. 'Aye, I'm getting off here,' and took a pipe and cap out of the pocket of his worn gabardine. 'All systems go now!'

The tram ground to its stop as he swayed and held on to the pole of the boarding platform. He stepped out laughing then crumpled face down onto the kerbstone, scattering pipe, flat cap, loose change from his coat pocket in the road. From nowhere a circle of people appeared.

'Get back! Let him breathe. Get back! He needs First Aid.' The conductor turned the man over, saw the face bruising and loosened the shirt collar.

A woman in a navy hat and coat pushed her way forward. 'I've done First Aid. Help me. Somebody call the police and an ambulance. Hold his head or put something under it. 'Ben, can you hear me?' The woman opened his jacket.

'She knows him.' They were whispering in the crowd.

'Can you hear me, Ben?' She patted his face and began pressing his chest.

'He's going!' The conductor sat back on the ground.

'Ssshhh ... here's the polis.'

A policeman knelt on the other side. He put his face to the man's mouth as if listening. The woman left off pumping. 'Let's try the arms to get his breath going.' They spread eagled the arms and brought them back over his chest. Another policeman arrived and they made way.

He looked for a pulse and shook his head. 'Seems like a stroke or heart attack, massive, but we'd better not move him till a medic gets here.' He felt the temples and neck again, picked up a wrist that hung limp. 'Anyone know this man?'

Someone pointed from the crowd. 'She does. That wifey.' The policeman turned to the woman in navy who was staring at the dead man's face.

'He was on his way to the Mining Institute.'

'How do you know?'

'I was going there myself ... for a meeting. It's Ben Hawthorne.'

'Who'd have thought it?' Hushed chatter started behind them. 'He's a family man. Yes, I know who he is.'

*

The organ played sweet consoling music, softened to a fall of notes and stilled. Would Ben have wanted a Christian burial? He never said, too much alive to be thinking of death. All this was for the living.

As the polished oak box was shouldered in by bearers in solemn procession and they stood in a rustle of clothing, Patricia was conscious of the smell of damp limestone from the church pillars, transforming a fresh perfume of flowers from life to a funeral.

John Hargraves' voice deep, echoing from the stone.   '... in sure and certain hope ...'

She listened and glanced at the coffin that seemed an affront. Her mother sat on one side of her, Andrew on the other. Mary clutched a thin blue airmail envelope from Christopher, on his way home but unable to be there. Louise looked well with her bump beginning to show. Diane, next to her husband was smart, in a fitted *Utility* suit, pleated skirt, dark bottle green, black trim. She sat still, pale faced next to her husband, twisting the rings on her finger, then on her other side Fred and Katharine with her strong healthy beauty even in mourning. Wilf sat behind them blowing his nose, openly weeping. No children were present.

The heavy scent of chrysanthemums was overpowering. Pews behind them were packed, women with hats, men bareheaded, people sighing, shuffling, paying their respects. From their street and from Ben's Union mates and friends there'd been a silver collection to help pay for the funeral, give him a 'proper send off'.

Andrew took her hand, two of his fingers missing.

In her mind she pictured Ben alive, smiling, debating, cantankerous, visionary in his way.

Goodnight, dad, God bless.

Acknowledgements

The Fellowship of Reconciliation was my initial inspiration for the period.

The present cover of the book was inspired from a design by Ricki Thaman

Thank you Rikki.

And I'd like to thank Roger for his patient support through many years of a writer faced with a computer screen and tearing her hair.

I was grateful to the late Fred Aspin for permission to draw from his personal journal covering years as a Conscientious Objector.

I've also been grateful to the late Margaret Alsopp for her oral memories of World War 2 and to members of the Durham Fellowship of Christian Writers who encouraged and advised. Thank you to Ivy Hudson for lending source material.

Thank you also to Lynne Thompson for enthusiasm after reading an early draft of the book and, of course, to David Hepworth for finally publishing it.